Found Money

JAMES GRIPPANDO

Found Money

WHEELER
PUBLISHING, INC.
ROCKLAND, MA
★ AN AMERICAN COMPANY ★

Published in Large Print by arrangement with HarperCollins Publishers, Inc., in the United States and Canada

Wheeler Large Print Book Series.

Set in 16 pt Plantin.

Library of Congress Cataloging-in-Publication Data

Grippando, James, 1958-
    Found money / James Grippando.
        p. (large print) cm.(Wheeler large print book series)
    ISBN 1-58724-069-6 (softcover)
    1. Single mothers—Fiction. 2. Physicians—Fiction. 3. Colorado—Fiction. 4. Wealth—Fiction. 5. Large type books. I. Title. II. Series

[PS3557.R534 F6   2001]
813'.54—dc21
                                                        2001026295
                                                            CIP

For you, Tiff, always

"Say not you know another entirely, till you have divided an inheritance with him."

—Johann Kaspar Lavater
Aphorisms on Man, c. 1788, no. 157

Acknowledgments

Thank you...

Tiffany, I love your honesty and everything about you.

Carolyn Marino and Robin Stamm truly took the book to another level, with a helpful assist from Jessica Lichtenstein. An author couldn't have better friends than Richard and Artie Pine; you take better care of me than I do. Joan Sanger, as always, left her very welcome mark. And the critics at large are getting better with each book: Eleanor Rayner, Carlos Sires, Jennifer Stearns, Dr. Gloria M. Grippando, Judy Russell.

A few friends lent their special expertise. James W. Hall, deputy sheriff, Yakima County Sheriff's Department. F. Clay Craig, probate attorney *extraordinaire* and lover of *béisbol*. Gerald J. Houlihan and Ron Hanes, two most talented criminal defense lawyers.

Some of the Colorado in this novel is real, some is made up (don't go looking for the Green Parrot or the Half-way Café). My thanks to the Colorado Travel and Tourism Authority; City of Boulder Housing Authority; the Boulder School District; the Lamar Chamber of Commerce; Jane Earle, manager of community relations, Denver Water (a/k/a "the water goddess"); the Denver Public

Library, especially Gwendolyn Crenshaw, senior librarian, and Don Dilley, Department of Western History/Genealogy; and the Department of Astrophysical and Planetary Sciences, the Fiske Planetarium and Sommers-Bausch Observatory, University of Colorado, Boulder. Keith Gleason deserves special mention for his entertaining and informative crash course on dying stars and the life of an astronomer. (I hope I didn't let you down.)

Prologue

It was dying. No way to save it. And Amy Parkens watched with a child's fascination.

The night was perfect. No city lights, not even a moon to brighten the cloudless sky outside her bedroom window. Billions of stars blanketed the vast blackness of space. Her six-inch Newtonian reflector telescope was aimed at the Ring Nebula, a dying star in the constellation of Lyra. Amy liked that one best. It reminded her of the smoke rings her grandfather used to blow with his cigar—a faint, grayish-green ring puffed into outer space. Death was slow in coming, over many millennia. It was irreversible. Astronomically speaking, the Ring Nebula was light-years beyond Geritol.

Amy peered through the eyepiece, pushing her hair aside. She was a tall and skinny eight-year-old with sandy-blonde bangs that dangled in her eyes. She'd often heard grown-ups say she was destined to be the Twiggy of the eighties, but that didn't interest her. Her interests were unlike those of most third graders. Television and video games bored her. She was used to spending time alone in the evenings, entertaining herself with

1

books, celestial maps, her telescope—things her friends would have considered homework. She had never known her father. He'd been killed in Vietnam before Amy could even walk. She lived with her mom, a busy physics professor at the University of Colorado in Boulder. A passion for the stars was an inherited fascination. Long before her first telescope, Amy would look into the night sky and see much more than twinkling lights. By the time she was seven she could name every stellar constellation. Since then, she'd even made some up and named them herself—distant constellations, beyond the reach of even the world's most powerful instruments but not beyond her imagination. Other kids might stare through telescopes all night long and never see Orion or Sirius, because the stars didn't line up exactly right for them. For Amy, it all made perfect sense.

Amy switched on her flashlight, the only light she needed in her small pink bedroom. With colored pencils she sketched out the Ring Nebula on her notepad, her own makeshift coloring book. She was the only kid in her class with no fear of the dark—so long as her telescope was nearby.

"Lights out, sweetie," her mother called from the hallway.

"Lights *are* out, Mom."

"You know what I mean."

The door opened, and her mother entered. She switched on the little lamp beside Amy's bed. Amy squinted as her eyes adjusted to the faint yellow glow. Her mother's smile was

2

warm but weak. Her eyes showed fatigue. She'd looked tired a lot lately. And worried. Over the last few days, Amy had noticed the change, had even asked what was wrong. Her mother would say only that it was "nothing."

Amy had gotten ready for bed hours ago, well before the celestial sidetrack. She was dressed in her yellow summer pajamas, her face washed and teeth brushed. She climbed down from the chair and gave her mom a hug. "Can't I stay up a little longer? Please?"

"No, honey. It's way past your bedtime."

Her face showed disappointment, but she was too tired to argue. She slid into bed. Her mother tucked her in beneath the sheets.

"Tell me a story, then?"

"Mommy's really tired tonight. I'll tell you one tomorrow."

Amy frowned, but it didn't last. "A good one?"

"I promise. It'll be the best story you ever heard."

"Okay."

Her mother kissed her on the forehead, then switched off the lamp. "Sweet dreams, baby."

" 'Night, Mom."

Amy watched her mother cross the dark room. The door opened. Her mother turned as if to bid a silent goodbye, then closed the door.

Amy rolled on her side and gazed out the window. No more telescope tonight, but this was one of those incredibly clear nights when the heavens were awesome even with the naked eye. She watched for several minutes until her vision blurred and the stars began to swirl. She was getting drowsy. Twenty minutes passed. Maybe longer. Her eyes closed, then opened. Her head sank deeper into the pillow. The strip of light from the hallway disappeared beneath her bedroom door. Mom was apparently going to bed. It comforted Amy to know that. The last few nights, her mother hadn't been sleeping.

She glanced out the window again. Beyond the trees, she saw the lights go out in the house next door. With eyes closed, she imagined the lights going out in house after house as the neighborhood, the city, the entire country went to sleep. The lights were off all around the world. But the stars burned bright. Amy was nearly asleep.

A loud crack pierced the night—like thunder, but it wasn't thunder. Amy jackknifed in her bed, as if kicked in the belly.

The noise had come from *inside* the house.

Her heart raced. She listened for it again, but there was only silence. She was too frightened to scream. She wanted to call for her mother, but words wouldn't come. It had been an awful sound, enough to make her fear the dark forever. Yet it took only a second to pinpoint the source. She knew the sound. There was no mistaking it. She'd heard it before, far from the house, the time her mother had driven her out to the woods and Amy had watched her practice.

It was the echoing clap of her mother's loaded handgun.

Part 1

SUMMER 1999

1

Amy wished she could go back in time. Not *way* back. It wasn't as if she wanted to sip ouzo with Aristotle or tell Lincoln to duck. Less than a fortnight would suffice. Just far enough to avert the computer nightmare she'd been living.

Amy was the computer information systems director at Bailey, Gaslow & Heinz, the premier law firm in the Rocky Mountains. It was her job to keep confidential information flowing freely and securely between the firm's offices in Boulder, Denver, Salt Lake City, Washington, London, and Moscow. Day in and day out, she had the power to bring two hundred attorneys groveling to their knees. And she had the privilege of hearing them scream. Simultaneously. At her.

As if I *created the virus,* she thought, thinking of what she wished she had said to one accusatory partner. He was miles behind her now, but she was still thinking about it. Driving alone on the highway was a great place to put things exactly as they should have been.

It had taken almost a week to purge the entire system, working eighteen-hour days, traveling to six different offices. She had everyone up and running in some capacity within the first twenty-four hours, and she ultimately salvaged over 95 percent of the stored data. Still, it wasn't a pleasant experience to have to tell a half-dozen unlucky lawyers that, like Humpty Dumpty, their computers and everything on them were DOA.

It was a little-known fact, but Amy had witnessed it firsthand: Lawyers *do* cry.

A sudden rattle in the dashboard snagged Amy's attention. Her old Ford pickup truck had plenty of squeaks and pings. Each was different, and she knew them all, like a mother who could sense whether her baby's cry meant feed me, change me, or please get Grandma out of my face. This particular noise was more of a clunk—an easy problem to diagnose, since torrid hot air was suddenly blowing out of the air conditioning vents. Amy switched off the A-C and tried rolling down the window. It jammed. Perfect. Ninety-two degrees outside, her truck was spewing dragon's breath, and the damn window refused to budge. It was an old saw in Colorado that people visited for the winters but moved there for the summers. They obviously didn't mean *this*.

I'm melting, she thought, borrowing from *The Wizard of Oz*.

She grabbed the *Rocky Mountain News* from the floor and fanned herself for relief. The week-old paper marked the day she had sent her daughter off to visit her ex-husband for the week, so that she could devote all her energy to the computer crisis. Six straight days away from Taylor was a new record, one she hoped would never be broken. Even dead tired, she couldn't wait to see her.

Amy was driving an oven on wheels by the time she reached the Clover Leaf Apartments, a boring collection of old two-story red brick buildings. It was a far cry from the cachet Boulder addresses that pushed the average price of a home to more than a quarter-million dollars. The Clover Leaf was government-subsidized housing, an eyesore to anyone but penurious students and the fixed-income elderly. Landscaping was minimal. Baked asphalt was plentiful. Amy had seen warehouse districts with more architectural flair. It was as if the builder had decided that nothing man-made could ever be as beautiful as the jagged mountaintops in the distance, so why bother even trying? Even so, there was a four-year waiting list just to get in.

A jolt from a speed bump launched her to the roof. The truck skidded to a halt in the first available parking space, and Amy jumped out. After a minute or two, the redness in her face faded to pink. She was looking like herself again. Amy wasn't one to flaunt it, but she could easily turn heads. Her ex-husband used to say it was the long legs and full lips. But it was much more than that. Amy gave off a certain energy whenever she moved, whenever she smiled, whenever she looked through those big gray-blue eyes. Her grandmother had always said she had her mother's boundless energy—and Gram would know.

Amy's mother had died tragically twenty

9

years ago, when Amy was just eight. Her father had passed away even earlier. Gram had essentially raised her. She *knew* Amy; she'd even seen the warning signs in her ex-husband before Amy had. Four years ago, Amy was a young mother trying to balance a marriage, a newborn, and graduate studies in astronomy. Her daughter and coursework left little time for Ted—meaning too little time to keep an eye on him. He found another woman. After the divorce, she moved in with Gram, who helped with Taylor. Good jobs weren't easy to find in Boulder, a haven for talented and educated young professionals who wanted the quintessential Colorado lifestyle. Amy would have loved to stick with astronomy, but money was tight, and a graduate degree in astronomy wouldn't change that. Even her computer job hadn't changed that. Her paycheck barely covered the basic living expenses for the three of them. Anything left over was stashed away for law school, which was coming in September.

For Amy, a career in law was an economic decision, not an emotional one. She was certain she'd meet plenty of classmates just like her—art historians, English literature majors, and dozens more who had abandoned all hope of finding work in the field they loved.

Amy just wished there were another way.

"Mommy, Mommy!"

Amy whirled at the sound of her daughter's voice. She was wearing her favorite pink dress and red tennis shoes. The left half of her very blonde hair was in a pigtail. The other

10

flowed in the breeze, another lost barrette. She peeled down the walkway and leaped into Amy's arms.

"I missed you so much," said Amy, squeezing her daughter tightly.

Taylor laughed, then made a face. "Eww, you're all wet."

Amy wiped away the sweat she'd transferred from her cheek to Taylor's. "Mommy's truck has a little fever."

"Gram says you should just sell that heap of junk."

"Never," said Amy. Her mother used to own that heap of junk. It was about the only thing she'd managed to come away with in the divorce. That, and her daughter. She lowered Taylor to the ground. "So, how is your dad?"

"Fine. He promised to come visit us."

"Us?"

"Uh-huh. He said he'll come see you and me at the party."

"What party?"

"*Our* party. For when you gradgy-ate law school and when I gradgy-ate high school."

Amy blinked twice, ignoring the sting. "He actually said that?"

"Law school takes a long time, huh, Mommy?"

"Not that long, sweetheart. It'll be over before we know it."

Gram came up from behind them, nearly panting as she spoke. "I have *never* seen a four-year-old run that fast."

Taylor giggled. Gram welcomed Amy back with a smile, then grimaced. "For goodness sakes, you're an absolute stick. Have you been living on nothing but caffeine again?"

"No, I swear I tried taking a little coffee with it this time."

"Get inside and let me fix you something to eat."

Amy was too tired to think about food. "I'll just throw something quick in the microwave."

"Microwave," Gram scoffed. "I may be old, but it's not like I have to rub two sticks together to heat up a late lunch. By the time you're out of the shower, I'll have a nice hot meal waiting for you."

Along with a month's supply of fat and calories, thought Amy. Gram was from the old school of everything, including diet. "Okay," she said as she grabbed her suitcase from the back of the truck. "Let's go inside."

The threesome walked hand in hand across the parking lot, with Taylor swinging like a monkey between them.

"Home again, Mommy's home again!" said Taylor in a singsong voice.

Amy inserted the key and opened the door. Home was a simple two-bedroom, one-bath apartment. The main living area was a combination living room, dining room, and playroom. Gram sometimes said "the girls" had turned it into one big storage room. Bicycles and Rollerblades cluttered the small entrance; the small ones were Taylor's, the big ones were Amy's. There was an old couch and matching armchair, typical renter's furniture. An old pine wall unit held books, a few plants, and a small television. To the right was a closet-size kitchen, more of a kitchenette.

Amy dropped her suitcase at the door.

"Let me get started in the kitchen," said Gram.

"I help!" Taylor shouted.

"Wash your hands first," said Amy.

Taylor dashed toward the bathroom. Gram followed. "Your mail's on the table, Amy. Along with your phone messages." She disappeared down the hall, right on Taylor's heels.

Amy crossed the room to the table. A week's worth of mail was stacked neatly in piles: personal, bills, and junk. The biggest stack was bills, some of them second notices. The personal mail wasn't personal at all—mostly that computer-generated junk written in preprinted script to make it look like a letter from an old friend. In the bona fide junk pile, a package caught her eye. There was no return address on it. No postage or postmark, either. It appeared to have been hand-delivered, possibly by a private courier service. For its size, it seemed heavy.

Curious, she tore away the brown paper wrapping, revealing a box bearing a picture of a Crock-Pot. She shook it. It didn't feel like a Crock-Pot. It felt like something more solid was inside, as if the box had been filled with cement. The ends had been retaped, too, suggesting the Crock-Pot had been replaced with something else. She slit the duct tape with her key and opened the flaps. A thick plastic lining encased the contents, some kind of waterproof bag with a zipper. There was no

13

note or card, nothing to reveal the identity of the sender. She unzipped the bag, then froze.

"Oh my God."

Benjamin Franklin was staring back at her, many times over. Hundred-dollar bills. *Stacks* of them. She removed one bundle, then another, laying them side by side on the table. Her hands shook as she counted the bills in one stack. Fifty per stack. Forty stacks.

She lowered herself into the chair, staring at the money in quiet disbelief. Someone—an anonymous someone—had sent her two hundred thousand dollars.

And she had no idea why.

2

Lazy swirls of orange, pink and purple hovered on the horizon in the afterglow of another southern Colorado sunset. From the covered wood porch of his boyhood home, thirty-five-year-old Ryan Duffy stared pensively at what seemed like nature's daily reminder that endings could be beautiful. The spectacle slowly faded into darkness, a lonely black sky with no moon or stars. The brief burst of color had nearly fooled him. He felt guilty now for having thought even for a moment that his father might be better off dead.

Ryan's old man had lived his sixty-two years by one simple rule: "last" was the most vulgar of four-letter words. For Frank Duffy, there was no such thing as second place, no ranking of priorities. Everything was first. God, family, job—he devoted unflagging energy to each. A tireless working slug who never missed a Sunday service, never let his family down, never left a job site before someone had said, "That man Duffy is the best damn electrician in the business." Only in the most important battle of his life did he seemingly *avoid* being first.

He was the last to admit that his cancer would kill him.

Not until the pain was unbearable did he finally concede he couldn't beat it on his own. Ryan was furious with him for shunning medicine. Being a doctor had only seemed to make his incessant pleas *less* credible, as if Ryan were just another one of those test-crazy physicians Frank Duffy had never trusted. As it turned out, treatment would only have prolonged the inevitable—two months, maybe three, tops. Ryan would have welcomed any extra time. Had the tables been turned, however, he knew he might well have displayed the same stubborn denial. Ryan enjoyed it when people said he was just like his father, and they looked so much alike that comparisons were inevitable. Both were handsome, with warm brown eyes. His father had long ago gone completely gray, and Ryan was on his way, with distinguished flecks of gray in his thick dark mane. At six-one he was the taller of the two, though he would have been the last to point out that his proud father was shrinking in his old age.

The sun was completely gone now, dipping below the flat horizon. After dark, the plains of southeastern Colorado were like a big ocean. Flat and peaceful, not a city light in sight. A good place to raise a family. No crime to speak of. The nearest shopping mall was in Pueblo, a blue-collar city a hundred miles to the west. The closest fancy restaurant was in Garden City, Kansas, even farther to the east. Some said Piedmont Springs was in the middle of nowhere. For Ryan, it was right where it ought to be.

Ryan had supported his father's decision to spend his few remaining days at home. Frank Duffy was well liked among the town's twelve hundred residents, but the two-hour trek to the hospital was making it hard for his oldest friends to say their final goodbyes. Ryan had set his father up in the rear of the house, in his favorite sitting room. A rented hospital bed with chrome railings and adjustable mattress replaced the rustic pine sofa with forest-green cushions. Beyond the big bay window was a vegetable garden with knee-high corn and bushy green tomato plants. Ash-oak floors and beamed cedar ceilings completed the cabin feeling. It used to be the cheeriest room in the house.

"Did you get it?" his father asked eagerly as Ryan entered the room.

Ryan smirked as he took the bottle from the paper sack in his hand: a fifth of Jameson Irish Whiskey.

His face beamed. "Good boy. Set 'em up."

He put two glasses on the bed tray in his

father's lap, then poured two fingers into each.

"You know the really good thing about Irish whiskey, Ryan?" He raised his glass in a toast, smiling wryly. "It's *Irish*. To your health, laddie," he said in an exaggerated brogue.

The hand was shaking, Ryan noticed, not from drinking but from his illness. He was even more pale today than yesterday, and his weakened body seemed shapeless, almost lifeless, beneath the wrinkled white sheets. In silence, they belted back one last round together. His father finished with a crooked smile of satisfaction.

"I still remember the first drink you ever took," he said with nostalgia in his eyes. "You were a spunky little eleven-year-old, pestering my old man for a sip. Your grandmother said go ahead and give it to him, thinking you'd spit it out like medicine and learn your lesson. You threw your head back, guzzled it right down and slammed the glass on the table, like some cowboy in the movies. You wanted to cough so bad your eyes were nearly popping out of your head. But you just dragged your sleeve across your lips, looked your grandma in the eye and said, 'Better than sex.' "

They shared a weak laugh. Then his father gave him a searching look. "That's the first time I've seen you smile in I don't know how long."

"Guess I haven't felt much like smiling. Didn't feel much like drinking tonight, either."

"What do you propose we do? Make a few phone calls, cancel the disease? Look," he said warmly, "the way I see it, we can either laugh in the face of death, or we can die trying not to. So be a sport and pour your old man another drink."

"I don't think you'd better, Dad. Painkillers and alcohol aren't a good mix."

"God, you're always so damned responsible, Ryan."

"What's wrong with that?"

"Nothing. I admire you for that, actually. Wish I were more like you. People always said we're exactly alike, but that's just on the surface. Not that it wasn't cute when you used to sit at the breakfast table and make like you were reading the sports section with me, trying to be just like Dad, even though you were two years old and didn't know how to read yet. But all that was just pretend. On the inside, where it counts—well, let's just say that you and I are far more different than you'd think."

He paused and placed his glass on the tray. All humor had left his face. He was suddenly philosophical. "Do you believe that good people can turn bad?"

"Sure," Ryan said with a shrug.

"I mean *really* bad, like criminals. Or do you think some things are so unspeakable, so heinous, that only someone who was bad from the very beginning could have done them?"

"I guess I don't think anyone's *born* bad.

People have their own free will. They make choices."

"So why would someone choose to be bad if they're not bad?"

"Because they're weak, I guess. Too weak to choose what's good, too weak to resist what's evil."

"Do you think the weak can become strong?" He propped himself up on his elbow at the edge of the mattress, looking Ryan in the eye. "Or once you turn toward evil are you like rotten fruit, gone forever?"

Ryan smiled awkwardly, not sure where this was headed. "Why are you asking me this?"

He lay back and sighed. "Because dying men take stock. And I am surely dying."

"Come on, Dad. You're devoted to Mom. Both your children love you. You're a good man."

"The best you can say is that I've *become* a good man."

The ominous words hung in the air. "Everybody does bad things," Ryan said tentatively. "That doesn't make them bad."

"That's the fundamental difference between you and me, son. You would never have done what I did."

Ryan sipped nervously from his empty glass, unsure of what to say, fearing some kind of confession. The drapes moved in the warm breeze.

His father continued, "There's an old chest of drawers in the attic. Move it. Beneath the floorboards, I've left something for you. Some money. A lot of it."

"How much?"

"Two million dollars."

Ryan froze, then burst out laughing. "That's a good one, Dad. Two million in the attic. And hell, all this time I thought you had it hidden in the mattress." He was smiling, shaking his head. Then he stopped.

His father wasn't smiling.

Ryan swallowed hard, a little nervous. "Come on. You're joking, right?"

"There's two million dollars in the attic, Ryan. I put it there myself."

"Where the hell would you get two million dollars?"

"That's what I'm trying to explain. You're not making this easy."

Ryan took the bottle from the tray. "Yup, I'd say that's about enough horsing around. Whiskey on top of painkillers has you hallucinating."

"I blackmailed a man. Someone who deserved it."

"Dad, cut it out. You were in no position to blackmail anybody."

"*Yes*, I was, damn it!" He spoke with such force, he started a coughing fit.

Ryan came to him and adjusted the pillows behind his back. His father was wheezing, gasping between coughs. The phlegm in his mouth was coming up bloody. Ryan pushed the emergency call button for the home care nurse in the next room. She arrived in seconds.

"Help me," said Ryan. "Sit him up straight so he doesn't choke."

She did as instructed. Ryan wheeled the oxygen tank alongside the bed. He opened the valve and placed the respirator in his mouth. Home oxygen supply was a drill the whole family knew well, as he'd suffered from emphysema long before the terminal cancer developed. After a few deep breaths, the wheezing subsided. Breathing slowly returned to normal.

"Dr. Duffy, I don't mean to question your professional judgment, but I think your father should rest now. He's had way too much activity for one night."

He knew she was right, but his father's eyes gave him pause. Ryan had expected the glazed, delirious look of a sedated man who was making up crazy stories about blackmail. But the dark old eyes were sharp and expressive. They not only spoke without words, they spoke intelligently. They had Ryan thinking, *Could he be serious?*

"I'll be back in the morning, Dad. We can talk then."

His father seemed to appreciate the reprieve, as if he had said enough for one night. Ryan pulled away, forcing a meager smile. He started to say "I love you," like he always did, fearful as he was that each conversation might be their last. This time he just turned and left the room, his mind racing. It was inconceivable, really—his father a blackmailer to the tune of two million dollars. Never, however, had Ryan seen his father more serious.

If this was a joke, it was frightfully convincing. And not the least bit funny.

Damn it, Dad, he thought as he left the house. *Please don't make me hate you.*

3

It was still dark when Amy woke. The drapes were drawn, but lights from the parking lot made them glow around the edges, the room's only illumination. Her eyes adjusted slowly. The twin bed beside hers was empty, already made. The usual morning noises emerged from the kitchen. Gram was always the first to rise, earlier and earlier with each passing year. Amy checked her alarm clock on the nightstand. Five-sixteen A.M.

She's probably fixing lunch by now.

Amy lay still, staring at the ceiling. She had done the right thing, she knew, by telling her. Gram would have wormed it out of her eventually. Amy had an incredibly expressive face, one that Gram had learned to read with ease. Truthfully, Amy wanted to tell her. She needed help with this one. Gram was old-fashioned, but few things were more reliable than old-fashioned common sense.

Amy slipped on her flannel robe and shuffled toward the kitchen, following the aroma of fresh strong coffee.

"Morning, dear," said Gram. She was already dressed. Overdressed, by her own historical standards. For almost half a century, Gram had lived in blue jeans in the winter, Bermuda shorts in the summer. Lately, she'd taken to pressed slacks and silk blouses, even for routine trips to the grocery store. Amy suspected a man was in the picture, though Gram vehemently denied it.

"Morning," said Amy. She pulled up a chair at the dining room table. Gram brought her a cup, no cream and two sugars, the way she liked it.

"I've made a decision," she said, taking the seat across from Amy. "We'll keep the money, right here."

"I thought you said you wanted to sleep on it, and that we'd discuss it in the morning."

"That's right."

"Well, this is hardly a discussion. You just announced a decision."

"Trust me, darling. Your grandmother knows best on these things."

The coffee was suddenly bitter. Amy measured her words, but there was resentment in her tone. "That's exactly what you said when you talked me into quitting astronomy for this computer job."

"And that has worked out beautifully. The law firm loves you so much they're willing to help send you to law school."

"It's not the law firm that loves me. It's Marilyn Gaslow. And the only reason she got the firm to cough up this partial scholarship is because she and Mom were old friends."

"Don't be cynical, Amy. Be realistic. With a degree in astronomy you would have been lucky to get a job teaching high school. You'll earn ten times more as a lawyer."

"Sure. And with spiked heels and a G-string I could make fifty times more than—"

"Stop," said Gram, covering her ears. "Don't be talking like that."

"I'm kidding, okay? Just making a point."

"There's no point in sass." Gram went to the kitchen and refilled her coffee cup.

Amy sighed, backing down, as usual. "I'm sorry, all right? It's not every day a box full of money comes in an unmarked package. I'd just like to talk it out."

Gram returned to her chair, then looked across the table, eye to eye. "What do *you* think we should do with it?"

"I don't know. Should we call the police?"

"What for? No crime has been committed."

"None that we know of, you mean."

"Amy, I'm surprised at you. How did you get so negative? Something good happens, and you immediately figure it has to be connected to something bad."

"I'm just considering all the possibilities. I'm assuming we don't have any rich relatives you've forgotten to tell me about."

Gram laughed. "Honey, in our family tree, not even the leaves are green."

"None of your friends have this kind of money to give away, do they?"

"You know the answer to that."

"So, if this is a gift, it came from someone we don't know, someone who's not even related to us."

"It could happen. Things like that do happen."

24

"When?"

"All the time."

"Name one."

"I can't think of one, but it happens. Somebody you met, somewhere along the line. You're a sweet person, Amy. Maybe some rich old man had a crush on you and you didn't even know it."

Amy shook her head. "This is just too strange. We should call the police."

"For *what*? We'll never see it again."

"If nobody claims it, I would think the police will give it back to us."

"That's not the way it works," said Gram. "A few years ago, I read in the newspaper about a minister who found over a million dollars in a suitcase on the side of the road. He turned it in to the police, thinking that if nobody claimed it, the cops would give it back to him, since he was the guy who found it. Sure enough, nobody claimed it. But you know what? The police said it was drug money, and they confiscated it under these drug laws they have now. They kept every penny of it. That's what will happen to us."

"I'm just worried. If it were just the two of us, maybe I'd be braver about this. But with Taylor living here, I'd feel better if we had a little protection."

"Protection from what?"

"Well, maybe it *is* drug money. Someone could have sent it to me by mistake, thinking I'm part of their distribution chain or something."

"That's preposterous."

"Oh, and some rich old man with the hots for me is perfectly logical."

"Look," said Gram, "I don't know who sent you this or why. All I know is that it couldn't have happened to a nicer person. So we keep the money, and we wait a couple weeks. Don't spend any of it, at least for a little while. Maybe in a few days a letter will come in the mail from someone that explains everything."

"Maybe the Mafia will come pounding on our door."

"Maybe. That's why we're keeping the money right here in our apartment."

"That's crazy, Gram. We should at least put it in a safe deposit box for safekeeping."

"Bad idea. Don't you watch the news? The quickest way to get shot in a robbery is not to have any money on you. It makes robbers very angry."

"What does that have to do with this?"

"Let's say it was criminals who sent you this money by mistake. Let's say they come looking for it. We tell them we don't have it. They think we're lying. They go berserk. Somebody gets hurt."

"But if the money is here, then what?"

"We just give it back to them. They leave happy, and we go on living the way we've always lived. The chances of anything bad like that happening are probably zilch. But in the worst-case scenario, I don't want any angry thugs accusing me of playing games. It's best if we can just hand over the money right on the spot and be done with it."

Amy finished her coffee. She looked away nervously, then back. "I don't know."

"There's no downside, Amy. If it's a gift, we're rich. If some creeps come to claim it, we just give it back. Just wait a couple weeks, that's all." Gram leaned forward and touched her granddaughter's hand. "And if things work out the way I think they will, you can go back to grad school."

"You certainly know how to push a girl's buttons."

"So, you're with me on this?"

Amy smiled with her eyes, peering over her cup. "Where do you want to stash our loot?"

"It's already in the perfect hiding spot. The freezer."

"The freezer?"

Gram smirked. "Where else would a crazy old woman keep a box of cold hard cash?"

4

Ryan spent the night in his old room, fading in and out of sleep. Mostly out.

As the only physician in town, Ryan hadn't taken a vacation in three years. For this, however, he'd managed to clear his calendar, referring all but the most pressing emergencies to clinics in neighboring towns.

Actually, he'd spent the last seven weeks living with his folks. He and his wife were legally separated, just the crack of a judge's gavel away from an official divorce after eight years of marriage. It was a classic case of unrealized expectations. Liz had worked as a waitress to help put him through medical school, thinking it would pay off after graduation. His friends from medical school had all moved on to mountainside homes and his-and-hers BMWs. Ryan had completed his surgery residency at Denver General Hospital and could have gone on to an equally lucrative career. He'd never been interested in pursuing the profits of "managed care," however, where HMOs and utilization review boards rewarded doctors for *not* treating patients. Over Liz's objection, he went back to his hometown to practice family medicine, the only doctor in town. Most of his patients were the real crisis in today's health care—children of lower-income workers or self-employed farmers who earned too much to qualify for Medicaid but who still couldn't afford health insurance. Liz eventually posted a sign in the office that said "PAYMENT DUE AT TIME OF SERVICE," but Ryan always looked the other way whenever someone needed credit. When the uncollected accounts receivable reached well into six figures, Liz couldn't stand it anymore. Ryan was running a charity. She filed for divorce.

So now he was home. His father dying. His wife moving to Denver. His boyhood memories staring down from the walls. With the end so near, he hadn't the time or inclination to redecorate and dissolve the past. Posters of quarterback Roger Staubach and the Super Bowl Champion Cowboys still covered the walls, abandoned by the kid who used to dream there almost three decades ago. He wondered what had happened to the famous one of Farrah Fawcett with her feathered hair and thin red swimsuit. Gone, but not forgotten.

Innocent times, he thought. Things didn't seem so innocent anymore.

Six A.M., and Ryan had hardly slept. He kept wondering, was it really the combination of booze and painkillers? Talk of blackmail and hordes of cash sounded like hallucination. But Dad was so damn serious.

Ryan had to check the attic.

He slipped out of bed and pulled on his jeans, sneakers and a polo shirt. The floorboards creaked beneath his feet. He stepped lightly. His mother was surely awake already, downstairs, at Dad's bedside. The morning vigil was their time alone. No one was going to deprive her of being with her husband of forty-five years at the moment of his death.

The door creaked open. Ryan peered into the hall. Not a sound. The attic, he recalled, was accessed through a ceiling panel at the end of the upstairs hallway. Ryan skulked like a prowler past the bathroom and guest bedroom, stopping beneath the two-foot length of chain hanging from the ceiling. He pulled. The hatch fell open like a crocodile's lower jaw. The big springs popped as the ladder unfolded. Ryan cringed at the noise, anticipating his mother's voice. But he heard nothing. Slowly, making not another sound, he extended the ladder to the floor and locked it into place. He drew a deep breath and began his ascent.

He was sweating almost immediately, besieged by yesterday's heat. Musty odors tickled his nostrils. A predawn glow seeped through the small east window, creating long shadows, illuminating cobwebs. Ryan tugged the string that dangled from the light socket, but the bare bulb was burned out. He waited, knowing that when his eyes adjusted, the morning light from the window would be sufficient.

Slowly, the past came into view. Ryan and his friends used to play up here, twenty-five years ago. Sarah, his older sister, always used to spy on them. She was the one who had discovered their coveted *Playboy* magazine. Ryan wasn't sure if Sarah liked being a good do-bee or if she just liked to see him punished. He wondered what Miss Goody Two-shoes would think now.

Each step across the attic triggered more memories. His first stereo, complete with vinyl records that had long ago melted in the attic's hundred-plus-degree heat. His sister's clarinet from the high school band. Seeing all this junk reminded him that soon he would begin his task as executor of the estate, taking inventory of his father's possessions—the simple belongings of a life-long wage earner. A rusty set of tools. Extra fishing gear. Stacks of old clothes. Furniture his dad had never gotten around to fixing. And if this was no joke, two million dollars in tainted funds.

It *had* to be a joke.

Ryan stopped at the old chest of drawers his father had described to him last night. He swallowed hard; its existence confirmed that his father wasn't completely delusional. But that didn't mean there was actually money beneath it.

He shoved the chest once. It wouldn't budge. He shoved harder. It moved an inch, then another. With all his strength, Ryan slid it a good two feet. He glanced at the floor. The boards it had once covered were not nailed down. Ryan knelt down and lifted the loose planks, exposing a layer of fiberglass insulation. He peeled it away. A suitcase was in plain view. Not the typical vacation suitcase. This one was metal, presumably fireproof, like the ones sold in spy shops. Ryan lifted it from the hole and laid it on the floor in front of him. It had a combination lock, but the latches weren't fixed. Dad had apparently left the tumblers set to the combination, making it easy for his son. Ryan popped the latch and lifted the lid, his eyes bulging at the sight.

"Ho-lee shit."

It was all there, just as his father had promised. Ryan had never seen two million dollars, but the neat stacks of hundred-dollar bills could easily total up to that much.

Lightly, Ryan raked his fingers over the bills. Although he'd never been driven by money, seeing and touching this much cash sent tingles down his spine. Last night, while lying in bed, he had tried to make himself fall asleep by pretending the money might actually be there and asking himself what he might do with it. In the realm of the hypothetical and highly unlikely, he had resolved to give it all away to charity. He wouldn't want the fruits of a crime—even if, as Dad had said, the man deserved to be blackmailed. But with all this green staring him in the face, the issues weren't so black and white. Had he not dedicated his career to a low-income community, he might easily have earned this much cash in a normal-paying medical practice. Maybe this was God's way of making him whole for a life of good deeds.

Get over yourself, Duffy.

He closed up the suitcase and put it back in the hole, covering it with the insulation and loose planks, just the way he had found it. He slid the heavy chest back in place. Quickly, he retraced his steps to the ladder. He'd deal with the money later. After the funeral.

After one more talk with Dad.

Ryan climbed down the ladder, into the hall. His shirt was dirty and soaked with sweat. He ducked into the bathroom and splashed cold water on his face. He threw his shirt in the hamper, then started toward his room for a clean one. He stopped as he passed the stairwell. It sounded like his mother sobbing in the living room. He hurried down the stairs. She was alone on the couch, shoulders slumped, still wearing her robe and slippers.

"What is it, Mom?"

She looked up, and he knew.

He came to her side, took her in his arms.

32

She'd always been petite, but never so frail.

Her body shook, her voice was quaking. "It was so...peaceful. His touch. His breath. His presence. It all just faded away."

"It's okay, Mom."

"It's like he was ready," she said, sniffling. "As if he'd just decided it was time."

Ryan bristled. *As if he'd rather die than face his son again.*

His mother shook harder in his arms, the tears flowing freely. He held her close, rocking gently. "Don't worry," he whispered, almost speaking to himself. "I'll take care of everything."

5

Amy took Monday morning off, arriving at the office during the lunch hour. After six straight days of nonstop work, three thousand travel miles among the firm's U.S. offices, and immeasurable abuse and aggravation from frantic attorneys, she felt entitled to a few hours with her daughter.

The Boulder office of Bailey, Gaslow & Heinz was on Walnut Street, filling the top three floors of a five-story building. Boulder was the firm's second-largest office, though with 33 lawyers it was a distant second behind Denver, which had 140. The office prided itself on doing the same quality work and generating the same billable hours per lawyer as

Denver. That was the minimum standard set by the new managing-partner-in-residence, a certified workaholic who had moved from Denver to Boulder to whip the satellite office into shape.

"Morning," said Amy as she breezed by a co-worker in the hall. She got a cup of coffee from the lounge, then headed back to her office. The thought of a week's worth of work piled up on her desk made her dread opening the door.

Her office was small, but she was the only non-lawyer in the firm who had a window and a view. Marilyn Gaslow had pulled strings to get it for her. Marilyn was an influential partner who worked out of Denver. Her grandfather was the "Gaslow" in Bailey, Gaslow & Heinz, one of the founding partners over a century ago. She and Amy's mother had been friends since high school—best friends until her death. It was Marilyn who had gotten Amy hired as the computer expert, and it was Marilyn who had committed the firm to pay half of Amy's tuition if she went to law school. The only condition was that Amy had to come back to work at the firm as an associate, putting her valuable law and science background to use in the firm's nationally recognized environmental law practice. At least, that was supposed to be the only condition. Ever since Amy had accepted the deal, the firm had treated her like slave labor.

She sat down behind her desk and switched on the computer. She had been checking her e-mail from outside the office for the past week, but she had some new messages. One was from Marilyn, just this morning. It read, "Atta girl, Amy. One hell of a job!"

Amy smiled. At least *one* of the firm's two hundred lawyers knew how to say thank you for salvaging the computer system. Somehow, however, it didn't mean quite as much coming from Marilyn, her mother's old buddy. She scrolled down to the next virtual envelope on her screen. It was from Jason Phelps, head of the litigation department in the Boulder office. Now, kudos from *him* would definitely be a breakthrough. She opened it eagerly.

SEE ME! was all it said.

She looked up from her screen and nearly jumped. He was standing in the doorway, scowling. "Mr. Phelps—good morning, sir. Afternoon, I mean."

"Yes. It is *after* noon. A big T-ball game for Timmy this morning, I presume?"

Her gut wrenched. It didn't matter how many nights and weekends she worked. It didn't matter if she was away on firm business. For a single mother, temporary unavailability always gave rise to the same negative inference.

"Her name is Taylor," she said coolly. "And she doesn't play T-ball. Her mother doesn't have time to take her."

"I need that joint defense network for the Wilson superfund litigation operable by three o'clock. No later."

"I have to work through the MIS directors of six different law firms. You want it in two hours?"

35

"I *wanted* it yesterday. Today, I *need* it. I don't care how you get it done. Just get it done." He raised a bushy gray eyebrow, then turned and left.

Amy sank in her chair. Things were picking up right where they had left off. *I'd like to play T-ball with your head, asshole.*

She would have liked to say it to his face, but he would surely pull the plug on the firm's promise to subsidize her tuition. Then she couldn't go to law school. And then she couldn't come back—to *this*.

"I need a life," she muttered. She wondered why she put up with it, but she knew the answer. Every two or three months, her ex-husband would remind her. He'd call with another one of his empty offers to pay half of something for Taylor if Amy would pay the other half. Sometimes he was just being disruptive, like the time he told Taylor he'd send her and Amy on a Hawaiian vacation if Mommy would just pay half. Taylor had pranced around the house in a plastic lei and sunglasses for a week before that one blew over. Other times he was just taunting Amy, like his standing offer to put ten thousand dollars into a college fund for Taylor if Amy would come up with the other ten. Things like that—things for Taylor's future—really made her wish she were in the position to call his bluff.

Maybe she was.

Her eyes lit with a devilish smile. She picked up the phone and dialed his office. His secretary answered.

"I'm sorry," she told Amy. "He's in a meeting. Can I take a message?"

The message was right in her head, ready to spring. Taylor's going to Yale. Pay half of *that*, you blowhard. But she realized it was premature. The money wasn't hers. Not yet.

"No message, thank you." She hung up and came back to reality.

She checked the clock. She'd have to clone herself to meet Mr. Phelps's three o'clock deadline. She drew a deep breath and returned to the computer, but not for Phelps's project. A financial planning program appeared on her screen.

She smiled thinly as the computer calculated the interest on two hundred thousand dollars.

The funeral was on Tuesday at St. Edmund's Catholic Church. Neither Ryan nor his sister were regular churchgoers. His parents, however, had attended nearly every Sunday for the last four decades. Here, Frank and Jeanette Duffy had exchanged marriage vows. It was where their two children had been baptized and taken their First Holy Communion. Ryan's sister, Sarah, had also been married here. In the last row of the balcony, a fellow altar boy had told Ryan where babies really come from. Behind the solid oak doors in the side chapel, Ryan used to confess his sins to an old Irish priest with a drinker's red nose. *"Bless me, Father, for I have sinned..."*

Ryan wondered when his father had last gone

to confession. He wondered what he'd confessed.

St. Edmund's was an old stone church built in the style of a Spanish mission. It wasn't an authentic Spanish mission. The old Spanish explorers hadn't bothered to go as far east as the Colorado plains in their search for the mythical Seven Cities of Gold. Places like the San Luis Valley and Sangre de Cristo Mountains in southwest and south central Colorado were filled with reminders of the legendary search for cities made of solid gold. The Spaniards seemed to have stopped, however, once the landscape turned interminably flat. Somehow, even sixteenth-century explorers must have sensed that no riches would lie in Piedmont Springs.

If only they had checked Frank Duffy's attic.

Ryan felt a chill. The church was cold inside, even in July. Dark stained-glass windows blocked out most of the natural light. The smell of burning incense lingered over the casket in the center aisle, rising to the sweeping stone arches overhead. The service was well attended. Frank Duffy had many friends, none of whom apparently had a clue that he was a blackmailer who'd socked away two million dollars in extortion money. Dressed in black, his mourners filled thirty rows of pews on both sides of the aisle. Father Marshall presided over the service, wearing a somber expression and dark purple vestments. Ryan sat in the front row beside his mother. His sister and brother-in-law sat to his left.

Liz, his estranged wife, had been "unable to attend."

The organ music ended abruptly. An ominous silence filled the church, pierced only by the occasional squawk of an impatient child. Ryan squeezed his mother's hand as his uncle approached the lectern to deliver a eulogy. Uncle Kevin was bald and overweight, suffering from heart disease, once the odds-on favorite to drop dead before his younger brother. He seemed the least prepared of all for Frank Duffy's death.

He adjusted the microphone, cleared his throat. "I loved Frank Duffy," he said in a shaky voice. "We all loved him."

Ryan wanted to listen, but his mind wandered. Months in advance they knew this day was coming. It had started with a cough, which he'd dismissed as the same old chronic emphysema. Then they found the lesion on the larynx. Their initial fear was that Dad might lose his voice. Frank Duffy had the gift of gab. He was always the one telling jokes at the bar, the guy laughing loudest at parties. It would have been a cruel irony, taking away his ability to speak—like an artist gone blind, or a musician turned deaf. The throat lesion, however, had only been the proverbial tip of the iceberg. The cancer had already metastasized. Doctors gave him three to four months. He never did lose his voice—at least not until the very end, silenced by his own sense of shame. His death brought its own irony.

The eulogy continued. "My brother was a workingman all his life, the kind of guy who'd get nervous whenever the poker ante rose above fifty cents." His smile faded, his expression more serious. "But Frank was rich in spirit and blessed with a loving family."

Ryan's heart felt hollow. His uncle's fond memories no longer seemed relevant. In light of the money, they didn't even ring true.

He heard his aunt sobbing in the second row. Several other mourners were moved to tears. He glanced at his mother. No tears behind the black veil, he noted with curiosity. She sat stone-faced, expressionless. No sign of sadness or distress of any kind. Of course, the illness had been prolonged. She must have cried it out by now, no emotion left.

Or, he wondered, *was there something she knew?*

6

Amy met Mr. Phelps's unrealistic three o'clock deadline. She always met her deadlines. This time, however, she was feeling abused. She went home when she finished.

She conjured up an image as she drove—a fantasy of sorts. It had to do with the money. She wouldn't just quietly give notice, she decided. She would drive her old truck to Bailey, Gaslow & Heinz, like any other day. She'd get her morning coffee, retreat to her office, and sit very calmly at her desk. But she wouldn't turn on her computer. She wouldn't even close the door. She'd leave it wide open—and just *wait* for someone like Phelps to come piss her off.

For the moment, however, the waiting was beginning to breed paranoia.

It had been Gram's idea to keep the money in the house and see what happened. Amy had a nagging instinct that someone was testing her, checking whether she'd do the honorable thing. She recalled the pointed questions on her application to law school. *Are you currently under investigation for any crime? Have you ever been convicted of a crime?* Before long she would face the same probing questions in her application to the Colorado State Bar Association. What kind of dim view might they take toward a candidate who had knowingly deprived the IRS of its fair share of a mysterious cash windfall? Worse yet, someone could be setting her up—someone like her ex-husband. Maybe he'd reported the money stolen, the serial numbers registered with the FBI. The minute she tried to spend it, she'd be arrested.

Now you're really being paranoid. Amy's ex-husband made a stink over paying five hundred dollars a month in child support. He certainly wouldn't risk shipping two hundred grand in a cardboard box. Still, the prudent course was to contact the police, probably even fess up to the IRS. But Gram would kill her. She'd kill herself, if she messed up her chance to beg off law school, return to her graduate studies and follow her dreams. It was time for Amy Parkens to live on the edge a little.

41

Amy walked to the kitchenette and opened the freezer door. She reached for the box of cash behind the frozen pot roast.

"Amy, what are you doing?"

She turned at the sound of her grandmother's voice. She felt the urge to lie, but she could never fool Gram. "Just checking on our investment."

Gram placed a bag of groceries on the table. She'd returned from the store sooner than Amy had expected. "It's all there," said Gram. "I didn't take any."

"I wasn't suggesting you had."

"Then leave it be, girl."

Amy closed the door and helped unload the groceries. "Where's Taylor?"

"Outside. Mrs. Bentley from three-seventeen is watching her. She owes us, all the times I've watched her little monsters." Gram paused, then smiled with a thought. "Maybe we can take some of the money and get Taylor a nanny. A good one. Someone who speaks French. I'd like Taylor to speak French."

Amy stuffed a box of Rice Krispies into the pantry. "Excellent idea. She'll be the only four-year-old in Boulder who orders *pommes frites* with her Happy Meal."

"I'm serious, Amy. This money is going to open a whole new world for your daughter."

"That's so unfair. Don't use Taylor to make me feel better about keeping this money."

"I don't understand you. What's so wrong about keeping it?"

"It makes me nervous. Sitting around, waiting for a letter in the mail or a knock on the door—anything that might explain the money. An explanation might never come. If the money was sent by mistake, I want to know. If it's a gift, I'd like to know whose kindness is behind it."

"Hire a detective, if you're that nervous. Maybe they can check the box or even the money for fingerprints."

"That's a great idea."

"Just one problem. How are you going to pay for it?"

Amy's smile vanished.

Gram said, "You could use some of the money. Take five hundred bucks or so."

"No. We can't spend any of it until we find out who it's from."

"Then all we can do is wait." She folded up the paper shopping bag, placed it in a drawer, and kissed Amy on the forehead. "I'm going to check on our little angel."

She grimaced as her grandmother left the apartment. Waiting was not her style. Short of hiring a detective and checking for fingerprints, however, she wasn't sure how else to go about it. Cash was virtually untraceable. The plastic lining had no identification on it. That left the box.

The box!

She hurried to the freezer, yanked open the door, and grabbed the box. She set it on the table and checked the flaps. Nothing on top. She turned it over. Bingo. As she had hoped, the box bore a printed product identification number for the Crock-Pot it had once contained. Amy had purchased enough small

43

appliances to know that they always came with a warranty registration card. She doubted, however, that they would freely give out names and addresses over the phone. After a moment to collect her thoughts, she called directory assistance, got the toll-free number for Gemco Home Appliances, and dialed it.

"Good afternoon," she said in her most affected, friendly voice. "I have a favor to ask. We had a potluck supper here at the church the other night, and wouldn't you know it that two women showed up with the exact same Gemco Crock-Pot? I washed them both, and now I'm not sure whose is whose. I really don't want to have to tell these women I mixed up their stuff. If I gave you the product identification number from one of them, could you tell me who owns it?"

The operator on the line hesitated. "I'm not sure I can do that, ma'am."

"Please. Just the name. It would save me a world of embarrassment."

"Well—I suppose that would be all right. Just don't tell my supervisor."

She read him the eleven-digit number from the box, then waited anxiously.

"Here it is," he said. "That one belongs to Jeanette Duffy."

"Oh, Jeanette." Amy wanted to push for an address, but she couldn't think of a convincing way to work it into her ruse. *Leave it be,* she thought, heeding Gram's advice. "Thank you so much, sir."

Her heart pounded as she hung up the phone. She had surprised herself, the way she'd pulled it off. It was actually kind of fun, exhilarating. Best of all, it had worked. She had a lead.

Now all she had to do was find the right Jeanette Duffy.

7

The kitchen smelled of corned beef and cabbage. So did the dining room. The living room, too. The whole house smelled of it. It was a Duffy family tradition going back as far as Ryan could remember, which was his grandfather's funeral. Just as soon as the body was in the ground, they'd file back to the house and stuff themselves, as if to prove that nothing was depressing enough to ruin a good meal. Somebody always brought corned beef and cabbage. Hell, anyone who could turn on an oven brought corned beef and cabbage.

Dad didn't even like corned beef and cabbage. Not that it mattered. Dad was gone. Forever.

"Your father was a good man, Ryan." It was Josh Colburn, the family lawyer. He'd been *every* family's lawyer for the last fifty years. He was no Clarence Darrow, but he was an honest man, an old-school lawyer who considered the law a sacred profession. It was no wonder his dearly departed client's last will and testament had made no mention of the stash in the attic. Colburn was the *last* person Dad would have told.

He was back in the buffet line before Ryan could thank him for the kind words.

Apart from the guests' black attire, the post-cemetery gathering had lost any discernible connection to a funeral. It had begun somberly enough, with scattered groups of friends and relatives quietly remembering Frank Duffy. As the crowd grew, so did the noise level. The small groups expanded from three or four to six or eight, until the house was so crowded it was impossible to tell where one group left off and the other started. The food had broken whatever ice remained—tons of food from mutton to whitefish, dumplings to trifle. Before long, someone was playing "Danny Boy" on the old upright piano, and Uncle Kevin was pouring shots of Jameson's, toasting his dearly departed brother and days gone by.

Ryan didn't join in. He just kept moving from room to room, knowing that if he stood still he'd be locked in conversation with someone he had no interest in talking to. In fact, he had no interest in talking to anyone. Except his mother.

Ryan had been watching her closely all day, ever since that eulogy that had moved everyone to tears—everyone but Jeanette Duffy. She had a detached look about her. In some ways it seemed normal. She wouldn't be the first widow to walk numbly through her husband's funeral. It was just so unlike his mother. She was an emotional woman, the kind

46

who'd seen *It's a Wonderful Life* at least fifty times and still cried every time Clarence got his wings.

Ryan caught her eye from across the room. She looked away.

"Eat something, Ryan." His aunt was pushing a plate of food toward him.

"No, thanks. I'm not really hungry."

"You don't know what you're missing."

"Really, I'm not hungry." Through the crowd, he tried to catch his mother's eye again, but she wouldn't look his way. He glanced down at his four-foot-ten-inch aunt. "Aunt Angie, does Mom seem okay to you?"

"Okay? I guess so. This is a very tough time for her, Ryan. Your father is the only man she ever—you know. Loved. What they had was special. They were like one person."

He glanced at his mother, than back at his aunt. "I don't suppose they would have kept any secrets from each other, would they?"

"I wouldn't think so. No, definitely not. Not Frank and Jeanette."

Ryan was staring in his mother's direction, but he'd lost focus. He was deep in thought.

His aunt touched his hand. "Are you all right, darling?"

"I'm fine," he said vaguely. "I think I just need some air. Will you excuse me a minute?" He started across the living room, toward the front door, then stopped. He sensed his mother was watching. He turned and caught her eye. This time she didn't look away.

Ryan worked his way back through the

47

crowd toward the dining room. His mother was standing at the head of the table full of food, busily cutting a piece of corned beef into toddler-sized pieces for some youngster. He stood right beside her, laid his hand on hers, speaking in a soft voice. "Mom, I need to talk to you in private."

"Now?"

"Yes."

She smiled nervously. "But the guests."

"They can wait, Mom. This is important."

She blinked nervously, then laid down the carving knife beside the plate of bite-size beef. "All right. We can talk in the master."

Ryan followed her down the hall. The door flew open as they reached the master suite. An old man came out, zipping his fly.

"Sorry," he said sheepishly. "Damn prostate, you know." He hurried away.

They entered together. Ryan closed the door, shutting out the noise. Like his own old bedroom, the master was a veritable time capsule, complete with the old sculptured wall-to-wall carpeting and cabbage rose wallpaper. The bed was the old four-poster style, so high off the floor it required a stepstool to get into it. He and his sister Sarah used to hide beneath it as kids. Dad would pretend he couldn't find them, even though their giggling was loud enough to wake up the neighbors. Ryan shook off the memories and checked the master bathroom, making sure they were alone. His mother sat in the armchair in the corner beside the bureau. Ryan leaned against the bedpost.

"What's on your mind, Ryan?"

"Dad told me something the night before he died. Something pretty disturbing."

Her voice cracked. "Oh?"

He started to pace. "Look, there's really no delicate way to put this, so let me just ask you. Did you know anything about some kind of blackmail Dad might have been involved in?"

"Blackmail?"

"Yes, blackmail. Two million dollars, cash." Ryan checked her reaction, searching for surprise. He saw none.

"Yes, I knew."

He suddenly stopped pacing, stunned. "You knew *what*?"

She sighed. It was as if she were expecting this conversation, but that didn't mean she had to enjoy it. "I knew about the money. And I knew about the blackmail."

"You actually let him do it?"

"It's not that simple, Ryan."

His voice grew louder. "I'm all ears, Mom. Tell me."

"There's no need for that tone."

"I'm sorry. It's just that we haven't exactly lived like millionaires. Now Dad's dead, I find out he was a blackmailer, and there's two million dollars in the attic. Who in the heck was he blackmailing?"

"That I don't know."

"What do you mean, you don't know?"

"He never told me. He didn't want me to know. That way, if anything ever went wrong, I could honestly tell the police I didn't know anything. I had nothing to do with it."

"But you were happy to reap the benefits."

"No, I wasn't. That's why the money's still in the attic. To me, it was tainted. I would never let your father spend a penny of it. Your father and I had some doozy fights over this. I even threatened to leave him."

"Why didn't you?"

She looked at him curiously, as if the question were stupid. "I loved him. And he told me the man deserved to be blackmailed."

"You believed him?"

"Yes."

"So that's it? Dad says the guy deserved it, so you let him keep the money. But you wouldn't let him spend it. That's crazy."

She folded her arms, suddenly defensive. "We reached a compromise. I didn't feel comfortable spending the money, but your father thought you and your sister might feel differently. So we agreed that he would keep it hidden until he died. Then we'd leave it up to you and Sarah to decide whether you wanted to keep it, leave it, burn it—whatever you decide. It's yours. If you can spend it in good conscience, you have your father's blessing."

Ryan stepped to the window, looking out to the backyard. Uncle Kevin was organizing a game of horseshoes. He spoke quietly with his back to his mother. "What am I supposed to say?"

"It's your call—yours and Sarah's."

He turned and faced her, showing no emotion. "Guess it's time I had a little talk with my big sister."

8

The Crock-Pot discovery had Amy in high gear. Just to be safe, she didn't want to use the law firm's computers or phones for the follow-up on Jeanette Duffy. A run through her standard Internet search engines on her home computer, however, had turned up hundreds of Jeanette Duffys nationwide, with nothing to distinguish any one of them as the possible sender. So she went to the University of Colorado law library for more sophisticated computerized capabilities. She wasn't technically a student yet, but a sweet smile and a copy of her acceptance letter for the fall class was good enough to gain access to the free Nexis service, which would allow her to search hundreds of newspapers and periodicals.

She figured she'd limit the search to Colorado initially, then expand out from there, if necessary. She typed in "Jeanette Duffy" and hit the search button, then chose the most recent entry from a chronological listing of about a dozen articles.

The blue screen blinked and displayed the full text of an article from yesterday's *Pueblo Chieftain*. Amy half expected to find that someone named Jeanette Duffy had just embezzled two hundred thousand dollars from the First National Bank of Colorado.

Instead, she found an obituary.

"Frank Duffy," it read, "62, longtime resident of Piedmont Springs, on July 11, after a courageous battle with cancer. Survived by Jeanette Duffy, his wife of 44 years; their son, Ryan Patrick Duffy, M.D.; and their daughter, Sarah Duffy-Langford. Services today, 10 A.M., at St. Edmund's Catholic church in Piedmont Springs."

Amy stared at the screen. A death made sense of things. Perhaps the two hundred thousand dollars was some kind of bequest. She printed the article, then logged off the computer, headed for the pay phone by the rest rooms, and dialed home.

"Gram, do you remember the exact day our little package was delivered?"

"I told you before, darling. I wasn't there when it came. It was just waiting on the doorstep."

"Think hard. What day was it when it just showed up?"

"Oh, I don't know. But it was right after you left. No more than a couple days."

"So, definitely more than a week ago?"

"I'd say so, yes. Why do you ask?"

She hesitated, fearing her grandmother's wrath. "I've been doing a little investigating."

"Amy," her grandmother said, groaning.

"Just listen. The money came in an old box for a Crock-Pot, right? Well, I took the serial number from the box and found out that the Crock-Pot belonged to Jeanette Duffy. Turns out there's a Jeanette Duffy in Piedmont Springs whose husband died five days ago."

"Don't tell me. They buried him in a Crock-Pot."

"Stop, Gram. I think I'm on to something. The obituary said he had a courageous battle with cancer. That means he knew he was dying. He could have sent it to me before his death. Or his wife could have sent it. Like a secret bequest or something that he didn't want their children to know about."

"Don't you think you're jumping to conclusions here?"

"Not really. All my fears about possible criminal connections seem off the mark, the more I think about it. Criminals wouldn't send money in a Crock-Pot box. No offense, Gram, but that sounds like something an old man or woman would do."

"So, what are you going to do now? Call this Jeanette Duffy just a few days after her dead husband is laid in the ground? Please, give the poor woman some time to grieve."

"Gosh, I hate to lose any time."

"Amy," she said sternly. "Show some consideration."

"Okay, okay. I gotta run. Love to Taylor." She hung up, tempted to snatch the phone right back and call Jeanette Duffy. But Gram was right. It was conceivable that Jeanette Duffy's husband had sent the money without his wife's knowledge. Or Amy could have the wrong Jeanette Duffy entirely. Either way, it would be cruel to confront a recent widow with a discovery like this. She checked the obituary again. A sly smile came to her face as she hurriedly dialed directory assistance.

"Piedmont Springs," she said into the phone. "Yes, I'd like the number and the

53

address for Ryan Duffy, M.D." She smirked as she jotted down the information.

The widow was off limits. But the son was fair game.

9

"We're rich!"

Sarah Langford's face beamed with excitement as she spoke. His sister would have leapt from her chair, thought Ryan, had she not been eight months pregnant.

Sarah was just five years older than Ryan, but to him she had always seemed old. In grade school, her beehive hairdo and sixties-style cat's-eye glasses made her look more matronly than their own mother. Kids used to tease that Ryan was prettier than his sister, more a slap to her than a compliment to him. Sadly, she hadn't really changed much over the past three decades, save for the gray hair, crow's feet around the eyes, and additional poundage. Sarah had been big before getting pregnant, which made her eighth month look more like her twelfth.

"Two million bucks!" She was literally squealing with delight. "I just can't *believe* it!"

They were alone in Ryan's old room. Their mother was downstairs with a handful of relatives who had decided to make dinner out of the leftovers from this afternoon's post-service feast. Ryan was sitting on the bed. Sarah

54

had squeezed into the nicked and scratched Windsor chair from his old desk. There had been no option but to tell her. Half the money was rightfully hers. Still, he hadn't expected her to go giddy on him. At least not on the very same day their father had been buried.

"Easy, Sarah. There is a catch."

Her excitement slowly faded. "A catch?"

"It's not really found money, so to speak. At best, it's tainted."

"In what way?"

"Dad got it by blackmailing somebody."

Her eyes widened once again, this time with anger. "If this is your idea of a joke, I'm—"

"It's no joke." In minutes, he explained all he knew—in particular, how neither he nor their mother knew who had paid the money. "The only thing he told Mom was that the guy deserved to be blackmailed."

"Then we deserve to keep it."

"Sarah, we don't know that."

"What do you want to do, give it back?"

He said nothing.

His sister shot him a troubled look. "You can't be serious."

"I just want to get some basic questions answered before we do anything. For all we know, Dad extorted some poor old fart for every cent he was worth. Or maybe he was forced to steal to meet Dad's demands. And what horrible thing did this guy do in the first place to make him vulnerable to blackmail?"

"Don't you think we owe it to our father to trust his judgment on those questions?"

"Hell, no. I loved Dad, but the bottom

line is, he was a blackmailer. Morality aside, this money raises some serious legal problems. If the IRS or FBI gets wind of the fact that Dad somehow came into two million dollars without winning the Lotto, someone—namely *us*—is going to have some serious explaining to do."

"Fine. Then give me my million, and you can do whatever you want with yours. I'll take my chances. But from where I sit, it seems like lawyers are pretty damn good at keeping millionaires out of trouble."

"I don't want to fight with you over this. We need a plan, one we both can stick to."

She struggled for a deep breath, shifting her pregnant body awkwardly in her chair. The slightest movement seemed to bring on discomfort. "Damn it, Ryan. You've got my hemorrhoids flaring up."

"I'll write you a prescription," he said dryly.

"Wouldn't do any good. I couldn't afford to get it filled. Look at the realities, Ryan. It's been a tough year for the whole family. On top of Dad's doctor bills, pretty soon we're going to have to figure out a way to take care of Mom. She depended on Dad for everything, so you can bet she'll look to us now. You're in the middle of a divorce, and even though Liz has been acting pretty civil toward the family, I think it says something that she didn't come to the funeral. From what I hear, she's gone out and hired a shark of a Denver divorce lawyer who has a reputation for leaving husbands flat broke."

"Sarah, I can deal with my own problems."

"Well, I've got my problems of my own. At my age, it ended up costing me and Brent a fortune to get pregnant. All these fertility drugs aren't cheap. We're up to our eyeballs in debt, and the baby isn't even born yet. And the way Mom keeps nagging, I shouldn't have to remind you that Brent hasn't worked since they closed down the plant."

"You think two million dollars can solve the world's problems?"

"No. But it can solve *ours*."

"It might create more problems than it solves."

"Only if you let it, Ryan. Now, if you don't mind, I'd like to see my million dollars."

He shook his head. "We can't split it up until we have an agreement on what we're going to do with it."

"It's my money. I'll do what I want."

"We have to stick together on this. There's all kinds of issues to resolve. Not the least of which is possible estate tax."

"Jeez, Ryan. Just take the money, and be happy."

"I'm the executor of the estate. It's my neck on the line. Blackmail is illegal, you know. We're talking about receiving the proceeds of criminal activity. If we're going to do it, we're going to do it the right way."

"And what is the right way?"

"I'll keep the money hidden until we find out who Dad blackmailed and why. In the meantime, we tell no one about it. Not Liz. Not Brent. That way, the secret won't slip out and the IRS won't come crashing down on our heads. In the end, if we're satisfied that Dad was right—if the man did deserve to be black-mailed—then we'll keep it."

"And if he didn't deserve it?"

"Then we make a two-million-dollar anonymous donation to charity."

"Get outta town!"

"That's the deal, Sarah."

"What if I don't like it?"

"I don't want to be a bully about this, but you don't know where the money is. I do. If anybody gets greedy, I've already picked out a very deserving charity."

"Shit, Ryan. That's like extortion."

"It must run in the family."

She made a face.

"So," he said. "We tell no one, not even Liz or Brent. *Especially* not Liz or Brent. Till I find out the truth. Do we have a deal?"

"I guess so," she said, grumbling.

"Good." He rose to help his sister from the chair. She waved him off, refusing his offer. He stepped aside as she waddled toward the door. He scratched his head and watched, wondering if the compromise was the right thing to do—and questioning the strength of Sarah's commitment.

Ryan knew his sister was angry. She left the house immediately after their conversation, barely taking the time to say goodbye to their mother. He didn't see any point in chasing after her. They'd each had their say. Hopefully she'd cool down on her own.

His mother and aunts were bouncing back and forth between the kitchen and dining room cleaning up. Staying busy was certainly one way to stave off the loneliness, the crying jags. Ryan escaped to the family room and switched on the evening news. A flood in India had killed eighty-six people. A convenience store clerk had been shot to death in Fort Collins.

A working stiff in Piedmont Springs just died in his sleep. The last one didn't make the news. No violence, no fascination, no news. *Should have jumped off a building, Dad.*

Ryan paused, wondering if his father had succumbed to the thinking that a life wasn't worthy unless it was *news*worthy. Dad had always shortchanged his own accomplishments, never fully seeing the beauty in the way he made others feel good about themselves, one person at a time. Most people didn't think the cashier at the grocery store or the gas station attendant were worth their time. Frank Duffy knew their names, and they knew his. He had the magic touch with everyone. *That* was something to be proud of. Yet Ryan remembered back in high school, when his acceptance letter had come from the University of Colorado. The first Duffy to go to college. His father had been more excited than anyone, embracing him so hard he'd nearly cracked a rib as he whispered in Ryan's ear, "Now the Duffys finally have something to be proud of." At the time, Ryan had thought it sad that his father didn't feel the pride he rightfully should have felt. Now he could only wonder what secrets had made him feel so ashamed.

The news was turning to sports when Ryan heard a knock on the front door. He rose from the couch and answered it.

"Liz," he said with surprise.

His wife stood in the doorway, tentative. "Can—can I come in?"

He stepped aside awkwardly. "Of course. Come in."

Liz was wearing a casual print sundress, not exactly mourning attire. It showed the figure she'd worked hard to maintain. She'd changed her hair, Ryan noticed. It was lighter, more blonde, making her eyes seem greener, her legs more tan. Physical attraction had never been the problem in their marriage. Maybe it was a classic case of wanting what you can't have, but to Ryan his wife had never looked better than in the last seven weeks, since she'd told him she was filing for divorce.

"Can I get you something?" asked Ryan. "Lots of food left. You know how funerals are in the Duffy family."

"No, thanks."

Ryan wasn't surprised. Liz never ate, it seemed, never needed sustenance. Eight years of marriage and he never did find that battery she must have run on.

Liz said, "Can we talk for a minute?"

She seemed to be shying from the noise in the kitchen. Ryan quickly surmised her visit wasn't family-oriented. She wanted some privacy. "Not to push you out the door," he said, "but how about the porch?"

She nodded, then led the way to the big covered wood porch that extended across the front of the house, overlooking the lawn. Ryan closed the door behind them. He started toward the wicker love seat near the picture window, but they both stopped short, thinking twice. Too many memories there, watching sunsets side by side. Liz took the old rocker. Ryan sat on the porch railing beside a potted cactus plant.

"I'm sorry I missed the funeral," she said, eyes lowered. "After all these years, I did love Frank. I wanted to go. I just thought it would have been awkward for the family. You, especially."

"I understand."

"I hope you do. Because I don't want us to end up enemies."

"It's okay. I promise."

She looked away, then turned her gaze toward Ryan. "I don't think Frank would want us to be enemies."

"Dad would want us to stay married, Liz. But this isn't about what Dad wants." Ryan paused. His words had sounded harsher than intended. "I do appreciate the way you helped me keep the lid on the divorce around Dad. There really wasn't any need for him to know."

She sniffed back a tear, nearly scoffed. It was a hopeless charade. Ryan had kept up for the sake of his dying father, never telling him that the marriage was over. "He must have known. For God's sake, we lived in Piedmont Springs. *Everybody* knew."

"He never said anything to me. To suggest he knew, I mean."

"We talked a couple of weeks ago. On the phone."

"I didn't know that."

"He didn't really come right out and say the word 'divorce.' But I think he sensed you and I were having money problems."

"What did he say?"

"Just before he hung up, he said something like, hang in there. Things will get better for you and Ryan. Money will come soon."

"Did you ask him what he meant by that?"

"I didn't push it. At the time, I didn't see the point." She paused, as if considering what she was about to say. "But I've been thinking about what he said. A lot. I guess that's why I drove all the way down here to see you."

Ryan bristled. "What have you been thinking?"

"I thought, if only that were true. If we could solve our money problems, maybe we wouldn't be where we are now." She looked up, catching Ryan's eye.

He blinked. She looked sincere, sounded like she meant what she was saying. Yet he somehow didn't trust her. Anger swelled inside him. It was the damn money. Either she was after it, and it was making her deceitful. Or she knew nothing about it, and it was making him paranoid. *The damn money.*

"Liz, I'd be lying if I said I'd lost all feelings for you. But I just buried my father today. I can't get on this emotional roller coaster."

"I'm sorry," she said, rising. "I didn't come here to mess with your head."

"I didn't mean to send you away."

She smiled sadly. "It's okay. I really should go. Give my love to Jeanette." She kissed him lightly on the cheek—just a peck, next to nothing.

"Thanks for coming by. It means a lot."

"You're welcome." She headed down the steps and crossed the lawn. With a half-turn she waved goodbye, then got in her car and drove away.

He watched as her taillights faded into the darkness. He was tempted to call her back and tell her about the money. But his sister's earlier warning echoed in his mind—how Liz had hired herself a shark of a Denver divorce lawyer. Maybe Liz was just fishing for assets, something to report back to her lawyer.

Ryan walked back inside, chiding himself. After coming down hard on Sarah to keep things quiet until they sorted out the truth, there he was ready to tell all to Liz at the first sign of a possible reconciliation. Still, he couldn't deny his feelings for Liz. What was so awful about a woman who wanted a little financial security?

He went to the living room and picked up the phone, ready to call her answering machine and tell her to call him as soon as she got in. He punched three buttons, then hung up.

Sleep on it, he told himself.

10

Two days had passed, and Amy was still working up the nerve to phone Ryan Duffy. Just one question—the two-hundred-thousand-dollar question—had her paralyzed: Did she have the right Duffys?

She had done some serious checking. Yesterday, she'd even taken a sick day from the firm and driven all the way to Piedmont Springs, looking discreetly for obvious signs of wealth, a lifestyle befitting a family that could spare an extra two hundred thousand dollars. She found nothing of the sort. The Duffys owned a simple house in a rural middle-class town. The only car in the driveway was an older Jeep Cherokee. Ryan's clinic had the street presence of an abandoned five-and-dime store, serving patients who looked like they might barter sheep for services. And Frank Duffy had worked for wages his entire life.

Her findings had so befuddled her that last night she'd gone back to the computer to check the remaining Jeanette Duffys on her list. No one, however, seemed more promising than the Duffys of Piedmont Springs. Amy figured that whoever had sent the money didn't just wake up one morning and decide to do it. *Something* had to trigger the decision—a traumatic and life-altering event, like Frank Duffy's illness and impending death. It couldn't be coincidence. It had to be *these*

Duffys. For whatever reason, they just didn't flaunt their money.

Amy had to be cautious in her approach. It simply wouldn't be smart to phone Frank Duffy's son and say, "Someone in your family appears to have sent me a box full of cash for no good reason." Greedy heirs weren't likely to explain why she'd gotten the money. They were more likely to say, "It's mine, give it back."

At lunchtime Thursday, Amy grabbed a Pepsi and an orange from the employee lounge and went back to her office. She peeled the orange and broke it into wedges as she glanced at the handful of snapshots she'd taken of the Duffy house. Eight of them were spread across her desk. It had seemed wise to take pictures, just in case she ever had to go to the police. Police were always taking pictures—at least that was her experience. She remembered when she was eight, when her mother died. The police were all over the house taking photographs.

Funny, but the Duffy house resembled her old house in some ways. An old two-story frame with green shutters and a big porch out front, the kind they didn't seem to build anymore. She wondered if Frank Duffy had died in that house, as her mother had died in theirs. She wondered who had found his body, the first to realize he was gone. The thought chilled her. There was something eerie about a house in which someone had died, which was only compounded when, as in her house, that someone had died so violently. Amy hadn't gone back to her old house since the night of the gunshot.

That is, she hadn't *physically* gone back there. In her mind, she'd relived that night many times. Now, alone in the silence of her office, the photographs of the Duffy house seemed to blur, drifting out of focus. Her mind, too, began to drift. The image in the photographs looked more and more like her old house, until she could see beyond the likeness, see right into her old bedroom. She saw herself on that unforgettable night, a frightened eight-year-old girl alone in her dark bedroom, shivering with fear on a warm summer night, unsure of her next move...

Amy was sitting on the window ledge, a tight little ball with her knees drawn up to her chin. She had waited for another gunshot, but there had been only one. Not another sound. Just silence in the darkness.

She didn't know what to do, whether to run or stay put. Someone could be out there, a burglar. Or Mom could need her help. She had to do *something*. It took all her courage, but slowly she lowered her feet to the floor. The wooden planks creaked beneath her feet, startling her. She took a deep breath and started toward the door. She stepped lightly, so as not to make a sound. If there was someone out there, she couldn't let them hear her.

The knob turned slowly in her hand. She pulled the door toward her. It opened a crack, then caught on something. She tugged harder. It would open no more than a two-finger width. With her cheek pressed against the door frame, she peered out the narrow opening.

She blinked, confused. A rope was tied to her bedroom doorknob. The other end was looped around the banister across the hall. With the door open just an inch, it was taut as a tightrope.

Someone on the outside had tied her *inside* her bedroom.

She closed the door, trembling. On impulse, she ran into the closet and shut the door. It was pitch dark inside. She was accustomed to the dark, all the nights she'd spent with her telescope. For the first time, however, she was truly afraid of it.

The flashlight, she thought.

It was in there, she knew, with her astronomy books. The third shelf. She groped in the darkness, sorting through her possessions by touch. Finally, she found it and switched it on. The brightness hurt her eyes, so she aimed it at the floor. The closet glowed. Her eyes adjusted. Shoes lay scattered on the floor. Her clothes hung on a rod directly above her head. To the side were the built-in shelves, reaching like a ladder from floor to ceiling. At the top was a panel—an entrance to the attic.

She had used it once before to make an escape, when she was playing hide-and-seek with her friends. It led to the guest room across the hall. When her mother had found out, she'd told her never to go up there again. Tonight, however, was clearly an exception.

Amy was frightened to go up alone but even more afraid to stay put. She swallowed hard for courage, then tucked the flashlight under her chin and climbed up the shelves.

...The phone rang on her desk, rousing her from her twenty-year-old memories. Just a friend calling for lunch. "Sure," said Amy. "Meet you in the lobby at noon."

She hung up, still distracted, connected to her past. It had taken a lot of courage for that little girl to climb out of that closet and see what lay outside her room. It was time to dig inside and find the same fortitude.

She picked up the phone and dialed Ryan Duffy at his clinic. This time, she stayed on the line when the receptionist answered, unlike yesterday when she'd lost her nerve and hung up. "May I speak to Dr. Duffy, please?"

"I'm sorry, he's with a patient."

"Can you interrupt him, please? This will take just a minute."

"Is this an emergency?"

"No, but—"

"If it's not an emergency, I'll have him call you."

"It's personal. Tell him it's about his father."

The receptionist paused, then said, "Hold one moment."

Amy waited, reminding herself of the dos and don'ts. Tell the truth to a point. First name only, not her last. No mention of where she lived.

"This is Dr. Duffy—"

"Hi," she said, somewhat startled. "Thanks—thanks for coming. I mean, for answering. The phone, that is." *Jeez,* she thought, cringing. *Taylor could have put together a better sentence.*

"Who is this?"

"You don't know me. But I think your father must have. Or maybe it was your mother."

"What? Is this some kind of crank?"

"I'm sorry. I'm not making much sense. Let me just start at the top, and you can decide what's going on for yourself. You see, I got a package a couple of weeks ago. It didn't have a return address, but I'm certain it came from either your father or your mother. I know your father passed away recently, and I didn't want to trouble your mother."

Ryan's voice suddenly lost its edge. "How do you know it came from my parents?"

"That's just something I figured out."

"What was in the package?"

"A gift."

"What kind of gift?"

"A totally unexpected one. I don't really want to get into it on the telephone. Could we maybe meet somewhere and talk about this?"

"I'd really like to know more about this gift."

"And I'd be more than happy to tell you," said Amy. "But please, not on the phone."

"Where do you want to meet?"

"Just someplace public, like a restaurant or something. Not that I don't trust you. I just don't know you."

"Okay. You want to meet here in Piedmont Springs? I can do it tonight, if you like."

Amy hesitated. It was a five-hour drive from Boulder each way, and she had just made the trip yesterday. Long trips in her clunky old truck were a complete roll of the dice, especially at night. And another day off from work was pushing it. "That's kind of far for me."

"Where are you coming from?"

"I'd rather not say."

"Well, tomorrow I'll be in Denver on a personal matter. Is that any better for you?"

Amy was sure she could think of *some* computer-related excuse to go to the firm's Denver office. "Yes, as a matter of fact it is. Do you know the Green Parrot? It's a coffee shop, dessert place at Larimer Square."

"I'm sure I can find it."

"Great," said Amy. "What time is good for you?"

"I have an appointment at two. Not sure how long it will last. Let's say four o'clock, just to be safe."

"Four it is," she said.

"Hey," he said, catching her before the hang-up. "How will we know each other?"

"Just give the hostess your name. I'll ask for Dr. Duffy when I get there."

"See you then."

"Yes," she said eagerly, "definitely."

11

Ryan ate an early lunch on Friday and drove alone to Denver. The radio was playing, but he hardly noticed. This afternoon's property settlement conference with Liz and her lawyer was enough to keep his mind whirling.

Now he could also look forward to the mystery woman and her four o'clock surprise.

Ryan had phoned Liz the morning after their Tuesday evening talk on the front porch. Having slept on it, he'd decided to feel her out before telling her about the money. He offered to ride together to Friday's meeting, hoping she'd suggest they simply postpone the whole divorce thing, maybe start talking reconciliation. But she declined the ride. Seemed she had to be in Denver three hours ahead of time to prepare with her lawyer.

Three hours? Who the hell did they think he was, Donald Trump?

His heart thumped with a sudden realization. Technically, he was a millionaire. But how would Liz know that? Ryan hadn't even told his own lawyer about the two million in the attic, which raised another set of problems. Eventually, the divorce would force him to disclose his net worth under oath, either in sworn deposition testimony or in his sworn statement of assets and liabilities. For the moment, however, he didn't consider the tainted cash an asset. At least not until he decided to keep it. Today, he would just have to finesse things. Later, if he did decide to keep it, he could figure out a way to tell Liz.

Unless she already knew. Somehow.

Seventeenth Street was the lifeline of Denver's financial district. Amid the shadows of more than a dozen sleek chrome and glass skyscrapers, Ryan drove slowly in search of parking rates that didn't cause cardiac arrest. It was futile. He parked in the garage of a

71

forty-story tower owned by the Anaconda Corporation, an international mining conglomerate whose *real* gold mine must have been parking revenue. A catwalk took him to the building's atrium, where he caught an express elevator to the thirty-fourth floor.

The doors opened to a spacious lobby. Silk wall coverings and cherry wainscoting lent the desired air of prestige and power. The floors were polished marble with elaborate inlaid borders worthy of the Vatican. A wall of windows faced west, with a breathtaking view of jagged mountaintops in the distance. Ryan would have guessed he was in the right place from the impressive decor alone, but the shiny brass letters on the wall confirmed his arrival at Wedderburn and Jackson, P.A.

A far cry from the clinic, thought Ryan.

Ryan felt sorely underdressed in his khaki pants and blazer, no tie. He had read somewhere that even stodgy law firms had caught on to the "casual Friday" dress code that was all the rage in the corporate world. If that was the case, the normal dress at this place must have been black tie and tails.

"Can I help you, sir?"

Ryan turned. The young woman at the reception desk had caught him wandering like a lost tourist. "I'm Ryan Duffy. My lawyer and I are supposed to meet with Phil Jackson at two o'clock. Mr. Jackson represents my wife. We're, uh, getting divorced."

She smiled. It was her job to smile. Ryan could have said he was a serial killer seeking advice on the disposal of body parts and she would have smiled.

"I'll tell Mr. Jackson you're here," she said cheerfully. "Please, have a seat."

Ryan walked toward the windows, taking in the view. He was twenty minutes early. Hopefully, his lawyer would arrive soon. He had a feeling they could use a bit more preparation than the usual two-minute drill at the water cooler.

In thirty minutes, Ryan went through every magazine in the waiting area. By 2:15, his lawyer was still missing in action. At 2:20, a sharply dressed man approached, looking straight at Ryan. "Dr. Duffy, I'm Phil Jackson."

Ryan rose from the leather couch and shook the hand of the enemy. He'd never met Liz's lawyer, but he certainly knew the name. "Nice to meet you," he lied.

Jackson said, "I called your lawyer's office to see if she was coming, but she has apparently been called into court on an emergency hearing."

"And she didn't tell me?" he asked incredulously.

"I'm sure she tried to reach you."

Ryan checked the pager on his belt. No message. *Emergency heating, my ass.* She probably left early on another long weekend. That settled it: he needed a new lawyer. "What about our meeting, Mr. Jackson?"

"We can reschedule for another day."

"I've already canceled my appointments for today. I can't lose another day."

"Then we'll just have to wait for your

lawyer to get here, which may be a couple more hours. However, I feel obliged to tell you my rate is three hundred an hour, including waiting time. I may represent Liz, but let's face it. Eventually, *you* pay."

Ryan glared. Jackson had taken obvious pleasure in that last remark. "You really have a way with people, you know that?"

"It's a gift," he said smugly.

"Let's just start without her," said Ryan.

"Sorry, can't do that. The rules of ethics prevent me from negotiating directly with you if you're represented by an attorney."

"I just fired my attorney. So now there's no ethical problem."

Jackson raised an eyebrow. "My, you surprise me, Doctor. I had you pegged for someone who definitely felt constrained to hide behind his lady lawyer's apron strings."

I'm feeling constrained to punch your lights out, thought Ryan. "Let's just get this over with."

"Right this way." He led him down a long hall to a glass-encased conference room. The door was open. Liz was seated on the far side of the table, her back to the window. A stenographer was already set up at the head of the table.

"Hello, Liz," he said. She replied with a weak smile.

Ryan glanced at the stenographer, then at Jackson. "What's the court reporter here for? I thought this was an informal meeting, not a deposition."

"No one is testifying under oath," said

Jackson. "She's just here to take down everything we say, so there's a record. It's basically no different than turning on a tape recorder or having my secretary take really good notes."

Right, thought Ryan. *Only fifty times more intimidating, you son of a bitch.* "I'd rather she not be here for this."

"Why?" Jackson asked with sarcasm. "Are you one of those people who will say something only if he can reserve the right to deny he ever said it?"

Ryan glanced at the stenographer. Her fingers were moving on the keys. She'd already recorded the first pointed volley. "Fine. She can stay."

Jackson maneuvered around the stenographer and took the seat beside Liz. Ryan took the chair on the opposite side of the table. He was facing the window. The blinds had been adjusted perfectly in advance of his arrival, so that the sun hit him directly in the eyes.

"Excuse me," he said, squinting, "but I left my welding visor in the car. You think we could fix the blinds here?"

Jackson smirked. "Gee, I'm sorry. Let me take care of it." He leaned back to adjust the blinds—but only a smidgen. In a few minutes, the sun would be right back in Ryan's eyes. It was part of Jackson's strategy, Ryan surmised. Every three or four minutes, Ryan would be staring into the sun. Anything to distract and annoy the opposition. *This guy's unbelievable.*

Jackson said, "Let's start by making it clear

for the record that Dr. Duffy has fired his attorney, so he is representing himself today. Is that true, Doctor?"

"Yes."

"Very well," said Jackson. "Let's start our discussion with a review of the documents."

"What documents?"

He handed one to Ryan. "This is something our accountants prepared for us. It's a more accurate assessment of your net worth and earning potential."

Ryan's eyes moved immediately to the bottom line. He nearly choked. "Seven hundred thousand dollars! That's ten times my annual income."

"Ten times your *reported* annual income. Although your tax return shows a modest five-figure income, we know differently."

Ryan glanced at Liz. *Did she know about the attic?* "What are you talking about?"

Jackson laid a file on the table. It contained a stack of documents nearly eight inches high. "Invoices," he said flatly.

"Invoices for what?" asked Ryan.

"During the last eight months of your marriage, Liz took over the billing practices of your clinic. She mailed these to your patients with delinquent accounts. You don't deny she did that, do you?"

"No, I don't deny it. It was Liz's idea. I told her we'd never collect, that these people couldn't pay. She sent them anyway. But you can't count uncollected invoices as income. That's absurd."

Jackson leaned forward, more than a little

confrontational. "We don't think they went uncollected."

"I don't understand."

"You knew Liz was unhappy. You knew this divorce was coming long ago. We intend to prove that you accepted cash payments from patients under the table so that you could hide the money from Liz and keep it for yourself."

"Have you lost your marbles?" He glanced at his wife. "Liz, tell him."

She looked away.

"Dr. Duffy, the bottom line is that you owe your wife seven hundred thousand dollars in a lump sum payment, plus monthly alimony commensurate with a thriving private practice."

"This is laughable."

"No one's laughing, Doctor."

"Liz, I can't believe you would set me up like this."

Jackson said, "I'd appreciate it if you would direct your comments to me, Doctor. Not to your wife."

"Naturally. I'm sure you're the one who concocted this scheme in the first place."

"No one has *concocted* anything."

"How long have you represented her? Eight months, I'll bet, ever since she started sending the invoices. Only with the encouragement of a shark like you would she re-bill patients who couldn't pay and then accuse me of accepting cash payments under the table."

"I won't sit here and trade insults with you, Doctor. This meeting will proceed on a professional level, or it won't proceed at all."

He rose and pushed away from the table. "Fine with me. This meeting's over." He glared at Liz. "It's definitely over." He turned and left the room.

Liz jumped up to follow. Her lawyer grabbed her wrist, but she shook free. "Ryan, wait!"

He heard her voice, but he didn't break stride. It shocked him the way Liz had changed since their pleasant talk on the porch three nights ago. The three-hour prep session with Mr. Congeniality had obviously tapped her negative energy. *Or maybe Tuesday was just a ruse.*

"Ryan!"

He continued through the lobby, never looking back. The elevator doors opened, and he hurried inside. Liz lunged forward as the doors were closing. She barely made it. The elevator began its descent with just the two of them aboard. Liz was red-faced and breathless from the chase. "Ryan, listen to me."

He watched the lights above the elevator doors, avoiding eye contact.

"This wasn't my idea," she said, pleading.

Finally, he looked at her. "What were you trying to do to me in there?"

"It's for your own good."

"My own good? *This* I gotta hear."

"It was my lawyer's idea to accuse you of hiding your income, just to put you on the defensive. I wouldn't let him use that ploy at a real deposition or in the courtroom, anyplace where it could embarrass you. But today was just a settlement conference. It's just posturing."

"*Posturing?* It's an outright lie. How could you let him pull a stunt like that?"

"Because it's time you woke up," she said sharply. "For eight years I begged you to get your career in order and earn the kind of money we deserved. You could have been a top-flight surgeon at any hospital you wanted, right here in Denver. You just gave it all up."

"I didn't give it all up. I'm still a doctor."

"You're a waste of talent , that's what you are. It's time you stopped playing Mother Teresa for all the poor sick folks in Piedmont Springs and started making some real money—for both of us."

"You and your lawyer are going to make sure of that. Is that the plan?"

"If forcing you to write a hefty alimony check every month is the only way to blast you out of Piedmont Springs, then by God, I'm going to do it. You brought this on yourself. I didn't work two jobs putting you through med school so that I could wake up every morning to the smell of cow manure blowing in from the fields. Piedmont Springs was *not* the future we talked about before we got married. I've waited long enough to get out of that hellhole."

The elevator doors opened. Liz started out to the main lobby. Ryan stopped her.

"Is that what's driving you, Liz? You just can't wait to get out of Piedmont Springs?"

Her eyes turned cold. "No, Ryan. What's driving me is that I'm sick and tired of waiting for you."

He swallowed hard, tasting the bitterness as she quickly walked away.

12

Friday afternoon traffic was heavy as Amy reached Denver. She parked near the Civic Center about a mile from the coffee shop, then walked a block to the 16th Street Mall and caught the free shuttle. The bus ride was part of her plan to conceal her identity, to the extent possible. It was conceivable that Ryan's father had sent the money to her without telling anyone, taking the name and address of Amy Parkens with him to the grave. She didn't want Ryan to find out who she was simply by checking her license plate.

She was getting nervous about meeting Ryan face to face. She wished she had a friend in law enforcement who could run a criminal background check on the Duffys, make sure the money was clean. She didn't. Snooping around was no way to get answers anyway. She had learned that from her marriage. Weeks of discreet, behind-the-scenes inquiries had brought only aggravation. The answer had come only after she'd invoked the direct approach and asked him point-blank, "Have you been screwing another woman?" No soft-pedaling it with the usual euphemisms—"seeing someone," "having an affair," or "cheating on me." It had hurt to hear the truth. But at least she knew.

The direct approach. In a pinch, there was no substitute.

The shuttle bus dropped her at Larimer

Square, a historic street that boasted authentic Western Victorian architecture. But for the determination of preservationists, it would have been bulldozed for yet another glass and steel skyscraper, like so many others that had sprouted in the days when Denver meant oil and the TV hit *Dynasty*. It had become Denver's most charming shopping district, home to specialty shops, cafés, and summer concerts in brick courtyards.

On the corner was the Green Parrot, a coffeehouse with a bird sanctuary motif, having been converted from a century-old drugstore. A big brass chandelier hung from a thirty-foot coffered ceiling. The soda fountain was now a busy espresso bar. The floor was old Chicago brick. Flowering orchids adorned each of the decorative wrought-iron tables. Bubbling fountains and an abundance of green plants made coffee klatches feel like a day at the park. Huge wire cages towered above the tables, some fifteen feet high, each displaying colorful exotic birds.

Amy checked her reflection in the plate-glass window before entering. She had chosen her outfit carefully. Nothing too sexy. She didn't want Ryan to infer that his old man had left a box full of money for his twenty-eight-year-old mistress. She wore a navy blue suit with a peach blouse, shoes with only a two-inch heel. No flashy jewelry, just faux pearls and matching earrings. Sincere, but serious. She entered the double doors and stopped at the sign that said, "WAIT HERE TO BE SEATED."

"Can I help you?" asked the hostess.

"Yes. I'm supposed to meet someone here at four. His name is Dr. Duffy."

She checked her clipboard. "Yes, he's here. He said he was expecting someone. Follow me, please."

Amy gulped. He had actually come.

Most of the tables were filled, and the after-work crowd was beginning to file in for wine and locally brewed beers as well as coffee. The hostess directed her to the booth by the window. The man rose to greet her. He looked younger than she'd expected. More handsome, too. A good-looking doctor. *Gram would be doing cartwheels.*

"Dr. Duffy?" she said as she approached.

They shook hands. "Right. And you must be..."

She hesitated. *No last name.* "Call me Amy."

"Okay, Amy." He didn't push for a surname. "Have a seat."

The waitress appeared as they slid into opposite sides of the booth. "Can I bring you something?" she asked.

"How about a decaf cappuccino?" said Amy.

"And for you, sir?"

Ryan paused. "I'll just have coffee."

"We have two hundred kinds."

"Pick any you like. Surprise me."

She rolled her eyes, jotted something on her pad, and left.

Amy took another look at Ryan. He really was handsome.

"Something wrong?" he asked.

She blushed, embarrassed that he'd caught her staring. "I'm sorry. I guess you just don't look anything like the small-town country doctor I was expecting."

"Well, I make it a point never to smoke my corncob pipe outside of Piedmont Springs."

She nodded and smiled, as if she'd deserved that. "Anyway, thanks for coming, Doctor."

"Call me Ryan. And you don't have to thank me. I'm pretty eager to find out what this gift is you're talking about."

"Then I'll just get right down to it. Like I said, I got a package a couple of weeks ago. When I tore away the brown paper wrapping, I found a box for a Crock-Pot. No return address, no card inside. I checked the serial number with the manufacturer and found out the warranty was registered in the name of Jeanette Duffy."

"That's my mom's name."

"Does she own a Crock-Pot?"

Ryan chuckled, thinking of the mounds of corned beef at the gathering at their house after the funeral. "You bet she does."

"A Gemco Crock-Pot, by any chance?"

"As a matter of fact, it is. I was with my dad when he bought it for her."

It was the added confirmation she needed. "Good. Anyway, I opened the box."

"I assume there wasn't a Crock-Pot inside."

"No." Her expression turned more serious. "There was money it. A thousand dollars." Amy watched his face carefully. She felt duplicitous, but it wasn't entirely a lie. It *did* contain a thousand dollars. She just didn't tell

83

him that it *also* contained 199,000 more. Not yet, anyway.

"A thousand dollars, huh?"

"I don't know if it was your mom or your dad who sent it. Either way, with your dad just passing away, I didn't want to bother or upset your mom. That's why I called you. Honestly, I'm not sure what to do."

"Keep it."

She was taken aback by the quick response. "No questions asked?"

Ryan shrugged. "I can't see my mother doing something like this. So I assume it was my dad. He obviously wanted you to have it. You may not have known him, but somewhere along the line you must have shown him some kindness, or maybe he felt sorry for you for some reason. My dad was that way. It doesn't surprise me he'd send money to someone like you. You seem nice enough. Hell, it wouldn't surprise me if he sent lots of people money after he found out he was sick."

The waitress interrupted. "One decaf cappuccino," she said, serving Amy. "And a cup of black sludge for the gentlemen." She smirked. "Just kidding. It's Brazilian blend. Anything else?"

"No, thank you," said Ryan. She turned and left.

Amy emptied a pack of Equal into her decaf. "Are you sure I should just keep it?"

"Hey, it's a thousand dollars. We're not talking Fort Knox here. Just don't tell my wife I let you keep it. She'd probably sue me."

Amy sensed an opening to the kind of personal details she wanted. "She's fond of money, is she?"

"That's an understatement. It's the reason we're getting divorced."

"I'm sorry."

"Yeah, me too. Fortunately, we don't have any children. Just money problems."

"Too much? Or not enough?"

Ryan raised an eyebrow. "Kind of personal."

"Sorry. It's just a familiar story, I guess." Amy hesitated. She didn't want him to know too much about her, but if she told him *something* about herself, perhaps he'd give her the insights she wanted into the Duffy family. "You might say I'm a bit of an expert on the subject of money and marriage."

"Is that so?"

"My ex-husband was an investment banker. Loaded. It only made him meaner, greedier, if you ask me."

"You're divorced now?"

"Yeah. And I'll be honest with you. We may not be talking about Fort Knox here, as you say. But I appreciate your generosity. I can definitely use the money."

"Your rich ex-husband doesn't pay enough alimony, I take it."

"Doesn't pay any. Not a cent."

Ryan kidded, "Do you have the name of his lawyer?"

She smiled, then turned serious. "Ted didn't need a lawyer. After I filed for divorce, he threatened to hide a bag of cocaine in my truck and get me arrested, then use the drug conviction to keep me from getting custody of our daughter. I wasn't sure if he meant it, but I couldn't take the risk. We settled. I got what was important to me—my daughter. Ted got what was important to him: he pays no alimony and hardly enough child support to cover the monthly food bill."

"Sounds pretty tough."

"Actually, I've never been happier in my life." She smiled, though it was another half-truth. Taylor was a total joy, but going to law school solely for the money made her feel like a hypocrite.

She raised her coffee mug. "A toast to your new life as a redneck."

"A redneck?"

"It's an acronym. Sounds like redneck, but it's R-D-N-K. Recently Divorced, No Kids."

Ryan smiled. "Never heard that one before."

"I made it up. Cheers."

"Cheers."

She caught him watching her over the rim of his cup. The sudden silence could have been uncomfortable, but his eyes put her at ease. She blinked, reminding herself to stay on the subject. "Getting back to this money thing."

"Of course. The money."

"I was pretty nervous about it at first. Now that I've met you, it's almost embarrassing to say what I was thinking. I was just afraid to keep it until I had some assurance that your dad was on the level."

"What do you mean?"

"Oh, I was having all kinds of crazy thoughts. Maybe your dad was a notorious bank robber or something."

Ryan smiled. "We're talking about Piedmont Springs. The last time we had a bank robbery, I think Bonnie and Clyde were the prime suspects."

She laughed lightly. "You're a hard one to figure out, you know that?"

"How's that?"

"A doctor who doesn't worship money and hasn't lost his sense of humor."

"I guess I get that from my dad."

"Were the two of you a lot alike?"

Ryan thought for a second. A week ago he would have given an unqualified yes. Now he hedged. "I think so. It's funny. I was looking through some family albums after the funeral. Some old pictures of my dad really struck me. He looked almost exactly the way I look now. Put him in some modern clothes, change the hair a little, he probably could have passed for me."

"That's eerie, isn't it?"

"Yeah. We're all like our parents in some ways. But when you see such a strong physical resemblance, it really makes you wonder how much of what you are is predetermined."

Amy got quiet. She'd often wondered that as well, the spitting image of her mother. "I know what you mean."

"Now that he's gone, I'm almost mad at myself for not getting to know him better. I'm not saying we weren't close. But I never asked him the kind of questions that might help me better understand myself."

"Sometimes we just don't have the opportunity," she said, thinking more of her own situation.

Ryan sipped his coffee. "Wow, this is getting kind of deep, isn't it? You probably think I need a shrink or something."

"Not at all."

They talked casually for another fifteen minutes. Conversation came easily, considering the awkward circumstances. It was feeling more like a date than a meeting about money.

"Refills?" asked the waitress, sneaking up on them.

They exchanged a look. The meeting could easily have been over, but neither seemed to want to end it.

"I don't have to be anywhere," said Ryan.

Amy checked her watch, then made a face. "Yikes. Unfortunately, I do. I have to pick up my daughter."

He looked disappointed. "Too bad."

"I guess I didn't think this would take very long."

The waitress laid the bill on the table. Ryan grabbed it. "I'll take care of it."

"Thank you. I'm sorry I have to run off like this."

"No problem." He took a business card from his wallet, then jotted a number on the back. "Let me give you my home number, just in case any other questions come to mind. About the money, I mean."

She took the card, rising. "Thanks."

There was humor in his eyes. "I would tell you to look me up if ever you're in Piedmont Springs, but I'm sure you know dozens of people there already, and I'd be way down on your list of people to call."

"Of course. Paris. London. Piedmont Springs. I have that problem wherever I go."

"I figured. Maybe I can send you another thousand dollars and see you again sometime."

She smiled, but her gut wrenched. Little did he know he had already prepaid for another 199 visits. She was suddenly flustered, not sure what to say. "You never know."

He shrugged, as if the response were a brush-off. "Well, it was very nice meeting you."

She stood and waited for a second, wishing it had ended on a different note. But it was hard to come back from a remark like *You never know.* She wasn't sure why she'd said it, wasn't sure how to fix it. "Nice meeting you, too, Ryan."

They exchanged one last smile, sadder than the others. She had an empty feeling of missed opportunity as she turned away and headed for the door.

13

From the Mile High City to the plains of southeastern Colorado, the ride was all downhill. Appropriate enough for a guy whose marriage was in a death spiral. Ryan drove the entire way to Piedmont Springs in silence, no stops and no radio, arriving at dusk. He was so consumed by his thoughts that he automatically turned on River Street, toward the house he and Liz had shared in their final years of marriage. Two blocks away, he realized his mistake. He didn't live there anymore. This afternoon had made it clear he never would again. He pulled a U-turn, heading back to his parents' house. Mom's house, actually. Dad was dead. Mom got the house.

Ryan got the headache.

Quite literally, his head was pounding. Throughout the trip home, his mind had replayed today's clash with Liz. It was a strange coincidence, the way her lawyer had cooked up the allegation that Ryan was hoarding huge sums of cash, keeping it from Liz. *If they only knew.*

His pulse quickened as he pulled into the driveway. *Could they know?*

They couldn't. Liz was so angry today, she surely would have said something. Her only demand was that Ryan start earning money in a high-paying practice. In no way did she lay claim to a secret stash in the attic.

He killed the engine and stepped down from his Jeep Cherokee. His thoughts turned to Amy as he headed up the sidewalk. He still couldn't figure what had gone wrong at the end. He thought he'd sensed a connection, seen something in her smile. For a while, she had him feeling not so bad about getting divorced. She seemed like a woman he'd like to get to know. But at the mere mention of possibly seeing each other again, it had all fallen apart. He couldn't help but wonder what was really going on. As recently as Tuesday night, Liz was still talking about his father's deathbed promise that "Money will come soon." Maybe this Amy was a friend of Liz, someone that sneaky lawyer had sent just to pump financial information from him. Or maybe she really did receive some money, but she was being nice just to wiggle even more cash out of the Duffy family.

Ryan fumbled for his key to the front door, thinking. Extortion money in the attic. Cash gifts to strangers. Promises to Liz. *What the hell were you trying to do to me, Dad?*

He glanced to the west. The afterglow of the setting sun was fading behind the mountains in the distance. He *assumed* there were mountains out there somewhere. He couldn't actually see them. From the dusty plains of southeastern Colorado, even fourteen-thousand-foot peaks were well beyond view. The utterly flat horizon reminded him of a late afternoon he and his dad had shared on the porch, just the two of them. It was a long time ago, when Ryan was small and his father chain-smoked the cigarettes that would eventually kill him. The sky had been unusually clear that day. On a hunch, his dad had brought out the binoculars, thinking rather naively that perhaps Ryan could get his first glimpse of the mountains to the west. Even on the clearest of days, however, they were still too far away. Ryan was disappointed, but he listened with excitement as his father described in detail the grandeur they were missing.

"Why don't we live *there?*" he had asked eagerly.

"Because we live here, son."

"Why don't we move?"

His father chuckled, puffing on his cigarette. "People don't just move."

"Why not?"

"They just don't."

"You mean we're stuck here?"

He looked toward the horizon. There was sadness in his voice. "Your roots are here, Ryan. Five generations on your mother's side. Can't just pull up roots."

Thirty years later, Ryan recalled the tone more than the words. Complete resignation, as if the thought of sunsets and mountains glistening to the west were a constant reminder that everything beautiful was outside the reach of tiny Piedmont Springs.

Thinking about it now, he could see why Dad and Liz had gotten on so well. He used to think it was because father and son were so alike. Maybe it was because they were different.

Ryan unlocked the front door and stepped inside. The sun was completely gone, leaving the house in darkness. He flipped on the light, then called out, "Mom, you home?"

No reply. He crossed the living room into the kitchen. A note was stuck to the refrigerator. It was the way the Duffys had always communicated. Civilization might have evolved from the beating tom-tom to e-mail, but nothing was more effective than a note on the freezer door. Ryan read it as he grabbed a beer from the refrigerator. "Went to dinner and a movie with Sarah," it read. "Be back around ten."

He checked the clock on the oven. Eight-thirty. It was good that Mom was getting out. Even better that she wasn't home to ask him how things had gone with Liz. He twisted off the cap and sucked down a cold Coors on his way to the family room. He switched on the lamp, then froze.

The furniture had been moved. Not rearranged in an orderly fashion. Moved. The couch was angled strangely. The wall unit had been pulled a few inches away from the wall, several drawers hanging open. The rug was curled up at one end. Clearly someone had been here. Someone who had been searching for something.

Someone, he feared, who knew about the money.

14

Stupid. That was how Amy felt. After all the mental preparation for her meeting with Ryan Duffy, she hadn't really accomplished what she'd set out to do. Her only objective had been to find out why Frank Duffy had sent her the money. She came away with no clear picture. Stupid, was all it was.

Not that it was so great to be smart all the time. She'd learned the downside of brains long ago, as a child. If you were stupid, no one blamed you. But people were suspicious of intelligence, as if you had done something wrong just by virtue of being smart. That reaction from others had bred shyness in Amy, a trait that had surely contributed to her blunder with Ryan. She didn't especially like that about herself, which was precisely the reason she could recall the very day she had begun her transformation from an outspoken little girl to a kid who was beyond humble, almost embarrassed by her own extraordinary abilities. A couple of years before her mother's death, she had tagged along to the doctor's office for her mom's annual checkup. Her mom sat on the table, so pretty, looking much like the woman Amy would become. Amy watched intently as the nurse rolled up her mother's sleeve and checked her blood pressure.

"Very good," said the nurse, reading from the gauge. "One-twenty over eighty."

"One and a half," Amy volunteered.

".One and a half what?" her mother asked.

"One-twenty over eighty. That equals one and a half."

The nurse looked up from her chart, almost dropped her pen. "How old is that child?"

"Six," said her mother. "Well, *almost* six."

More than twenty years later, the look on that old nurse's face was still unforgettable. Over and over, throughout her childhood, Amy would see that same spooked expression. Hearing the amazing things that came out of her mouth, people would think she was just small for her age. Then they'd find out how young she really was and look at her like some kind of walking gray-matter freak. "You're special," her mother would tell her, and she had always made Amy feel that way. Until she was gone, and then things really got difficult. Amy learned to be tough, both physically and emotionally. Especially with boys. In elementary school, they would pick fights with her on the playground, just to show her the limits of being so smart. As pretty as she was, she had plenty of dates in high school, but not many second dates. Brains were a scary thing to some people, from that nurse in the doctor's office, to the boys on the playground, to her jerk of an ex-husband.

Somehow, it didn't seem like that would ever be an issue for a guy like Ryan Duffy.

Admittedly, the meeting with Ryan wasn't the smartest thing she'd ever done. Even her own mother would have told her that, had she been alive. Yet dismissing the whole thing as stupid rang hollow in her heart. She had a good feeling about Ryan. He'd made her smile, put her at ease in a situation that could have been far from easy. To her surprise, she found herself wishing they met under different circumstances, another time in their lives. She wasn't sure what was percolating inside of her, but ever since she'd left the restaurant, she'd thought more about him than the money.

If that was what it felt like to finally feel stupid, stupid wasn't such a horrible thing.

What was really stupid was her remark right before she'd left, when he'd asked to see her again. *You never know.* Three little words that, to any reasonable human being, translated roughly to "In your dreams, buddy."

Enough self-flagellation. She had his phone number. And she did have to call him. She at least had to tell him the truth. This wasn't just a matter of a thousand dollars, as she had led him to believe. She had ignored the very pep talk she had given herself outside the Green Parrot, when she'd promised herself to use "the direct approach." It was time to practice what she preached.

And then just see where things led from there.

She picked up the phone, took a deep breath, and dialed the number.

The phone rang, piercing the silence. Ryan stopped in the hall. He had checked the entire house. He was definitely alone. Whoever had been there had left some time ago. Still, he had a strange sensation that somebody was watching the house—that whoever had broken in was on the phone, calling him, taunting him. He went to the kitchen and answered in a harsh tone.

"What do you want?"

"Ryan, hi. It's Amy. Did I catch you at a bad time?"

He knew he sounded stressed, but he sure wasn't going to tell her about the break-in. "Sort of. No, I'm sorry. Go ahead."

96

"I'll make this quick. I've been thinking about our conversation, and I felt like I needed to set something straight. But I can call back later, if you want."

"No, really. What is it?"

She struggled, not wanting to sound like a complete liar. "One comment you made really stuck in my mind. You said it didn't surprise you that your dad gave me some money. You said you wouldn't be surprised if your dad had given away money to lots of people after he learned he was sick."

"I was just talking off the cuff."

"But let's say he did give away money to more people like me. Maybe lots more. I don't mean to offend, but from what I can tell, your father didn't appear to be super wealthy."

He leaned against the refrigerator, curious. "What are you getting at?"

The direct approach, she reminded herself. *Use the direct approach.* Her voice tightened as she asked, "Where would he get that kind of money?"

Ryan hesitated. *Did she know something?* "I could only assume he saved it."

"But what if it were a lot more than a thousand dollars? Just hypothetically speaking."

"I don't really see your point."

"Just bear with me. You seemed like a nice guy when we talked. I guess I need to know just how nice you really are. Let's say the box had…five thousand dollars in it. Would you still tell me to keep it?"

"A thousand, five thousand. Whatever. Yeah, keep it."

"What if it were fifty thousand? Hypothetically speaking."

He swallowed with trepidation. "I guess it wouldn't make a difference. Not if that was what Dad wanted."

"How about a hundred thousand?"

He said nothing, as if it were unthinkable.

"No," said Amy, "let's say it was *two* hundred thousand dollars. Would you let me keep it?"

A nervous silence fell over the line. "Hypothetically?" asked Ryan.

"Hypothetically," she said firmly.

He answered in a low, even tone. "I'd want to know where in the hell my dad got the money."

She answered in the same serious voice. "So would I."

He sank into a bar stool facing the kitchen counter. "What do you want from me?"

"I just want this to be on the level. I'd love to keep the money. And as you say, for some reason your father apparently wanted me to have it. But if it's dirty, I don't want to be connected to it in any way."

"I don't know where my dad would get two hundred thousand dollars, if that's what you're asking me."

"All I'm really asking is whether your father was an honest man."

Ryan only sighed. "I may need a little time to answer that."

"I don't understand."

"Neither do I. There are some things I need to check into."

"What kind of things?"

"Please, give me a week, just to get things in order. Family stuff."

She didn't answer immediately, but she didn't see a choice. Not if she wanted to keep the money. "All right. I'm not looking to upset your family or ruin your dad's good name. But if I don't see some bank records or something that proves this money is from a legitimate source, I'm afraid I'll have to turn it over to the police."

"You could just give it back to me."

"I'm sorry. But it came to my house, touched my hands. If it's tainted money, I have to turn it in. Maybe the police can figure out where it came from."

"That sounds like a threat."

"I know it does. Believe me, that was the last thing I intended when I made this phone call. I was hoping...."

"Hoping what?"

The words caught in her throat. There was no point telling him she had hoped to see him again. Not if he couldn't give a straight answer to a simple question like *Was your father an honest man?*

"Nothing. I just hope you can come up with something to put me at ease. You can have a week, Ryan. I'll call you then," she said, then hung up the phone.

15

Ryan hung up, then froze. He heard a creak in the floorboard just a few feet behind him. He whirled, clutching the phone like a weapon.

His moment of panic turned quickly to relief. It was his brother-in-law. Sarah must have given him her key. "Damn it, Brent. What the hell you doing, sneaking up on me?"

"Not sneaking," he said in a thick, gravelly voice. He smelled of spilled beer, a half-empty Coors in one hand.

Ryan peered through the kitchen window to the driveway. Brent's car was a few feet behind his, parked at a careless angle. He must have pulled up while Amy was on the phone. "Did you drive here in that condition?"

He grinned widely, as if it were funny. "I don't remember." Typical Brent. Still proud of the way he could polish off a six-pack faster than a drunken frat boy.

Brent was actually four years younger than Ryan, but he looked older. He had been handsome once—he still was, to a lesser degree, at least on the two or three days a week he was showered, shaved and sober. His glory days had passed with high school football, rekindled briefly in his late twenties with delusions of becoming a bodybuilder. Ryan got him to quit the steroids, but then he turned to alcohol. The muscles softened, the personality hardened. Now he was just a large, angry man, like the overweight and over-the-hill wrestlers on television—except that Brent had no job. Ryan had never been thrilled with Sarah's choice of a mate, but five years ago she'd panicked, nearly forty years old and never married. She'd latched onto Brent, good looking and nine years younger, winning him over by playing his live-in maid-servant. Now she was forty-something and pregnant, stuck with a shell of a man who slept off a hangover every morning as his pregnant wife trudged off to work at WalMart for minimum wage.

"You were here earlier, weren't you?" asked Ryan.

"Yup. Waited over an hour for you."

Ryan noticed the empty beer bottles on the kitchen table. He counted eight. "Way to go, buddy," he said with sarcasm. "I see you're cutting back."

Brent's face was flushed. He was clearly buzzed. He offered Ryan his half-empty bottle. "Want some?"

Ryan pushed it away, his tone harsh. "What were you doing here?"

He went to the refrigerator, got himself a fresh beer. The head went back, the bottle was emptied. Twelve ounces in twelve seconds. He wiped his chin, then looked at Ryan. "Looking for the money."

The word hit like a sledgehammer, but Ryan kept a straight face. "What money?"

"Don't play dumb on me. Sarah told me."

Ryan flushed with anger. *Good ol' Sarah, always great with secrets.* "What about it?"

"I need fifty thousand dollars. And I gotta have it tonight."

"What for?"

"None of your damn business, that's what for. It's Sarah's money. And I want it."

"Sarah and I had a deal. Neither one of us takes any of the money until we know exactly where it came from."

Brent's eyes narrowed. "How do we know you haven't already spent it?"

"You're just going to have to trust me."

"I'm still trusting your ass for nine hundred and fifty thousand. Just give me the fucking fifty grand."

"No. Who do you think you are, Brent? Coming into my mother's house, looking for money."

He rose, threatening. "It's Sarah's money. Give it to me!"

"I said no."

Brent wobbled toward him. "Give me the fucking money, man, or I'll—"

Ryan silenced him with a steely glare. "Or what, Brent?"

Brent knew better than to take on Ryan drunk. Still, he had a crazed look in his eyes, as if the eight empty beers on the table were merely a footnote to a full day of bingeing. "Or," he said with a slur, "I may be forced to hit a pregnant woman."

Something snapped in Ryan. He lunged forward and grabbed him by the throat, knocking him to the floor. "I told you I'd kill you, Brent! You ever touched her again, I'd fucking kill you!"

Brent wriggled and clawed, trying to break Ryan's grip around his throat. His face was turning blue. Ryan squeezed harder, spurred by the memory of stitching up his own sister after the blows from her husband. He should have settled the score then, but Sarah begged him not to.

"Ry-an," Brent was wheezing, barely conscious. His eyes were bulging.

Ryan stopped, suddenly realizing what he was doing.

Brent pushed him off and rolled on his side, coughing and gasping for air. "You coulda killed me, you crazy bastard."

Ryan was shaking. He *could* have killed him.

Brent rose slowly, whining pathetically, a drunk on a crying jag. "I want my money. I *need* it, bad. Please, Ryan, I gotta have it."

Ryan's hands were shaking. Since the funeral, all anyone talked about was money. Liz would divorce him for it. Brent would beat his sister for it. And Amy—who the hell knew what she was up to.

"You want it?" he said bitterly. "Fine. I'll give you the damn money. Wait here." He stormed out of the room and raced upstairs, gobbling up two and three steps at a time. He yanked down the ladder to the attic and climbed up. He went straight to the old dresser and shoved it aside. In seconds he popped the floorboard and grabbed a bundle of bills—a few thousand, easy, but he didn't even count it. He scurried back down the ladder and ran downstairs. He was huffing like a sprinter as he raced past the living room, then stopped short. He suddenly had an idea. It was as if Liz, Amy and now Brent in the same day had brought everything to a head. His father's betrayal. The greed all around him.

He called out to the kitchen. "Come get your money, Brent. It's all here."

Brent hustled eagerly into the living room. He stopped cold at the sight across the dimly lit room. Ryan was standing beside the fireplace. He had a stack of bills in one hand. A long, burning matchstick was in the other. An open can of lighter fluid rested on the mantel.

Brent's voice shook. "What—what you doing?"

"Easy come, easy go." He brought the match to the stack of bills, lighting the corner.

"No!"

The bills burst into flames, thoroughly soaked with lighter fluid. Ryan tossed them into the fireplace. Brent rushed forward. Ryan grabbed the fireplace poker, cocking it like a baseball bat. "Not another step, Brent!"

He stopped in his tracks, his face filled with anguish. The money was burning, but Ryan looked deadly serious. He was nearly in tears. "Ryan, man. Please don't burn it."

Ash fluttered up from the fireplace. The bills burned quickly. Ryan didn't budge. "You lay a hand on Sarah, I'll burn it all. I swear, I will burn every last bill."

"Okay, man. Just be cool, okay?"

"It's the rule," he said, as if to remind himself as much as Brent. "No one gets the money. No one tells anyone else about the money. Not until we find out who paid it to my father and why."

Brent backed away slowly. "Okay, my friend. You're the man. You make the rules. I'm going home now. Just don't burn any more of that money. That's fair, right? You and me just pretend like this little episode never happened."

Ryan kept the poker cocked, ready to crack Brent's skull if he had to.

Brent stepped backward to the door. "No problem here. If you say that's the rule, that's the rule. I'll just go home and tell Sarah we gotta play by the rules, that's all."

"Get the hell out of my sight, Brent."

Brent gave an awkward nod, then hurried out the door. Ryan went to the front window and watched him pull away. He glanced back at the fireplace. The money was a glowing pile of smoldering ash. Thousands of dollars. Gone. Strangely, he felt good about that. He glanced up the staircase, toward the attic. There was still plenty more to fight over.

Or plenty more to burn.

He checked the clock on the end table. Mom wouldn't be home for another hour. He stoked the ash with a shot of lighter fluid, then threw on some kindling and a dry, split log. As the fire hissed and flames reached upward, he closed the screen and started up the stairs.

16

At 9:00 P.M., Amy had a date. With Taylor.

The Fiske Planetarium at the University of Colorado was the largest planetarium between Chicago and Los Angeles. All summer long, Fiske sponsored Friday night programs in astronomy, followed by public viewings at the observatory. The evening programs were way over Taylor's head, more on the level of college students than a four-year-old girl. She had loved the Wednesday morning family matinees, however, learning how runaway slaves had used the Big Dipper to find freedom, and taking a tour of the solar system with a make-believe robot. The simulated displays inside the dome were impressive enough, but Amy had promised to take her to the observatory for a look at the real nighttime sky. Tonight was the night.

They spent more than an hour at the Sommers Bausch Observatory, viewing double stars and galaxies through a sixteen-inch telescope. The big hit, however, was simply viewing Saturn and its rings through a much smaller telescope on the deck. Taylor was full of questions. Her mother had all the answers. Forty hours of graduate study in physics and infrared astronomy hadn't gone completely to waste.

"This is so cool," said Taylor.

"You like astronomy?"

"Only if I get to stay up late every night."

Amy smiled. It sounded like something Amy would have said to her own mother years ago. Taylor had interest, no doubt, but she didn't show the passion for astronomy that Amy had shown as a kid. Then again, ever since she'd started working at the law firm, Amy hadn't given her the same level of encouragement her own mother had given her. There just wasn't time.

She had tried not to show it in front of her daughter, but her focus had been elsewhere most of the night. She was thinking about Ryan, though not about the money. Something he'd said at the restaurant had stuck in her mind. She found it intriguing how he wished he had known his father better, thinking it might help him better understand himself. She knew that exact feeling, the eerie sense that you are what your parents were, the fear of making the same mistakes they'd made. In Amy's case, the same deadly mistake.

Amy walked toward the edge of the observation deck, toward a little two-and-a-half-inch telescope. She pointed it due overhead, where Lyra passed Boulder on summer evenings. She quickly found Vega, the brightest and most prominent star in the constellation. Just below, she knew, was the Ring Nebula—the star she had lingered over on that summer night her mother had passed away. The one that was dying, like her childhood dreams and everything her mother had encouraged her to do.

She hadn't taken a good look at the Ring Nebula since that night. She didn't have to. Modern astronomers didn't gaze into the sky to do their studies. They aimed the telescope and let their instruments do the looking. Not that Amy didn't enjoy looking at the stars. She did. It was just this one, in particular, she couldn't bring herself to look at.

She lowered the telescope a few degrees. She used averted vision, looking out of the corner of her eye, the best way to see faint objects in the sky. The greenish-gray rings came into view. She blinked hard. Part of her wanted to look away, another part wouldn't let her. Staring into space, it looked exactly as it had twenty years ago. It even felt the same. Cold. Lonely. The memories were flooding back. The Ring Nebula had opened a window to her past. She could see an eight-year-old girl shivering with fear as she climbed the shelves in her bedroom closet, reaching for the attic that would be her escape...

The ceiling panel popped open easily, quietly. She pushed it up and to the side, opening her passage to the attic. The trapped air felt hot, heavy. With one last boost she was in.

The flashlight pointed the way. She remembered from the last time, when she and her friends had been playing, that another entrance panel was just a few feet away. That one led to the spare bedroom across the hall. On hands and knees she crawled across the rafters, taking care not to drop the flashlight.

She stopped when she reached the other panel, lifted it with one hand, and looked down from the attic. The closet was exactly like hers— a clothes rod on one side, built-in shelves on the other. She tucked the flashlight back under her chin and climbed down, again using the shelves as a ladder. When she reached the bottom, she crouched into a ball and took a minute to orient herself. If there was an intruder in the house, he might not find her here. She could just stay put, hide out. But the thought again crossed her mind—what if Mom needed her? What if she was hurt?

She rose slowly. She had to go out there. And she couldn't take the flashlight. If someone was in the darkness, it would give her away like the North Star in the night sky.

She switched off the flashlight and opened the closet door. The hall was just a few steps away, beyond the bedroom door. She covered them quietly, then peered down the hallway. She saw nothing. She waited a few seconds. Still nothing. Her heart was in her throat as she stepped from the safety of the spare bedroom.

Her mother's room was upstairs, like Amy's, but on the opposite end of the house. It was dark, but Amy found her way. She was relying more on memory than her sense of sight. She could hear the oscillating fan in her mother's bedroom. She was getting close. She stopped at the doorway. The door was open just a foot. Amy took another step and peeked inside.

The lights were out, but the streetlight on the corner gave the room a faint yellow cast. Everything looked normal. The TV on the stand. The big mirror over the bureau. Her eyes drifted toward the bed. It was a mound of covers. Amy couldn't really make out her mother's shape. But she saw the hand. It was hanging limply over the edge of the bed. A sleep far deeper than Amy had ever seen.

"Mom?" she said with trepidation.

There was no answer.

She said it again. "Mom. Are you okay?"

"Mom, Mom!"

The sound of Taylor's voice roused her from her memories.

"Mommy, let me look!" Taylor was yanking on her arm, climbing up to the telescope.

Amy stepped back and hugged her tight.

Her daughter wiggled away. "I wanna see."

Amy turned the scope away from the Ring Nebula, away from her past. She trained it downward, pointing toward the Fleming Law Building, just a little farther south on campus. The lights were still burning in the library. Probably someone from the law review. She lifted Taylor up to look.

"That's where Mommy will go to law school in September."

"Do you get to look through telly scopes?"

"No. Not in law school."

"Then why do you want to go there?"

She struggled with the lump in her throat. "Let's go home now, Taylor."

They were on the road by ten-thirty, but Taylor was asleep in her car seat before they'd left campus. By day, a drive on U.S. 36 offered magnificent views of Flagstaff Mountain and the Flat Irons, the much-photographed reddish-brown sandstone formations that marked

110

the abrupt border between the plains and the mountains. At night, it was just another dark place to be alone with your thoughts and worries.

Tonight, money was on her mind.

She parked her truck in the usual spot and carried her sleeping beauty up to the apartment. She entered quietly and took Taylor straight to her room. It was a little dream world for both of them. Amy had painted the ceiling with stars and moons. The colors, however, had been selected by Taylor. They had the only planetarium in the world with a Crayola-pink sky.

Amy did the best she could to remove the shoes and get Taylor into pajamas without waking her. She kissed her good night, then switched out the light and quietly closed the door.

It had been a good night, mostly. Overall, the visit to the observatory had only raised her hopes that Ryan Duffy would come through. If the money were legitimate, she could say goodbye to law school and go back where she belonged.

Money—the *need* for it—would no longer be her trumped-up excuse to run from the demons that lurked in the sky she had loved since childhood.

17

The money was burning. But only in his mind.

The metal suitcase full of cash was heavier than Ryan had expected. He'd carried it down the ladder, then down the stairs. He'd moved so quickly that the flame in the fireplace was still going strong when he returned. He dropped to his knees right at the hearth, unzipped the bag, and jerked back the metal screen. His hand shook as he reached for the money. He was determined to go through with it. And then he froze.

Two *million* dollars.

Both the heat and nerves had him dripping with sweat. Still on his knees, he looked back and forth from the money to the flame as he weighed his decision. It was making him crazy. It was making them *all* crazy. His father had been dead less than a week. His wife was clawing at his throat for a huge divorce settlement, spurred on by his father's dying words. His greedy brother-in-law was threatening to beat up his pregnant sister, prompting Ryan to torch the equivalent of a month's salary. And some mysterious woman claimed his father might have sent her as much as two hundred thousand dollars for no reason at all. The money was evil, no question about it. Burning it was the right thing to do.

He grabbed a stack of bills and held it over the fire. His brain commanded him to drop it, but the hand wouldn't listen. Or maybe it was the heart. He just *couldn't*.

His eyes closed in shame and anguish. He'd never felt the power of money. He'd never felt so weak.

A sudden noise roused him from his thoughts. It had come from outside. He jumped up from his knees and hurried to the window. In the darkness, he saw Brent's Buick coming up the driveway.

He's back.

Ryan turned away in panic. The money. He had to hide the money. He grabbed the suitcase and paused for a split second, searching in his mind for a good place to stash it. He heard a car door slam. No time to spare. He stuffed it under the couch. Out of the corner of his eye he saw the fire still burning. The money should have gone with it—which gave him an idea. He grabbed the newspaper from the couch and pitched it into the fire. It burned immediately, leaving the flaky residue of burned paper. It could pass for burned money. Not many people were crazy enough to know what burned money actually looked like.

Ryan stiffened, thinking through the possibilities. It wasn't likely that Brent would come back to talk. It wasn't likely he'd sobered up. He was probably even more drunk, more fired up. He'd be looking for the money. He would have come back only for a showdown. Ryan didn't own a gun, but his father had. Ryan had inventoried everything in the estate. He knew where everything was, right down to the last two million dollars. Down to the last thirty-eight-caliber bullet.

He sprinted down the hall to the master bedroom. The old Smith & Wesson was in the dresser, top drawer. The bullets were in the strongbox in the closet. Ryan grabbed the revolver first, then the ammunition. He loaded all six chambers and wrapped his hand around the pearl handle, the way his father had taught him. The gun was not a toy, he'd always warned Ryan, it was only for protection. Protection from drunken in-laws who were after the Duffy millions.

Ryan heard footsteps on the front porch, then a key in the front door. He switched off the safety on the revolver and started for the living room.

Gun in hand, he waited by the staircase, watching the front door. He heard keys jingling. He watched the lock turn. He raised the gun, taking aim, ready on the defense. The door opened. Ryan's finger twitched. His heart pounded. His whole body stiffened, then suddenly relaxed.

"Mom?" he said, seeing her in the doorway.

She sniffed the smoky room. Her face went ashen. "Don't tell me you really burned it."

He was tongue-tied with surprise. His mother had always been intuitive, but to infer from the mere smell of smoke that he had burned all the money was downright clairvoyant. He lowered the gun, deciding to play dumb. "Burn what?"

She closed the door and went straight to the fireplace. "The money," she said harshly. "I

114

was at Sarah's house and Brent came home all hysterical. Said you'd gone crazy and were burning the money."

"Is he out there now?" ask Ryan. "I thought I saw his car."

"Sarah drove me over." She glanced at the ash in the fireplace. "I can't believe you did this."

He discreetly stuffed the gun into his pocket, hiding it from his mother. "What did Brent tell you?"

"He said you burned at least ten thousand dollars in the fireplace. That you threatened to burn it all."

"That's true."

His mother stepped toward him, looked him in the eye. "Have you been drinking?"

"No. Brent's the drunk. He came in here like a burglar looking for the money."

Her tone softened. "They're afraid you're going to cheat them out of their half."

"I'm not cheating anyone."

She looked again at the ashes in the fireplace. "Ryan, you can do what you want with your share of the money. But you don't have the right to burn your sister's."

"Sarah and I had a deal. The money would stay put until we figured out who Dad was blackmailing and why. She wasn't even supposed to tell Brent. Obviously she did."

"You had to figure she'd tell her own husband."

"Why?"

"Because he's her husband."

"By that logic, Dad should have told you who he was blackmailing."

She seemed to shrink before his eyes. "I told you. I don't know any of the details. I didn't want to know, and your father didn't want to tell me."

Ryan stepped closer and took her hand. "Mom, I came this close to burning two million dollars tonight. Maybe you would agree with that move, maybe you'd disagree. But I deserve to know everything you know before I do something that final."

She turned away and faced the fireplace. The flickering flames were reflected in her dark, troubled eyes. She answered in a soft, serious voice, never looking up. "I do know more. But I don't know everything."

Ryan was beginning to sense why his mother hadn't cried at the funeral. "Tell me what you know."

"Your father—" She was struggling for words. "I think I know where you can find the answers you're looking for."

"Where?"

"The night before he died, your father gave me a key to a safe deposit box."

"What's in it?"

"I don't know. Your father just said that if you had any questions about the money, I should give it to you. I'm sure the blackmail will become clear once you open it."

"How can you be sure?"

"Because even though your father couldn't say it to your face, he apparently wanted you to know. And I know of no place else to look."

He searched her eyes, as if scrutinizing her soul. He'd never looked at his mother that way before, never had to watch for signs of deception. He found none. "Thank you, Mom. Thank you for telling me."

"Don't *thank* me. Can't you see how afraid this makes me? For you, for all of us?"

"What do you want me to do?"

She grimaced, as if in pain. "That's up to you. You can be like me and just stay away from it. Or you can open the box and deal with whatever comes with it."

He paused for a moment until their eyes met. "I have to know, Mom."

"Of course you do," she said in a voice that faded. "Just don't tell *me* about it."

18

Panama. Until now, it had meant nothing to Ryan but a famous canal and an infamous dethroned dictator named Noriega. When his mother had told him about the safe deposit box, he'd figured it might be as far away as Denver.

What the hell was Dad doing with a safe deposit box in Panama?

The key and related documentation were in a locked strongbox in the bedroom closet, right where his mother had said they would be. Box 242 at the Banco Nacional in Panama City. There was even a city map. Dad's passport was in there, too. Ryan didn't even know he'd owned one. He thumbed through the pages. Most were blank. The passport was like new, stamped only twice. A trip to Panama nineteen years ago and a return to the United States the very next day. Not much of a vacation. It had to be business.

The business of extortion.

Ryan took the box up to his room and spent most of Friday night in bed awake, his mind racing. He ran though every human being he'd ever seen his father with, every man and woman his father had ever mentioned. He couldn't come up with a single person who had the financial wherewithal to pay two million dollars in extortion. He certainly couldn't think of anyone with connections to Panama.

At two in the morning he finally formed a semblance of a plan. He rose quietly and peeked in his mother's room, making sure she was asleep. Then he sneaked downstairs. The money was still under the couch, where he'd stashed it when his mother had pulled up unexpectedly. He had a mini-warehouse near the clinic where he stored extra supplies, some old office furniture. Not even Liz knew it existed. Like a cat burglar, he slipped silently out the front door, pushing his Jeep Cherokee to the end of the driveway so that the engine noise wouldn't wake his mother. He drove straight to the warehouse and hid the money in the bottom drawer of an old file cabinet. It would be safe there. Both the cabinet and the metal suitcase his father had left him were fireproof. He returned home, went straight to bed, and waited for the sun to rise.

He rose early Saturday morning, having managed only a couple of hours of sleep. He showered, dressed, and brought the box down to the kitchen. His mother was sitting at the table, drinking coffee and reading the *Lamar Daily News,* a local paper put out by the nearest "metropolis"—Lamar, population 8,500. It was usually no more than sixteen pages, three or four of which would typically be devoted to a photographic recap of the annual Granada High School class reunion or the 4-H Horse Show. The sight of his mother and her small-town news made it all the more absurd, the thought of his father flying to Panama and opening a safe deposit box.

"I've looked everything over," said Ryan.

His mother stared even more intently at her newspaper.

"Don't you want to know exactly what's in there?" he asked.

"Nope."

Ryan stood and waited, hoping she'd just look at him. The wall of newspaper between them seemed impenetrable. Fitting, thought Ryan. Most people in Piedmont Springs at least once in a while read the *Pueblo Chieftain,* the *Denver Post,* or even the *Wall Street Journal.* Not Mom. Her world was filtered through the *Lamar Daily News.* Some things she just didn't need to know.

"Mom, I'm going to take all this stuff with me, if that's okay with you."

She didn't respond. Ryan waited a full minute, expecting her at the very least to ask where he was going. She simply turned the page, never making eye contact. "I'll be back late tonight," he said on his way out the kitchen door.

He put the box in the backseat of his Jeep Cherokee and fired up the engine. The sun was just rising over the cornfields. Miles and miles of corn, all for animal feed, not the sweet corn grown for human consumption. A cloud of dust kicked up as he sped along the lonely dirt road, a shortcut to Highway 50, the first leg of the two-hundred-mile trip to Denver.

The air conditioner in Amy's truck was still broken, making the Saturday afternoon traffic jam even more unbearable. According to historians, Arapaho Indian Chief Niwot once said that "people seeing the beauty of the Boulder Valley will want to stay, and their staying will be the undoing of the beauty." Inching toward the fourth cycle of the traffic light at 28th Street and Arapahoe Avenue, Amy was beginning to see the truth in what locals referred to as "Niwot's curse."

Amy had a twelve-thirty lunch reservation at her favorite restaurant. Gram had graciously agreed to babysit until three o'clock. For Taylor, that meant nonstop reruns of *Three's Company* and *The Dukes of Hazzard*, at least until she went down for her afternoon nap. It made Amy feel a bit like a child abuser, but tomorrow she'd figure out some way to reverse the brain damage.

She parked near Broadway and walked up to

the Pearl Street Mall. For all its natural beauty, Boulder was ironically quite famous for its mall. The four-block open-air walkway was the city's original downtown area, converted for pedestrians only. Historic old buildings and some tastefully designed new ones lined the brick-paved streets, home to numerous shops, galleries, microbreweries, offices, and cafés. The mall was prime people-watching territory, especially on weekends. Jugglers, musicians, sword swallowers, and other street performers created a carnival atmosphere. Amy smiled as she passed "Zip Code Man," a virtual human computer who, with no more information than your zip code, could identify and often even describe your neighborhood, no matter how far away. Taylor had stumped him last December, using the zip code she'd posted on her letter to Santa Claus.

Narayan's Nepal Restaurant was a sizable downstairs restaurant right on the mall, offering a distinctive mountain fare at bargain prices. As a graduate student, Amy had shared many a lunch and dinner at Narayan's with Maria Perez, her old faculty advisor from the Department of Astrophysical and Planetary Sciences. Together, they'd plotted the course of her doctoral research over stuffed roti or the ever-popular vegetable sampler. Amy hadn't seen much of Maria since she'd left astronomy. Even though she still considered her a friend, she found it hard to just pick up the phone and give her a call. Partly, she felt she'd let Maria down. Mostly, she felt she'd let herself down.

Maria was waiting at the entrance when Amy arrived.

"How are you, stranger?" she said as they embraced.

"So good to see you," said Amy.

They kept right on talking as the hostess led them to a small table near the window. There was lots of catching up to do. Maria had recently bagged her eighth fourteener—Colorado lingo, meaning she'd climbed eight of the state's fifty-four mountain peaks that exceeded fourteen thousand feet. Maria was a bona fide fitness fanatic, a fairly common breed in a city where winter snowplows sometimes cleared the bicycle paths before the streets. She never ate meat and actually had a chin-up bar in her puny office. Amy was the only one in the department who had even come close to keeping up with her on the jogging trail.

The waitress took their orders, and then they marveled over the latest pictures of Taylor while sipping house Chardonnay. Finally, the conversation wound its way down the career path.

"So, are you ready for law school this fall?"

"I guess."

Maria smirked. "I'm glad to see your enthusiasm has grown since last we talked."

"Actually, I have some potentially good news on that front."

"What?"

"It's highly confidential. If I tell you, you can't tell anyone. Not even your husband."

"Don't worry about Nate, honey. I could

tell him I just uncovered the secret formula for Coca-Cola, and his response would probably be something like, 'That's nice, sweetie. Have you seen my car keys?' Come on," she said eagerly. "What's the big secret?"

Amy paused for effect, then said, "I may be re-enrolling in the fall."

Maria shrieked. Heads turned at neighboring tables, but she kept on gushing. "That's great! It's better than great. It's *fabulous*. But why is it a secret?"

"Because the law firm I'm working for is giving me a partial scholarship to law school. If they find out I'm having second thoughts, I'm afraid they'll pull the scholarship. If my astronomy plans don't work out, then I'd be screwed all the way around."

Maria gestured, zipping her lip. "Your secret is safe with me. When will you know for sure?"

"By the end of the week, hopefully."

"God, I'm so happy you've had a change of heart."

"My heart never changed. It's more a change in circumstances. Money, to be exact."

"What, somebody died and left you a fortune?"

"Actually, yes."

Her smile faded. "Great. I mean, I'm sorry about the death. But good for you, in a way. Hell, you know what I mean."

"It's okay. I didn't really know the guy."

"Somebody you didn't know is leaving you a pot of money?"

"Possibly, yes. I met with his son yesterday

123

to make sure everything checks out. It's a little sticky. He's in the middle of a divorce."

"Oh," she said. It was an ominous "oh."

"Why the look?"

"Some guy you don't know dies and leaves you money. His son is in the middle of a divorce. Don't you think you're being a little optimistic about enrolling in the fall? Those kinds of legal problems can drag out indefinitely."

Amy hesitated. It was even more complicated, but it was best to keep it simple. "He promised to have everything cleared up by next Friday."

"Friday," she said, drumming her fingers on the tabletop. "To be honest with you, that might not be soon enough."

"What do you mean?"

"Don't get me wrong. No one would be more excited than me to see you come back. But it's already mid-July. I'm not sure we can line things up for the fall term."

"What's the big deal? I just pick up where I left off."

"It's not that simple. With most of your coursework already behind you, your primary focus this fall is your independent research. There's already a lot of research being done in the field on the birth and death of stars and the possible existence of other planetary systems around them. If you're going to generate a dissertation of publishable quality, the best place to conduct your research is the Meyer-Womble Observatory on Mt. Evans."

Amy was aware of that. At better than four

thousand meters above sea level, they were pulling images from Mt. Evans that rivaled Hubble Space Telescope quality. "What do we have to do to get me in?"

"The site is operated by the University of Denver under a U.S. Forest Service special use permit, so the department will have to work out some kind of collaborative research arrangement with DU. That needs to be done well in advance. It's not just a question of access to the telescope. It's also a matter of getting to and from the observatory. Living accommodations are limited on the mountain, especially if you're going to take your daughter and grandmother with you. You can't be driving back and forth from Boulder every day. It's not only time-consuming, but come November, the roads could be impassable."

Amy sipped her wine, thinking. "I promise to let you know by next Friday."

"I can't guarantee anything."

"Come on. Cut me a little slack, okay? What's the absolute deadline?"

"Yesterday. Or to be even more precise, last month. If I'm going to bust my political hump to work you back into the fall program, I need a commitment from you. And I need it right away. I'm being straight with you, Amy. As a friend."

She snagged her lip with her tooth. She had agreed to give Ryan Duffy a week to pull together the records, but that wasn't written in stone. "Okay," she said with a quick nod. "I'll let you know by Monday."

19

By midafternoon, Ryan could see the Denver skyline from the interstate. A hint of the infamous brown cloud hovered over the city. Despite serious clean-up efforts, Denver hadn't completely shaken the ghost of air pollution. The worst Ryan had seen it was a year ago last winter. That was the last time he'd come to visit his old friend Norman Klusmire.

The once inseparable twosome had met as freshmen at the University of Colorado—roommates, in fact, though it was just the luck of the on-campus housing lottery that had thrown them together. They didn't exactly seem destined to become life-long friends. Ryan was the more serious student, with an eye on med school from the first day of orientation. Norm had chosen UC because it was close to the ski slopes, a curious move for a native of southern Mississippi who had absolutely no use for ice, save for mint juleps. His grades were lousy in one sense; astounding if you considered he never went to class. On a dare he took the Law School Admissions Test and scored in the top one-half of one percent. The sea change was complete when he met another transplanted southerner, the radiant Rebecca—though he nearly blew it with her right on their wedding day. In probably his only lapse of judgment since his twenty-first birthday, Norm put his hell-raising older brother in charge of his bachelor party. Norm awoke an hour before the ceremony with a permanent nipple ring big enough to set off a metal detector and absolutely no memory of how it got there. Ryan did the emergency removal in the basement of the church. The stitches blended nicely with the chest hair. Rebecca never knew. They'd been married ever since.

Norm had always said that if Ryan were ever in a crack, he could count on Norm to return the favor. It was intended as a joke. Norm's specialty was criminal defense.

Ryan called from the truck stop just outside Denver to say he needed to cash in on that old offer. Norm laughed, recalling the old joke. Ryan didn't laugh with him. Norm immediately dropped everything and invited his old buddy over to the house.

Norm lived on Monroe Street in the Cherry Creek North subdivision. A million dollars didn't buy what it used to in Denver, but Ryan still thought it should have bought more than Norm's five-bedroom, mausoleum-like home with no yard to speak of. It had that multilevel, overbuilt look that the same builder had achieved in a dozen other new homes in the neighborhood, all in the hefty million-plus price range. For the money, Ryan preferred the restored Victorian jewels in the Capitol Hill area.

Ryan parked behind the Range Rover in the driveway. Norm came out to greet him. He wore baggy Nike shorts and a sweaty T-shirt, much like his three sons. They were having a game of two-on-two basketball. Norm had been a decent athlete at one time, but he'd put on a few pounds since Ryan had last seen him. Lost a little more hair, too.

They exchanged their usual greeting—a big bear hug from Norm, never mind the sweat.

Ryan stepped back, making a face. "What was that BS you used to give me? Southerners don't sweat. They glisten."

"It's absolutely true," said Norm, giving him another wet hug. "Just some of us glisten our ass off."

Norm toweled off as he led his friend around back to the patio, where they could sit and talk in private. The housekeeper brought them a pitcher of iced tea that had been sweetened in the extreme, another of Norm's connections to his southern roots. Norm poured as they talked about the funeral he was sorry to have missed. Then the conversation turned serious.

"So," Norm said between gulps of tea. "What's the terrible crisis that brings you all the way to Denver to talk to a big-shot criminal defense lawyer?"

"This is all attorney-client, right?"

"Absolutely. Completely privileged and confidential. The fact that we're friends and this is a freebie doesn't change that."

"I can pay you for your time, Norm. I wasn't really looking for charity."

"Nonsense. Trust me when I say you can't afford me. And please don't take that as an insult. Hell, if I needed a lawyer, I couldn't afford me."

"That's kind of why I'm here, Norm. I could afford you. Seems my dad left me some money."

His interest piqued. "How much?"

"More than you'd think."

"I see. Seems like you'd want a probate specialist. Who are you using?"

"I was planning on using the same lawyer who drafted Dad's will. Josh Colburn. Kind of local legal beagle."

"You mean legal eagle."

"No. I mean beagle. Not too smart, loyal as a puppy dog. Basically he does everybody in Piedmont Springs. But it's starting to look like this is way over his head."

"In what way?"

"I have some real questions about the source of the funds."

"What kind of questions?"

Ryan hesitated. Suddenly the fact that he knew Norm and Norm had known his father was a hindrance. It had nothing to do with trust. An acute sense of shame kept him from uttering the word "extortion." He skipped ahead, glossing over it. "My dad had a safe deposit box in Panama."

"The country of Panama?"

"*Sí*," said Ryan.

"That doesn't mean anything by itself."

"Norm, cut the politically correct bullshit. We're not talking about a high-rolling international businessman. We're talking about a sixty-two-year-old electrician from Piedmont Springs."

"I see your point."

"He rented the box almost twenty years ago. Went down on a Tuesday, came back the following day. As far as I can tell from his passport, he never went back."

"You know what's in it?"

"Supposedly there are some papers inside that will explain the source of the money."

Norm shook his head, confused. "You gotta give me a little more information here. When you say money, you talking stocks, bonds, gold doubloons—what is it?"

"Cash. Seven figures."

His eyes widened. "Congratulations, old buddy. You *can* afford me."

"What do you know about Panamanian banks?"

"It all depends. Back in the days of dictatorship, things were different than they are now. Very strict bank secrecy. Frankly, a lot of drug money was laundered through Panamanian banks. Some would say it's still prevalent to this day, just that it's no longer sponsored by the government."

"This is so crazy."

Norm leaned closer. "I don't mean to alarm you, *amigo*. Even though I do mostly criminal work, I've done enough probate to know you're in somewhat of a crack yourself."

"What do you mean?"

"You're the executor of the estate, right? That means you have ethical and legal obligations of your own. For starters, where did the money come from?"

"I don't know exactly."

"Where do you *think* it came from? Be honest with me."

Ryan still couldn't say it—he couldn't call his father a blackmailer. "I'm afraid it may turn out that Dad wasn't entitled to this money."

"All right. Just so we can have an intelligent conversation here, let's say your old man cheated somebody. I presume he didn't pay income tax on the money."

"Definitely not."

"There's problem number one. The IRS has absolutely no sense of humor about these things."

"So I suppose I'll have to report the money on some kind of estate tax form."

"Not just that. The probate court requires you to file a schedule of assets. And you have to give legal notice to potential creditors, who then have the right to file a claim against the estate. If your dad did cheat somebody, I suppose the victims would be considered creditors. In the strictest ethical sense, you would be obligated to send them a notice so they could get their money back, if they wanted to make an issue out of it."

"What if I don't know who they are?"

"You're the executor of the estate. It's your duty to find out. Within the exercise of reasonable diligence, of course."

The mention of a legal duty only heightened Ryan's sense of moral responsibility—not to mention his curiosity. "I just can't believe my dad would be involved in anything...unsavory. I always thought he was such a good person."

"That's what we always want to think. We think that about ourselves. Then one day, opportunity knocks. And that's when we find

131

out. Are we truly honest? Some people are. Some people are hard-core crooks. Those are the extremes. Most of the people I defend are in the middle. They've done the right thing all their life, but only because the fear of doing time outweighs the rewards of the crime. For them, morality boils down to simple risk analysis. The thing is, you never know which way those people will turn until the right opportunity comes along."

"I'm afraid my dad may have flunked the test."

"It's not a test, Ryan. At least not the kind you can cram for the night before, like we did in college. It's a question of what you're made of. Now, I don't know where your dad got that kind of money. Maybe it's totally legitimate. Maybe it's not. But maybe he still had a damn good reason for doing what he did."

"I don't know the complete picture yet."

"Then you have a couple of choices. You can go down to Panama and open the box. Or you can ignore it. My hunch, however, is that if you go down there, you're going to find out what your father was made of. Can you handle that?"

"Yeah," he said without hesitation. "I have to."

"Okay. That was the easy one. Here's where it gets complicated."

"What do you mean?"

"Once you start chasing the money trail, you might well find out what *you* are made of. So before you hop on an airplane, you need to ask yourself: Can you handle *that*?"

Ryan looked his friend in the eye. "I brought my passport," he said flatly. "That question was answered before I got here."

20

On Sunday morning Amy called Ryan Duffy again. An elderly-sounding woman answered, his mother. Amy hadn't realized that the doctor she had found so interesting had formally moved in with his mother, but she quickly cut him some slack. She knew better than anyone what a divorce could do for your living arrangements.

"He's not here," said Mrs. Duffy.

"Do you know when he'll be back?"

"He had to go out of town on business. Can I take a message?"

"I can call again. You think he'll be back tomorrow?"

"Probably not. He called me from the Denver airport last night and said he'd be away for a few days. Are you a friend of his?"

"Yes, sort of. Thank you for your time, ma'am. I'll check back later." She hung up before the next question.

Amy sat on the edge of her bed, her thoughts churning in her head. It was a bit unnerving to hear Jeanette Duffy's voice, the voice of the widow. It was Jeanette's Crock-Pot, after all, that had given Amy her first link to the Duffy family. In that light, it seemed interesting

133

now that Ryan had been so quick to dismiss the possibility of his mother's involvement—his off-the-cuff comment that his father but definitely not his mother would be the type to give away money to strangers. And now the phone call. Evasive, at best.

Amy hurried to the closet and dug out her tennis shoes. If Mrs. Duffy was lying and Ryan was still at home, she had to talk to him. If he was really out of town, this was her chance to talk directly to Jeanette Duffy.

It was time for another visit to Piedmont Springs.

The temperature rose as morning turned to afternoon and the mountains gave way to the eastern plains. Five hours on the highway had brought Amy down from an elevation of 5,400 feet to just over 3,000. The typical July humidity and scattered afternoon thunderclouds marked her entry into Prowers County.

Amy knew the way to the Duffy house from her earlier trip, when she had scouted out the family in advance of her meeting with Ryan. Her second trip to Piedmont Springs in a week had her somewhat concerned about her old truck. So long as she traveled by day, however, she felt safe.

She reached the Duffy residence around two o'clock. The Jeep Cherokee she'd seen in the driveway last time was nowhere to be seen. Maybe Ryan really was gone. Another car was in its place, a white Buick. Amy parked right behind it. She drew a deep breath and headed up the walkway toward the front door.

Wind chimes tinkled in the lazy breeze as she climbed the porch steps and knocked lightly. The screen door was locked with a metal latch. The heavy wood door behind it was wide open for ventilation. Through the screen, Amy could see across the living room, almost to the kitchen. Her palms began to sweat as she waited for a response. She had spent the last five hours in the truck rehearsing exactly what she would say—Plan A and Plan B, depending on whether Ryan or his mother came to the door.

Amy was about to knock again when she heard footsteps from inside the house. Actually, it was more of a shuffling sound. Slowly, a large woman came into view. As she crossed the living room, it was clear she was pregnant. Very pregnant.

"Can I help you?" she asked, still shuffling forward.

Amy smiled. She had this notion in her mind that people in small towns always smiled. It was a nervous smile, however, as this woman's voice didn't match the voice on the phone. Amy had no Plan C.

"I—uh. Is Ryan here?"

She stopped on the other side of the screen door and caught her breath. "No."

"Are you—you're not Jeanette Duffy, are you?"

"I'm Sarah. Ryan's sister." She turned decidedly suspicious. "Who are you?"

She thought for a second. Last Friday, she had told Ryan her first name. It would be interesting to know if the name meant anything to his sister. "My name's Amy."

"You a friend of Ryan's?" Neither the tone nor her expression raised a specter of recognition. Apparently Ryan hadn't told his sister a thing.

"I wouldn't say I'm a friend, really. To be honest, you might be as much help to me as Ryan. Maybe even more."

"What are you talking about?"

"It has to do with money. Money that I think may have come from your father."

Sarah's eyes widened. Amy noted the reaction. "Can I come inside and talk for a minute?" asked Amy.

Sarah didn't move, said nothing.

"Just for a minute," said Amy.

"Let's talk out here." The screen door creaked as Sarah stepped onto the porch. She directed Amy to the wicker rocking chair in the corner. Sarah took the hanging love seat swing in front of the window. She looked about as miserable as pregnant-in-July could possibly look.

"I'm listening," said Sarah. "What money are you talking about?"

Amy wasn't aware of it, but she was on the edge of her chair. She was apprehensive, unsure of how to play this. She settled on a replay of her meeting with Ryan. "I received a package a few weeks ago. There was money inside. No return address, no card. But as best I can tell, I think it came from your father."

"Did you know my father?"

"I don't ever recall meeting him."

"How do you know it's from my father?"

"It came in a Crock-Pot box. I checked the registration from the product number on the box. It was registered in your mother's name. I suppose it could have come from your mother—"

"No," she interrupted. "Couldn't have come from my mother. How much money was in the box?"

"At least a thousand dollars." She flinched at the white lie—but again, it wasn't a total lie. There was *at least* a thousand dollars. "Honestly, I'm not sure what to do with it."

Sarah leaned forward in the swing, speaking sharply. "I'll tell you what you do with it. You put the money back in the box. Every bit of it. And you bring it right back. You have no right to keep it."

Amy froze in her rocker. It was as if she'd stepped on a rattlesnake. "I didn't come here to make trouble."

"I won't let you make trouble. Ryan and me are the only heirs. Our father didn't leave no will, and in two months of dying, he sure as hell didn't mention no Amy."

"Are you sure?"

"I'm positive."

"Is your mother home? I'd like to talk to her. Maybe your father mentioned my name to her."

"Don't you go near my mother. This has been hard enough on her. I don't need you poking around like some long-lost illegitimate child trying to weasel her way into an inheritance."

"Who said anything about *that*? All I'm trying to do is figure out why your father would have sent me some money in a box. I'd like to know where the money came from."

"It doesn't matter where it came from. All that matters is that it comes back where it belongs. I want that money back, Miss Amy. I hope you have the good sense to see me eye-to-eye on this."

"I really wish you would just let me talk to your mother, maybe clear things up."

Her eyes narrowed. "There's nothing to clear up. I told you what to do. Now *do* it."

Amy stared right back, but there was nothing more to say. "Thank you for your time," she said, rising. "And your hospitality."

She stepped down from the porch and headed for her car.

It nearly maxed out his Visa card, but Ryan booked a flight to Panama City through Dallas. Getting out of Denver was the easy part. Apparently the plane for the second leg of the journey had come down with malaria or some other mysterious Panamanian ailment. He spent the night and most of Sunday in the terminal at the Dallas-Fort Worth International Airport, waiting on a mechanically sound 737 to take him and the other two hundred stranded passengers the rest of the way to Panama.

Ryan had no luggage to check, just his carry-on bags. Norm had loaned him some extra clothes, which accounted for the mono-

138

grammed polo player on his shirt. He took several naps in the waiting area, no more than twenty minutes at a stretch, keeping both arms wrapped around his bag at all times. The last thing he needed was someone to walk off with his passport. His bladder was bursting, but he didn't dare get up from his seat. The flight was overbooked, and one trip to the airport rest room would mean having to sit on the floor until boarding time. The family camped out on the floor beside him spoke no English, so he used the opportunity to practice his Spanish. He was rusty, but it pleased him to see he could still get his point across. He'd treated a number of Spanish-speaking patients over the years, mostly migrant workers from the melon fields west of Piedmont Springs.

At 3:35 the woman at the check-in counter announced that Flight 97 to Panama would begin boarding in fifteen minutes.

Promises, promises. Ryan grabbed his bag and made a final preboarding break for the rest room. On his way out, he stopped at the bank of pay phones in the hall for one last domestic call home, just to check on things. He punched out the number and waited. Sarah answered.

"Hi, it's Ryan," he said. "Everything okay?"

"Yeah, fine."

"Mom's okay?"

"Yup."

"You'll stay with her tonight, right?"

"I've been with her all day, Ryan. Yes, I'll spend the night."

"Be firm about it. She'll tell you she's fine alone and tell you to go home. But she's still depressed. She left the damn gas burner on yesterday. She's just not all there. She's gonna hurt herself if there isn't somebody there looking after her."

"Ryan, I said I'd stay."

"Okay. Thanks."

"When you coming home?"

"Possibly Monday night. Tuesday at the latest."

The airport speakers crackled with another announcement. Ryan's flight would begin boarding in five minutes. "I gotta go, Sarah. You're sure everything is okay?"

"Yes," she said, almost groaning. "Just a typical dull day in Piedmont Springs."

"What do you mean by that?"

"Nothing, Ryan. Nothing at all. I assure you, everything is perfectly A-okay."

21

Her truck was dying at the Sand Creek Massacre.

Just north of the town of Chivington, to be exact, near the small stone monument that marked the spot where in 1864 Col. John Chivington and his citizens' militia annihilated an entire reservation of peaceable Indians, including unarmed children running from the scene. Amy recalled that disgraceful tale from grade school history. At the moment, however, she could think only of her own disaster.

Steam was spewing from beneath the hood, growing thicker with each tick on the odometer. The engine sputtered. The truck was losing speed. Amy cranked on the heater inside the cab. Through experience she'd learned that turning on the heat could help cool down an overheated engine—at the driver's expense, of course. The midafternoon's flirt with a hundred degrees had thankfully passed, but the temperature was still unbearable. The heater was blasting on high. The plains stretched for miles in all directions, not a building or car in sight. Just acres of soybeans on either side. For miles ahead, mirages danced on a sun-baked road as straight as string. Amy felt like she might pass out. She stuck her head out the window for some cooler air. The truck limped along at twenty miles an hour. She had to make it to the next town. A deserted highway was no place to spend the night.

"Come on, baby. You can do it." Talking to her truck had always seemed to help. It sure couldn't hurt.

Somehow she managed to make it a few more miles, all the way to a town called Kit Carson. She didn't know precisely where she was, but it was hard to feel lost in a town named after Colorado's most famous scout. Luckily there were a few service stations, particularly where Highway 40 intersected with 287. Her truck rolled into the station with just barely enough momentum to make it to the garage door. Unfortunately, it was Sunday. No mechanic would be on duty until Monday morning. One way or another, Amy was stuck on the plains for the night. She left a note under the windshield telling the mechanic she'd be back at 6:00 A.M., when the garage opened. Down the road she noticed a small motel. The sign proclaimed "vacancy." From the looks of the place, it *always* had a vacancy. She locked the truck and headed up the gravel shoulder along the highway.

The Kit Carson Motor Lodge was a simple one-story motel designed for one-night stays. Each room had its own outside entrance. Rooms in front faced the highway. Rooms in the back faced the gravel parking lot. Only the back rooms had air conditioning, rusty old wall units that stuck out beneath the windows. Amy took the one room with a unit that actually worked.

Amy showered and washed her clothes in the sink. She was able to buy a toothbrush and toothpaste at the front desk. She wrapped herself in the flimsy bath towel and hung her clothes on the shower rod to dry. The television didn't work, which was just as well. She lay on the bed, exhausted, but she couldn't let herself sleep until she called home.

She sat up and dialed, thinking with the phone to her ear as she counted the lonely-sounding rings on the other end of line. Gram was totally up to speed. This morning, Amy had decided that if she was going to make contact with the Duffys in Piedmont

Springs, Gram should know about it. One thing had led to another, as it always did with Gram, and before Amy hit the road Gram knew all about the meeting with Ryan in Denver. Gram wasn't happy about any of it—which had Amy bracing for her wrath.

"Gram, it's me."

"Where the heck are you, girl?"

"I'm at the Kit Carson Motor Lodge. My truck died on the way home."

"I told you to get rid of that junk."

"I know, I know. I think it's just a water hose. But I can't get it fixed till tomorrow, so I'll have to spend the night."

"What about work? You want me to call the law firm and tell them you're sick?"

"Gram, this isn't grade school. I can call them." She instantly regretted the sarcasm. Gram only meant well, even if she did sometimes treat Amy as if she were Taylor's age.

Gram let it go. "By the way, did you get to talk with Mrs. Duffy?"

"No."

"Just as well."

"I talked to her daughter. A woman named Sarah. She said she wants the money back."

"Doggone it, Amy. I told you not to stir the pot. Now look where we are."

"I didn't tell her I had two hundred thousand dollars. I only told her it was about a thousand."

"Good girl."

Amy blinked. The woman who'd taught her right from wrong was now praising her for telling half-truths. "Gram, I don't think I have the stomach for this."

"Nonsense. We're over the hump now. You talked to the son. You talked to the daughter. You tried to talk to the widow. You've done everything you can to try and find out where the money came from. Your conscience should be clear. Just give that Sarah character her thousand dollars and everybody will be happy."

"There's more to it than that."

"Like what?"

"I don't know how to describe it. I just got some strange vibes from Sarah. Downright hostile."

"How do you mean?"

Amy had not forgotten the feeling she'd gotten when talking to Sarah—the way Sarah had treated her like the gold-digging illegitimate heir. Still, it was a touchy subject to raise with her grandmother—the mother of her father. "I'm sure it's nothing. I'm just being a nervous Nellie."

"You really are. Now promise me you'll be careful getting home."

"I will. Let me talk to Taylor for a minute, okay?"

"She might be asleep already. Let me check."

The wait triggered a wave of thoughts, again about Sarah. An inheritance would explain the money. Amy had no list of every man her mother had ever known intimately. Perhaps Frank Duffy was among them. Maybe the money was his way of acknowledging Amy was his. Why else would he have been so seemingly careless as to send the money in a used Crock-Pot box, which made it possible

144

for her to track down the sender with just a little and perseverance? Maybe his mind had said make the gift anonymously, but in his heart he *wanted* her to find out it was from her real father.

She was suddenly queasy about the instant attraction she'd felt toward Frank Duffy's handsome son.

"She's asleep," said Gram, back on the line. "Poor little angel must have put a hundred miles on her roller skates today. Call us in the morning before you get on the road. And be careful. I love you, darling."

"I love you, too."

She hung up the phone, torn inside. She did love her Gram. She'd always love her. Even if it turned out she wasn't her *real* grandmother.

22

Ryan woke at 5:30 Monday morning, Mountain Time. He reset his wristwatch ahead two hours to local time in Panama City. Butterflies swirled in his belly. The bank would open in thirty minutes.

He showered and dressed in record time. Room service brought him a quick continental breakfast. He managed a few sips of *café con leche* while shaving but didn't have the stomach for food. Overnight, something inside him had changed. He felt different. Staring at his reflection in the mirror, he even looked at himself differently. From the moment he'd left Piedmont Springs almost forty-eight hours ago, his mind had strategically diverted his attention from the real problem. He'd been thinking of his mother and her small-town preference never to know anything that wasn't fit to print in the *Lamar Daily News*. He'd met his friend Norm to talk out the legal niceties of Panamanian banks. He'd made small talk with a Panamanian family in the airport. He'd done everything but come to terms with the fact that his father was a blackmailer—and that the box would tell him why.

This morning, there was no more dodging the truth. He felt like a son who had never known his father. Today, he would meet him for the very first time.

Ryan checked out of the hotel at 7:50 A.M. and checked his garment bag with the concierge. He would pick it up later on his way to the airport after visiting the bank. He took the small carry-on with him, a leather shoulder bag that made him look like a camera-toting tourist. Whatever he might find inside the safe deposit box, the bag would enable him to carry it out in conceal-ment.

Sweat soaked his brow the minute he stepped outside the hotel. Besides the great canal and those namesake hats that were actually made in Ecuador, Panama was known for its rainfall. It got more than any other Cen-tral American country, mostly between April and December. Today's rain was not yet

146

falling, but the heavy tropical heat and 90 percent humidity foreshadowed the inevitable. Ryan considered hailing a taxi to beat the heat, but the drivers were beyond aggressive; they were downright reckless, notorious for their many accidents. The buses weren't much better, called the Red Devils not just because of their color. Ryan would just have to hoof it.

His pace was swift, partly because he was eager to open the box, partly because he was uncomfortable in the neighborhood. There seemed to be more beggars than anything else on the sidewalks. Street crime in Panama City was a serious problem. It surprised him that his father had actually come here. His mother never would have come.

The thought jarred him.

Maybe that was the point. Dad had chosen to hide his ugly secrets in a place Mom would never look—even if she knew where they were and she desperately wanted to know them.

The neighborhood improved considerably as he turned on Avenida Balboa. Banco Nacional de Panama was a modern building on the lively thoroughfare, one of literally hundreds of international banks in the burgeoning financial district of Panama City. Ryan climbed the limestone steps slowly, bemused by the fact that he was retracing his father's steps. The bank itself was medium-size, slightly larger than the typical branch bank in the States. The entrance was formal and impressive, a tasteful mix of chrome, glass, and polished Botticino marble. An armed guard stood at the door. Two others were posted inside. Business hours had started just fifteen minutes ago, and the place was already bustling. Behind velvet ropes, lines of customers snaked toward the tellers. Bank officers were busy with clients or on the phone. With business all over the world, the bank transcended time zones.

Ryan crossed the spacious lobby and headed for the sign marked LAS CAJAS DE SEGURIDAD— SAFE DEPOSIT BOXES. The boxes were located in a small, windowless wing behind the tellers, part of the private banking section. Ryan left his name with the receptionist and took a seat on the couch, absorbing the surroundings. The well-dressed man seated beside him was reading a French magazine. The receptionist appeared to be a descendant of a local Indian tribe. One of the tellers was black; the other, Chinese. Ryan had read somewhere that Panama was not a melting pot but a *sancocho* pot. As in the local dish, the various "ingredients" contributed their own flavor but retained their own individual identity. The meaning was beginning to come clear.

"Señor Duffy?"

Ryan looked up at the woman in the doorway. *"Buenos dias, señora. Yo soy Ryan Duffy."*

She smirked, obviously sensing from his accent that Spanish was his second language—a *distant* second. She answered in English. "Good morning. I'm Vivien Fuentes. Please come with me."

Though not perfect, her English was fairly good, which helped account for his father's selection of this particular bank. Ryan followed her to the small office around the corner. She offered him a chair, then closed the door and seated herself behind her desk. She smiled pleasantly and said, "How can I help you?"

"I'm here on family business, I guess you'd call it. My father recently passed away."

"I'm so sorry."

"Thank you. As the executor of his estate, I'm accounting for all of his assets. It's my understanding that he has a safe deposit box here at your bank, which I'd like to access this morning."

"Very well. I'll need to see your passport and power of attorney."

"Sure." Ryan opened his leather bag and removed the power of attorney his father had executed when he became ill. He handed it over with his passport.

"Thank you." She flipped right to the photo ID, then glanced at Ryan. She seemed satisfied. "Your father's full name?" she asked, poised to enter it on her computer keyboard.

"I believe it's a numbered account."

"It's numbered as far as the outside world is concerned. We do have the names in our internal data bank."

"Naturally," he said, feeling a little stupid. "His name was Frank Patrick Duffy."

She typed in the name and hit ENTER. "Here it is," she said, checking the screen. "Yes, he does still have a safe deposit box with us."

"Box Two-Forty-Two," said Ryan as he pulled the key from his bag.

"That's what your key says. It's actually Box One-Ninety-Three. It's coded for security purposes."

"Whatever it is, I'd like to get into it as soon as possible."

"First, I need to check your father's signature on the power of attorney against the signature specimen on file here. Standard procedure. It will take only a second." She clicked her mouse, bringing up a signature on her computer screen. She fed the signature page from the power of attorney into a document scanner on her desktop. In seconds, as she had promised, it verified the signature as genuine.

"Let's go," she said, rising.

Ryan followed her out the door and down the hall. They stopped at the security checkpoint, where another armed guard was posted. He unlocked the glass door to allow Ryan and his escort to pass. The safe deposit boxes were all in one secured area, arranged from floor to ceiling like a locker room. Everywhere he looked was another stainless steel box. The large ones were on the bottom. Smaller ones were on top. Ms. Fuentes led Ryan to Box 193, which was one of the smaller ones. It had two locks on the facade. She inserted her master key into one lock and turned it.

"Your key is for the other lock," she said. "I'll leave you alone now. If you need me, check with the guard. There's a room with a table and chair to your left. You can take the whole box with you and open it there, if you wish. No one else will be allowed in here until you're finished."

"Thank you," said Ryan.

She nodded, then turned and walked away.

Ryan stared straight at the shiny stainless steel box. He could only shake his head. His father had led a simple life. So simple, his secrets were locked in a cold steel box in Central America.

To his surprise, he felt numb, nearly paralyzed. Even just five minutes ago, he had been so eager to open the box that he thought he might conceivably break the key in the process. Now, however, he wasn't so courageous. He felt his mother's trepidation. Norm's warning haunted him. He did have a choice. He could open the box. Or not. It wasn't just a matter of wanting to know the truth. The question was, could he deal with it?

Slowly, he brought the key to the lock and inserted it. With a turn of the wrist, the tumblers clicked. He grabbed the handle and tugged. The box slid forward a few inches, opening like a small drawer. He froze. He felt a sudden impulse to shove it back in place, closing it forever. There was still time to turn back. He could not yet see inside. He hadn't come this far just to pay homage to the past, however, leaving it safely buried.

With a steady pull he removed the box from its sleeve. He laid it on the bench behind him. It was no larger than a shoe box, sealed all the way around. With the truth so close, curiosity took over. He didn't bother taking

151

the box to the back room with the table. His heart quickened. He flipped the latch and opened the top.

He stared inside. He wasn't sure what he had expected, but this didn't look like much. Just some papers. He reached inside and removed the top sheet. It was a bank record for yet another Panamanian bank, the Banco del Istmo. Ryan read it closely. He recognized his father's signature at the bottom. It was an application for a numbered bank account. Attached to the back was a deposit slip. Ryan shuddered.

The deposit was *three* million dollars.

"Holy shit," he uttered. His mind raced. The two million he'd already found in the attic was possibly part of the three million. Or perhaps the three was in addition to the two. The thought made him dizzy.

He reached inside the box for the remaining contents, which were in a large manila envelope. He opened the flap and removed a document. It looked old, tattered around the edges. It was old. Forty-six years old, to be exact.

Ryan scanned it from top to bottom. It was the information his mother had intuitively feared. A copy of a sealed record from the juvenile courts of Colorado. A criminal sentencing report for "Frank Patrick Duffy, a minor." Not only had his father committed a crime, he'd apparently been convicted. In fact, he had pleaded guilty. Ryan felt chills as he read the charge aloud in quiet disbelief.

"One count sexual assault in violation of Colorado Statutes, section..."

His heart was in his throat. Before opening the box, he had hoped for many things. *This* was not on his wish list.

At age sixteen, Frank Duffy had raped a woman.

23

Ryan Duffy, M.D., S.O.R.—son of a rapist.

That was the identity with which he had to come to terms. He felt anger, resentment, betrayal—a flood of emotions. He and his father had always been close. Or had they? Certainly Ryan was proud to be his son. In truth, however, there had always been a safe emotional distance between them. Dad was a great buddy—a regular guy who would share a round of Irish whiskey on his deathbed. On that level, he and Ryan were close. Hell, on that level, Frank Duffy had been "close" with half the male population of Prowers County. But there were things Ryan and his father had never discussed, things they probably should have talked about. Not just the rape, the money, or the extortion. Other things, too.

Like the *real* reason Ryan had chucked a promising career in Denver and moved back to Piedmont Springs.

Secrets, it seemed, were a bit of a Duffy family tradition. Maybe it was genetic. As a child, he had emulated his father, wanting only to be more like him. How much, he wondered, *were* they alike?

Ryan returned to the hotel around 6:00 P.M. He had already checked out of his room, but his flight wouldn't leave Tocumen International Airport for another four hours. He decided to kill some time in the bar in the main lobby.

"Jameson's and water," he told the bartender.

He sat alone on a stool at the end of the mahogany bar. It had been a long day. First the safe deposit box at the Banco Nacional, which had led him to a second Panamanian account at the Banco del Istmo—which had turned out to be a veritable bonanza. The two million dollars in the attic hadn't been withdrawn from that account or even laundered through it, whatever the correct terminology was. The funds were completely separate sums, though inextricably related. Ryan had found an *additional* three million dollars that his father had obtained through extortion. The total was now five.

The bartender poured his drink. "*Salud*," he said, then returned to his televised soccer game at the other end of the bar. He and some other fanatics were screaming at the set. Ryan was oblivious to the game, the shouting. He guzzled his drink and ordered another, a double. With each sip, the background noises were retreating further into oblivion. He was beginning to relax. The bartender served him another drink.

"No, *gracias*," said Ryan, waving it off. "Reached my limit."

"Is from the young lady at the table over there." He pointed discreetly with a shift of the eyes.

Ryan turned in his bar stool. The bar was dimly lit, but not so dark that he couldn't see her. She was surprisingly attractive. Very attractive. Ryan glanced back at the bartender. "Is she a...you know."

"A hooker? No. You want one? No *problemo*. What you like, I can get it."

"No, that's not what I meant," he said with mild embarrassment.

"Berry good-looging," he said with a smirk.

Ryan checked his reflection in the big mirror behind the bar. No woman had ever bought him a drink before. Bars had never been his forte. He was too shy. He felt like the only man in America who had actually never gotten a woman's phone number in a bar, not even in college. *Maybe I should have been hitting the happy hours in Panama.*

He looked her way to thank her, raising his glass. She smiled—not too much, barely perceptible. A subtle smile that invited him over.

His battered ego swelled. It had been a long time since a woman had looked at him that way. Liz hadn't wanted him for months. Amy had sparked him for a few minutes at the Green Parrot, then backed off like a squirrel. Flirting, however, was the last thing he felt like tonight. Still, her interest was flattering. He at least had to be polite, thank her properly. He started across the room toward her table. The closer he got, the better she looked.

She was in her early thirties, he guessed. Her

straight hair was shoulder-length, a rich black sheen beneath the dim bar lights. The eyes were equally dark, not cold but mysterious. She wore a tan fitted suit, probably French or Italian. Her jewelry was gold and sapphire, clearly expensive but still professional. A stunning international businesswoman. Ryan was amazed she was alone.

Don't see many women like this in Piedmont Springs.

"Thank you for the drink," he said.

"You're quite welcome. Don't take this the wrong way, but you looked like you could use it. That's a very stressful look on such a handsome face."

"Kind of a tough day."

"Sorry." She offered the empty chair. "Care to commiserate?"

He considered it, then thought better. Nothing good could come from confiding in some stranger, however beautiful. "I appreciate the invitation, but my wife has this thing about me meeting women in bars. Can you imagine that?"

She smiled thinly. "I understand. That's very decent of you. Your wife's a lucky woman."

"Thanks."

"Does she know how lucky she is?"

It was an oddly personal question, the kind that sounded rehearsed. Ryan guessed it was a tried-and-true *modus operandi,* the gorgeous woman in the bar who made married men feel the need to spend time with a woman who could appreciate them. "Thanks for the drink," he said.

"Any time."

He turned and headed back to his bar stool. The irony nearly choked him—using Liz as an excuse *not* to meet an attractive, interesting woman. Instinct, however, had him questioning everything and everybody. Especially with what he was carrying in his bag.

My bag!

He froze just a few steps from his bar stool. He didn't see his leather bag. He'd forgotten it had even been there until now. The come-hither looks had made him forget all about it and leave it behind when he'd walked over to her table. He was sure he'd left it on the floor.

He checked the other bar stools and the floor all around. It was nowhere to be found. Panic gripped him. The bag contained everything. His passport. His plane tickets. Photocopies of *everything* from the two Panamanian banks.

"Bartender!" he said urgently. "Have you seen my bag? It was right beside the stool."

"No. Sorry."

"Did somebody pick it up, maybe by accident?"

"I don't see nobody."

He wheeled around for a look at the woman. Her table was empty. She was gone.

"Damn it!" He ran from the bar to the lobby, weaving through the crowd, skidding on the marble floors. He nearly knocked over a bellboy laden with baggage. "Have you seen a woman in a tan suit? Black hair?"

The man just shrugged. "Many peoples, *señor*."

Ryan was about to try in Spanish, but his mind was racing too fast to translate. He sprinted across the lobby and pushed through the revolving doors at the main entrance. Outside it was dusk. City lights were flickering, a neon welcome for the night life. Cars and taxis clogged the motor entrance to the hotel. Pedestrians filled the sidewalks on both sides of Avenida Balboa. Ryan ran to the curb and looked up the busy street, then down. For blocks in either direction, throngs of shoppers flowed in and out of stores that would remain open well into the evening. Ryan picked out several tan suits in the crowd, but no one stood out. In Panama, that woman's jet-black hair was hardly a distinguishing feature.

He clenched his fists in anger, mostly at himself. She was clearly a designed distraction. He'd been robbed. Scammed was more like it. Undoubtedly, the woman had gone in one direction. Her partner had run off in another—with Ryan's bag.

He rolled his head back, looking up toward the darkening sky. "You *idiot*."

24

It took longer than Amy had expected to fix her truck. She didn't get on the road until the late morning. It wasn't just a leaky water hose. The radiator had holes in it. Not rust holes. They were small and perfectly round, evenly spaced apart, as if the metal had been punctured by something. Or someone. The mechanic suggested it might have been kids, possibly a prank—rowdy teenagers with nothing better to do on the plains in the summertime.

Amy wasn't so sure.

She drove straight to Boulder from Kit Carson, stopping only once for gas and to make phone calls. Nothing urgent at work. No answer at home. That didn't surprise her. Gram took Taylor to the youth center three afternoons a week, always on Monday. She would play cards with the other seniors. Taylor would jump rope or play kickball, though most of her time was spent running from the boys who felt compelled to pull the hair of the prettiest girl on the playground.

At 5:20 Amy reached the outskirts of Boulder. She would have liked to go directly to the youth center to pick up Taylor, but during the peak of rush hour she couldn't have gotten there before the place closed at six o'clock. She went home to the Clover Leaf Apartments, where she'd wait for Gram and her little girl.

Amy inserted her key in the lock, but the deadbolt was already open. That was surprising. Gram *never* left the door unlocked. She turned the knob. It felt different, the way it turned. The door creaked open by itself, just a few inches. She realized what was wrong.

The lock had been picked. Someone had been there.

Logic told her to run, but maternal instinct wouldn't let her. She was worried about her daughter. "Gram, Taylor!" she called out.

There was no reply. She nudged the door, swinging it open slowly. Her eyes widened with horror as the scene unfolded.

The apartment had been ransacked—*completely* torn apart. The sofa had been butchered, the cushions sliced open. The television was smashed. Shelves had been emptied, books and mementos strewn across the carpet. They had been searching for something.

"Taylor!" she called, but all was quiet. Amy knew they were *supposed* to be at the youth center, but something told her differently. The *smell*. The whole apartment had that smell.

She ran to the bedroom. Broken glass from picture frames crackled beneath her feet. It was an obstacle course of broken furniture, shattered memories. "Taylor, where are you!"

Amy shrieked at the sight. Taylor's bedroom was destroyed, her mattress shredded. The dresser was overturned, her little clothes thrown everywhere. But no sign of her daughter.

"Taylor, Gram!" She ran to the other bedroom. It was the same scene—completely destroyed. The cordless phone lay on the floor beside the shattered lamp. She snatched it up to dial 911, then stopped. They couldn't tell her what she needed to know. She tried the youth center first, speaking as fast as she possibly could.

"This is Amy Parkens. I'm looking for my

daughter, Taylor. And my grandmother, Elaine. It's an emergency. My grandmother should be in the senior recreation room."

"I'll check," said the woman on the line.

"Hurry, please." Amy's eyes scanned the wreckage as she waited, but the wait wasn't long. Gram was on the line.

"What is it, darling?"

"Gram, are you okay?"

"Yeah, I'm up five bucks."

"Someone broke into our apartment. The place is destroyed."

"You're not serious."

"Yes, I'm here right now. Where's Taylor? Is she with you?"

"She's—I left her with the counselor. Outside. Let me see." Gram went to the window and scanned the playground. Kids were tumbling and running in every direction. She searched the swing set, the monkey bars. Finally she saw her. "Yes she's right outside playing on the teeter-totter."

"Oh, thank God."

"What about the money?" asked Gram.

Panic struck. "I didn't even think to look. Let me check." She hurried to the refrigerator, cordless phone in hand, stepping like a hurdler over toppled furniture. She stopped in the kitchen doorway. The cabinets had been emptied. Appliances had been yanked from the walls. Gram's favorite dishes were broken, the pieces scattered everywhere. The doors to the freezer and refrigerator were wide open. Their food covered the floor. The odor was pungent—meat or something was rotting in the heat. That was what she had smelled earlier.

Amy checked the bottom shelf of the freezer, where Gram had stashed their nest egg.

Her hand shook as she spoke into the phone. "It's gone. The box, the money. *Everything* is gone."

Gram could barely speak. "What do we do now?"

"What we should have done in the first place. We call the police."

Part 2

25

Ryan didn't call the police. Sure, he'd been robbed—robbed of the paper trail that could prove his father was an extortionist. He needed help, but not from law enforcement. He needed a lawyer. A good one.

From a phone booth in the hotel lobby, he called his friend Norm back in Denver. With the two-hour time difference, he was still in his office at the end of the business day, feet up on the desk, leaning back in his leather chair.

"Norm, I need your help."

"What'd you do, steal the locks off the canal?"

"This is no joke. I've been ripped off."

He straightened in his chair. "What happened?"

In a matter of minutes, he told Norman everything. The extortion. The rape conviction. The scam at the hotel. Saying it all on the phone was less agonizing than in person. Knowing his father had committed rape made it almost easy; he seemed less deserving of protection.

Silence lingered after Ryan had finished, as if the pensive lawyer was still absorbing it. Finally, he spoke: "It's curious."

"Curious?" he said, chuckling with frustration. "It's a nightmare, Norm."

"I'm sorry. I know it's awful. What I meant was, the extortion is curious. Your father commits a rape, and then twenty-five years later *he* blackmails somebody for five million dollars. It doesn't make sense. You would think someone would have been blackmailing *him*, threatening to expose the sealed juvenile records or something along those lines."

"What does that mean exactly—the records are sealed?"

"It means they're absolutely confidential. By law, nobody can find out what crimes a person committed as a juvenile."

"So it's possible that even my mother wouldn't know?"

"Definitely. Would your mother have married a rapist? That's why it makes sense that somebody could have blackmailed your dad. Not the other way around."

"Except that my father wasn't exactly the kind of rich man you's target for extortion. I don't know what's going on, really. All I know is that some woman is walking around Panama right now with every bit of information I came down here to get. Not to mention my plane tickets and my passport."

"Did you have any original documents in the bag?"

"Just copies. I left the originals in the safe deposit box."

"Good. Here's what we do. First thing, we get you a new passport. I'll take of that tomorrow. Do you have any kind of photo ID?"

"Yeah, driver's license. They didn't get my wallet."

"Excellent. Go back to the bank tomorrow. If you talk to the same person who helped you this morning, your license should be sufficient to get you back in the box. Especially if you tell them your passport was stolen. Make another set of copies of the juvenile record, the account statements, everything that was in your bag. But don't take any documents from the bank—not even the copies. Have the copies made right there on the premises, then bundle it up and ship it overnight to me. I don't want you carrying anything on your person."

"Then what?"

"I'll get the passport to you through the embassy. But you're probably stuck down there for at least another day."

"Good. Maybe I can find that woman."

"I wouldn't go to the police, if that's what you're thinking. The political climate in Panama today is far different from the dictatorship that existed when your father opened these accounts. They may not look too favorably on the heir to extortion money."

"I wasn't going to call the police. I thought I'd just cruise the major hotels. I know her MO. Maybe I'll spot her hitting on another stupid American who thinks with his crotch."

"Something tells me you won't see this woman cruising bars around the city. This is bigger than that."

"What do you mean?"

"The woman was a diversion, obviously. She got your attention while someone else walked off with your bag. Thieves work in teams like that all the time. But we can't assume that's all there is to this."

"You don't think it was a random hit, then."

"Do *you*?"

"I think it was triggered by my visit to one of the banks today, but I'm not sure how."

"It's possible somebody got a tip from a bank employee that you came in and opened your father's safe deposit box. Maybe that somebody wanted to know what you had removed from it."

"You're saying I'm being followed?"

"We're not talking nickels and dimes here, Ryan."

"Yeah, but you're making it sound like some big conspiracy."

"Call it whatever you want. But if these people can afford to pay your father five million dollars, they can sure as hell afford to put a tail on you."

"Or worse," said Ryan, his heart suddenly in his throat.

"A *lot* worse. Take my advice. Don't waste your time looking for some mysterious woman in a tan suit. Let's focus on the three million dollars in that second account. We need to find out where the money was transferred from and who transferred it. That's the root of the extortion."

"All the banker at Banco del Istmo would tell me is that it came from another numbered account in the bank. Bank secrecy laws prohibited him from giving me the name of the other account holder."

"I suppose that's right," said Norm. "The bank owes a fiduciary obligation to both account holders. They can't disclose one to the other without the consent of both customers." He drummed his fingers on his desktop, thinking. "Somehow we have to persuade him to tell us more."

Ryan thought for a moment. "I bet that woman in the tan suit can help us."

"I hardly think she would."

"Maybe she already has."

"I don't follow you."

Ryan was smug. "It's probably better that way."

"Careful, my friend. The last time I heard that tone in your voice you nearly got me kicked out of college. We're not talking dormitory pranks here. You're in a Third World country with no passport, and God only knows who may be watching you. Don't be taking stupid chances."

He remained silent, the wheels turning in his head.

"Ryan, come on. I don't know what you're thinking, but it's like I told you before you left. You're executor of the estate. Eventually you'll have to represent to a court that you've accounted for all the heirs and inventoried all the assets. What the hell are you going to say about the two million in the attic and three million more in Panama? I'm your friend and I want to help you, but I can't help any client break the law."

"I'll call you tomorrow. I promise, I'm not going to break any laws." He hung up the phone. *At least not the laws of the United States.*

Ryan stepped out of the phone booth and crossed the busy lobby, back to the hotel bar. A few more customers had gathered around the television, glued to the soccer game. It was nearing the end of the match, score tied. The bartender looked as if he hadn't moved. The lone waitress was equally riveted. No one had been tending to the tables since Ryan had left. He glanced toward the table at which the woman had been seated.

Her empty glass was still there.

Ryan smiled to himself. *So far, so good.*

26

The Boulder police arrived in minutes. Curious onlookers gathered outside the apartment and in the parking lot, near the squad cars. Two officers searched the outside perimeter of the complex. Two others marked off the crime scene with yellow police tape.

A detective interviewed Amy in the doorway. She would have invited him inside, but there wasn't a chair left unbroken. He had salt-and-pepper hair and deep lines in his face, the kind that came from too much work or too much drinking, perhaps both. He was a serious type, with not much of a bedside manner. The closest he came to an expression of sympathy was a clipped "Hope you got insurance, lady." He took notes on a small spiral pad as he moved from question to question in a plodding, matter-of-fact manner.

Gram arrived in the middle of the interview. The emotion in her eyes touched her granddaughter. They embraced in the hall, just outside the open doorway.

"It's okay, Gram." Those same words from her grandmother had never failed to comfort Amy as a child. They felt a little strange flowing the other way.

"Thank God we weren't home."

Amy took a step back. "Where's Taylor?"

"I didn't want her to see this. She's over in three-seventeen with Mrs. Bentley."

Together, their eyes drifted inside to the living room. For Amy, the second look was worse than the first. Details stood out in what before was just wreckage. The potted plants Gram had babied along forever were upside down on the floor. Taylor's box of toys was a pile of splintered lumber.

Gram spoke quietly, as if at a funeral. "I just can't believe they did this. They destroyed everything we own."

"Excuse me," said the detective. "Who is 'they'?"

Gram blinked, confused. "I'm sorry—what?"

"You said you can't believe *they* did this. Who is 'they'?"

"It was just a figure of speech."

"Do you have reason to believe more than one person did this?"

"I can't really say."

"Do you have any idea who *would* do it?"

"No."

He looked at Amy. "You told me you were divorced, right?"

"That's right."

"What kind of relationship do you have with your ex-husband?"

"We're civil."

He paused, taking mental note of the word choice. "Would *he* know who *they* are?"

"Why are you harping on that? My grandmother told you it was just a figure of speech."

"To be blunt, miss, I don't think you've been telling me everything there is to tell."

Gram stepped forward and said sharply, "Are you calling my granddaughter a liar?"

He shrugged. "Wouldn't be the first time a woman lied to keep the father of her child from going to jail."

"My ex-husband would never do something like this."

The detective nodded, though not in agreement. "Let me explain where I'm coming from. I've been a cop for almost twenty-five years. This is one of those crime scenes that you don't have to be a genius to analyze. Doesn't look like your typical burglary. This has the flavor of personal anger to it. Like someone trying to get even with you for something. Trying to scare you."

Amy bristled at his insight, but she said nothing.

"In fact," he continued, "I wouldn't be a bit surprised to find out that burglary isn't the motive at all."

"I told you exactly what happened. I came home, the place was a wreck. I don't know why they did it."

"There *they* go again," he said, smirking.

Gram glared. "Stop harassing us."

"It's all right," said Amy. "I can see where this might look a little...unusual."

The detective handed her his business card. "I'm gonna take a look around. Why don't you give yourself a little time to calm down, get over the initial shock. Then give me a call. I have a few more questions."

"I'll answer whatever questions you have."

"Good. Because I'd really like to put this burglary thing to bed. Once the crime scene is cleared, I'd like you to take stock of your things. Tell me if anything's missing. Anything at all."

Gram looked confused. "What do you mean, tell you if anything is missing? Of course something is—"

A glance from Amy stopped her cold—subtle but effective.

"You were saying?" said the detective.

Gram hesitated. "I was saying, uh, just look at the place. Something's bound to be missing."

"Yeah," he said flatly. "You let me know. You

173

got my card." He raised an eyebrow, then walked away.

Gram pulled Amy aside, speaking softly as they walked alone down the hallway, away from the crime scene. "You obviously didn't tell him about the stolen money."

"Not yet. I was about to, but I froze up."

"He *is* a jerk."

"It's more than that. For all the reasons I thought we should have told the police at the very beginning, I was afraid it might get us into even more trouble to admit we've been hanging on to it, essentially hiding it from the IRS and everybody else. I felt like I needed some advice first. Some professional advice."

"From who?"

"There's only one lawyer I would trust with something like this. That's Marilyn Gaslow."

"You sure you want someone in the law firm to know about this?"

She stopped and looked Gram in the eye. "It's not just someone. It's Marilyn."

From a comfortable hotel suite, she watched as Panama City came alive at nightfall. Steam from a hot shower still hovered in the room. A bath towel wrapped her shapely young body. Her wet hair was wrapped in a smaller towel, turban style. A long black wig lay atop the dresser. Ryan Duffy's leather bag lay open on the bed. She reclined on the pillow beside it as she spoke into the telephone.

Her voice had more of an edge than the soft, coy bar talk she had used with Ryan.

"I got his bag. For a hundred bucks the bartender ran a little diversion scam with me."

"I told you not to involve anyone else."

"He's not *involved*. I'm sure he's played this same game with half the hookers in Panama City. He just grabbed the bag when Duffy had his mind on other things, so to speak."

"What's in it?"

"Bank records, some other papers. Nothing you didn't already tell me about." She braced the phone with her neck and shoulder, then zipped the bag closed.

"Did you talk to Duffy?"

"Yeah. But he didn't bite. Never went beyond some brief bar banter."

"You losing your edge or something?"

She checked herself in the mirror, then answered in an affected, throaty voice. "What do you think?"

"Guy must be a homo."

She laughed lightly. "So, what happened in Boulder?"

"I think I got the point across."

"What does that mean?"

"That's not your concern."

"Come on. I hate working in the dark."

"Really? And all this time I thought you were leaving the light on for my benefit."

"Cute. But a crack like that's going to cost you, asshole. When you are least prepared to pay. Unless you make amends."

"What do you have in mind?"

"Tell me what happened in Boulder."

"You're being too nosy for your own good."

"Maybe. But if I'm going to do my part of the job right, I need to see the big picture."

"All right, all right. Your instincts were dead on. That happy hour with Amy Parkens you observed at the Green Parrot back in Denver evidently wasn't just a casual meeting between friends. I found two hundred grand in her apartment. Cash."

"Whoa. I guess Saint Amy has broken her vow of poverty."

He asked, "Are you sure you didn't see Duffy give her anything at that restaurant?"

"I'm sure. I tailed him the whole day, just like you told me. Never took my eyes off him."

"Somebody must have given it to her before the old man died. I don't see where the hell else she could have gotten that kind of cash."

"So, what does all this mean? You want me to keep tailing him?"

"Definitely. But from here on out, you need to be extra careful. With me hitting Parkens and you hitting Duffy at the exact same time, I'm sure we took them both by surprise. But they're on guard now. I want you to act under the assumption that the two families are sharing both wealth and information."

"And risk," she said coolly.

"That too."

She rose and stepped to the window. The busy streets below were an endless string of lights. "What do you want me to do next?"

"Just stay there until Duffy leaves, keep an eye on him. And keep that buffoon out of trouble. I want to deal with him when he gets back. So make sure he *gets* back."

"Got it." She was about to hang up, then caught herself. "Oh, one other thing."

"What?"

"I *do* leave the lights on for *your* benefit," she said, then hung up the phone.

27

Ryan returned to the Banco del Istmo on Tuesday morning. It was only half a block away from the Banco Nacional, where he'd found the records for the three million dollar account in the safe deposit box. Yesterday, he'd made the journey in a state of disbelief, almost in a stupor. Only today did he even notice the logo on the doors, the narrow isthmus of Panama, which explained the bank's name—literally, the Bank of the Isthmus.

Ryan waited almost an hour in the lobby. He waited alone. Not a single customer came or went. The building was much older than the Banco Nacional, the decor less impressive. No artwork on the walls, no plants to dress up the hallways or offices. No air conditioning, either, at least not the modern kind. Through the open windows seeped traffic noise and exhaust fumes from the busy city streets. A wobbly old paddle fan rattled overhead, as if trying to shake itself free from the ceiling. Ryan got the distinct impression that very few customers did their business in person at the Banco del Istmo.

Ryan went through two cups of coffee while he waited. He could have spoken to several bank officers during that time period, but he wanted to meet with the same vice president he had spoken to yesterday. At 11:15, Humberto Hernandez finally emerged from his office.

"Dr. Duffy?" he said with an apologetic smile. "Sorry to keep you waiting. I just couldn't get away from the telephone."

Ryan rose and shook his hand. "I understand."

"Please, come back to my office."

Ryan followed him down the hall into his small cubicle. Hernandez wore a short-sleeved dress shirt with no jacket or tie, very practical in the heat. He had thick black hair that he combed straight back. It glistened with some kind of oil, as if he'd just jumped out of the shower. He stood almost a foot shorter than Ryan but was easily fifty pounds heavier. Tiny remnants of an early lunch of rice, beans, and sausage rested in the center of his cluttered desk.

"Please, have a seat," he said as he sank into his Naugahyde desk chair.

"Thank you." Ryan took the only available chair, on the other side of the desk.

"How can I help you today, Doctor?"

"I'd like to follow up on something we were talking about yesterday."

"Yes, go on."

"It has to do with the source of the three million dollars that was transferred into my father's account."

"I am very sorry, sir. I already explained. That is something I cannot help you with."

"If I may, I'd like to explain my situation. I think it might make a difference."

He seemed unmoved. "Go on, please."

"I'm the executor of my father's estate. It's my job to distribute the assets of the estate in accordance with my father's wishes. I cannot in good faith distribute those assets if I don't know where they came from."

"Why not?"

"Because my father was not the kind of man to have three million dollars in a numbered account in the Banco del Istmo."

"Sir, we run a legitimate bank here. I do not appreciate your suggestion to the contrary."

"I didn't mean to insult. I just meant that my father wasn't the kind of man to have three million dollars in *any* bank."

"Perhaps you don't know what kind of man your father was."

"What are you implying?"

"Nothing."

"Did you know my father?"

"No. Did you?"

Ryan narrowed his eyes. "I need to know where this money came from. Period."

Hernandez leaned forward, his hands atop the desk. He was polite but firm. "As I explained yesterday, the funds were transferred from another numbered account in this bank.

Just as your father's identity was protected by the laws of bank secrecy, that other account holder is entitled to the same protection. I cannot breach that confidentiality just because you walk in and demand to know."

Ryan glared, then opened the paper bag he'd brought with him. "I have something for you, Mr. Hernandez."

"Oh? What?"

Ryan reached inside with a handkerchief. Carefully, he removed the bar glass and set it on the desk. "This cocktail glass is from the lounge in the Marriott Hotel."

He was baffled, unsure of what to say. "Did you get a set of bath towels for me as well?"

"This is not a joke. After I left this bank yesterday, someone followed me to my hotel and robbed me. They took my bag and everything in it."

"I'm sorry to hear that."

"I believe it was an employee of this bank who followed me."

"That's ludicrous."

"I can prove it. The woman who followed me was drinking from this glass. Her fingerprints are still on it."

"Have you done a fingerprint analysis?"

"Of course not. Not yet."

"So the analysis could very well prove that the culprit is not one of our employees."

"Or it could prove that she is. It all comes down to the question of what risk do you want to take."

"Risk?"

"Yes, risk. If I give this glass to the authorities

and there is no match, you're in the clear. But if there is a match, the legal problems will be the least of your worries. Competition is brutal among international banks these days. This is the kind of misfortune your competitors could seize upon, I'm sure. It couldn't be good for business if your customers were to hear that a law-abiding American doctor with three million dollars in your bank was stalked by one of your employees and robbed. You're going to have one huge customer relations problem on your hands. I guarantee it."

His right eye twitched. "Sir, I admit that the Banco del Istmo does not have a past that is, as you Americans say, squeaky clean. But in recent years we have worked very hard to change that image. I beseech you, do not slander our good name."

"It's in your hands. If you're a hundred percent confident that it wasn't an employee of this bank who followed me to my hotel, then you can send me on my merry way to the police. But if there is the slightest doubt in your mind, the glass is there for the taking. Consider it a gift."

He glanced at the glass, then at Ryan. "Of course, it would make me feel terribly guilty to accept a gift from a friend without giving something of myself in return."

"You know what I want."

"I told you. It's against the law."

"I've never been a big fan of laws that allow criminals to shield themselves behind banks. This is not negotiable."

Hernandez seemed in agony, like a man with

a gun to his head. Suddenly he swiveled in his chair, faced his computer and typed in the account number. "I have here the entire transaction history for your father's account. It shows every deposit, every withdrawal. Including internal transfers from other account holders at the bank."

Ryan couldn't see the screen from his chair. As he rose to take a look, Hernandez said, "Stay right where you are."

Ryan retreated to his chair, confused.

Hernandez said, "As I explained, I cannot give you this information. That would be a crime. That is my final word on the matter." He rose, then continued, "Now, I'm going to take this glass, go to the snack room, and get myself a cool drink of water. I will be back in exactly five minutes. You can remain here while I'm gone, if you wish. Whatever you do, do *not* look at that computer screen. I repeat: Do not look at that screen."

The banker had cleared his conscience. He took the glass and quietly left the room. The door closed behind him.

Ryan remained in his chair, staring at the back of the computer monitor. It chilled him to think the answer was right around the desk, flashing on the screen. Yet to learn who had paid the blackmail, he would have to break the law of bank secrecy. It wasn't an American law. It wasn't even a law he much respected, having seen it abused by drug lords and tax evaders. Breaking *any* law, however, was a dangerous road. The first step had a way of leading to the second.

He paused to weigh his alternatives. He could walk away, perhaps never to know who his father had blackmailed. Or he could step around and have a look.

He waited only another moment. Then he took that first step.

28

Amy drove to Denver on faith. She didn't actually have an appointment with Marilyn Gaslow, but she was confident she would see her. Few people had a full appreciation of the personal history between Amy and the firm's most influential partner.

The main offices for Bailey, Gaslow & Heinz were on five contiguous floors some forty stories above downtown Denver. Theoretically, the Denver headquarters and six branch offices operated as one fully integrated law firm. Amy made sure that was the case with state-of-the-art computer links between cities. Still, there was no technological or other way to transport completely the high-charged atmosphere of the main office to its satellites. Each visit to Denver reminded Amy that it wasn't the satellites in Boulder or Colorado Springs that made this Rocky Mountain law firm comparable to the finest firms in New York or Los Angeles.

Amy approached the secretarial station outside Marilyn's office with some trepidation. Her secretary was a notorious snob who protected Marilyn like royalty.

"Good morning," said Amy. "Is Marilyn here?"

The secretary raised an eyebrow, as if Amy's use of the first name was utter insubordination. "She's here, yes. But she's not available."

"Is she with someone?"

"No. She's simply unavailable."

"When will she be available?"

"That depends."

"On what?"

She almost glared at Amy, invoking her most snotty tone. "Whether a client calls. Whether her partners need her. Whether Jupiter aligns with Mars."

"Please tell her Amy Parkens is here, that it's personal, and that it's very important."

She didn't budge.

Amy met her stare. "If she gets angry, you can personally type my letter of resignation."

Smugly, she buzzed Marilyn on the intercom and delivered the message exactly the way Amy had worded it. A look of surprise washed over her face. She hung up and muttered, "Ms. Gaslow will see you now."

Amy smirked. *Never underestimate the power of an astronomer to align the planets.*

Marilyn Gaslow had an impressive corner office on the forty-second floor with breathtaking views of both the mountains and the plains. The furnishings were French antiques. Museum-quality artwork decorated one wall. Another was covered with plaques and awards she had accumulated over the years, marking a lifetime of achievement that included every-thing from first woman president of the American Bar Association to a four-year stint as chairwoman of the Commodity Futures Trading Commission. Scattered among the wall of glory were photographs of Marilyn with every president since Gerald Ford, each signed and inscribed with a warm personal message. Behind her desk was a more personal touch—a framed but faded old snapshot of two smiling teenage girls. It was Marilyn and Amy's mother.

"So good to see you, Amy." She rose and gave her a motherly hug.

In some ways, Marilyn was like a mother, at least when they were together. Marilyn had been her mother's closest friend at one time and, in her own way, had taken an interest in Amy's well-being after the sui-cide. Whenever Amy wasn't right before her eyes, however, Marilyn was simply too busy to notice that she lived from paycheck to paycheck in a tiny apartment with her daughter and grandmother. Marilyn was a career woman to the exclusion of *any* personal life. Her only marriage had ended in divorce twenty years ago, and she had no children of her own.

Amy gave her the latest on Taylor as they settled into their chairs. Amy sat on the couch. Marilyn took the Louis XVI arm-chair. Marilyn was pleasant but clearly pressed for time.

"So what's this personal and important matter you've come here to talk about?"

185

"Our apartment was broken into yesterday. The place was completely wrecked."

"My God, that's terrible. Do you need a place to stay?"

"We're okay. Fortunately we had rental insurance. We'll just have to impose on the neighbors until the place gets cleaned up."

Marilyn reached for the telephone. "I know the chief of police in Boulder. Let me give him a call, make sure there are more patrol cars in the area."

"Marilyn, that's not necessary. I just wanted your advice."

"On what?"

"The burglars took some money."

"How much?"

"Two hundred thousand dollars. Cash. It was in the freezer."

She did a double take. "What were you doing with that kind of money in the freezer?"

"It's a long story." Over the next few minutes, Amy summed it up. The Crock-Pot box from the anonymous source. The meeting with Ryan Duffy. The meeting with Sarah and the breakdown in Kit Carson. Finally, the demolished apartment and stolen money. It was difficult at first, but then the words began to flow. Gram was great, but it was nice to have someone like Marilyn on your side.

Marilyn leaned back in the armchair, seemingly overwhelmed. "So right now, the police know nothing about the money?"

"Nothing," said Amy. "I'm not sure what to tell them. That's why I'm here. I wanted your advice."

"For starters, don't put large sums of cash in the freezer. But as they say, that bit of advice is a day late and two hundred thousand dollars short."

"That was Gram's idea."

"Doesn't matter. Let's just talk this out. You say you got the money in a Crock-Pot box. You don't know who sent it. You think it was a guy named Frank Duffy, whom you have never met. You have no idea why he'd give you the time of day, let alone two hundred thousand dollars. He was a middle-class family man, no outward signs of wealth. He sent it to you right before he died."

"That's right."

"Your first problem is obvious. It doesn't pass the time-honored *'What in the hell have you been smoking?'* test."

"You don't believe me?"

"*I* believe you. Barely. And that's only because I know you."

"Why would I make something like this up?"

"Who knows? Sympathy? Desperate single mother goes on the evening news, says her house was ransacked and the burglars made off with two hundred thousand dollars in cash. Before you know it, people are mailing in checks to the television studio to replace the stolen money. I'm not saying it could work. But a skeptic might say that's your angle."

"You know that's not me."

"Of course. But we have to worry about the way others might perceive this."

"I'm not worried about perceptions."

"Well, I surely am. And you should be, too. You are a valued employee of this law firm. Everything you do is a reflection on the institution. How old did you say Mr. Duffy was?"

"Sixty-two."

"Great. A dying, married old man gives two hundred thousand dollars in cash to a stunning twenty-eight-year-old woman. And she has no explanation for it. To put it bluntly, do you really want people calling you a whore, Amy?"

"Marilyn!"

"I'm not making accusations. Just playing out the possible ramifications. Perceptions aside, you've got even bigger problems. The basic question is, who is this Frank Duffy character? For all you know, he or his son or someone else in that family was a scumbag drug dealer. Why would you want to report missing money that could link you to somebody like that?"

"Because I have nothing to hide."

"Like I said, no one's going to believe you got that much money for doing absolutely nothing. You could have the Boulder police and maybe even the FBI watching you for the rest of your life. And remember, you don't have to be *convicted* of a crime to be denied admission to the Colorado Bar. If you raise enough questions about your character, you could end up spending three years in law school and never become a lawyer."

"You really think that could happen?"

"Possibly. One thing's for sure. You'll have

big problems right here in this office. I went to bat for you to get the firm to underwrite your tuition so you could start law school this fall. How are you going to explain to the partnership that while you were claiming poor-mouth, you actually had a spare two hundred thousand dollars laying around the apartment?"

"It was recent."

"Sure. And if it hadn't been stolen, would you have ever bothered to tell the firm?"

Amy paused. She could have said law school would have lost out to astronomy if the money hadn't been stolen—but now didn't seem like the time. "I see your point."

Marilyn checked her watch. "I'm sorry to cut this short. I have to run to a luncheon. I'll think more about this later, but my gut reaction is pretty solid."

"What do you suggest I do?"

"Above all, keep perspective. At this stage in your life, two hundred thousand dollars sounds like all the money in the world. Ten years from now, you'll be a partner in this law firm and it won't even be a down payment on a house. And no matter what you do now, you'll never recover the cash. It might as well have burned. You have a wonderful future ahead of you. There's just no point in making yourself a lightning rod for trouble."

Marilyn leaned forward and touched Amy's hand, looking her in the eye. "Listen to me, Amy. It was found money. Now it's lost. Forget about it. And you and I will forget we ever had this conversation."

Amy had no time to respond. Marilyn was on her feet, phone in hand, speaking to her secretary. Amy rose and started for the door.

Marilyn covered the mouthpiece. "Give my love to Taylor," she blurted across the room, then returned to her phone conversation. Amy forced a smile and let herself out. That was Marilyn. Already on to the next client, the next set of multimillion-dollar problems.

While Amy battled the little problems of her own.

Liz Duffy went to lunch at Spencer's, a quick place for salads on the 16th Street Mall. She sat alone at a table for two. A newcomer to Denver, she was still trying to meet new friends and build a new life without Ryan. She was picking at a grilled chicken Caesar and starting chapter two of a dog-eared paperback when her cell phone rang.

It startled her at first. She had never owned a cell phone before. Her lawyer had gotten it for her. Jackson had said it was for emergencies, just in case he needed to reach her. So far, he'd used it only to call and say hello—at least twice a day. Liz was flattered by all the personal attention. Jackson had a lot going for him. Brains. Looks. Money. Lots of money.

"Hi," he said. "What are you doing?"

"Eating lunch. Are you calling just to bug me again?" she asked with a smile.

He turned the corner in his Lexus, merging into downtown traffic. "Actually, this is a legitimate business call. What do you know about your brother-in-law, Brent Langford?"

"Total loser. Hasn't held a decent job as long as I've known him. Hasn't had any job for at least six months. Why?"

"My private investigator has some interesting intelligence on him. Seems Brent was over in Pueblo shopping for a brand-new Corvette, over fifty thousand dollars' worth of auto-mobile. Later the same day he was at the Piedmont Springs Bar & Grill, bragging about how he's coming into some serious money."

"That's interesting. Amazing, actually."

"Maybe Frank Duffy wasn't delirious after all when he promised you all that money."

Liz winced, uncomfortable with her lawyer's characterization. As far as the so-called promise went, she had told Jackson the same story she had told Ryan after the funeral, out on the front porch. "You know, I'm still not sure you'd call it an actual promise. Like I told you, Frank was trying to keep me and Ryan together. He just told me to hang in there, the money would come soon, or something like that."

"Liz," he said in a soft but stern voice. "Remember how important I told you it was that Frank made an explicit oral promise of money to you while he was alive?"

"Yes."

"Remember what I said happens to waffles?"

She smiled. "They get toasted."

"That's my girl. So knock off the waffle voice, okay?"

"Okay."

"Good. Now you work on that memory of yours. If you do your part, I'll do mine."

"What's your plan?"

He stopped at the traffic light, checking himself in the rearview mirror. "One step at a time. This latest development could seriously raise the stakes in our property settlement negotiations. I was thinking I'd just take ol' Brent's deposition. Put him under oath and see if we can get some idea just how much money is out there."

Out of respect for Frank, Liz thought before dragging the family into the divorce. But Brent was a Langford, not a Duffy. Hell, if she had asked Frank, Brent wasn't even a human being, let alone family. "Liz, what do you say?"

"Go for it, counselor. You'll eat that moron alive."

29

At noon Ryan called Norm from the Panama City Marriott. He had taken a room through tomorrow, until his new passport was ready. The passport, however, wasn't his first order of business.

"I got it," said Ryan, seated on the bed. "I got the scoop on the three million that was transferred to my father's account at Banco del Istmo."

"How'd you pull that off?"

"All it took was a little persuasion."

"Something tells me I'd rather not hear the details."

"And I don't think I want to tell you. At least not on the phone."

"What did you find out?" asked Norm.

"Believe it or not, the money was transferred in three hundred installments of nine thousand nine hundred ninety-nine dollars, and then one last installment of three hundred dollars for an even total of three million. It was spread out over a fifteen-year period. The last one was made a little over a year ago."

"Sounds like they were trying to avoid some financial reporting requirements."

"How do you mean?" asked Ryan.

"Banks are required to file a CTR—a currency transaction report—for any deposit of ten thousand dollars or more. That raises a red flag for the regulatory authorities. It's a way of keeping track of the big money flow between banks."

"But these transfers weren't between two different banks. They were internal transactions, from one account holder at Banco del Istmo to another. Why would that attract anyone's attention?"

"I'm sure the intra-bank transfer was the last layer of protection in a series of deposits and wire transfers that crossed several national borders. No doubt at least one of the banks along the way did business in the United States, which meant it would have been required to file a CTR for deposits of ten thousand or more. The final internal transfers at Banco del Istmo were each less than ten thousand dollars because they mirrored the amount of the inter-bank transfers."

"That makes sense, I guess. It also explains why the name on the account at Banco del Istmo doesn't mean a thing to me."

"Who is it?" asked Norm.

"It's a foreign corporation registered in the Cayman Islands. Jablon Enterprises, Ltd. I don't have a clue who that could be."

"Quite possibly, you never will. No doubt it's just a shell corporation."

"But even if it's a shell, aren't they required to have real human beings as officers and directors? Somewhere that has to be a matter of public record, doesn't it?"

"Yeah, but the only place those records would be is in the Cayman Islands."

"Then that's where I need to go."

"You'll need a passport first. You should be able to pick it up at the embassy tomorrow morning."

Ryan grimaced. "I hate to lose a day just waiting around."

"Frankly, I hate to see you go. You've already been robbed, Ryan. And that was just for checking on your father's account. If you start snooping around the Cayman Islands for the names behind this shell corporation, they may not be so polite the next time around."

"I can be discreet."

"Sure you can."

"Can you do me a favor?"

"What, notify your next of kin?"

"Don't be a wiseass. I need your help sorting this out. I've been thinking about this rape conviction. The fact that those documents were in the safe deposit box with the other bank records makes it clear that the extortion is somehow connected to the rape, agreed?"

"I don't think it was purely coincidence that those records were in the same box, if that's what you're saying."

"Exactly. Now, if you think about it, there are a limited number of people on this planet who can afford to pay five million dollars in extortion money."

"It's a big world out there, Ryan."

"Not that big. Especially when you consider that whoever that person is, somewhere along the line he had to come into contact with my father. More than likely it dates back to the rape."

"That's logical."

"Agreed. So the only sensible thing we can do is reconstruct that period of my father's life—when Frank Duffy was sixteen. Let's go back in time and look at the people my father knew back then. And let's find out where they ended up. Specifically, let's see if any of them turned out to be the kind of person who could afford to pay five million dollars in blackmail."

"How do you suggest we go back forty-five years?"

"School is probably the best way. I called the school superintendent's office this morning.

Unfortunately, they don't have any class lists going back that far. The only way to figure out who was in my dad's class is to look at the actual yearbooks."

"Did your dad have one?"

"I went through all his possessions after he died. I didn't see one. I have a feeling that was a time in his life he preferred to erase. But they keep them at the high school, in the records department."

Norm paused. "So you want me to drive all the friggin' way down to Piedmont Springs to look at forty-five-year-old yearbooks?"

"It's easier than that. My mom's family goes back five generations in Prowers County. But my dad didn't move there until after the rape—probably in shame, which explains why he was never really happy there. I can remember when I was a kid. The best reason he could give me for staying in Piedmont Springs was because my mom's side of the family had roots there. I guess he felt like he was living in exile."

"So where did he go to high school? Until he was sixteen, I mean?"

"Dad grew up in Boulder. He would have been a student at Boulder High School when the rape took place."

"So you want me to go to Boulder?"

"It's less than an hour's drive for you, Norm."

"All right, I can do it this week."

"I'd like you to go today. Just copy the books and get your investigator to check these people out. There can't be that many of my dad's classmates who ended up being millionaires."

Norm checked the appointment calendar on his desk and made a face. "Shit. Okay. I'll juggle things around and do my best to get over there this afternoon. If it's that important to you."

"Thanks," said Ryan. "It's really that important."

Brent Langford was stretched out on the couch in the living room, wearing only gym shorts. Even half-naked he was overheated, his body glistening with sweat. The hottest point of the afternoon had passed hours ago, yet it only seemed to be getting hotter inside the house. The old window-unit air conditioner had been busted since last summer, still no money to fix it. A fan turned lazily in the open window, sucking in hot air from the plains. It had been the summer's stickiest day so far. So hot, Brent hadn't ventured outside all day. He had spent most of the day right on the couch, flipping through the brochures for the new Corvette.

A convertible, he thought, smiling to himself. *Gonna get me a convertible. And that blonde in the bikini to boot.*

A knock at the front door disturbed his fantasy. Brent didn't move. He just turned the page, undecided between the yellow or the red one.

A second knock, louder this time.

He grabbed the remote control and lowered

the volume on the television. "Sarah!" he shouted. "Answer the door already!"

Half a minute later, Sarah crossed the room. The heat had her almost immobilized. Her obstetrician had told her to stay home from work today and elevate her ankles. It had struck Sarah as funny in a twisted way. She hadn't *had* any ankles since about the seventh month.

She breathed extra-heavy as she passed Brent on the couch, exaggerating just a little to make him feel guilty. He didn't notice.

The front door was already open. She spoke through the screen door to the stranger on the porch. "Can I help you?"

He nodded respectfully. "Afternoon, ma'am. Is this here your permanent residence?"

"Yes."

He glanced at her pregnant belly. "And I presume you're over fifteen years of age."

She scoffed. "Yeah."

He pulled an envelope from his shirt pocket. "I have something here for you from the Prowers County Sheriff."

Sarah opened the screen door and took it.

"What—" she started to ask. But the man ran away the second she touched it, as if there were a bomb inside. She watched as he jumped into his car and sped down the road.

Brent called from the living room. "Who is it, Sarah?"

She was reading from a document as she walked from the foyer to the living room. "I don't know who that was. But he just left us a subpoena."

"A subpoena?"

"Yeah. It's from Ryan's divorce case. Looks like it's from Liz's lawyer. Issued to Brent Langford. You are hereby commanded to appear for deposition—"

"Deposition!" He jumped up and snatched the subpoena from her hand. He stared at it for a moment, then threw it on the couch. "Damn, I don't want to give no deposition. What did you take that thing for?"

"I didn't know what it was."

"Well, dumbshit, did you even think to ask?"

"He said it was from the sheriff."

"If he had said it was from the president, would you believe him? Don't answer that. You probably fucking would."

Sarah took a step back, wary of his tone. "Just calm down, okay? It's no big deal. I'll talk to Ryan and find out what this is all about."

"It's about money, you idiot. It's all about Liz trying to get her hands on my money. Why didn't you just slam the door in that guy's face? Just slammed it!" He went to the door and slammed it so hard the windows rattled. "That's all you fucking had to do!"

"How was I to know?" she said timidly.

"Common sense, that's how. If you had any."

Her eyes welled with tears. It was a cumulative emotion. Anger. Frustration. Fear at the thought of Brent as the father of her child.

"Oh, stop your sniveling, woman."

"Maybe—maybe I can get Ryan to cancel the deposition."

"Just stay the hell out of it. You screwed things up enough already." He went back to the couch, moving the car brochures aside with care. "I'll handle this myself. This is one deposition they ain't never gonna forget."

30

It was getting late on Colorado's Front Range. Clouds drifted across the night sky in long, tattered strands, as if shredded by the mountaintops on their journey toward Boulder.

Amy watched in silence from the balcony off her bedroom. She was alone for the night. Gram and Taylor were staying with a neighbor for a few days, until they could replace the sliced-up mattresses and other busted furnishings. Amy had been cleaning up their ravaged apartment all afternoon, working into the evening. Little was salvageable. The insurance adjuster had come and gone hours ago. The check would come in a few days, he'd promised, though it wouldn't help much. Most of the furniture was much more than ten years old and had almost zero depreciated value. For what it was worth, the adjuster seemed to agree with the detective's assessment. This was no simple burglary. Someone had wanted to send her a message.

The question was, what was the message?

All her life, Amy had been exceptional at solving problems of any kind, from calculus to crosswords. Ever since she'd opened the box of money, however, she'd felt completely clueless. She hated that helpless feeling, that inability to figure things out. She'd felt that way only once before in her life. Many years ago.

Right after her mother died.

"Amy, you okay here tonight?" It was Gram.

Amy was leaning on the balcony rail. She glanced over her shoulder, back into the bedroom through the sliding glass door. "Yeah, I'll be okay. Taylor asleep?"

Gram joined her on the balcony. "Like a log. I just wanted to come up and see how you were doing, check on things."

"Not much to check on, is there?"

"Aww, forget it. I've been meaning to get rid of a lot of all this old junk anyway. We'll be fine."

Amy smiled with her eyes. "What is that you used to tell me? Our guardian angel owes us one?"

Gram smiled back. "It's been a long time since I said that. That's quite a memory you have there."

"I don't forget much. Just certain things."

Gram looked at her with concern, as if she sensed what her granddaughter had been thinking. "Amy, darling. When something bad happens, it's natural to think back on the past, to other sadness."

She nodded, looking up to the sky. "I can see Vega."

"Where?"

"Right overhead. It's the brightest star in the constellation of Lyra. See it?" she said, pointing. "It forms a harp, or lyre, with those four other faint stars that are positioned like a parallelogram."

"Yeah," Gram said, smiling. "I do see it."

"That's the constellation I was looking at the night Mom died."

Gram's smile faded. She lowered her eyes.

Amy said, "I have a very spotty memory of that night. Certain things are clear. Other things are fuzzy. Some things I can't remember at all. I remember the noise, the sound of the gunshot. I remember waiting in my room, pitch dark. Going up in the attic, then down the hall and into Mom's room." She drew a deep breath. "And I remember the hand hanging over the side of the bed."

They stood in silence at the rail. Finally Gram spoke. "We found you in your room. I found you. You were curled into a tight little ball, shivering. In shock, I think. You were on that padded ledge of the bay window. Right by your telescope."

"I don't remember any of that."

"That's normal. It's probably best."

"No," she said sharply. "It drives me nuts. I can't figure it out. I'll *never* figure it out if I can't remember what happened."

"What happened was tragic. You don't need to go back there."

"Do you really think she killed herself?"

Gram made a face, as if the question surprised her. "Yes. No one's ever questioned that."

"I've *always* questioned it."

"You were eight, Amy. Suicide wasn't something you could accept."

"No, it's more than that. Think about it. Why would Mom shoot herself in the head while I was in the house?"

"That's why she tied that rope to your door, I suppose. I think the police were right about that. She didn't want you to come out and find the body."

"That doesn't hold up, Gram. Mom had caught me playing in the attic just a few months before that. She was completely aware that I knew how to get out of my room with the door shut. She knew about the ceiling panel in my closet."

"Maybe she forgot. She was obviously in a very tortured state."

"But she wasn't *suicidal*."

"That's a pretty tough judgment for an eight-year-old girl to make."

"Not really. I remember the conversation Mom and I had before she died. I asked her to read me a story. She said she was too tired. But she promised to read me one the next night. She promised it would be the best story I ever heard."

"Who knows what was going through her mind?"

"That just doesn't sound like something a woman would say to her daughter an hour before she kills herself. She never even said goodbye, Gram."

"Amy, you don't know what happened after she tucked you into bed."

"*Exactly*. I don't know, because there are things I can't remember about that night. I try to remember. You know what happens? I get numbers in my head. M 57. You know what that is? It's an astronomical designation for the Ring Nebula, the dying star I was looking at the night Mom died. Here I am trying to sort out the death of my mother, and all my overeducated brain can bring into focus is M 57, the fifty-seventh object in Charles Messier's eighteenth-century catalog of fuzzy objects in the sky. It makes me crazy, Gram. Look at the sky right now. You can pick out the constellation of Lyra where the Ring Nebula lives, but you can't see the Ring Nebula with the naked eye. We're looking right at M 57, but we can't see it.

"That's the way I feel about the explanation for Mom's death," said Amy, her voice fading. "I'm looking right at it. But I just can't see it."

Gram looked into her troubled eyes, then gave her a gentle hug. "It's not your fault that you don't remember. Sometimes we don't figure everything out. Sometimes we just never know."

Amy wiped a tear from the corner of her eye. She knew Gram was trying to make her feel better, but it wasn't working. That was Amy's greatest fear in the world. The fear of never knowing.

Together, they turned away from the night sky and headed back inside.

31

From his hotel room late Tuesday night, Ryan called his voice mail at the clinic for messages. He had canceled his appointments for the week and routed his patients to the clinic in Lamar. Still, he wanted to make sure there were no emergencies. The first message was definitely nothing to worry about. Ninety-year-old Marjorie Spader wanted to know if she could use her own prescription cough medicine to help her cat dislodge a fur ball. Ryan shook his head. That was the crazy thing about Piedmont Springs. Folks would let a deadly cancer grow inside them for years, completely untreated. But let their cat start hacking on a fur ball and they were immediately on the phone to the doctor.

The fifth message got his attention. It was from Liz.

"Ryan, just calling as a courtesy to let you know that my attorney is planning to take Brent's deposition. The subpoena was served today, but I didn't want to start taking depositions of family members without giving you a call first. Take care."

He cringed. *Courtesy my ass.* She had called to gloat. He hung up and called Norm at home. He was already in bed, half asleep, half watching the late news. He grabbed the cordless phone on the nightstand. "Hello," he grumbled.

"Sorry to bug you at home," said Ryan.

He was groggy, forcing himself awake. "Yes, I did go to Boulder and I did copy the stupid yearbooks. It'll take a couple of days for my investigator to run background checks on all your dad's classmates."

"Good. But that's not why I'm calling. I need to talk to you."

"Just a sec," Norm said softly. He rolled out of bed and walked into the big walk-in closet, so as not to disturb his sleeping wife. "What's up?"

"Liz's lawyer is going to depose Brent, my brother-in-law."

"Tonight?" He was being facetious.

"No, wiseguy. But the subpoena has already been served. I have to move fast if I'm going to stop it."

"What does he know?"

"Not everything, but enough."

"Walk me through it. Does anybody besides you and your mom know about the safe deposit box, the money?"

"As far as I know, my mom and I are the only ones who know about the safe deposit box at the Banco Nacional. The only one who knows about the three million at the Banco del Istmo is me. But Sarah knows about the two million in the attic. So does Brent."

"What does Liz know?"

"Hard to say. She had a talk with my dad a few weeks before he died. I don't remember exactly how she put it, but she claims he made some remark that money would come her way soon."

Norm took a seat on the clothes hamper behind the closet door. "So that's their angle."

"What?"

"They're trying to say the money was a gift from your dad while he was alive, rather than an inheritance that passes through the estate after death."

"What's the difference? From Liz's standpoint, I mean."

"Huge. If it's an inheritance, it's what the law calls a special equity. She can't get her hands on it in the divorce. But if it was a gift made before your father died, that might be a different situation. Especially if she can show that your dad expressly promised it to *her*."

"Meaning she *can* get it in the divorce?"

"It's a tough argument. But it's their only argument."

Ryan rose from the hotel bed and began to pace. "A few weeks ago, I wouldn't have believed Liz would reach like this. But I'll believe anything after the wringer her lawyer ran me through in his office."

"Who's her lawyer?"

"Phil Jackson in Denver."

"Oh, man. That guy's a shark."

"You know him?"

"Hell yes. He has his own publicist, for crying out loud. His mug is on the front page of the legal fish wrappers every other day. He's slick. I think he's downright dishonest. In fact, it wouldn't at all surprise me to hear that one of his overly zealous investigators is behind the disappearance of your bag."

"How could that be?"

"Let's say Liz knows there's money in Panama. Maybe your dad told her that much. She tells Jackson. He hires an investigator to watch you, letting you lead him straight to the money. Bingo. He's hit the mother lode."

Ryan shook his head. "I don't know. Liz may have gone off the deep end, but I don't think she would ever authorize someone to follow me to Panama and swipe my bag."

"Jackson could have talked her into it. Or he could have done it without her authorization. He could be just biding his time, waiting for the right moment to show Liz a copy of that three-million-dollar bank book you lost."

"So what should I do?"

"You need to talk to your divorce lawyer."

"I fired my divorce lawyer."

"Then you need to get a new one."

Ryan was silent.

Norm read his mind. "Uh-uh, no way, no how. I'm a white-collar criminal defense lawyer. I quit that divorce shit years ago. Too nasty for my taste. If I want to get bloody, I take on an occasional murder case. That's my limit."

"Who else can I trust with this? Don't make me go into some stranger's office and tell them my dad was a blackmailer with two million dollars in his attic and another three in Panama."

"You're asking me to go up against one of the toughest divorce lawyers in Denver. I'm rusty, at best."

Ryan's voice dropped, more serious. "Norm, I'm calling in the favor."

The tone made it clear this was not about wedding days and nipple rings. Three years ago, Ryan had forced him to get a biopsy on a strange-looking mole on his back. But for that, Norm would have died of skin cancer two years ago. Ryan never thought he'd play that card. Then again, he never would have foreseen *this*.

"All right," Norm said with a sigh. "Let me ease into it. I'll handle the deposition, see how it goes."

"Thanks, buddy. You're a lifesaver."

"Guess that makes us even."

"Touché." Ryan checked the alarm clock beside his bed, ready to set it. "So, what time will my passport be ready tomorrow?"

"Stop by the embassy some time around mid-morning. It should be there by then. Call me if you hit any snags."

"You know I will."

"Yeah." Norm chuckled. "You're becoming my best client."

"No offense, but aren't most of your clients in jail?"

They laughed together, then stopped in awkward silence. It suddenly didn't seem funny anymore. Ryan said good night. But the thought stayed with him after the call had ended.

His best client. *What a dubious distinction.*

Phil Jackson rose at 5:00 A.M., the start of his

usual eleven-hour workday. People abhorred his style. Colleagues begrudged his celebrity-like status in the Denver legal community. No one denied he worked hard for his success. He had to. A flashy reputation lured clients through the door. Results paid the rent.

Jackson was showered, dressed, and out the door in forty-five minutes. It was a lonely routine for him, though he rather enjoyed the solitude of an entire neighborhood asleep. The sun wouldn't rise for a few more minutes. No traffic disturbed the quiet street. Even the morning paper had yet to arrive.

He stepped carefully across the lawn. The brick pavers on the sidewalk were slick with the morning dew, and the path was darker than usual. The decorative lamp outside the garage had apparently burned out.

The transmitter on his key chain activated the garage door opener, raising the middle door of his three-car garage. He felt like the 800 series Mercedes today. The black car, however, was barely visible this morning. The garage was unusually dark. The light inside was burned out, too.

What is this, an epidemic?

He entered the garage and started toward the driver's side. The alarm chirped as it disengaged by keyless remote. The car lights blinked. He reached for the door. Something rattled behind him. He turned to look. His briefcase went flying with the first blow to the head. He swung wildly in self-defense. Someone had him by the neck. His head snapped forward. His face slammed into the windshield. He was stunned, blinded by the hot rush of blood. Another quick jerk of his head put a crack in the windshield.

His legs buckled, but his attacker held him up. He was pinned against the car, barely able to breathe beneath the man's weight. The stranger's hot breath coursed down the back of his neck. His attacker was right on him, as if poised to say something. A ringing filled his ears, but he could hear the rough words, a voice like gravel, undoubtedly disguised.

"It's family business. Don't make it yours."

The lawyer's head slammed against the windshield one last time. Red rivulets of blood ran down to the wipers. Jackson fell to the cement floor. He could see nothing. He heard only footsteps, faintly, until he heard nothing at all.

The numbness took over as he drifted away.

32

Ryan slept in his hotel room until noon. He'd been awake all night, having last checked the alarm clock at 6:55 A.M. Rest was something that no longer came easy, not since his father's death. Each time his busy mind drifted toward sleep, the images came. He would think of his father. Dead, not alive. He could see him in the ground, sleeping peacefully beneath so many tons of earth. Beside him in the coffin was a noticeable void, a hole much deeper than the one in which they'd buried him. It was a vast underground cavern, like the ones he'd shown Ryan long ago in New Mexico, big enough for the secrets he should have taken to the grave.

The phone rang. He was standing at the bathroom sink, dressed only from the waist down, splashing away the soapy remains of his morning shave—though it was actually the afternoon. He dried his face with a towel as he crossed the room and answered on the half-ring.

"Hello."

"They're coming for you. Get out of the hotel."

It was a woman's voice. It sounded vaguely familiar—like the woman who'd scammed him in the hotel bar. "Who is this?"

"You've got thirty seconds, no more. Get out of the hotel. *Now*."

The line clicked.

Ryan stood frozen. It *was* the same voice, he was sure of it. *Which means this is probably another scam.*

He pulled on a shirt and went to the door. He opened it quickly but carefully, just a crack, not even as far as the chain lock would allow. The door frame blocked his view to the left. To the right, however, he could see all the way down the long corridor, clear to the elevators. About thirty other rooms separated his from the exit. The halls were quiet and empty, save for an unattended maid's cart. A few doors were open for cleaning. The clang of the elevator bell signaled an arrival. Ryan watched from afar as the doors slid open.

Five men stepped out. Their pace was brisk, purposeful. All were dressed in the beige and brown uniforms of the Panamanian military police.

Ryan closed the door, nearly fell against it. *Son of a bitch.*

His mind raced with possibilities. It had to be a setup orchestrated by the very same woman who had teamed up to steal his bag. She'd called them herself. But why would she have called to warn him? Maybe the banker at Banco del Istmo had called them. This was his payback for the way Ryan had bullied him into violating Panamanian bank secrecy. Ryan just didn't know. And he didn't intend to hang around and find out.

He double-checked the lock on the door and raced across the room. His garment bag was already packed and on the bed, but baggage would slow him, and it wasn't worth saving. He grabbed only his smaller bag and ran to the window. He was on the second floor, in one of the cheaper rooms that faced the alley. For once he was glad to have the room without a view. He paused to think twice. He could stay put and try to explain. But with no passport and three million dollars in a numbered bank account, he wasn't looking forward to a police interrogation. The dictatorship was gone, but Panama was still the third world.

Boot steps rumbled in the hall, like a charging cavalry. No time to think. He opened the window and climbed out on the ledge.

It was a narrow alley, barely wide enough for compact cars. Ryan's room faced a seafood restaurant. Garbage lined both sides, some of it in big overflowing bins, most just scattered in the gutter. The odor suggested that it had been there for some time. He wasn't sure what to do. He could jump straight to the pavement and risk breaking an ankle. Or he could let the trash break the fall and risk smelling like week-old mahi-mahi.

A hard knock on the door announced their arrival. *"La policía! Abre la puerta!"*

Ryan paused. If he jumped, there was no turning back. *If I stay...*

The knock was suddenly a thud—then a crash. The door burst open just a crack, caught by the chain. They were breaking down the door.

Staying is not an option.

He took a deep breath and jumped from the ledge, flying, amazed at how long it took to fall just three stories. His feet skidded on the pavement. Momentum sent him rolling across the alley between the trash piles. He kept his bag close to protect the breakables inside. From the ground, he looked up toward his room.

The police were at the window, shouting something in Spanish.

Ryan sprang to his feet and ran up the alley, weaving between trash bins and a few makeshift bungalows for the homeless. His knee was throbbing from the fall, but it didn't slow him down. At a dead run it was difficult to see in the shadows. He kept his eye on the daylight just ahead, where the alley fed into a busy thoroughfare. He heard shouting behind him. The police. A burst of adrenaline quickened his pace. Finally he reached the street, clutching his bag like a football.

The sidewalk was a two-way stream of pedestrians, nearly shoulder to shoulder. It was impossible to run. Better not to run, thought Ryan. *Just blend with the crowd.*

A shrill whistle cut through the usual city noises. Ryan glanced over his shoulder. It was a police whistle. They were coming from the alley.

His eyes darted, searching for an escape. He was itching to turn and see if they were closing in. He couldn't run without giving himself away. But maybe they had a bead on him. His only chance might be an all-out run for it.

Ryan spotted a cab pulling up at the corner. He nearly broke into a run. The moment the previous passenger stepped out, Ryan jumped in the backseat and slammed the door behind him.

"El embassy de los Estados Unidos," he said in bad Spanish. He dug all of his money from his bag and showed it to the driver. *"Pronto, por favor."*

The cabby hit the gas so hard it threw Ryan against the backseat. Ryan looked out the rear window. The police were in the street, shouting at each other. One of them pointed at the taxi as it sped away.

Ryan glanced ahead through the windshield. The American embassy was just a few blocks away. That was his best bet. The local police had no jurisdiction there. If he'd done something wrong, he'd face the music in his own country. He just didn't want to spend the night—or longer—in a Panamanian jail.

Sirens blared behind them. The police were in pursuit.

"Hurry, please!" said Ryan.

The cab screeched to a halt. The driver was shouting in rapid-fire Spanish. Ryan couldn't understand the words, but the point was clear. He wanted no part of a police chase. Ryan tossed him some money for the ride and jumped out at the curb.

The embassy was just a half-block ahead, between Thirty-eighth and Thirty-ninth streets on busy Avenida Balboa. The main building, which housed the ambassador, faced the blue-green Bay of Panama. Ryan was fairly certain that his new passport was waiting in the administrative offices a few blocks away, but right now he had other priorities. He slung his bag over his shoulder and sprinted up the avenue, toward a large circular intersection. Traffic fed in from five different directions, then wound around a small park in the center. By car, the police would have to go the long way around the perimeter. Ryan was better off on foot. He cut across the diameter, running straight through the park. Just six lanes of traffic separated him from U.S. soil. The police car was nearly on two wheels as it raced around the circle, weaving in and out of cars. Ryan dodged a few cars as he cut across the street. An old Chevy swerved and slammed on its brakes, nearly flattening him. Ryan leaped to the sidewalk and never stopped. The police car screeched to a halt in front of the embassy. Ryan kept going. The police jumped out and ran across the sidewalk, then stopped at the gated entrance to the embassy grounds—the end of their jurisdiction. He glanced back, relieved to see they had given up.

A security guard stopped him at the outside gate. Ryan was so winded he could barely speak. "I'm an American citizen. My passport was stolen. I need help."

"Come with me," he said.

The guard escorted him onto the compound, where a U.S. Marine met him at the entrance to the main building. Outside the embassy were privately hired guards; inside, the Marines took over. Ryan felt relief at the sight of the American flag in the lobby. Even the picture of the president he hadn't voted for made him feel at home.

"Thank you so much," he said.

The young Marine was as stiff as his starched and pressed uniform. He wore a tan shirt and dark blue pants with a red stripe down the side. A pistol and metal handcuffs were on his belt. He drew neither, but he did little else to put Ryan at ease. They passed the elevators and the entrance to the ground-floor offices. The directory on the wall listed everything from the ambassador and the legal attaché to the Coast Guard and Drug Enforcement Agency. Ryan wasn't sure where they were headed. He just followed. They stopped at a set of double wood doors at the end of the hall. The Marine opened the door on the right.

"Please, step inside, sir."

Ryan went in. The Marine posted himself outside and closed the door behind him. The room was sparsely furnished, just a rectangular table and chairs. A fluorescent light hummed overhead. Two men rose from the chairs on the opposite side of the table. One looked young and Hispanic. The other was more WASP-ish and mature. They were dressed alike in white shirts and dark blue blazers. Both were stone-faced as they looked at Ryan.

"Dr. Duffy?" the older one said. His voice almost echoed off the cold bare walls.

"Yes."

The man reached inside his pocket and flashed his credentials. "Agent Forsyth. FBI. Agent Enriquez and I would like to ask you some questions. Just take a few minutes. Could you have a seat, please."

Ryan remained standing, shifting nervously. "I'm just down here on business, you know. Somebody stole my bag."

"What's that on your shoulder?"

"Oh, this? I bought it here in the city. At the hotel, actually. As a replacement."

He seemed skeptical. "Did you report the theft to the Panamanian police?"

"No, I didn't. I, uh, just didn't get around to it."

"Why were you running from the police?"

"What do you mean?"

His gaze tightened. "You heard me."

"Look, this whole thing is getting way out of hand. My passport was stolen. I just wanted to get back to my own country as quickly as possible. Why would a guy who has anything to hide run straight to the U. S. embassy? If you think I was running from the police, that's your perception. But I have no idea why the police would be following me."

"We asked them to pick you up," said Forsyth. "That's why they were following you."

Ryan looked confused. "The FBI *asked* them?"

He nodded. "It's not unusual for the FBI to ask the local police to pick up a subject."

"A suspect? Suspect of what?"

"I said subject, not suspect. You're not a suspect. Please, sit. We'd like to talk to you."

Ryan had watched enough cop shows on television to know there was something magic about the term "suspect." At the very least, a suspect had to be advised of his legal rights—which was probably why they weren't calling him one. At least not yet.

"What do you want to know?" asked Ryan.

"For starters, let's talk about the three-million-dollar account at the Banco del Istmo." Forsyth leaned forward, watching Ryan carefully. "You must have really pissed off that bank officer you were dealing with. These days it's a little easier to pierce bank secrecy than it used to be under the dictatorship. But even so, this is the first time we've ever gotten the cooperation of the Banco del Istmo. They sent all the records straight to the financial intelligence unit here in Panama, which sent them to us." He picked up a file from the table before him, apparently reading from something. "Three hundred transfers in the amount of nine thousand nine hundred ninety-nine dollars. A rather unimaginative way to circumvent the ten-thousand-dollar currency transaction reporting requirements, if I do say so myself."

Ryan blinked, saying nothing.

Forsyth continued to read from his file. "According to the bank officer, you told him—quote—'My father was not the kind of man to have three million dollars in a numbered account in the Banco del Istmo. My father wasn't the kind of man to have three million dollars in *any* bank.' End quote." He looked up from the file. With a quick glance, he directed Ryan to the empty chair at the table. "Have a seat, Dr. Duffy. I'd really like to give you an opportunity to explain that statement."

Ryan started to sweat. Part of him felt the need to say something. Part of him felt the urge to get the hell out of there. He didn't know his rights, but he knew someone who did.

"I'll be happy to talk to you," he said. "After I talk to my lawyer."

33

They were out of lettuce. For nine straight days, Sarah's late-morning snack had consisted of the same unique sandwich delicacy. Peanut butter, sliced bananas, mayonnaise, and iceberg lettuce on rye bread, grilled on both sides until the mayo was bubbling and the lettuce went soft. *Dee-licious.* But it just wasn't the same without the lettuce.

She slumped with despair as she stood staring into the open refrigerator. She made one more attempt to bend her pregnant body and check the bottom vegetable bin. Definitely no lettuce. Her hormones took over. She was suddenly on the verge of tears.

The phone rang. She paused, unsure whether it was worth the effort to answer. The wall phone was all the way on the other side of the kitchen. Her swollen ankles were worse today than yesterday, and the cold air from the open refrigerator was feeling mighty good.

It kept ringing. Seven, eight times. Somebody really wanted to talk to her. She stepped away from the fridge and slowly crossed the room, grimacing with each step. She answered in a clipped tone. "Yeah."

"Sarah, it's Liz. Where is Brent?"

"Not here."

"I didn't think so. Where is he?"

Sarah checked the clock on the oven. "Probably halfway back from Denver by now."

Liz hesitated. "I appreciate your candor."

"Excuse me?"

"I didn't expect you to actually admit he came here."

"Liz, what are you talking about? He went to Denver to see *you*."

"Me?"

"He left early this morning. Real early. Like two A.M. Said he wanted to catch you before you went to work. He couldn't sleep. Was up thinking about that deposition your lawyer wanted him to give. He needed to talk to you about it."

"I never saw him."

"That's funny. Then I don't know where he is."

"Neither do I. But I have a pretty good idea of where he's been. Somebody beat the daylights out of my lawyer this morning. Jumped him right in his garage on his way to the office."

"Oh, my word. Is he hurt bad?"

"Bad enough to land in the hospital."

"Gosh, Liz. That's terrible. I'm sorry."

"Are you?"

She stiffened at the accusatory tone. "Wait a second. You don't think Brent—what *are* you thinking?"

"Just look at what happened. Yesterday, Brent was served with a subpoena. It made him so mad he couldn't sleep. He jumped in his car in the middle of the night and drove to Denver, supposedly to talk to me. Next thing we know my lawyer's in the emergency room getting his face stitched up."

Sarah's hand shook nervously. "Just slow down. I know this looks bad. But let's not jump to conclusions."

"This is hardly a jump. Brent's in trouble this time, Sarah. Big time. All I can say for you is that I hope you had nothing to do with it."

She was about to respond, but the line clicked. Her hands shook harder. She gripped the phone, paralyzed with confusion. The dial tone hummed in her ear. Liz was gone. Brent was unaccounted for.

And Sarah felt completely alone.

Ryan insisted on a thoroughly private line for his call to his lawyer. Agent Forsyth offered the use of an embassy phone, but somehow that sounded about as private as dialing into a talk radio station. The only viable option was a pay phone on the street. Forsyth wasn't happy about it, but he didn't seem prepared to arrest him to prevent him from walking out of the building. The Panamanian police were no longer a threat, since their only apparent objective had been to assist the FBI in bringing him to the embassy. Ryan found a public phone right on Avenida Balboa. Cars and buses rumbled by on the busy street. He closed one ear with his finger as he dialed Norm's private line.

"Where are you?" his lawyer asked.

"About a block from the embassy. I'm at a pay phone, but they're expecting me back inside when I finish talking to you. I've been sort of detained for questioning by the FBI."

"What?" He sounded as if he was coming through the phone.

"You heard me." Ryan gave him the two-minute summary, filling in the gaps since their talk last night.

"First off," said Norm, "I suppose it tells us something that you ran into the FBI instead of the DEA. The FBI does do drug work, but if the government thought the three million dollars at Banco del Istmo was drug money, I would think DEA would have detained you rather than the FBI."

"Does that mean they know the money is from extortion payments?"

"I wouldn't go that far, but I will say this. It's puzzling that the FBI went to all the trouble of coordinating with the local police to question you in Panama. It would have been much easier just to wait for you to return to the United States."

"Except that last night I booked a flight to the Cayman Islands so I could check on that offshore corporation that transferred the money to my father's account. Maybe the FBI wasn't so sure I was coming back to the states."

"That's possible. But the FBI doesn't have unlimited resources to chase people around the globe. If these agents were based in Panama, that's one thing. But if they flew down from the States just to talk to you, this thing may be bigger than your father even knew."

Pedestrians hurried past on the sidewalk. In a moment of paranoia, Ryan wondered if any were FBI. "Let's take this one step at a time. What do I do right now?"

"Step one is to get your new passport. It should be ready and waiting for you right there at the embassy, and they can't withhold it."

"Then what?"

"Legally, you have no obligation to talk to anyone. The FBI has no right to detain you. But we have to be concerned about appearances. After you leave, the FBI agent will fill out a Three-oh-two report that makes a record of your conversation. We don't want that Three-oh-two to state simply that on the advice of your attorney, you refused to talk to the FBI. That sounds like you're hiding something. We want you to sound as cooperative as possible, short of talking to them. So here's what you do. You go back to the embassy and tell the agent that you fully intend to cooperate. But now isn't a good time to talk. Your bag was stolen along with your passport. You're upset and you're tired. Ask them for their business cards. That's important. I need to know which field office these agents are from. Tell them your lawyer will contact them about an interview in Denver after you've returned to the States."

"So you want me to come straight back to Denver? No stop in the Cayman Islands?"

"Do *not* go to the Cayman Islands. I'll have my investigator check out that lead discreetly. Everything you do from here on out, you have to assume the FBI is watching."

"This is getting so nuts."

Norm sensed his frustration. "Ryan, take it easy. You've done nothing wrong. If a crime has been committed, it was your father. The

FBI can't send you to jail for something your father may have done."

"The FBI may be the least of my problems. Obviously someone has been tailing me all over Panama, maybe even followed me from Denver. And I still can't figure out why the same woman who scammed me out of my bag at the hotel bar would then warn me that the police were coming to my room to pick me up."

"Are you sure it was the same woman?"

"Sounded just like her. If it wasn't, that's even more baffling. It is strange, though. Why would someone who essentially robbed me suddenly decide she's on my side?"

"Maybe she's not exactly on your side. Just that in certain respects your interests coincide."

"What do you mean?"

"The essence of blackmail is the secret. Neither side wants the secret to get out. If it does, the blackmailer loses his cash cow, and the person paying the blackmail has to suffer the consequences of the world knowing the truth about him."

"You think she's protecting the person who was blackmailed?"

"I think she knows who paid the money. And I think it's her job to make sure nobody finds out."

Ryan swallowed hard. "Then why doesn't she just kill me?"

"Probably for the same reason she didn't just kill your father. He must have worked out some arrangement where the secret would be revealed if anything untoward happened to him or his family. It's a fairly common safety valve in any extortion case."

"How would it work?"

"Hypothetically, let's say your father had photographs of a famous TV evangelist having sex with his German shepherd. This is not the kind of thing that advances an evangelist's career. Your father blackmails the evangelist, but he's afraid the bad guys might kill him rather than pay him five million dollars. So he sends copies of the photographs to some third party, along with explicit instructions. If Frank Duffy dies under suspicious circumstances, the photographs are to be sent immediately to the *National Enquirer*. That way, killing the blackmailer accomplishes nothing. The only option is to pay the money."

"So in my situation, this third party would be...who? My mother?"

"Not likely a family member. Maybe a friend. Maybe someone with no apparent connection to your father at all."

Ryan fell silent, pensive. Maybe somebody like Amy Parkens. Maybe that was why she had balked at his hints to move their relationship beyond business.

"You still there?" asked Norm.

"Yeah, I'm here. I was just thinking. This third party you mentioned. They probably wouldn't work for free, right?"

"It would be typical to give them a cut of the extortion money."

"Say two hundred thousand dollars?"

"I guess. Whatever they negotiate. What are you driving at?"

"Maybe it's best I'm not going to the Cayman Islands after all. There's something I need to check out back in Denver."

Norm stiffened, concerned. "You're getting that funny sound in your voice again. What are you thinking?"

He smiled with his eyes. "I'm thinking that things are just beginning to make sense."

34

Visiting hours at Denver Health Medical Center started at 7:00 P.M. Liz reached Phil Jackson's private room at 7:01.

She was eager to see him and make sure he was okay. She walked briskly, then slowed steadily. A journey down the busy hospital corridors triggered memories of Ryan's medical school residency, back when DHMC was called Denver General Hospital. She remembered the night he'd decided to be a surgeon. She remembered the following nights, too, the years of sacrifice. Ryan worked twenty-hour shifts for wages that didn't even come close to paying his student loans. They lived week to week on Liz's paycheck. They saw each other once a day for dinner right at the hospital, usually a ten-minute burger break between her night job and her day job. Ryan had invested so much. *She* had invested just as much. All for the glorious payoff of life without parole in Piedmont Springs.

For Liz, it was a return to failure. She had grown up dirt poor, one of seven children in a dilapidated four-bedroom farmhouse. She was the only one in her family who had ended up staying in Piedmont Springs. It was a bitter irony. Her heart had been broken when Ryan had gone away to college without her. She was seventeen and left to play mom to six younger siblings, an experience that had taught her never to want children of her own. Four years later, her friends had been so jealous when Ryan invited her up to Denver and asked her to marry him. A medical student. A future surgeon. He could have been her way out. No one had told her it was a round-trip ticket. In hindsight, she should have smelled trouble when it took five years of living together to move the engagement to the wedding.

"Knock, knock," said Liz as she appeared in the doorway.

Jackson was sitting up in bed and conscious. He looked battered but better than expected. The right side of his face was swollen with purple and black bruises. A bandage covered eleven stitches above his right eyebrow. Painkillers and a glucose solution fed intravenously into his needle-pricked forearm. His dinner rested on a tray over his lap. It had hardly been touched. At his side was a yellow legal pad and a case file his secretary had brought from the office.

"Phil?" she said softly.

He waved her in and tried to smile, but the movement of any facial muscles seemed to cause him pain.

"You poor man."

"Nothing a good dose of work can't cure."

"Don't you ever stop?"

"Don't complain. It's your case I'm working on."

She nearly shivered with gratitude. "You have no idea how relieved I am to hear you say that. I was so afraid you would drop my case."

"Why would I do that?"

She shrugged impishly. "I spoke to your paralegal this afternoon about the phone conversation I had with Sarah Langford. Didn't she tell you?"

"She told me everything. Honestly, I figured it was Brent long before you even called."

"And you're still sticking with me?"

He laid his legal pad aside and took her hand lightly, looking her straight in the eye. "Let me tell you something. I have deposed everybody from Teamsters to gangsters—and ripped them to shreds. I have had my tires slashed, my house vandalized, my life threatened. If I were easily intimidated I'd be sitting in an office at some big law firm doing bond work. I'm more committed to your case than ever. Nobody threatens Phil Jackson. Least of all a punk like Brent Langford."

She squeezed his hand, then pulled away shyly.

"Don't be embarrassed," he said. "You can't help yourself. All women find men with purple faces absolutely irresistible."

"It is a very nice shade of purple."

He smiled, then turned more serious. "You know, I'm not the only one who has to gear up for a fight. You need to brace yourself as well."

She nodded tentatively. "I'll do what I have to do."

"Good. Because this is going to get nasty. And I don't just mean Brent's deposition. The whole Duffy family is going to feel the pressure. In fact, the FBI should be taking a pretty close look at them already."

"The FBI?"

"One of my most satisfied former clients is now a special agent in the Denver field office. I called her this morning from the hospital and asked her to poke around a little. Brent's attack is a federal offense—obstruction of justice. The FBI has much bigger fish to fry, but with a little friendly encouragement and factual embellishment, I think I piqued her interest. Ryan's phony invoices at his clinic. Frank's talk of all the money he was going to leave you. Brent's statement that it was 'family business.' It probably won't amount to anything, but it doesn't hurt to have your husband squirming under the microscope of a possible federal racketeering investigation."

She blinked nervously. "That's pretty harsh, don't you think?"

"Do you want to win or don't you?"

"Yeah, I want to win. But—"

"No buts. Now do me a favor. Take this," he said as he handed her a slip of paper. It had two phone numbers written on it.

"What's this?"

"My secretary got a call today from the law office of Norman Klusmire. He's your husband's new divorce attorney. The top number is his beeper number. On your way home tonight, stop at a pay phone and dial his beeper. Be sure to use a pay phone so there's absolutely no way of tracing the call back to you. Just enter the other number and hang up."

"Whose number is it?"

"It's the home phone number for the judge in your case. He's a crusty old fart who goes ballistic whenever lawyers call him at home. He won't even give Klusmire a chance to explain he was answering a bogus page. This is the kind of stupid little thing that'll have Judge Novak riding his ass all the way to trial. It should teach a hotshot criminal lawyer like Klusmire to think twice before taking on another divorce case."

"That's too clever," she said as she tucked the piece of paper into her purse.

"I can't take full credit. I sort of stole the idea from one of my clients. Whenever she suspected her husband was off with his mistress, she used to beep him with their rabbi's home phone number."

"Do you always steal from your clients?"

"Sometimes."

"What are you going to steal from me?" she asked coyly.

He raised an eyebrow till it hurt. "We'll see."

35

Amy had taken her daughter to Denver only a dozen times or so in her young life, and each time it seemed their destination was LoDo—short for lower downtown. It had two of Taylor's favorite attractions: the world-renowned roller coaster at Elitch Garden Amusement Park and the Colorado Rockies professional baseball team at Coors Field. Of special moment that Wednesday night was "hat night" at the ballpark. The first ten thousand fans through the gate would receive a free baseball cap. Taylor was certain that fans would be coming from places as far away as Pluto for such a tempting giveaway. Mommy *had* to take her. On the heels of the break-in at their apartment, some time away from Boulder would do them both good.

Built of red brick and green steel, Coors Field was one of the league's new breed of "baseball-only" stadiums that had the aura of an old ballpark. A natural grass playing field and intimate seating arrangement gave ball games the feeling they used to have, before domed stadiums and artificial turf became so popular. Even the nostalgia buffs, however, appreciated the modern touches, such as big-screen scoreboards, plenty of concession areas, and enough rest rooms to ensure that a second-inning trip with Taylor to the potty didn't mean a return sometime after the seventh-inning stretch.

It was a cool summer evening, perfect for a ball game. They sat in the cheaper seats in right field. Taylor brought her baseball mitt to catch any long home runs. The free cap was several sizes too big and kept falling over her eyes, completely blocking her vision. Every twenty seconds it was "What's happening now, Mommy?" Amy had to play radio announcer for the entire first inning until Taylor finally tired of the silliness and agreed to lose the hat.

By the sixth inning, Taylor's eyes were getting heavy. She was starting to slump in her seat. Amy, too, had drifted away from the game. She was thinking of the conversation she'd had with Marilyn Gaslow. She could actually see Marilyn's office from the stadium. The lights burned late on the forty-second floor. She wondered if Marilyn was still there. She wondered if Marilyn had spoken to anyone about their conversation.

She quickly shook away her doubts. Talking to Marilyn was like talking to Gram. Without the guilt.

Still, it was bothersome that Marilyn didn't quite seem to believe her. Amy wasn't sure which part of the story had been so difficult for Marilyn to swallow. Maybe she didn't believe a word about the two hundred thousand dollars in the first place. Maybe she didn't believe Amy had no connection to the dying old man who had sent it. Worse yet, she wondered if Marilyn had conveyed her own hidden sentiments when she'd warned that others might call her a whore.

Good thing she hadn't mentioned that his son Ryan was a heartthrob. It would only have fueled Marilyn's suspicions.

"Me tired," said Taylor. She was half in her own seat, half in Amy's lap.

Amy stroked her daughter's forehead, then took her in her arms. "It's time to go anyway."

"I didn't catch a ball yet."

"Next time."

They walked hand in hand down the cement ramps. Taylor was struggling to keep up as Amy walked with purpose, on the verge of a decision. It was time to regroup. Astronomy was history. She had already missed the Monday deadline to reenroll in the doctoral program for the fall, and she had lost the cash that would have made that possible anyway. The job now was to regain Marilyn's confidence and prove she wasn't making up stories about the money. That was something Ryan Duffy could help her with. Last time they'd talked, she had given him one week to come up with a legitimate explanation for the money. The deadline was Friday. She would go through with the follow-up meeting, she decided, even though the money was gone. She would tape-record their conversation and let Marilyn listen. It wouldn't bring the money back, but it would restore Marilyn's faith.

A roar of the crowd disrupted her thoughts. The Rockies had scored. She and Taylor kept walking, leaving through the turnstile and chain-link gate to the north parking lot.

Amy had never taken Taylor to a night game before. Leaving early had a different feeling at night than in broad daylight. Vapor lights gave the grounds an eerie yellow glow. Trash bins at the gate were overflowing with cans and bottles that had been confiscated from fans on their way in. Ticket stubs lay scattered on the ground. The crowd noise faded behind them. The parking lot was jammed, without another soul in sight. It was an uneasy feeling of solitude, as if forty thousand people had vaporized with the sunset, leaving Amy and Taylor alone in a sea of cars.

Amy picked up her sleepy daughter and walked faster toward her truck.

The walk back to the parking space always seemed farther than the walk to the stadium. That was never more true than when you were alone in the parking lot with a sleepy four-year-old in your arms. They passed row after row of empty vehicles. Amy was certain she was in section E, but the rows all looked alike. For the second time she saw the same red Honda. She headed in the other direction this time, searching for her distinctive old truck. Taylor was sound asleep on her shoulder. Amy's arms were getting tired. Her back was aching. Taylor wasn't such a little girl anymore. Finally, she spotted her truck in the next row.

She cut between two parked cars and dug out her key. She opened the passenger door with one hand and placed Taylor in the car seat. She closed the door and hurried around the back to the driver's side. She stopped short, startled by a noise. A blur leaped from behind the truck. Someone jumped up and grabbed her from behind. She started to scream, but a huge hand covered her mouth. A cold knife was at her throat.

"Don't move," he warned.

She was shaking but unable to move, pinned against the truck.

He spoke right into her ear from behind her. "We saw the police report. You didn't mention the money. Smart move."

She didn't even breathe. It was her worst fear—the thugs behind the money.

"Stay smart, lady. Tell no one about the money. And stay away from the cops." He twisted her arm, heightening the pain. "Now get in your truck and get the hell out of here. You scream, you *ever* talk to the police again, it's your daughter who pays."

He knocked her to the ground and sprinted away. Amy hurried to her feet and looked around, gasping for breath. She didn't see him anywhere. She reached for the rape whistle on her keychain and brought it to her lips, then stopped. His warning stayed with her.

She jumped in the truck and started the engine. Taylor was still asleep in her car seat. The sight of her little one brought emotions to a head and moisture to her eyes. She leaned over and hugged her with one arm while steering with the left. Her whole body trembled as she drove quickly from the parking lot.

36

Ryan's flight landed at Denver International Airport at 11:50 P.M. He hadn't bothered to retrieve his garment bag from the hotel room in Panama, so he had no checked baggage, just the small carry-on he had purchased to replace his stolen bag. He'd already passed through customs at the plane change in Houston. Norm met him out front, near the curbside check-in at the United Airlines terminal. The motor was running in the Range Rover as the passenger door flew open. Ryan jumped inside, laid his bag gently at his feet. After a day that included a run through the streets from Panamanian police, a run-in with the FBI, and nine hours of international travel, he nearly melted into the leather upholstery.

"Man, am I glad to see you," he said as he slammed the door.

Norm checked his disheveled appearance. "You look like Steve McQueen in that old movie about Devil's Island."

"*Papillon?*"

"Yeah. What did you do, float in from Panama on a sack of coconuts?"

"Shut up and drive, Norm."

A whistle blew, startling them. The DIA traffic gestapo was about to issue a parking citation, as if they expected passengers to catch their rides on the run. Norm hit the gas and quickly pulled back into traffic. They spoke as the truck weaved between car rental buses and stopped cars on the way to the airport exit and Pena Boulevard.

"You made it out smoothly, I presume," said Norm.

"I told them exactly what you told me to say. Got their business cards, too. Forsyth is a field agent here in Denver. The other guy isn't FBI. He's from Washington. The criminal tax division of the IRS."

"I figured it was only a matter of time before they showed up." Norm steered onto the expressway ramp. "I've been doing a little legwork myself while you were traveling. Called a friend over at the U.S. attorney's office."

"What would they know about this?"

"In any investigation, the FBI's legal counsel is an AUSA—an assistant U.S. attorney. A routine subpoena for documents, for example, would be handled at a ministerial level by a junior AUSA. But if your case was assigned to an AUSA who specializes in money laundering, for example, that would tell us something about the focus of the investigation."

"What did you find out?"

"Your case is under the major crimes section."

"Major?" he asked with concern.

"Don't let the name fool you. Everything is major. It's a slush pile for cases that are too new to be routed to a more defined area of specialization."

"Where do you think it's headed?"

"Could be strictly a tax investigation. You

said your old man didn't pay taxes on the money. Or if the FBI gets wind of the extortion, it could go to the public corruption section. If it's money laundering they smell, it could go to economic crimes. Too early to tell."

"All this because I pissed off a stupid bank officer at Banco del Istmo."

"Actually, it wasn't just him who brought in the FBI. From what I gathered from the AUSA, your wife's lawyer is also behind it."

"Jackson?"

Norm nodded as he changed lanes. "He's in the hospital. Gonna be okay. Looks like Brent may have punched his lights out in retaliation for scheduling his deposition."

"What a jerk."

"You mean Jackson or Brent?"

"Both," Ryan scoffed.

"Anyway, Jackson has managed to pitch this in a way that has piqued the FBI's interest. Three million dollars in a Panamanian bank account isn't necessarily front-page news. But when a high-powered attorney starts poking around and lands in the emergency room, it puts a different spin on the case. Especially a guy like Jackson. Believe it or not, he has friends. And if you're not his friend, he probably has dirt on you. You remember that hypothetical I gave you about the photographs of the TV evangelist having sex with his German shepherd?"

"Yeah."

"Jackson is the kind of guy who would actually *have* those photographs. File drawers full of things on everybody from the gov-

240

ernor of Colorado to your pet goldfish. He's like the J. Edgar Hoover of the legal profession. He can make things happen. And your brother-in-law Brent has given him every reason to pull out the stops."

"Terrific. Does this mean Jackson knows about the money?"

"Only if someone at the FBI leaked it, which I doubt. But he's sure getting close."

They rode in silence for a moment. The city lights of downtown Denver were coming closer.

"What's happening with the yearbook search? Find any millionaires in my dad's high school class?"

"Nothing yet. Still working on it.

"What about the Cayman corporation? I brought a lot of grief on myself trying to find out who transferred that money into my father's account. I definitely want to follow up on that."

"My investigator is on it. Hopefully he won't actually have to go all the way to the Caymans."

"How am I going to pay this investigator of yours? He's racking up some serious hours."

"Don't worry about it. He's on retainer. You'll just have to cover his out-of-pocket expenses."

"How 'bout that. Some good news."

*"Don't be so negative. Let's hear what the FBI's concerns are. If they say your dad owes back income tax, you pay the penalty and you're on your way. We just don't know yet."

"You think the FBI knows about the two million in the attic?"

"I don't see how they would. If they don't, we still have some time to decide what you should do about that. As the executor of your father's estate, you have ninety days to file your Seven-oh-six with the IRS. That's the form on which you would have to disclose the money."

"But what do I tell them at this meeting you're supposed to set up? We can't put that off for ninety days."

"The first meeting I was just planning on listening. I don't even want you to be there."

"I'll be there," he said firmly.

"As your lawyer, I don't recommend it. It's best if I go alone and find out what their focus is. Then we can regroup and decide whether you should talk to them."

"Norm, I trust you like a brother. But I have to be there. I have to."

He sighed, but he didn't fight it. "If you go, you can't say anything. Don't roll your eyes, don't scowl."

"I can do that."

"Good. We have to approach this meeting like a business negotiation, quid pro quo. It's like I said before, my gut tells me that this thing is bigger than even your father knew. If that's the case, I seriously doubt that you're a target of the FBI's investigation. But they'll want to put pressure on you to name names, to help them find out who's behind the money. And if they find out about the extortion, they'll want to know everything about that, too."

"The only person I can name is dead."

Norm glanced away from the road, looking

Ryan in the eye. "I knew your father. As far as I could tell, he wasn't savvy or dishonest enough to orchestrate a five-million-dollar extortion scheme on his own. The FBI will want to know who he was working with."

"Well, that puts us behind the eight ball. Because I have no other names to give them."

"Names aren't essential. Just give them something to go on. What about that woman who scammed you in Panama?"

"I have no idea who she was."

"There must be something you could tell the FBI to help find her. I'm not saying we walk into the very first meeting and spill our guts. But if it gets to the point where we're forced to negotiate for immunity for you or anyone else in your family, it's essential that we have something to offer the government in return."

Ryan reached down into his bag. "I may have something we can offer."

"What's that?"

Ryan folded away the plastic bubble wrap. "It's the glass from the bar at the hotel. The one that woman was drinking from."

"You told me you gave it to the bank officer at Banco del Istmo."

"I wasn't about to give up the only piece of evidence I had that could lead me to the person who had followed me. I gave him a glass from the hotel. I didn't give him *this* glass."

Norm was about to chew him out for having lied to his lawyer, but he was more intrigued than angry. "You think any of her fingerprints are actually left on it?"

"I did my best not to smudge it. I bought this bag and bubble wrap right at the hotel especially for it. I was hoping it might help me find that woman eventually. But if things go sour, as you say, maybe the FBI will be interested to see how good I am at preserving evidence."

"Depending on where the investigation goes, the FBI could be very interested." Norm looked closer and inspected the dried lipstick along the rim. "There might actually be enough dried saliva here for a DNA analysis."

"I take it we now have something to negotiate with?"

"It's a good start. We could always use more."

"That's pretty much it," said Ryan.

Norm sensed something in Ryan's voice. "You're holding back, aren't you?"

Ryan looked away. It was time to tell Norm about Amy. It only took a minute.

Norm pounded the steering wheel and drove angrily off the highway. The truck stopped in the parking lot to a motel. "Damn you," he said harshly.

"What?"

"I'm fed up already. The glass was one thing. Hiding this Amy from me is another. You keep acting like you're the know-it-all doctor and I'm the stupid patient. You tell me only what you think I need to know. That won't work. I'm your lawyer. You're my client. I need to know everything."

"I'm not playing games with you, Norm. I

244

just don't want to get Amy involved with the FBI."

"Why not? Hasn't it occurred to you that she might be the safety valve I talked about? Maybe she has the information that your father used to extort the five million dollars. Maybe it was her job to release the information to the public if anything untoward ever happened to your father."

"Yes, I did think of that. But it's not fair to get her involved until I've ruled out one other possibility."

"What's that?"

Ryan lowered his eyes, speaking softly, almost ashamed. The fact that he had felt some early chemistry with Amy made it even more difficult to explain. "I need to know if she's connected to the victim. Of the rape, I mean."

"What are you thinking?"

"I'm not sure. We know my father was convicted of rape as a juvenile. That means there had to be a victim. Obviously, Amy is too young to have been the victim herself. But maybe her mother or her aunt or someone in her family was raped. I just want to make sure that the money my father gave to Amy wasn't Dad's way of making amends for that, a way of easing his own guilt."

Norm nodded, seeming to understand. "Problem is, those court records are sealed. Hell, they were probably destroyed years ago. By law, juvenile records are destroyed once the offender reaches a certain age, usually somewhere in his twenties. I don't see how you could ever verify the victim's name."

"Right now, it's my number-one priority. When we met last Friday, she gave me a one-week deadline to prove that the money came from a legitimate source. That means she should be calling me tomorrow or Friday."

"What are you going to do?"

"I don't know," he said, staring out the window. "But by tomorrow, I better think of something."

"That's a pretty short fuse. What if you're stumped?"

He glanced at Norm, troubled by the thought of telling anyone his father was a rapist—let alone a woman who might have known the victim. "Then I'll do the only thing I can do."

"What?"

He looked away again. "I'll ask her."

37

On Thursday morning, Ryan was ready to call home. His father wouldn't answer.

That was a fact Ryan had not yet gotten used to. His father had always been the one to answer. Mom hated talking on the phone. Frank Duffy used to love it. You could hear it in his voice, the way he would answer. Not a lazy "Hello." It was a distinctive and energetic "*Hay*-low," a genuine greeting to anyone who did him the favor of dialing his number. It had been somewhat of a joke among friends,

246

the way people would call for Ryan, Sarah, or their mother and end up speaking to Frank. He always wanted to hear what was going on.

Ryan wondered if he was listening now.

Last night had been tough. He'd spent most of it thinking how best to tell his mother what he'd learned, especially about the rape. There was no easy way. Face-to-face was probably best, but with the FBI on his tail he at least had to bring her into the loop.

At the first sign of daylight, he placed the call from Norm's spare bedroom. It hadn't occurred to him that his mom would be anything but wide awake and dressed for the day—and it wasn't just because of the neighbor's blasted roosters that rattled the Duffy homestead with every sunrise. Jeanette Duffy wasn't a Duffy at all. She was a Greene, part of a pioneer family that more than a century ago had planted roots on the plains with two mules and a sod house. She had always been an early riser, as if genetically programmed to get up before dawn to milk the cows and feed the chickens, even if they didn't own any cows or chickens. Since the funeral, she'd been rising even earlier than usual. The big house was empty without Frank and his booming voice. Lying around in bed could only make it seem emptier. The image saddened Ryan. The loss had siphoned her frontier spirit. She looked older to him now, even in his mind's eye. He envisioned her sitting at the kitchen table with the phone to her ear, watching her morning toast and coffee get cold as Ryan tried to tell her the truth about the man she had married.

"I don't want to hear it," she said again, firmly.

It was a worn-out refrain, repeated like a mantra throughout their conversation. Ryan couldn't give her any details. She wouldn't allow it, threatened to hang up. It was as if she had fulfilled her promise to Frank by telling Ryan about the safe deposit box, and now she was done with it. It had been Ryan's decision to open the box. Now he had to deal with the consequences. Not her.

"Mom, at least let me say this much. It's possible the FBI will contact you."

"Oh, my God."

"Don't get nervous. I said it's possible, not definite. Yesterday, Norm notified the assistant U.S. attorney that he is the legal counsel for the entire Duffy family. They shouldn't contact any of us directly now that we have a lawyer."

"What do I say if they do call me?"

"Tell them they should call me or Norman Klusmire. Period. Don't try to be polite and helpful. You need to be firm on this."

"All right."

"Sarah needs to hear this, too. I've been trying to call her since late last night. Nobody answers at her house. Is she okay?"

"As far as I know, yes. She's okay."

"If you see her, tell her exactly what I told you. And have her call me as soon as possible. I'll be at Norm's house or at his office the rest of the day. We need to talk about Brent."

"Brent came back yesterday."

"So you heard what he did in Denver?"

"Uh—when are you coming home, Ryan?"

He paused. She obviously didn't want to talk about Brent. She didn't seem to want to talk about anything. "Maybe tomorrow. I have a few things to take care of here in the city."

"What are you doing about the clinic, son?"

"Don't worry about that. I'm referring my patients to Dr. Weber in Lamar."

"Oh, he's a fine doctor. And his receptionist is just lovely. Sweet and very pretty. Maybe you can give her a call once you and Liz are legally—"

"*Mom*," he groaned. His mother seemed to focus on the goofiest things in times of crisis. "Goodbye, Mom. I love you. Just remember, none of us has anything to be ashamed of. We've done nothing wrong."

"Yes," she said in a voice that quaked. "I'll try and remember that."

Sarah waited for the click on the other end of the line, then hung up the phone. She'd heard it all, without Ryan's knowledge.

Yesterday's attempt to confront Brent about the attack had proved disastrous. She'd spent the night at Mom's, giving her hotheaded husband some time to cool off. She and her mother had spent most of the night talking about Ryan. Sarah was suspicious. Partly it was because of things Brent had said, but not entirely. It seemed Ryan was keeping her in the dark, maybe for his own purposes. Jeanette had let her eavesdrop on this morning's phone call to ease her concerns.

Her slippers shuffled along the floor as she moved from the living room to the kitchen. She stopped in the doorway and glared at her mother. She was accusatory, not quizzical. "Why didn't you let him talk?"

Jeanette sipped her coffee, then grimaced. It was cold. "What do you mean?"

"You wouldn't let him tell you what he found out."

"I didn't want to know."

"Well, *I* want to know."

"I'm sure he'll tell you."

Sarah groaned, exasperated. "That was the whole point of letting me listen in on the phone call, Mom. To see if he would tell you things he wouldn't tell me."

Jeanette refilled her coffee cup and returned to her chair. "I'm sorry. I'm not going to get involved in this just to eliminate your crazy suspicions about your own brother."

"It's not crazy." Her eyes narrowed. "Are you with him on this?"

She stopped in mid-sip. "What?"

"Neither one of you wants me to know what's going on."

"That's ridiculous."

"You two are together on this. As soon as I walk out that door, you'll call him right back and get all the information. You're leaving me out of the loop."

"Sarah, get hold of yourself. This is your family you're talking about."

"Mom, I was on the phone. I heard, okay? All he had to do was mention Brent's name and you start talking about some silly receptionist in Lamar. Is that the problem? You're afraid of Brent? Or do you not trust *me*, either?"

"Of course I trust you, Sarah. And your brother does, too."

"Then why didn't he tell me about that woman named Amy?"

"What woman?"

"The woman who Dad sent some money to in a box. She went to see Ryan, and he never told me. Then she came to see me."

Jeanette shook her head vigorously. "I don't want to know about that. I'm sure Ryan had his reasons."

Sarah came to the table and sat across from her. It was clear her mother didn't want to discuss it, but she wouldn't let it go. "She came here to Piedmont Springs. I talked to her. Says Dad sent her a thousand dollars in a box. I got bad vibes from that woman. Real nervy-like. I didn't like her. Didn't like her at all."

Jeanette said nothing.

Sarah said, "She had an attitude. Came on too strong for my taste. Like she was entitled to something. Like she was part of the family or something."

Jeanette stared down into her coffee cup. Her hands were shaking, as if she were bracing herself for the worst.

"Mom, I need to ask you something. Was Dad ever unfaithful to you?"

Silence fell between them. Sarah tried to catch her eye, but her mother wouldn't look up. Finally, she answered in a voice that was almost inaudible. "That's a very personal question."

"Was he?"

"I don't see what that has to do with anything."

"A man can't have an illegitimate Amy, unless he was unfaithful."

She nodded slowly, reluctantly. "Now that you put it that way, I'll answer as best I can."

Sarah watched her mother struggle for words, then put her question more firmly. "Well, was he?"

Jeanette looked her daughter in the eye. "I think he could have been."

At 7:35 A.M. Amy was on her way to the office. Morning traffic was heavy on Arapahoe, but she was traveling on automatic pilot, deep in thought.

She had been up all night. The drive home from Coors Stadium had seemed like a blur. It wasn't until 3:00 A.M., hours after she'd put Taylor to bed, that she'd even stopped shaking. She couldn't talk about it, didn't even tell Gram. Four different times throughout the night she'd picked up the telephone to call the police. Each time she'd hung up before she'd finished dialing, the words of her attacker echoing in her ear.

You ever talk to the police again, it's your daughter who pays.

252

She wondered who the man was, if he had children of his own. Could one parent actually utter such words to another? Of course. That was how children grew up to be creeps like this. They were everywhere, she knew, people who could hurt children. No one had ever threatened *her* child, however, at least not directly. She remembered how horrified she'd felt when another pretty little girl had been murdered in Boulder. It had happened miles from their apartment when Taylor was just a baby. As a mother in the same city, she had felt threatened, even violated. This morning, she felt terrified.

But she had to do something.

She stopped at the traffic light. A restaurant marquee across the street advertised a Friday fish fry. Tomorrow *was* Friday—one week after her meeting with Ryan Duffy. The deadline was up. He was supposed to explain the money. Maybe he could explain who had jumped her in the parking lot.

And to think she had initially hoped to get to know him better. *Fool.*

She steered into the corner filling station and stopped at the pay phones by the vending machines. She checked her Filofax for the number and dialed it. On the fourth ring, she got an answering machine.

She thought before speaking. She wanted to get her point across, but she had to be vague in case a secretary or someone other than Ryan retrieved the message.

"Dr. Duffy," she said in a businesslike tone. "It's time for our follow-up appointment.

Meet me at the Half-way Café in Denver. Tonight at eight o'clock. I'm sorry this can't wait until tomorrow. It's important."

She hung up and drew a deep breath. *Very important.*

38

Amy arrived in Denver a few minutes early. Traffic out of Boulder wasn't as bad as she had expected, and, unlike most days at the office, no one had snagged her on the way to the elevator with some end-of-the-day crisis.

The Half-way Café was a trendy downtown restaurant-bar off Larimer Square. It had started as a popular lunch spot for the office crowd, which explained the name. "Meet me at the Half-way" was a cutesy play on "meet me halfway," a saying often heard in business. The owners, however, soon found that the "halfway" theme offered endless possibilities. Half-priced dinners. Half-priced drinks. It all contributed to a booming business. Amy had picked it for tonight's meeting only because it was a well-known place, easy to find. In hindsight, she worried that Ryan might read something into her selection of the Half-way, like the makings of a deal—or a relationship.

Amy reached the restaurant at 7:50. She considered leaving her name with the hostess, but Ryan already knew what she looked like. He could find her easily enough. She walked past the lively restaurant section to the bar and took the last available booth in the back. She waited alone, surrounded by oxblood leather. The music was a little too upbeat for her mood. At the table beside her, a foursome was laughing over salty popcorn and draft pilsners from the microbrewery. Two other guys were making fools of themselves arguing over a game of electronic darts. Behind the century-old oak bar was a big-screen television. The baseball game was playing. Amy looked away, harrowed by the reminder of last night's attack in the parking lot. She checked the blackboard menu without interest. She was suddenly too nervous to read, let alone eat.

The waitress arrived in less than half a minute—another hallmark of the Half-way Café. "Just one tonight?"

Amy started, then relaxed. "No, I'm waiting on someone."

"Can I bring you something to drink in the meantime?"

"I'll just have coffee, please."

"Half-cup or full cup?"

She gave a funny look. "Full, of course."

"One double coffee," the waitress mumbled as she scribbled in her pad.

"No, not a double. Just one regular-size cup."

"A double is one cup."

"That's confusing."

"Not if you're at the Half-way Café."

"Ah," said Amy. "So a half-cup would actually be a quarter-cup?"

"No. A half-cup would be a half-cup."

"But you just said a double cup is a single cup."

"No. A double *coffee* is a single cup. A double *cup* is two cups. A single coffee is a half-cup and—"

"I think I got it," Amy interrupted. "Why don't you just bring me the pot?"

"Half-pot or—"

"Never mind."

Amy rolled her eyes discreetly as the waitress walked away. *Should have called this place the Half-brain Café.*

"May I join you?"

Amy turned at the sound of his voice. It was Ryan.

"Please," she said.

He slid into the booth and sat directly across from her, nearly banging his head on the low-hanging Tiffany-style lamp. Amy took a good look at him, studying his features more intently this time. If ever she were required to describe him, she wanted to do an ample job. A general "handsome" wouldn't do.

Ryan caught her stare. "I feel like I'm in a police lineup," he said, making light.

"Should you be?"

"Whoa. Not exactly picking up where we left off last week, are we?"

"Here we are..." The cheery waitress brought Amy her coffee, then glanced at Ryan. "Something for you, sir?"

Amy jumped in, averting another go-round with Half-Brain. "He'll have what I'm having.

Not half of what I'm having. Not double what I'm having. *Exactly* the same thing."

"*Sor-ree.*" The waitress backed away, then disappeared.

Ryan asked, "What was that all about?"

"My apologies," she said with a hint of sarcasm. "I've had a pretty tough week. As I'm sure you're aware."

"I honestly don't have any idea how your week was."

"Do you expect me to believe that?"

"Yes."

She watched his expression, searching for signs of deception. The fact that he had even shown up, she realized, said much about that. Why would he have even bothered to come if he'd known her apartment had been ransacked and the money stolen?

She tried another tack. "Your sister is definitely an interesting person."

"My sister?"

"You two seem very different."

"You...talked to my sister?"

She checked his eyes this time. He seemed genuinely unaware. "We talked while you were away on your business trip. At least your mother said it was a business trip."

"You talked to my mother, too?"

"Just on the phone. I tricked her, actually. She didn't know who I was."

"So you met Sarah separately?"

"Yeah. I went down to see her. Don't you Duffys talk to each other?"

"Evidently not."

The waitress brought Ryan his coffee, gave Amy a half-smile, then disappeared.

Amy asked, "So, how was your so-called business trip?"

"Interesting."

"What a word. Interesting. Sex is interesting. The Holocaust is interesting." She glanced at the game on the television set. "Baseball is interesting. In fact, the walk back to your car after the game can be very interesting."

"What in the world are you talking about now?"

She searched again. Either he really knew nothing, or he was an extremely talented actor. "Nothing," she said. "I assume your business trip had something to do with our talk last Friday. Can you prove to me that the money came from a legitimate source?"

"Unfortunately, no."

"We agreed that if you couldn't prove it was legitimate, I'd go to the police."

"That's not in either of our interests."

Amy leaned forward, bluffing. "I'm not fooling around, Ryan. If you can't prove to me that it's legitimate, I have to turn this money over to the police."

"I believe you. I swear I do."

She played it cool. *He really doesn't know I no longer have the money.* "I hope you aren't just stalling."

"I'm not. What I'm trying to do here isn't easy. And to be honest, I'm sensing a lot of hostility from you that wasn't there last week, and it isn't making this any easier."

"Okay," she said, backing off a bit. "What is it you're trying to say?"

He lowered his eyes, unable to meet hers. "I have a feeling this whole thing is leading to something that is very personal to both of us."

She withdrew, confused. She had come here expecting a confrontation. Instead, he was soft-spoken, considerate, seemingly honest. The circumstances were horrible, but maybe the nice guy she remembered from the Green Parrot was the real Ryan after all. *He's definitely cute.* "Personal?" she said, flustered.

"Yes."

It sounded as if he was about to ask her on a date. "You mean—you and me?"

He looked lost, then embarrassed. "Oh, no. I wasn't suggesting—you know."

"No, of course not. That would be...inappropriate. Don't you think?"

"Highly."

"Yes. Absolutely."

They shared an anxious glance. Amy seemed troubled by the way that exchange had just gone. Ryan seemed troubled by what he was about to say.

"What is it?" asked Amy.

"I hate to go into this, but I have to."

Her anxiety only heightened. "Go on."

"Maybe it's just my nature, but I can't help but ask, *why* did this money bring you and me together?"

What was he getting at—destiny? "I don't know."

"From my standpoint, the more I look into the money, the more I learn about my father. So I'm just wondering if you might learn something, too. About somebody in your own family. Maybe there's a relative you have always wondered about. Somebody you'd like to know more about."

Her thoughts immediately turned toward her mother. "Maybe."

"This might be your chance. That's all I'm saying."

Her eyes narrowed. This was suddenly headed in a direction she had never anticipated. Ryan had hit her most sensitive nerve. "If you know something about my mother, say it."

"So, there is something you'd like to know about your mother?"

"Please, don't taunt me."

He hesitated, unsure of how far to take this. "Before I say anything more, Amy, I'd like to know something. Just answer this one question, okay? My dad was sixty-two years old when he died. How old is your mother?"

"My mother is dead."

"I'm sorry. How old would she have been if she were alive today?"

She thought for a split second. "Sixty-one."

"When did she die?"

"You said you had just one question."

"Sorry. This could be important for both of us. Just tell me, when did she die?"

"Long time ago. When I was eight."

"Did she ever live in Boulder?"

That was way too close to home. "What's

going on here? What does all this suddenly have to do with my mother?"

Ryan blinked nervously.

Her eyes turned soulful. She wasn't sure what he knew—or if he was just pushing her buttons. But after twenty years of wondering, she couldn't let an opportunity pass. "If you know something about my mother, I have a right to know."

His voice dropped. "Was your mother ever involved in a rape?"

"How do you mean, 'involved'?"

"I mean, was she ever the victim?"

Stunned silence. "Are you saying my mother was raped?"

His throat tightened. "It's possible. A long time ago. When she was a teenager."

"That far back? How would you know about it?"

He said nothing. Amy's tone sharpened. "How would you *know*?"

Ryan was struggling. "It's like I said. We're both learning some things here."

Her hands began to tremble. Her voice quaked. "Are you telling me that your father raped my mother? That's why he sent me the money?"

"I—" He couldn't say it. He could hardly think it, sitting right across from the daughter.

Her face reddened. A flood of emotions took over—rage toward the Duffys, disgust with the way she had earlier flirted with Ryan. "Oh, my God."

"Look, Amy."

"*Don't* even say my name." She slid out of the booth.

"Where are you going?"

"Away. Far away from you and your whole godforsaken family." She hurried from the table, nearly running from the bar.

"Wait, please!"

She heard his pleas but just kept going. A tear ran down her cheek as she burst through the double entrance doors. She turned at the sidewalk and headed the wrong way, any way at all, just to get away. More tears followed. Tears for her mother.

Great tears of sorrow for a rape that may have led to suicide.

39

Ryan didn't follow her out. Numbness took over, shutting out the sounds of a bustling bar. Amy's outrage had deepened his sense of shame. Until tonight, he'd focused mainly on the way a father's crime shaped the feelings of a son. Only now did he come to grips with the real victims.

It seemed repulsive now, the subtle way in which he had been taken with Amy the first time he had laid eyes on her. The son of a rapist attracted to the victim's daughter. Ironically, back at that first meeting in the Green Parrot, they had even talked about children who were destined to be like their parents. He wondered if something in his subconscious was fueling the demons inside him, flooding his mind with loathsome thoughts of his father raping her mother, thoughts of the son raping the daughter. Was there something genetically wrong with him? Or was this situation simply too weird for any man?

He wondered how and where it had happened. The backseat of a car? Somebody's house? Had his father used a weapon, some other form of coercion? Dad was a strong man. He was no lush, but he did drink more than most, especially at parties. Even so, Ryan had never seen him in a fistfight, never seen him abuse anyone, physically or verbally. He seemed happy with the man he was.

Seemed happy. Now that he was gone, it was looking more like an act. Dad had been happiest in group settings, making friends laugh, singing loudest at the piano. People loved him the way an audience loved a performer. Put him in a crowded room, and Frank Duffy would never shut up. Keep the topic light, and he was even great on the telephone. But face-to-face in a serious conversation, he wasn't much of a talker. On reflection, Ryan had gotten very few glimpses into his father's true feelings. Over the years, however, those little windows had stuck with him. Like the talk they'd had nearly two decades ago, on his parents' twenty-fifth wedding anniversary.

His father had been in a funk all day, working on the house, repairing some outdoor wiring under the roof easements. Ryan had always thought of his parents as happily married. On this momentous occasion, however, Dad wasn't exactly acting as if he would have done it all over again. Ryan caught up with him outside, standing twenty feet up on the ladder directly beneath the exposed wires. Ryan was on the ground, looking up.

"Dad, what are you doing up there?"

"Fixing this floodlight."

"That's not what I meant. Don't you think you should spend the day with Mom?"

He fumbled for his wire clippers, saying nothing.

"Dad, you're hurting Mom's feelings."

He paused. It was the most serious pause Ryan had ever seen in his father. Ryan was just eighteen years old and ready for college, trying to decide what to do about Liz, his high school sweetheart. Maybe his dad had sensed it was about time for some advice.

His father pointed at the wires dangling over his head. "See these?" he said from atop the ladder. "One of them's hot. Could even kill a man."

"Dad, be careful. Let me shut off the circuit breaker."

"Ah, don't worry. Let's just see what happens if I grab one."

"Dad, no!"

He grabbed it. "Nothing," he said, releasing it. "But what do you think will happen if I grab this other one?"

"Dad, stop playing around."

"What will happen, Ryan? What did I used to tell you, back when you wanted to be an electrician like your dad, rather than a college boy?"

"Dad, please just come down."

He smiled devilishly—then grabbed the wire.

"Dad!"

His father laughed. Nothing happened.

"Damn it! You scared the crap out of me. You said it was live."

"It is. But I'm standing on a fiberglass ladder. I'm not grounded. If you're not grounded, you can grab all the live wires you want. Understand what I'm saying?"

"Yeah, I get your point."

"Make sure you do, son. That Liz is a nice girl. But think ahead. Think twenty-five years ahead. Once you're grounded, that's it. No more wires."

Twenty years later, the analogy seemed just as crude—women as hot wires. But it was about as deep as Frank Duffy ever got. And now, with the rape come to light, it told Ryan much about the way his father felt about his own life choices, the decision to marry right out of high school and devote himself to one woman. It shed light on an even earlier conversation, when he and Ryan were admiring the mountains in the distance, when he'd told Ryan it wasn't his fault they were stuck in Piedmont Springs. His mother was the one with roots so deep she would never move away. Five generations of family history in Piedmont Springs. Because of that, they were *all* trapped here.

It was a grim excuse for living where they lived, as if his dad had banished himself to life on the plains. A man with one woman in an isolated world, where temptations were few.

It was a sentence of sorts. A self-inflicted punishment for one who had eluded formal judgment.

In the abstract, it seemed like a crazy notion. But now that Ryan was older and had made mistakes himself, he could relate. A real man had no tougher judge than himself. Like father, like son. But with one important distinction.

Ryan knew his father's sin. His father would never know Ryan's.

The waitress brought the bill. He paid quickly, then walked to the back of the bar near the rest rooms and stopped at the pay phones. He dialed Norm at home, getting right to Amy.

"How'd it go?" asked Norm.

"Better than expected. At least she didn't throw her scalding hot coffee in my face."

"That bad?"

"That bad."

"You want to talk about it?"

A young woman smiled at him on her way to the rest room. Ryan looked away. "Not right this second. Maybe in the morning. I think I'm going to spend the night at your place again, if that's all right."

"Sure. I'll wait up."

"See you in a few," he said, then hung up the phone.

From the doughnut shop across the street, she watched as Ryan Duffy emerged from the Half-way Café. She wore blue jeans, a baggy Denver Broncos sweatshirt, and a

266

shoulder-length blonde wig instead of the long black one. Her look was more like that of a college student than the businesswoman she'd played at the hotel in Panama City. It was unlikely that she'd be recognized. Still, she took pains not to flaunt her attractive face, peering over the top of the magazine.

Her eyes followed Ryan as he headed down the sidewalk and crossed the street. She rose from a table by the window, prepared to move in. She stopped in the doorway. The dark sedan at the corner was suddenly coming to life. The engine started. The lights went on. It slowly pulled away from the curb. She had first noticed it when Ryan had gone inside. For a good twenty minutes, the driver had just sat there. Now she knew why—the way it sprang into action the minute Ryan had passed.

Only a cop would be so obvious about a tail. *Son of a bitch.*

She stepped onto the sidewalk and headed the other way. She wasn't sure who had tipped off the police, Ryan or Amy. It didn't matter.

Whoever it was, they would both regret it.

Amy's old truck took her from Denver back to Boulder in record time. There was no real urgency. No one was chasing her. It was as if something horrible about her mother had been spilled back in Denver. Amy just couldn't get away fast enough.

She parked haphazardly in the last available space outside her apartment and hurried upstairs. For a split second she was thinking how good it felt to be home, but she quickly realized it was a home she no longer recognized. It had never been luxurious by any stretch of the imagination, but she and Gram had worked hard to make it pretty. The Bokhara rug they had saved for. The pink sky and stars she'd hand-painted in Taylor's bedroom. Antiques from the flea market, decorative things Gram had collected over the years. All their extra little touches had been trashed in the break-in. Now it *looked* like the cheap subsidized apartment it really was, with junky rental furniture that belonged in a ghetto.

Amy stopped outside her door to collect herself. She thought of Taylor inside, sleeping like an angel. She *was* an angel. *So stop feeling so damn sorry for yourself.*

She unlocked the door and stepped inside. Gram was sitting at a card table chair watching a Thursday night sitcom. They had no replacement couch yet. Amy walked to the TV and shut it off.

Gram looked startled. "I thought it was Taylor who had the limit on television time."

"Is she asleep?"

"Yes. About thirty minutes now."

"Good." She pulled up another chair and faced her grandmother. "I have to ask you something. It's important."

Gram looked at her with concern. "Have you been crying, dear?"

"I'm okay. Gram, you have to be completely straight with me. Do you promise?"

"Yes, of course. What is it?"

"This may sound like it's out of left field. But I have to know. Was my mother ever raped?"

Gram seemed to sway in her chair, overwhelmed. "What makes you think she was?"

"No, Gram. That's not being straight with me. I can't have questions answered with questions. Let's try it again. Was my mother ever raped?"

"I'm not being evasive. I just—"

"Straight. Yes or no."

"I don't know. How *would* I know? You keep asking me like I should know. I don't. I swear I don't."

Amy fell back in her folding chair. It was like hitting a brick wall. "I'm sorry. I didn't mean to sound so accusatory. If anyone would know, I just thought it would be you."

"I'm sorry. I don't. It's horrible if it's true. But why is it suddenly important?"

She scoffed, as if the answer should have been obvious. "Because I've been wondering all my life why Mom would kill herself. This doesn't explain everything, but it's the only promising lead I've ever come across."

"Where did it come from?"

"I talked to Ryan Duffy again. I think that's why they sent me the money. I think his father raped my mother."

Gram turned philosophical. "The price of easing a dying man's conscience."

"That's what I'm thinking."

"I wish I could help," said Gram.

"So do I. The people who definitely would

know are all gone. Mom's dead twenty years now. Grandma and Grandpa have been dead even longer. I don't know if Dad would have known or not. I guess I was hoping you'd heard something from someone."

Gram shook her head. "You and I are close, dear. We tell each other everything. But don't let that give you a false impression of the relationship I had with your mother. It wasn't a bad relationship. But basically, I was her mother-in-law."

"I understand."

"There must be another way to tackle this. When was the rape supposed to have happened?"

"Before Mom and Dad ever met. Sometime when she was a teenager, Ryan said."

"Then that's where you need to look. Go back in time. Check with people your mother might have confided in. Her classmates, her girlfriends."

The word hung in the air, as if the mere mention of "girlfriends" had struck the same chord in both of them.

Gram asked, "Are you thinking what I'm thinking?"

Her eyes brightened. "Only if you're thinking of Marilyn Gaslow."

40

Ryan sat in silence amidst a seventy-inch television screen and surround-sound speakers that stood four feet tall. With all the electronic toys turned off, the media room was the ideal place in Norm's huge house for a confidential conversation. It was soundproof with no windows, putting even the most paranoid at ease. In here, Norm had heard some of the most acoustically perfect confessions in the history of American criminal defense law—including one from Ryan eight years ago.

Tonight, however, Ryan had only Amy on his mind.

"Want a beer?" asked Norm.

Ryan was sitting on the couch, still shell-shocked from the full-blown explosion at the Half-way Café. "Huh?"

Norm took that as a yes and grabbed two from the minibar. He handed Ryan an open Coors and sat in the leather recliner facing the blank television screen. "Let's hear it. Tell me what the mysterious Amy had to say."

Ryan peeled the label on his bottle. "Not a whole lot. She was just...angry is the only way to describe it. Which is understandable. She thinks my father raped her mother."

"So, let me get this straight. She knew her mother had been raped, but she didn't know your father had done it?"

"No. I don't think she knew anything about a rape at all. I implied that my father might have raped someone she knew. She inferred it was her mother. It was the age similarity, I guess. Her mom is dead, but she would have been about the same age as my father. When I asked if her mother ever lived in Boulder, she wouldn't say. But I got the impression the answer was yes."

"Too bad we don't know Amy's last name. We could check those old yearbooks from Boulder High School, see if your father and her mother were classmates."

"Amy's name isn't the key. We need to know her mother's maiden name." Ryan sipped his beer, thinking. "You know, it might be worth a look at those yearbooks anyway. It's a long shot, but maybe Amy looks like her mother. I might be able to pick her out."

"You're right. That is a long shot."

"You got a better idea?"

Norm shrugged. "We can check them out tomorrow. The copies I made are photo-quality, so I don't see any burning need to drive all the way to Boulder to check the originals."

"I'd like to do it tonight. You want to go downtown?"

"They're not in the office. My investigator has them. He's still working on that background search of your father's classmates, looking for the kid who grew up rich enough to pay five million dollars in extortion."

"Call him. Maybe he can bring them by here. If I'm going to look for a woman who looks like Amy, I'd really like to do this tonight, while Amy's face is fresh in my mind."

Norm checked his watch. Not quite

nine-thirty. "I guess it's not too late to ask. He lives just a few minutes away from here."

Ryan only half listened as Norm placed the call. He leaned back on the couch and waited. He noticed his reflection on the dark television screen. It was barely perceptible. Norm's was even fainter, standing in the background and talking on the phone. It was a blurry image, yet in some ways it seemed clear. It was like watching himself from another time—déjà vu on the big screen, taking him back to the last time he had sought advice from his friend Norm. It didn't feel like eight years ago. Ryan was a resident at Denver General. A prominent professional athlete had checked into the hospital for surgery. Turned out he was HIV-positive. Back then, infected athletes worried about being banned from the playing field. His illness was a well-guarded secret. He'd told Ryan, as his doctor, to make sure it stayed a secret. He forbade Ryan to tell anyone—even the unsuspecting wife.

"All set," said Norm. "My investigator will be here with the yearbooks in ten minutes."

Ryan was still staring at the dark screen, not really focusing.

Norm snapped his fingers. "Hello, Earth to Ryan."

He looked up, smiled with embarrassment. "Sorry. Spaced out for a second there."

"Where'd you go?"

He sighed, not sure he wanted to tell. "Little time warp. I was just thinking about that time I came here eight years ago. Back during my residency."

"Ah, yes. The night you began your descent into Purgatory Springs."

"You mean Piedmont Springs."

"No, I mean purgatory. That's what it is for you, isn't it? You work for hardly any pay, do good deeds for the needy little people of the world, earn your place back in heaven. Sounds like purgatory to me."

"That's ridiculous."

"No, it's not. You and Liz were on the verge of having it made. Then poof, you walk away from it and go back to Piedmont Springs. I said it before, and I'll say it again. It's not your fault that guy's wife ended up with AIDS. The law prohibited you from telling anyone that your patient was HIV-positive."

"Yeah," he said with sarcasm. "I sure played that one right by the book."

"I don't know how else you could have played it. You had a duty to your patient."

Ryan shook his head, exasperated. "Just like I have a duty to my dad, right? A duty of loyalty. I'm supposed to keep my mouth shut and tell no one his dirty little secrets, even the people who have the right to know."

"I don't think the two situations are quite the same. But even if they were, you went the other way this time. You told Amy about the rape."

"Exactly. Last time I followed my technical duty right down the line. Which turned out to be a death sentence for an innocent woman. So this time I crossed the line. I put the victim ahead of my sense of duty. And it blows up in my face. Amy seemed totally

274

shocked to find out her mother had been raped. Her mother obviously had never told her. Presumably, that was the way her mother wanted it. What right did I have to step in and upset her mother's wishes?"

"These are tough dilemmas, Ryan. Both situations. Very tough."

"And I made the wrong decision both times."

"So what are you going to do now? Pack up your clinic in Purgatory Springs and move to Siberia?"

Ryan glared. "You think this is a joke?"

"No. You're being too hard on yourself. You're dealing in areas where there are no right answers. I take that back," he said, raising a finger for a case in point. "There was one option that would have been clearly the wrong decision. Ten years ago, you could have blackmailed that jock after you learned he was HIV-positive."

"That wasn't an *option*," he said, scowling.

"Your father might have considered it."

"Go to hell, Norm."

"Sorry. Let's just forget I said that, okay?"

"No, let's not forget it. If you think my old man was a scumbag, just come out and say it."

"I'm not passing judgment. I suppose sometimes even blackmailers have their reasons."

"But you can never justify rape."

He could see the pain in Ryan's face. "No, you can't."

"That's why I had to tell Amy—or at least

try to tell her. It seemed like the right thing at the time. Now when I see the agony this must be causing her, I'm not so sure. Maybe she was better off not knowing."

"Do yourself a favor, Ryan. Put it behind you. Telling Amy about the rape wasn't the hard decision anyway. You'll get a second chance to think this through and do the right thing."

"What do you mean?"

"We still have to meet with the FBI. The tough question is, do you tell *them*."

Ryan looked away, shaking his head. "Another one, huh?"

"Another one what?"

He answered in a hollow voice. "Another situation where there's no right answer."

41

Amy called Marilyn Gaslow at her home in Denver, but her housekeeper said she was out of town through Monday. Fortunately, Amy was on the standing short list of people who could reach Marilyn anywhere in case of a true emergency. It was a privilege Amy had never invoked—until tonight.

"Miss Marilyn is staying at the Mayflower Hotel in Washington," said her housekeeper.

Amy got the number, thanked her, and dialed the Mayflower. The hotel operator put her through to the room.

Marilyn's seventh-floor suite was furnished with handsome early-American reproductions. The shirt-stripe wallpaper was Laura Ashley. A tasteful fox hunt photograph hung over the desk. Marilyn was alone in the king-size bed, clad in her favorite chenille robe, sitting up against the headboard with her feet propped up on a pillow. It was after midnight in Washington, but she was still awake and reading as the phone rang.

"Yes?"

"Marilyn, do you have a minute?"

"Amy?" she said, the familiar voice registering. "Is something wrong?"

"There's something very important I have to ask you. I wanted to it in person, but it really can't wait. At least, *I* can't wait. Is now a good time?"

Two black-binder notebooks lay on the bed beside her. Another was in her lap. "Amy, I don't mean to be difficult, but I have a big day ahead of me tomorrow. I'm still preparing, and I have to get some sleep."

"I'm sorry. I forgot you were two hours ahead of me."

"It's okay." She pushed the notebook aside. "Go ahead. What do want to ask me?"

"There's something I need to know about Mom."

The silence was suddenly palpable. Marilyn scooted to the edge of the bed, sitting erect. "Okay. What is it?"

"I met a man for coffee tonight. I think his father knew my mother."

"Who is he?"

"His name is Ryan Duffy. His father was Frank Duffy. It's the same Duffys I was telling you about before—the ones who gave me the money that was stolen from my apartment."

"I told you to let that go."

"I know. But I couldn't. And now look what I found out."

"Amy, please. Just listen to me, okay? Stay away from Ryan Duffy. Stay away from the whole Duffy family."

"You *know* them?"

"Just stay away from them."

Amy's voice shook. "So...it's true?"

"What's true?"

"Frank Duffy raped my mother."

"What?"

"That's what I think Ryan was trying to tell me. His father raped my mother."

"Frank Duffy didn't rape your mother."

"How do you know? Did you know Frank Duffy? Tell me if you did."

"Yes. I knew him when I was in high school."

"You went to high school together?"

"No. He went to Boulder High, I went to Fairmont."

"But you met him?"

"Yeah. You could say that."

"Why didn't you tell me before? You just sat there and pretended you didn't know him."

"I—I just couldn't."

"Because he raped my mother. And Mom didn't want me to know. That's *why*."

"Amy, I told you. Frank Duffy didn't rape your mother."

"How do you know that?"

"Your mother and I were best friends. We told each other everything."

"Mom never told you she was raped?"

"Never."

"That doesn't mean it didn't happen."

"Amy, I know it didn't happen."

"How could you possibly know for sure?"

"Trust me. I know."

"Marilyn, don't be coy with me. If this man raped my mother, I have a right to know."

"He didn't."

Her voice turned shrill, the way only family would shout at one another. "You're lying! Why are you lying to me?"

"I'm not lying."

"Then how do you know he didn't rape her?"

"Because..."

"Because *why*?"

"Because he raped *me*, Amy. Frank Duffy didn't rape your mother. He raped *me*."

Amy's hand shook as she gripped the phone. "Oh, my God. Marilyn, I'm sorry. I had no idea. I hope—"

"Forget it. Just forget all about it. It was a long time ago. I've put it behind me. And that's where I want it to stay. Promise me, Amy. We will never talk about this again. To anyone."

"But—"

"Amy," she said sternly. "*Never* again. I don't need this back in my life. Not now. Especially not now. Do you understand?"

Amy swallowed the lump in her throat. "Marilyn," she said weakly, "I only wish I understood."

42

Ryan stayed in the media room all night, studying the old yearbooks of Boulder High School. Norm had said the copies were photo quality, which didn't say much for the quality of the original photos. Eight hundred grainy black-and-white mug shots were enough to make anyone's eyes blurry. Even after a pot of coffee, it was difficult to stay focused. He'd never seen so many kids wearing glasses—*ugly* eyeglasses at that. A lot of people said television or the airplane was the greatest invention of the twentieth century. Some of these geeks made a pretty compelling case for contact lenses.

After a few hours, Ryan had developed a system. He would check the eyes first. Amy had bright, almond-shaped eyes. Then the bone structure. Amy's face was heart-shaped, the makings of a natural beauty. From there, the task got more difficult. Most of the girls in the yearbook were smiling. It made him think of his first meeting with Amy, how pretty her smile had been. He imagined her mother's was much the same.

Though neither Duffy had given them much to smile about.

By 5:00 A.M., Ryan had lost track of the number of times he'd been through the photographs. He'd studied so many faces he was beginning to forget what Amy actually looked like. He'd narrowed it down to about thirty possibilities, but he didn't feel confident that any of them were actually Amy's mother. He was about to close the book when something caught his eye. It was a name, not a face. A boy, not a girl.

Joseph Kozelka.

It was an unusual name, Kozelka. Yet it was familiar to him. After a moment, he placed it. There was an entire hospital wing in Denver that bore the same name—the Kozelka Cardiology Center. Ryan had seen the plaque in the lobby years ago, during his residency.

He looked carefully at the photograph. A nice-looking kid. Well dressed, one of the few wearing a coat and tie that actually seemed to fit him. How many Kozelkas could there possibly be in Colorado? If this kid was related, he was one rich son of a bitch. Rich enough to pay millions in extortion.

Ryan nearly leaped from the sofa and hurried out the door. The elevator was right outside the media room, but it was way too slow. Ryan hurried up the dark stairwell and tapped lightly on the door to Norm's master suite.

The door remained closed, but he could hear Rebecca's sleepy voice from inside. It was muffled, as if she were calling from beneath the covers. "Tommy, please go back to sleep. You're getting too old for this."

Ryan whispered, more out of embarrassment than anything else. "Uh, Rebecca. Sorry. It's Ryan. I have to talk to Norm."

He waited. Inside, there was mild grumbling,

then footsteps. The door opened about six inches. Norm was wearing a robe. That long strand of hair that covered the ever-growing bald spot was standing on end. His face was covered with stubble. "What the hell time is it?" he asked, yawning.

"Early. Sorry. I think I might have found someone at Boulder High who was actually rich enough to pay my dad the extortion money. Can we get on your computer?"

"Now?"

"Yes. This could be the break I've been waiting for."

Norm rubbed the sleep from his eye, slowly coming to life. "All right," he said as he stepped into the hall. "This way."

Norm led him down the hall to the upstairs office. A computer terminal rested atop a small built-in desk that was covered with bills and magazines. Ryan spoke as it booted up.

"His name's Joseph Kozelka. Unusual name. I'm hoping we can pull up something on the Internet about him."

"Who is he?"

"I'm thinking he has to be related to the family who established the Kozelka Cardiology Center in Denver. They gave millions of dollars for construction and operation—*tens* of millions."

The screen brightened and Norm logged on. He went directly to an Internet search engine. "How do you spell his name?"

Ryan leaned forward and typed it in, then hit Enter. They waited as the computer searched databases all over the world for any information on Joseph Kozelka. It seemed to be taking forever.

Norm said, "It's conceivable we'll get goose eggs."

"I know. But if this guy has the kind of money I think he has, his name is bound to be out there at least a few times."

The screen flashed the results. Both Ryan and Norm did a double take. The computer-generated message read: "Your search has found 4,123 documents."

"Holy shit," said Ryan.

Norm scrolled down the abstracts of materials that mentioned Joseph Kozelka. Many of them were in Spanish. "Looks like he lived outside the States for a while."

"He wasn't just living there. Looks like he was head of the entire Central and South American operations for some company—K&G Enterprises. I never heard of them."

"Me neither. But if they do a lot of business south of the border, that might explain the Panamanian bank."

Ryan took the mouse from Norm and scrolled down himself, scanning the next group of entries.

"He sure has a lot to do with farming."

"When you get to his level, Norm, I think they call it commodities. Look at this."

The full text of a *Fortune* magazine article filled the screen. The title read "All in the Family." It was an exposé on a handful of "family-run businesses" whose sales rivaled companies like Coca-Cola.

" 'Joseph Kozelka,' " Ryan read aloud. " 'CEO and principal shareholder of K&G Enterprises, third-largest privately held corporation in the world. Estimated sales of over thirty *billion* dollars a year.' "

Norm said, "These are the kind of empires people never hear about because they're family owned. The stock isn't publicly traded. No public filings with the Securities Exchange Commission, no shareholders to hold them accountable. Nobody really knows how much they're worth."

Ryan scrolled further down the list of matches, then stopped when he saw something related to the Cardiology Center in Denver. He pulled up the full text. It was a description of the center, with bios of its directors—including Joseph Kozelka, president emeritus.

"Excellent," said Ryan. "This is what I wanted. A full bio."

"Yeah, I'll bet 'graduate of Boulder High School' is right up there on the top of his resumé."

"Shut up, Norm."

The bio slowly appeared on the screen, more than words. There was a photograph. It was the face of a man in his sixties. It was the aging smile of the kid in the yearbook.

"Look at those eyes," say Ryan. "That chin. Gotta be him." He scanned the bio for pertinent details. "Place of birth," he read aloud, "Boulder. Date of birth—same year as my dad. They had to be classmates."

"Fine. He's rich and he's your dad's age.

That doesn't mean he's the guy who paid the extortion."

"It's more than just that. Kozelka was born and raised in Boulder. He's my dad's same age. That means he and my dad were classmates the same year my dad committed rape. We know the extortion has something to do with rape, or the records wouldn't have been down in the safe deposit box in Panama. Logically, whoever paid the extortion should meet two criteria. One, he probably knew my dad in high school. Two, he definitely has to be financially secure enough to pay five million dollars. I defy you to find someone other than Joseph Kozelka who meets those criteria."

"Your logic is sound. But only if your criteria are correct."

"It's all I have to go on, Norm. Work with me."

They exchanged glances. Norm said, "Okay, it's possible. But where do we go from here?"

"We dig in. There's a ton of material right here on the computer. Something has to give us a clue as to whether he and my dad ever crossed paths."

"That could take a long time."

"I'm up for it."

Norm settled into his chair, thinking. "Maybe we can shortcut it."

"How?"

"I say we meet with the FBI, like we're supposed to. You remember what I said about quid pro quo, right?"

"Yeah."

"Well, before we take on a corporate shark

as big as Kozelka, let's see who else is fishing. And let's find out what they're fishing for."

Amy woke with fur on her face. It tickled at first, then frightened her. She swung her arm wildly, launching her attacker.

Taylor giggled as a stuffed Winnie the Pooh went flying across the bedroom. Amy sat up in bed, relieved it wasn't the real-live rat she had imagined.

"Don't you like bears, Mommy?"

"Yes, I love bears. But I like it better when *you* kiss me good morning."

Taylor crawled onto the bed and kissed her on the cheek. "Come on," said Taylor. "I'm making breakfast for you and Gram before you go to work."

"Thank you so much. I'll be right there in ten minutes." She sent Taylor off, then headed to the bathroom to brush her teeth. After a quick shower, she wrapped her wet hair in a towel and threw on her robe. She was awake, but she didn't quite feel like it. Last night's phone conversation still had her mind swirling. Marilyn had certainly put the kibosh on the theory that Ryan's father had sent Amy money to make amends for the rape of her mother. Things no longer made sense.

"Mom, breakfast!"

Taylor was shouting loud enough to invite the neighbors. But she was allowed. Gram didn't often turn her kitchen over to a four-year-old, and Taylor was always so proud of the special menu she came up with. Amy put her makeup bag aside and headed for the kitchen table. Her business face was not required for Cap'n Crunch and Kool-Aid.

Gram was seated at the table, eating her cereal and watching the morning news on television. Another place setting was arranged neatly beside her. Taylor was pouring the milk. "Skim milk for you, right Mommy?"

"That's right," she said with a smile. She pulled up a chair, then froze. A handsome young reporter on television was standing in front of the Mayflower Hotel in Washington D.C.

Gram said, "Hey, listen to this. They're talking about Marilyn."

Amy's pulse quickened. She reached forward and turned up the volume.

The reporter was saying something about Washington's worst-kept secret. "According to White House sources," he said, "Ms. Gaslow met yesterday with several of the President's high-ranking advisors. She will be meeting this morning with the President. If all goes well, we could possibly hear an announcement by the end of the day. Assuming she meets Senate approval, that would make Marilyn Gaslow the first woman ever to serve as chairman—make that chairwoman—of the Board of Governors of the Federal Reserve System."

The Denver anchor broke in, fumbling with his earpiece. "Todd, most of us hear about the Federal Reserve every day, but few of us understand it. Put Ms. Gaslow's appointment in perspective for us. How significant is this?"

"Very significant. The Fed is often referred to as the fourth branch of government, and that is no understatement. Through its seven-member Board of Governors, it sets the nation's monetary policy. It controls the money supply, it sets interest rates, it regulates the federal banking system, it engages in a host of activities that affect market conditions. Historically, it has received blame for the severity of the Great Depression in the thirties, and it has received credit for the relatively stable economic conditions of the sixties. In short, it determines the overall economic well-being of the most powerful nation on earth. If Marilyn Gaslow is approved as chairman, she would arguably become the most powerful woman in America."

"Are there any signs of Senate opposition to Ms. Gaslow's appointment?"

"None yet," said the reporter, "but in Washington, things can change in a hurry."

"Thank you very much," said the anchor, closing out the live report. The local coverage shifted to a traffic report.

Amy didn't move.

"Mommy, are they talking about the same Marilyn you work for?"

Amy nodded, but she was deep in thought.

"The most powerful woman in America," said Gram. "Boy, isn't that something?"

Amy blinked nervously. She had honored Marilyn's request to tell no one about their conversation—not even Gram.

"Yes," she said in quiet disbelief. "That is really something."

Part 3

43

At 10:00 A.M. Joseph Kozelka reached the K&G Building, a modern highrise that towered above downtown Denver. The ground-floor lobby was buzzing with men and women in business suits, the clicking of their heels echoing off the polished granite floors. Four banks of elevators stretched from one end of the spacious atrium-style lobby to the other. The first three were for tenants who leased the lower thirty floors from K&G. The last was for K&G visitors and employees only, floors thirty-one through fifty.

Kozelka stopped at the security check-point before the special employee elevators. The guard smiled politely, almost embarrassed by the routine.

"Good morning, sir. Step up to the scanner, please."

Kozelka stepped forward and looked into the retinal scanner. The device was part of K&G's high-tech corporate security. It could confirm an employee's identity based on the unique pattern of blood vessels behind the retina, like a fingerprint.

A green light flashed, signaling approval. The guard hit the button that allowed passage to the elevators.

"Have a good day, sir," he said.

Kozelka nodded and continued on his way.

It was the same silly charade every morning, part of Kozelka's self-cultivated image as a regular guy who tolerated no special treatment for anyone, including himself. Indeed, he never missed a chance to recount the story of the *former* security guard who had greeted him one morning with a respectful "Good morning, Mr. Kozelka," allowing him to sidestep the scanner. Kozelka fired him on the spot. To his cigar-smoking friends over at the Bankers Club, it was a perfect illustration of how, in Kozelka's eyes, the CEO was no better than anyone else. Never mind that a fifty-year-old faithful employee with a wife and three kids was suddenly on the dole. Kozelka didn't much care about the real-life sufferings of the peons he used to promote his image.

And it was all image. Equality and accountability simply weren't part of the K&G corporate lexicon. K&G had just two shareholders. Joseph held fifty-one percent. A trust for his children held the other forty-nine. The occasional talk on Wall Street of taking the company public never failed to make his lawyers giddy, but Kozelka wasn't interested. Shareholders would mean the loss of control. Kozelka didn't need the money he'd get from the sale of his stock. It was the control that drove him—control over a corporate empire that in one way or another was connected to one out of three meals served in North America daily, be it pesticides, produce, fertilizers, feed, grain, livestock, fish farms, or any other link in the food chain. The real money, however, came from commodities trading. Some would even say manipulation. Minute-by-minute activity on the market flashed beneath the crown moldings in Kozelka's penthouse office.

The elevator stopped on the thirty-first floor. Kozelka stepped off and transferred to a private executive elevator that took him to the penthouse office suite.

Half the top floor was his. The other half was divided among the remaining senior corporate officers—nonfamily members who served at the whim of Kozelka. No decorating expense was spared on either side of the hall. The doors were polished brass. The walls were cherry paneling. Sarouk silk rugs adorned floors of inlaid wood. The mountain views were nothing short of breathtaking, though Kozelka was thoroughly immune to them. For twenty years he'd commanded the same magnificent view, ever since his father had died and turned the desk, the office, and the thirty-billion-dollar family-owned company over to his son.

"Good morning, Mr. Kozelka," his secretary said.

"Morning."

She followed him into his office, taking his coat and briefcase. She had his morning schedule laid out on the desk for him, beside his coffee. Fridays were typically light, ever since his doctor had warned him about his blood pressure. He reviewed the schedule as he reclined in his leather chair.

His secretary stopped in the doorway on her way out. "One other thing, sir."

"Yes?"

"I wasn't sure I should even mention this, but there's a man in the visitor's lobby who says it is very important that he see you this morning. When I told him he would need an appointment, he said you would be expecting him. He's been waiting two hours. I was going to call Security, but I wanted to check with you before making a scene."

"Who is it?"

"He's a doctor. Dr. Ryan Duffy."

Kozelka said nothing, showed no emotion.

"Sir, what would you like me to tell him?"

"Nothing," he said, reaching for his phone. "Just close the door on your way out, please. I'll take care of this myself."

Norm had an early-morning hearing in criminal court and didn't reach his office until mid-morning. It seemed to have come as somewhat of a surprise to Ryan, but he actually did have other clients with other cases. Norm hung his suit coat behind the door. He was only halfway to his desk when his secretary appeared in the open doorway.

"Judge Novak's chambers is on line one," she said.

"Novak?"

"The judge in Dr. Duffy's divorce case."

What now? he thought, then picked up. "Hello."

The judge's deputy was on the line. "Mr. Klusmire, I have Phil Jackson on a conference call. Since Mr. Jackson's injuries prevent him from coming to the courthouse in person, the judge has agreed to hold a telephonic hearing on his emergency motion to reschedule the deposition of Brent Langford. Please hold for the judge."

Norm heard the click of the hold button. He and Jackson were alone. "Emergency motion? What kind of rescheduling you talking about?"

"If you knew anything about practice in family court, Klusmire, you'd know that the rules don't allow us to take a deposition on a Saturday. I originally set Brent's deposition for Thursday of next week, but I have to depose him tomorrow."

"Why?"

"Because his depo could lead to evidence that your client is responsible for the injuries that put me in the hospital. If that proves to be the case, I need to get a restraining order issued as soon as possible to protect both me and my client from any further abuse at the hands of Dr. Duffy."

"What in the world are you talking about?"

"It's all in the papers I filed. Check your in box, chump."

Norm hadn't even checked the morning mail. He riffled through the pile, found an envelope from Jackson's office, and tore it open. It took only a second to see what Jackson was really up to. The rescheduling of the deposition was secondary. His primary objective was simply to poison the judge's mind with wild accusations against Ryan.

That son of a bitch.

The judge joined them on the line. "Good morning, gentlemen. I've read Mr. Jackson's papers. Excellent, as usual. Mr. Klusmire, on what grounds are you opposing the motion?"

"Your Honor, if I could just have a minute to read through it. I haven't really had a chance to consider it."

Jackson jumped in. "Judge, the motion was hand-delivered to Mr. Klusmire's office last night. It was plainly marked as urgent. In my cover letter I urged him to call me here at the hospital by 9:00 A.M. if he would agree to let me take the deposition on Saturday instead of Thursday of next week. I hate to burden the court with an emergency motion on a simple scheduling matter, but Mr. Klusmire never called me. I had no choice but to petition the court."

The judge grumbled. "Mr. Klusmire, I've never met you, but this is the second time we've talked on the telephone. The first time was the other night when you called me at home, in direct violation of my rules against *ex parte* communications."

"Judge, I swear I was paged by—"

"*Never* interrupt me," he said harshly. "I don't like the way you practice, Mr. Klusmire. Good lawyers don't call judges at home. And they don't force other lawyers to seek emergency relief from the court where good old-fashioned courtesy and cooperation should enable the lawyers to work things out themselves."

"That's what I always say," said Jackson.

"Now," the judge continued, "I've read the

affidavit Mr. Jackson submitted in support of his motion, and I must say I am deeply disturbed. If Dr. Duffy and his brother-in-law are in any way responsible for this attack against Mr. Jackson, I want to put a stop to this before somebody else gets hurt. The request to take the deposition of Brent Langford a few days early is entirely reasonable. In fact, if Mr. Jackson weren't injured, I would dispense with the deposition and proceed directly with a hearing on whether a restraining order should be imposed against Dr. Duffy."

"Judge," said Jackson, "I'm feeling better already. If the court has room on its busy calendar for an evidentiary hearing, I owe it to my client to be there."

"Are you sure you're up for it? Physically?"

"Yes. It was a mild concussion. Believe it or not, having your face smashed against a windshield looks a lot worse than it is."

The judge growled. "I can't believe they did this to you. I rarely schedule a Saturday hearing, but in this case I'll make an exception. Can you have your witnesses here at ten o'clock tomorrow?"

"I believe so."

Norm said, "Your Honor, Dr. Duffy will certainly be there. But if Mr. Jackson intends to question Mr. Langford, I can't guarantee he will attend. I have no control over him. He's not a party and he's not my client."

"Mr. Klusmire, if you know what's good for you, your client will *make sure* that his own brother-in-law is in my courtroom tomorrow morning. Do I make myself clear?"

"Yes."

"Thank you, Judge," said Jackson.

"Good day, gentlemen." The judge disconnected, leaving only the lawyers on the line.

Norm shook his head. "You're everything people say you are, aren't you, Jackson?"

His face hurt, but Jackson managed a smile. "Everything—and then some."

"This hardball stuff really isn't necessary."

"But it is," he said, his smile fading. "This isn't the Liz and Ryan Duffy soap opera anymore. *This* is personal. I'll see you in court."

44

The wait was going on two and a half hours. Ryan took it as a good sign that he hadn't been thrown out of the building yet. Even better, he hadn't been thrown *off* it. He could wait all day, if he had to. The visitors' lobby was certainly comfortable enough. The leather couches weren't the stiff grade found in family rooms. These were as soft and supple as driving gloves.

Ryan had thought hard before coming directly to K&G headquarters. Last night, Amy's reaction had convinced him of one thing. He couldn't live with the money without knowing the truth. There was no honor in profit at the expense of a raped woman. He had to know how the rape was connected to the extortion.

Ryan's father was dead. Amy's mother was dead. The only living person who could possibly hold the answer was the man his father had blackmailed. Ryan couldn't be a hundred percent sure that it was Joseph Kozelka, but Norm's investigator had not identified a single other person in the Boulder High yearbook who had acquired the financial wherewithal to pay that much money. True, he and Norm had agreed they would talk to the FBI before moving on Kozelka. Waiting, however, would deprive Ryan of his leverage. The threat of *going* to the FBI and dropping Kozelka's name seemed like the only way to get Kozelka to tell him if he in fact had paid the money to Frank Duffy—and more important, *why*.

He knew what Norm would say. It was risky, maybe even dangerous. Somehow, however, his father had managed to keep the scheme going and keep himself alive for some twenty years. Ryan would take those odds. Still, he couldn't tell Norm in advance and give him the chance to talk him out of it. This time, Ryan was on his own.

"Dr. Duffy?"

It was a baritone voice from behind. Ryan rose from the couch and turned. The sheer size of the man suggested he was from corporate security. "Yes," said Ryan.

"Come with me."

They walked side by side down the hall in silence. Ryan stood over six feet, but he felt small next to this guy. He was easily six-five and solidly built. Not like those upper-body freaks at the gym with Herculean chests and legs like Bambi. This man's build was proportional, more athletic. Ryan suspected a military background.

"Where are we headed?" asked Ryan.

He stopped and opened the solid oak door to a conference room at the end of the hall. "Inside, please."

It was an interior conference room, no windows. Eight leather chairs surrounded a rectangular walnut table. The lighting was soft and indirect.

He directed Ryan to the other side of the table. "Sit there."

Ryan noted how evenly his voice had carried. The sound in the room was like Norm's media room—acoustically perfect. The room had that sleek look of those counterespionage corporate conference rooms he'd seen in magazines, with cameras hidden in wall clocks and anti-bugging devices throughout. Ryan was glad he hadn't come wired. It surely would have been detected.

The guard sat across from him. "Why did you come here?"

All doubts as to whether he had come to the right place were quickly evaporating. "I thought it was time we started a dialogue."

"Why?"

"Simply to put some issues to rest."

"There are no unresolved issues."

"There are for me. And I think Mr. Kozelka could clear them up for me."

"That's not going to happen."

"Why not?"

He leaned forward, shooting a steely glare. "Because Mr. Kozelka has no time for you."

Ryan was unfazed but suddenly noticed something. Just over the man's shoulder, behind him on the wall, was a very strategically placed painting. It was a hunch, but he felt certain that Mr. Kozelka was not only listening but watching—and probably recording.

With everything on tape, he had to be careful. The last thing he needed was to come off as an extortionist—like his father.

"I want you to give Mr. Kozelka a message. Tell him the woman in Panama who stole my bag made a big mistake. Tell him I have her fingerprints on a bar glass."

"Mr. Kozelka has no idea what you're talking about."

"Yes, he does. But that's not why I'm here. I came to thank him personally for all the advice he gave to my father over the years. No self-respecting small-town electrician should be without the services of an experienced consultant on matters of international bank secrecy."

The man's face reddened, but he said nothing.

Ryan said, "I'm almost embarrassed to say it, but I could use Mr. Kozelka's good advice, too. Ever since that mishap in Panama, the FBI wants to know all about my father's bank account in Panama. They are determined to find out where all that money came from."

Ryan checked for any reaction. It was subtle, but the mention of the FBI seemed to have hit a nerve.

"Now, I'll ask you again. Can I count on you to deliver a message to Mr. Kozelka?"

"I don't make promises."

"Fine." Ryan rose and faced the portrait on the wall—the hidden camera. He spoke directly to it. "Tell Mr. Kozelka I don't care about the money. I didn't ask for it, and I'm not here to ask for more. I'm not a criminal, and I'll do the right thing with or without the help of the FBI. All I want is a straight answer to a very simple question. Why. That's all I want to know. Tell him I want to know *why*."

He headed for the door and opened it, then stopped and glanced back. "And tell him one more thing. Tell him my appointment with the FBI is Monday. Ten o'clock.

"I can find my own way to the elevator," he said, closing the door behind him.

Amy took an early lunch off the beaten track of Boulder's Pearl Street Mall. With her mind still buzzing from Marilyn, she didn't necessarily want to be alone, just someplace where she was certain not to run into anyone from the law office.

She went to the Sink, one of her old college hangouts. In fact, it had been *everybody's* college hangout since the thirties, achieving a genuine claim to fame when a young Robert Redford quit as janitor, bagged UC-Boulder, and decided to try his hand at movies. The decor was organized graffiti. Youthful exuberance was the only way to describe the atmosphere. The food was of the munchies variety, with self-described "Ugly Crust Pizzas" a heavy favorite. Amy took one with pineapple topping and grabbed a small table by the window.

She glanced at the table beside hers. Two guys barely old enough to drink were making small talk with the girls, planning the weekend. Amy thought back to the days when weekends started after the last class for the week, sometimes on Thursdays if you could fix a schedule with no Friday classes. She hadn't had a real three-day weekend since—well, since college.

The television in the corner caught her attention. Noise from the lunch crowd made it inaudible, but she didn't need audio to know what was going on. Marilyn was standing beside the President outside the White House. A semicircle of smiling onlookers were applauding. It was official. Marilyn Gaslow had her nomination as chairwoman of the Board of Governors of the Federal Reserve. Now all she had to do was withstand the congressional approval process.

"Mind if I join you?"

Amy looked up. The face triggered no recognition. The only thing for sure was that he was the only person in the restaurant older than Amy. *Way* older. From the corduroy jacket and Bugle Boy pants, she would have guessed he was a professor.

"Do I know you?"

He put down his soda and joined her at the table. He extended his hand, introducing himself. "Jack Forsyth. FBI."

All she could say was "Oh."

"I hate to interrupt your lunch, but I would like to talk to you."

Amy froze. The warning outside the baseball stadium was all too fresh in her mind—how her daughter would pay if she talked to the police. But it was too late to get up and run. "Talk to me?" she asked innocently. "What about?"

"I think you know."

"I think you'd better tell me."

"We've been watching Ryan Duffy for several days now. And we've been monitoring his phone calls. We heard the message you left at his clinic. And we saw you meet with him last night in Denver."

Amy tried not to flinch. Her message had been intentionally vague, she recalled, just in case someone other than Ryan had listened to it. "So?"

"So, we've checked you out as well. We understand you were robbed recently. We spoke to the detective from the Boulder police. Says you were acting strange during his interview, as if you were holding back something."

"That's his opinion."

"Yes. It is a matter of opinion. But you know what? Just sitting here and watching your face for the last two minutes, I've formed the same opinion."

Amy looked away. It was a curse, that expressive face of hers. It wasn't just Gram who could read it.

The agent leaned closer. "Tell me. What are you doing with a guy like Ryan Duffy?"

She could sense his stare, but she didn't look, couldn't meet his eyes. She had too many reasons *not* to talk to him—the threat outside the stadium, and now Marilyn. She had promised Marilyn never to talk to anyone about the rape, and she knew that was where this would lead if she let the FBI in the door.

She gathered up her tray and rose, spilling her soft drink. "I have nothing to say to you," she said, flustered.

"You will. Take my card," he said, handing it to her. "Call me when you're ready."

Amy gave him a long look. She took the card without a word and walked away, never looking back.

45

Ryan went directly from K&G headquarters to Norm's office. Norm was working alone in the conference room, preparing for tomorrow's courtroom showdown. That Brent's deposition had blossomed into a full-blown evidentiary hearing came as a surprise to Ryan. Norm wanted to talk strategy with his client. Ryan, however, unloaded a surprise of his own—the meeting with Kozelka, or at least with his right-hand man.

Norm listened without interruption, but Ryan could tell he was steaming.

"Big mistake," said Norm. "I don't see an upside to a stunt like that."

"You got a better way to find out how my father committed rape and then turned it into blackmail?"

"You'll never find that out. Not from Kozelka."

"Had I already gone to the FBI, I would agree with you. But I made it very clear that I haven't said anything to the FBI yet. Kozelka can keep the FBI out of this just by giving me the information I want."

"Ryan, he's not an idiot. If you don't already know what information your father used to blackmail him, he's not going to tell you. He'd be giving you carte blanche to pick up where your father left off and keep on black-mailing him. He's probably back in his office doing cartwheels, delighted that your old man took the secret to the grave."

Ryan fell silent. "I hadn't really thought of it that way."

"Of course you haven't. You're a brilliant guy, but you haven't had a good night's sleep since sometime before your father died. You've hardly slept at all in the last four days. Your wife's divorcing you. Your block-headed brother-in-law appears to have beaten the crap out of her lawyer. Your sister's a pregnant squirrel. Your mother has her head in the sand. Your father's a convicted rapist. You've been chased by the Panamanian police. The FBI and the IRS are breathing down your neck. Need I go on? You have too much to think about. That's why you should listen to *me*, damn it. Or do you want to add 'FBI Most Wanted' to your list of woes?"

"So maybe I could have thought this through a little better. But Kozelka does appear to hold the key. I was afraid that once I went to the FBI, he might never talk. I'd never find the truth."

"The truth is, you made a terrible mistake. And you made it for one reason: you're still protecting your father."

"What are you talking about?"

"Your obsession right now is to find out why Kozelka paid your father all that money. One option is to cooperate with the FBI and let them interrogate Kozelka, but then you'd have to tell them your father was a rapist and extortionist. The other option is to barge into K&G headquarters like an idiot and demand to speak directly to Joe Kozelka yourself."

Ryan was suddenly angry, pacing the room. "Is it really that crazy to wonder why a man like Kozelka would pay a rapist five million dollars?"

"You're way too consumed by this rape question. Step back. You might even realize the blackmail has no connection at all to the rape."

"Then why would the rape conviction record have been in the same safe deposit box as the Panamanian bank records?"

"Maybe the rape simply explains why your dad gave a two-hundred-thousand-dollar chunk of the money to Amy Parkens. You said it yourself before—it could have been his way of making amends for what he did to Amy's mother. But the rape might have nothing to do with the reasons Kozelka or anyone else paid your father five million dollars."

Ryan considered the theory quietly, saddened by its plausibility. He could think only of the horrified look on Amy's face yesterday. "That would mean my father really did rape Amy's mother."

"Stop protecting your father, Ryan. It's time to start worrying about your own neck."

Ryan wanted to deny it, but the more the silence lingered, the more he realized: Norm was right. He answered in a calm, much quieter tone. "What's done is done, I guess. The good news is, I've at least confirmed that Kozelka is the source of the funds."

"And the really bad news," said Norm, "is that you still have no idea what your dad used to blackmail Kozelka. Yet you marched right into his building and left him with the distinct impression that the Duffy family is still blackmailing him."

"No way. I made it very clear that I wasn't after money."

"Blackmail doesn't have to involve money. In a general sense, any time you use threats to cause someone to act against their own free will, it's a form of extortion."

"I didn't threaten him."

"It was a veiled threat, Ryan. In essence, you told him to come up with the information you want by Monday at ten A.M., or you give Kozelka's name to the FBI."

"That's extortion?"

"Legally, it's a gray area. But if I were Kozelka, I'd take it that way."

"What should we do?"

"Wait. And brace ourselves. We're about to find out how Kozelka takes to threats."

Joseph Kozelka sat behind his desk, still fuming. The entire exchange in the conference room had been caught on camera, broadcast on closed circuit to the television monitor in his office. To say Dr. Duffy had angered him would be a gross understatement. Kozelka, however, wasn't the type to rant and rave. He stewed. Never alone. Always in the presence of those he held responsible. It was a power tactic that left subordinates melting with apprehension.

This afternoon, Nathan Rusch was one of those subordinates. He sat nervously on the couch, awaiting his boss's reaction.

Job security was a rare luxury at K&G, especially for someone like Rusch, whose job was totally result-oriented. Rusch wasn't part of K&G's regular corporate security. He was a special security operations consultant, a term that covered just about anything. If Kozelka needed protection on a trip to a Third World country, Rusch could assemble a team that rivaled the Secret Service. If a disgruntled former employee threatened to expose K&G trade secrets, Rusch was faster, cheaper and far more effective than any team of rabid lawyers. And if Kozelka was faced with blackmail, Rusch would tell him when to pay—and when to fight back.

Kozelka spoke in a controlled but biting tone.

"How could she be so stupid as to leave a glass with her fingerprints behind in the bar?"

"I don't know, sir."

"You're the one who hired her."

"It was on the quick. She came highly recommended."

"I don't see why you used her in the first place. You should have just snatched Duffy's bag yourself."

"We were hoping for more than just the bag. She's a very talented woman. We thought he'd be tempted. Maybe go back to her room, where she could get him talking. It didn't work out that way. Duffy didn't take the bait."

"Whatever. What's the worst-case scenario?"

Rusch hated to deliver bad news, but he was always honest with Kozelka. "Duffy gives the glass to the FBI at their meeting on Monday morning. The FBI gets a match on the prints and apprehends her. After that, it's in her hands."

"What do you mean, *her* hands?"

"She either tells the FBI nothing. Or she talks."

"What can she tell them?" He raised an eyebrow, threatening. "You didn't tell her anything. *Did you?*"

He gulped. "She couldn't operate totally in the dark. I told her a few things."

Kozelka leaned back in his chair. He didn't scream; it wasn't his style. But this time he was stewing so hard his eyes were bulging. "What did you tell her?"

"Just the essentials. Like I said, we were

hoping Duffy would pick her up in the bar, have a few drinks, get to talking. We had to give her some idea of what to pry out of him."

"Have you been in contact with her since Panama?"

"Yeah. I used her on surveillance here in Denver. For obvious reasons, I preferred to involve as few players as possible in this operation. Since she was already in the loop, I figured I'd use her again. She is good. Or so I'm told."

"Does she know too much? Is she dangerous?"

"I wouldn't go overboard with worry. This should take the FBI nowhere. All the glass proves is that she had a drink with Ryan Duffy in the bar. That's it."

Kozelka folded his hands atop the desk. "Unless she panics. Unless there's a warrant out for her arrest on six other unrelated scams we don't know about. Unless the FBI offers to wipe her slate clean if she'll tell them who hired her and what's going on in this case."

"That's possible. But it's premature."

"I have just one thing to say to you, Rusch." He leaned forward, staring him in the eye. "Don't let it happen."

46

The courthouse on Saturday was like church on Monday. Row after row of empty seats. Utter quiet in the halls. Lights and air conditioning were on in limited areas only. It had a way of making the proceedings seem both more and less important. It brought everyone in on their day off, but it was the last place anyone wanted to be.

With the exception of Phil Jackson. He seemed energized, if not happy.

Ryan tried not to look his way. He sat quietly beside his lawyer at the old mahogany table farthest from the jury box. Liz sat at the other table next to Jackson. While waiting for the judge, Ryan had glanced her way several times. He couldn't help it. She had yet to make eye contact.

"All rise," said the bailiff.

Judge Novak entered from a side door and stepped up to the bench. Norm had said he was old, but he looked even older than Ryan had expected. Huge age spots dotted his balding crown, like the markings on a globe. Hearing aids protruded from both ears. As he passed, Ryan noticed that he'd forgotten to zip up the back of his robe. Ryan looked away. It was hard to take a judge seriously knowing that his bony butt was clad in plaid Bermuda shorts. *So much for the judicial mystique.*

"Good morning," said the judge. "We're here

on the petitioner's emergency motion for a temporary restraining order. As I'm sure the lawyers have explained to their clients, there is no jury in this proceeding. I am the trier of both law and fact. A word of caution to the lawyers. Spare me the usual histrionics you might use in a jury case. I'm eighty-one years old. I've seen it all.

"Mr. Jackson, please call your first witness."

Jackson rose slowly, as if a little stiff in the joints. His face was slightly puffy. Other than the bandage over his eye, however, he showed few outward signs of the beating. Only on close examination was the faint purple discoloration on his cheekbone evident. It was hidden beneath the makeup. How vain did a guy have to be to wear makeup to an empty courthouse on a Saturday morning?

"Your Honor, our first witness is the petitioner, Elizabeth Duffy—"

Ryan did a double take. No wonder she hadn't looked at him.

The judge scooted forward in his chair. "Another word of caution," he said in a lecturing tone. "You may call your client to the stand, Mr. Jackson. But bear in mind that I have allocated only forty-five minutes for this hearing. I don't intend to sit here and listen to everything that was wrong with the Duffys' marriage. That is for another day. Keep the testimony limited to the issue in this hearing—that is, was Dr. Duffy involved in the attack on the petitioner's lawyer, and should a restraining order be imposed against Dr. Duffy to prevent any further attacks."

"Your Honor, I have one limited area of testimony I would like to cover with Mrs. Duffy. I promise it will take only a minute."

"Proceed."

Ryan watched carefully as Liz took the oath. She was dressed sharply in a Chanel suit. Either she'd sold her car or somebody had been fronting her some wardrobe money. She seemed nervous as she slid into the witness box. She still wouldn't look at him.

"Ms. Duffy, please state your name."

"Elizabeth Frances Duffy."

"And you are married to the respondent, Dr. Ryan Duffy, correct?"

The judge interjected. "Let's move it along. We can all stipulate they're married, she wants a divorce, blah, blah, blah. Get to the heart of the matter."

"Ms. Duffy, did you know Frank Duffy?"

"Yes, very well. Frank was Ryan's father. He died of cancer just two weeks ago."

"Did you have any conversations with him before he died? Specifically, any conversations about money?"

Norm sprang to his feet. "Objection. What does *that* have to do with the issues just framed by the court?"

"Your Honor, I would ask for a little latitude. If I fail to tie it all together with my next witness, you can deny my motion, hold me in contempt of court, and throw me in jail."

"*This* I can't wait to see," said the judge. "Proceed."

"Ms. Duffy," said Jackson. "Did you have any conversations with Frank Duffy about money?"

"Yes. We spoke on the telephone about two weeks before he died."

"Give us the gist of that conversation, please."

"Objection, hearsay."

The judge grimaced. "Isn't it enough that Mr. Jackson said I could throw him in jail if he didn't tie this together? Overruled."

Liz lowered her eyes, speaking softly. "Frank knew that over the years, Ryan and I had many disagreements over money. He always wanted me and Ryan to stay together. So, in this last conversation, he told me to hang in there. He said money would come soon."

"Did he tell you how much money?"

"No."

"Did he do anything to identify any specific funds?"

Liz looked up, glancing briefly at Ryan. Then she looked at her lawyer. "Yes."

Ryan felt a chill—more like a stabbing sensation. He recalled his conversation with Liz out on the front porch the night of the funeral. She hadn't mentioned *this*.

Jackson continued, "How did he identify the funds?"

"He gave me a combination."

"You mean for a lock?"

"Yes. He didn't say what it was for exactly. It was a very short conversation. He just, you know, intimated it had something to do with the money. He told me to check with Ryan. He would know."

"What was the combination?"

"Thirty-six-eighteen-eleven."

"Thank you, Ms. Duffy. That's all for now."

Liz rose slowly. Ryan watched, stunned. The numbers were right on. It was the exact combination to the briefcase in the attic. Dad had given her the combination. Not him. *Her.*

The judge looked across the courtroom. "Mr. Klusmire? Any cross-examination?"

Ryan caught his lawyer's eye. They could read each other's minds. This was dangerous territory. The FBI did not yet know about the two million dollars in cash in the attic. Any further examination could bust that secret wide open.

"No, Your Honor," announced Norm. "No cross."

"Mr. Jackson. Your next witness, please. And remember," he said, smiling thinly. "If you don't tie this together, there's a nice cold cell waiting for you."

"I'm confident I'll be sleeping in my own bed tonight, your honor. The petitioner calls Brent Langford."

Norm rose, speaking in his most apologetic tone. "Your Honor, I took your admonition on the telephone yesterday very seriously. We tried to bring Mr. Langford here. We called him repeatedly, never getting a response. Despite our most diligent efforts—"

He stopped in midsentence. All heads turned as the doors swung open in the rear of the courtroom. Brent was coming down the aisle. Norm and Ryan exchanged glances. The looks on their faces made it clear: This could not be good.

Brent's footsteps echoed in the near-empty

courtroom. He stepped through the swinging gate that separated the lawyers from the gallery, keeping his eyes straight ahead, looking at no one. His face was strained with concentration, even before he'd uttered a word. He looked like a school kid before an exam, trying to remember all the right answers.

As the bailiff administered the oath, Ryan could barely stomach the sight. There was Brent, promising to tell the truth, the whole truth, and nothing but the truth. Ryan had been there the last time Brent had staked his sacred honor before God and witnesses—a deadbeat pledging to love, honor, and cherish a woman he had beaten before and would beat again. Vows meant nothing to Brent. Nor did oaths.

"Mr. Langford, please state your name."

"Brent Langford."

"You are Dr. Duffy's brother-in-law, correct?"

The judge interjected again, louder. "Stipulations, Mr. Jackson, stipulations. I don't need the family history."

"Yes, Judge. Mr. Langford, you were served with a subpoena to appear at a deposition in this case, were you not?"

"Yes, I was. At my house in Piedmont Springs, last Tuesday afternoon."

"And it was your understanding that the person responsible for issuing that subpoena was me, correct?"

"That was my understanding."

"What did you do after the subpoena was served?"

He shrugged. "I'll be honest. I wasn't happy about it."

"Did you talk to anyone about it?"

"My wife."

"Anyone else?"

"Yes. Dr. Duffy."

Ryan's eyes widened. He knew Brent was a liar. He had no idea how big a liar. He quickly scribbled a note to Norm: *This is bull!*

"How did that conversation come about?"

"Ryan called me that night on the telephone."

"What did he tell you?"

"He said, 'Brent, this deposition can't happen. There's too much at stake.' "

"Meaning what?"

"Objection," said Norm, rising. "Calls for speculation."

"Let me rephrase," said Jackson. "What did you understand him to say?"

"Same objection," said Norm.

The judge leaned forward. "There's no jury in this proceeding, Mr. Klusmire. Let's hear the evidence. The witness shall answer."

"It was my impression that he had some serious money he didn't want Liz to find out about."

"How did you get that impression?"

"Because Sarah told me about it."

"Objection," Norm shouted. "Judge, now we're moving from speculation to hearsay."

"Sustained. Mr. Langford, you can tell us what you know firsthand, and you can tell us anything Dr. Duffy may have told you. But don't go telling us things other people may have said."

Brent replied in his most respectful tone. "Yes, Your Honor."

Jackson continued, "Mr. Langford, are you sure it was your wife who told you about the money? Or was it Dr. Duffy, himself?"

"Objection. This is ridiculous. He's coaching the witness right on the stand."

"Overruled."

"Come to think of it," said Brent, "it might very well have been Ryan who told me about the money. Yeah. It was Ryan. Definitely."

"Good," said Jackson. "Now that we've cleared that up, I'd like to get a little more specific about this money Dr. Duffy wanted to keep from his wife. Do you know if that money was ever kept in any kind of suitcase or storage container that had a combination lock?"

"I don't know."

"Could it have been?" Jackson pressed.

"Objection."

"Sustained."

"Your Honor," said Jackson, "I'm just trying to show that Dr. Duffy had motive to stop the deposition. He was concerned that if it went forward, Brent might tell me about the money that Dr. Duffy is trying to hide from my client."

"The objection is sustained," said the judge. "No need to stretch, Mr. Jackson. You've made your point and tied things together. You won't be going to jail tonight."

"Thank you, Judge." He checked his notes, then returned to the witness. "Mr. Langford, let's turn back to this late-night telephone conversation with Dr. Duffy. After he told you the deposition had to be stopped, what did you say?"

"I told him I'm not a lawyer, I can't stop the deposition from happing."

"What did Dr. Duffy say to that?"

"He said this wasn't about legal stuff. The only way to stop this deposition was for me to teach Liz's lawyer a lesson."

"Could you be more specific as to what he said?"

"Yes. I remember exactly what he said."

"Please, tell us Dr. Duffy's exact words."

He blushed, as if embarrassed. "I don't like to use profanity."

Ryan nearly burst inside. Brent was *walking* profanity.

The judge added, "It is very important for us to hear Dr. Duffy's exact words."

"Okay. His exact words. He said, 'Brent, I want you to beat the living shit out of that ass-hole Phil Jackson and teach him a lesson.' "

"What did you say?"

"I said forget it. No way."

"How did you leave it with Dr. Duffy?"

"He got mad. He called me—a pussy. Some other things that don't bear repeating. And then he said, 'All right, I don't need you. I'll get someone else to do it.' "

"Did he say who he would get?"

"No."

"What did you do next?"

"I didn't know what to do. I was up the rest of the night worrying about it."

"Why didn't you warn Mr. Jackson?"

"That's what I finally decided to do. I got up in the middle of the night and drove to Denver. Mind you, I was breaking ranks with my wife's brother. It wasn't something I could just do lightly. He's family. I didn't want to just call the police on him. I was going to talk to Liz and tell her about it."

"But you didn't get there in time."

"No. I didn't think Ryan would hire somebody that fast. Next thing I knew, you were in the hospital. After I heard what had happened, I got scared. I hung out in Denver that morning, not sure what to do. And then I just came home."

"Thank you, Mr. Langford. I know it's not easy to testify against someone in your own family. We appreciate your coming here today."

"Cross-examination, Mr. Klusmire?"

Norm rose. "Your Honor, as I'm sure you've surmised, we're surprised Mr. Langford is actually here this morning. And frankly, we're flat-out stunned by his testimony. May I have a fifteen-minute recess to confer with my client?"

"Tell you what," said the judge. "Take all the time you need. I was going to call a bladder break myself, but it appears the problem may run deeper than that, if you know what I mean. At all events, I've heard enough testimony for a Saturday. This is a preliminary hearing, and the rules don't require me to hear everything live in the courtroom before making a ruling. In the interest of fairness, however, I will defer my ruling until five P.M. Monday. The respondent shall have until that time to submit any written affidavits he may wish the court to consider."

"But Judge—"

"Court's in recess," he said with a bang of the gavel.

"All rise!" shouted the bailiff.

Ryan stood at his lawyer's side, confused. "I don't believe this."

The judge disappeared into his chambers through the side door. Brent stepped down from the witness stand and hurried past the lawyers. Ryan started toward him, as if to head him off. Norm stopped him.

"Let him go," he said quietly. "Don't look at him, don't look at Jackson, and don't look at your wife. You're bound to say something you'll regret. And believe me, they're taking notes."

Ryan swallowed his anger and let him pass.

Jackson gathered his papers into his briefcase. Liz was at his side, almost hiding behind her lawyer. He paused on their way out. "Welcome to Family Court, gentlemen."

It took all his strength, but Ryan said nothing. He just watched as Jackson led the way with Liz in tow. She took his arm as they passed through the swinging double doors in the back of the courtroom. Inertia kept the doors swinging back and forth several times before coming to a halt. On the third swing, he saw Brent and Jackson shaking hands in the hallway. Liz was there too, smiling. All three were smiling.

It was the Three Musketeers. "I *really* don't believe this," he said softly.

47

The drive back to Norm's house seemed to take forever. Ryan rode in the passenger seat, venting. Norm was behind the wheel, just listening. Ryan wasn't criticizing his friend. He was more critical of the process.

"It's totally bizarre," said Ryan. "One minute Judge Novak is threatening to throw Jackson in jail, the next minute he's throwing us out of court."

"I see that kind of posturing in criminal court. Judges are always threatening to hold the prosecutors in contempt and throw the case out. It creates the illusion of fairness before they stick it to the defendant. Whenever I hear that nonsense, I know my client is in for a nice long all-expenses-paid trip to Club Fed. I guess the same holds true in Family Court—though at least you're not in jail."

"That's the irony of it. Brent is the one who should be locked up. Instead, he and Jackson are buddies."

"There's no doubt in my mind that Brent put Jackson in the hospital. But somehow—probably through his FBI contacts—Jackson must have found out about the three-million-dollar bank account. Big money has a way of healing old wounds. They've clearly cut a deal."

"What kind of deal?"

"Jackson probably gave him two choices. One, Brent could help Liz get her share of the money. Or two, Jackson could bring the FBI down on Brent's head and make sure he spends the next three to six years in jail."

"You think Brent told them about the two million in the attic?"

"It's possible. Jackson was very careful with his questions. He didn't get too specific about the amount of the money, where it was kept, whether it was cash or in some other form. When it comes to money, he knows he's not helping his client by raising a red flag for the FBI or the IRS. He doesn't want to kill the proverbial goose that lays the golden egg."

"I can't believe Liz would be part of this. She never even liked Brent."

"He's all she's got. Look at it from her standpoint, Ryan. You never told her about the money. She had to hear it from her lawyer that your father had three million dollars in a foreign bank account. And she may not like Brent, but she may very well believe his story that you hired someone to beat up Jackson. To top it all off, your father gave *her* the combination to the lock. Don't you think it's natural she'd feel a little entitled?"

Ryan shook his head. "That combination just frosts me. I don't understand what my father was trying to do."

"What's to understand? Your old man loved Liz. Honestly, I think he felt sorry for her going way back to when you went away to college and left her behind in Piedmont Springs."

"Dad was the one who talked me into leaving her. I told you that story, didn't I? My dad's very sophisticated hot-wire analogy. Once you're grounded, never grab another."

"Maybe he felt guilty for giving you bad advice."

"Or bad metaphors."

"Whatever. The bottom line is he wanted you and Liz to stick together. So he told you where the money was, and he gave her the combination. He was forcing you two to work together."

"Except he screwed up. He didn't scramble the tumblers after he closed up the briefcase. It was still set to the combination when I found it. It opened right up."

"So, his intent was clear. The execution could use some work."

Ryan glanced out the window. "A lot of work. What do we do now?"

"This hearing is a lost cause, so I don't want to submit an affidavit from you. Jackson was attacked while you were in Panama, so the only way to oppose Brent's testimony is to account for every minute of every day while you were there. It makes no sense to pin you down under oath with the FBI snooping around."

"So you're just going to let the judge rule?"

"I'll call Jackson and try to negotiate an agreed order for the judge to sign. Something that makes no finding that you actually were responsible for the attack, but nonetheless says you agree not to get within a hundred yards of Jackson or your wife for the duration of the case."

"Wonderful. For years Brent has been abusing my sister, and now *he's* the key witness who gets a restraining order against *me*."

"The order might not technically protect Brent. Just Liz and her lawyer. But my advice to you is to stay clear of your brother-in-law anyway."

"I will," said Ryan. "Just as soon as I break his friggin' neck."

Jeanette Duffy came home from the beauty shop around two o'clock. It was her regular Saturday ritual. She pulled the car all the way up to the garage, toward the rear of the house. A light rain sprinkled the walkway to the kitchen door. She dug out her keys and took small, quick steps up the stairs, trying to save her hair from the weather. She aimed the key for the lock, then froze. The glass panel on the door was broken. The door was already unlocked.

Jeanette scurried down the stairs, spurred by fear. She yanked open the car door and jumped inside. Her hand was shaking so badly she could barely insert the key. Finally, she got it in and raced out of the driveway.

The dirt road was slick from the rain. The car fishtailed in a mud puddle, but she regained control. A hundred yards down the road was the McClennys' farm, her closest neighbors. She pulled in the driveway and ran to the front door. Mr. McClenny answered.

"I think I've been robbed!" she shouted. "Can I use your phone?"

McClenny seemed stunned for a half-second.

No one ever got robbed around here. "Sure," he said as she opened the door. "It's right in the kitchen."

"Thank you." She hurried through the living room and grabbed the phone. She started to dial the police, then stopped. It suddenly occurred to her that this could be another chapter in the feud between Ryan and Brent—a family matter. Maybe Ryan had threatened to burn the money again, and Brent had come looking for it.

She dug in her purse for the number Ryan had given her—Norm's house. She dialed nervously. Norm's wife answered and brought Ryan to the phone. Her composure broke at the sound of her son's voice. "Ryan," she said, sniffling. "I think we've been robbed."

"What?"

"Our house. I think somebody broke in. The window was broken on the back door."

"Are you hurt?"

"No."

"Did you see anybody?"

"No."

"Where are you now?"

"At the McClennys'."

"Good. Stay away from the house, Mom. Go stay with Sarah. No, on second thought, Brent's on his way home. Can you just stay with the McClennys a few hours?"

"I think so. I'd do the same for them."

"Okay. I'll leave now. I should be there sometime after dark."

"Should I call the police?"

He thought for only a split second. "No,"

he said firmly. "Don't call the police. I'll be home tonight. I'll handle it."

Amy phoned several times Saturday, only to hear that Marilyn was unavailable. She left messages, but a return call never came. She knew Marilyn was back from Washington, since the local news had photographed her stepping off the airplane at Denver International Airport on Saturday morning. By four o'clock, she could wait no longer. She laid it on the line to Marilyn's housekeeper.

"Tell her I've been contacted by the FBI," she said. "I must talk to her."

Within twenty minutes, Amy had a call back. Marilyn sounded less concerned than expected. She was actually apologetic.

"I wasn't avoiding you, Amy. It's just that everything's been a whirlwind since the announcement. I must have received a thousand congratulatory phone calls in the past twenty-four hours."

"I'm sorry. I should congratulate you, too. It's just that my enthusiasm has been overshadowed by the FBI."

"It's nothing to be concerned about," said Marilyn. "The FBI runs routine checks on all presidential appointees. It's their job."

"I don't think this is routine."

"Trust me. Once the appointment is announced, the FBI moves very quickly on these background investigations."

"No, listen to me. I was eating lunch, watching you and the President on television, when the agent came up to me at the restaurant. It wasn't triggered by your appointment."

"Then what *did* trigger it, Amy?"

She struggled, dreading what she had to say. "He wanted to know about my contact with Ryan Duffy."

"Oh, my God. Amy, I told you to stay away from those people. Do you have any idea what kind of scrutiny I'm under right now? Everyone around me is a reflection on my character. Especially someone like you. It's no secret you and I are close."

Amy's voice tightened. "Just how close are we?"

"Very close. You know that."

"I do, yes. But I'm confused. I was up all night. I couldn't stop thinking about what you told me yesterday. I flat-out do not understand it. I have to ask: why would a man rape you almost forty-six years ago, and then send me two hundred thousand dollars just before he dies?"

"I have no idea."

"Marilyn, are we...related?"

Stunned silence. Finally she answered. "I told you we can never talk about this. Please don't try to force me."

"I just have so many questions."

"Sometimes questions are better left unanswered."

"Better for you, maybe."

"Better for both of us. Don't make me ask you again, Amy. Do not go down this road. It's a dead end."

"Marilyn, please."

"Goodbye, Amy."

Amy was about to make one more plea, but the line clicked in her ear. It had caught her off guard. She gripped the phone, staring in disbelief.

For the first time in her life, Marilyn Gaslow had hung up on her.

48

Driving alone at night on Highway 287 was an exercise in monotony. It plunged south through the quiet eastern plains at insufferable stretches, flat as the oceans of darkened cornfields, moving only imperceptibly to the east or west. It was like being stuck on a treadmill. The only scenery was oncoming pavement that reached as far as the headlights. With the brights on you could see the first row of corn just beyond the gravel shoulder, maybe count telephone poles as they rushed by, one after another.

Brent switched on the squeaky wipers again. It was a little game he played with the misty rain. Tiny drops collected on the windshield one at a time. He'd hold his speed steady at seventy miles per hour and see how far he could go without having to wipe it clean.

Eleven miles that time. A *new world record.*

He cut off the wipers and played with the

radio dial. The Denver stations had long since faded. He was almost home. He didn't need road signs to know it. Where civilization ended, Piedmont Springs began.

Between static, he found a country music station and cranked up the volume. He glanced at the dial to check the numbers. His eyes were away from the road just an instant—just long enough to hit the piece of lumber in the road at full speed.

The tires popped on the long row of nails. The car swerved out of control. Brent steered left, then right, trying to bring it back. The car slid into the left lane, hit the gravel shoulder and spun completely around. He came to a sudden stop facing back toward Denver.

He had a death grip on the steering wheel, unable to let go. Finally, he took a deep breath and lowered his arms. He was shaken but unhurt. For a moment, he just sat.

The rain collected on the windshield. The headlights beamed deep into the cornfield. The plains seemed even darker now that the car wasn't moving. He switched off the headlights and turned on the emergency flashers. He unlocked the door and stepped outside. Two tires were flat, front and rear on the driver's side.

"Damn it," he said as he kicked the dirt.

He walked back to the trunk and popped it open. The little light inside was barely sufficient, enhanced only marginally by the intermittent orange flash of the emergency blinkers. He knew he had a spare, one of those mini-wheels that looked like they were from a go-cart. Hopefully Sarah had one of those fix-a-flat spray cans back there, too. He peeled back the carpeting to check, rattling the tire irons, turning things upside down. He was leaning over, inside the trunk from the waist up.

He didn't notice the footsteps behind him.

"Need a hand?"

Brent started at the voice, hitting his head on the open trunk lid. He turned around quickly. The man was a mere shadow in the darkness a ways down the road, just beyond the reach of the flashing taillights. "Yeah," he said nervously. "Got a flat. Two of 'em."

"What a shame."

The tone hardly put him at ease. Brent could barely see in the darkness. At this distance, the blinking orange taillights were actually a hindrance, playing tricks with his eyes. He squinted to focus, but he didn't see another set of car lights. Come to think of it, he hadn't even heard him pull up. The man seemed to have come from nowhere.

Survival instinct took over. He reached for the tire iron inside the trunk.

In one fluid motion, the stranger's arm came up, the gun came out. A single shot pierced the night. Brent's head jerked back. He fell to his knees, then flat on his face. Blood pumped from the hole that was once his right eye, spilling onto the asphalt. It gathered in a pool that drained to the shoulder, then gradually stopped.

All was quiet, save for the corn leaves rustling in the gentle breeze.

The gunman lowered his weapon and took a dozen steps forward. He stepped only on the pavement, not on the gravel shoulder, so as not to leave footprints. In the orange blinking lights his huge hands looked prosthetic, covered in the rubber gloves of a surgeon—there would be no fingerprints. He took aim at Brent's head and squeezed the trigger once more, shattering the back of his skull. The job done, he pulled a plastic evidence bag from his pocket and placed the weapon inside.

He walked toward the car and stopped at the left front tire. On one knee, he reached up inside the wheel well and yanked out the tiny transmitter he had attached while Brent was on the witness stand. The electronic pulse had allowed him to track the Buick all the way from Denver, telling him when to place the spiked board on the highway.

He rose and opened the car door. He reached inside and flashed the car lights. On cue, a car pulled onto the highway about fifty yards ahead.

It had been parked in a narrow agricultural side road, sufficiently hidden by shoulder-high cornstalks. It raced toward him and stopped alongside the Buick. The passenger door opened. He jumped in.

The car sped away, back toward Denver, leaving the bloody corpse in the highway. He glanced back at his work, then took the murder weapon from his coat. He admired it in the dim light from the dashboard, leaving it in the plastic bag. A Smith & Wesson revolver with a mother-of-pearl handle. It wasn't his, but he sure liked the way it had performed.

Frank Duffy had himself one fine piece.

49

Ryan's pager chirped just north of Eads, about an hour from home. He kept one eye on the lonely highway as he checked the number on his belt. He didn't recognize it. A Saturday evening page usually meant someone was awfully sick. Something told him, however, that this was no *medical* emergency.

He stopped at a gas station, went straight to a pay phone, and dialed the number. The rain seemed to fall harder with each push of the button. He moved closer to the phone, beneath the small overhang. It wasn't much shelter. Thankfully, it took only one ring to get an answer.

"Brent's dead."

The pattering rain made it hard to hear. "*What* did you say?"

"Your brother-in-law's dead. Shot twice in the head. His body's laying on Highway 287, about a half-hour from your house."

Ryan recognized the voice. It was that security guy at K&G. "You killed him."

"No. *You* killed him. With your father's gun."

He immediately thought of the break-in at his mother's house. "You broke in and stole the gun."

"Yeah," he scoffed. "Like the police are going to buy that one."

"How'd you find it? How did you even know my father *had* a gun?"

"Registration records. And let's face it. Isn't the top drawer in the master bedroom the first place you'd look?"

"You bastards. You won't get away with this."

"Don't be so sure. Listen to this."

There was a click on the line, followed by Ryan's own voice. It was a tape recording of his conversation with Norm after the hearing. Ryan listened in stunned silence as Norm's words were played back to him. *"My advice to you is to stay clear of your brother-in-law."* He braced himself for his own reply: *"I will. Just as soon as I break his friggin' neck."*

The recording was over. Ryan closed his eyes in disbelief. "You bugged Norm's truck."

"Not me. It probably was that bum who bumped into you outside the courthouse. Must have dropped something in your coat pocket. We heard the whole courtroom disaster—and everything since."

Ryan reached frantically into his coat pockets, left, then right. A tiny microphone was buried at the bottom. He pulled it out and crushed it, erupting with anger. "Stop this! What do you people want from me!"

The reply was smug, unemotional. "Stay away from the FBI. And forget you ever heard of Joe Kozelka."

"Or what?"

"Or the police are going to find this gun.

They're going to hear this tape. And they're going to come knocking on your door."

Ryan had no chance to speak. The line clicked, followed by the dial tone. He put the phone in the cradle but didn't let go. The rain started to blow, soaking his hair and face. He didn't know who to call first. Sarah. His mom. Norm. As he lifted the phone, he was certain of just one thing.

Definitely *not* the FBI.

Nathan Rusch hung up the pay phone and started back to the car. As an added precaution, he was taking the long way back to Denver, west to Pueblo and up I-25. He'd driven as far as Rocky Ford, the self-proclaimed melon capitol of the world. Banners and painted signs along the road heralded the upcoming Arkansas Valley Fair, held every August when the melons were in season. All the watermelon hoopla reminded Rusch of those old David Letterman shows where the host would drop big twenty-pounders off buildings in Manhattan, splattering them on the pavement. The result was not unlike Brent's head on the highway.

Melonhead Langford. Twenty years in the business, he gave all his jobs a name. He especially liked this one.

The parking lot outside Denny's restaurant was nearly full. Melons might have been the local claim to fame, but the Grand Slam breakfast was apparently a Saturday-evening hit. He crossed several rows of parked cars, then stopped alongside a white Taurus. The driver's window slid down. His partner was behind the wheel. She wore neither the black nor the blond wig tonight. She was her natural brunette.

"Did you reach him?" she asked.

"Yeah."

"Good." She slid across the bench seat to the passenger side. Rusch opened the door and got behind the wheel.

"I guess we're a pretty good team, huh?"

He started the engine, showing not a hint of friendly agreement as he steered out of the parking lot. "You fucked up again, Sheila."

"No way. I did everything I was supposed to do."

"It wasn't supposed to be such an obvious break-in. The whole key to the frame-up is that Duffy used his father's gun. If it looks like somebody broke into the house and stole it before Brent got whacked, we got nothing."

"The house was locked. What was I supposed to do? I thought I did a damn good job of finding the gun as quickly as I did."

"It wasn't that brilliant, Sheila. Nine out of ten people keep their handgun in a bedroom dresser drawer."

She glanced out the window. "You never give me credit."

"Credit for what? You go to Panama, you leave your damn fingerprints all over a cocktail glass. You go to Duffy's house, you break in like an amateur." He shook his head, grumbling. "I must have been crazy to think I could promote you from bedroom detail."

She leaned closer, narrowing her eyes. "We all have our own strengths," she said as she ran her fingertips along the inside of his thigh. "And we all have our weaknesses."

He knocked her hand away. "That's not going to work this time. I can only carry you so far. Kozelka doesn't tolerate mistakes."

"What are you telling me, Nathan?"

He glanced her way, then back at the road. "Mr. Kozelka was very concerned that Duffy would take that cocktail glass to the FBI and implicate you. He was even more concerned that you might turn around and drop the name Kozelka. Now, there were two ways for me to make sure that didn't happen. One was to make it impossible for Duffy to meet with the FBI. The other...well, I think you understand the other."

She glanced nervously at his hands on the steering wheel, as if suddenly aware of how huge they were. "Under the circumstances, I wish the frame-up were a little tighter."

"It should work in the short run. Even with your botched break-in, I can't see Duffy running to the FBI before he and his lawyer have a chance to sort this out."

"Then what?"

"Then we reevaluate."

She managed a weak, awkward smile. "Sure hope this works."

"Yes," he said coldly. "I know you do."

Ryan's first call was to his mother. She was still at the McClennys', where he had told her to stay until he returned from Denver. The rain continued to fall as he filled her in on everything from the courtroom disaster to the threatening phone call. By the time he'd finished, he was barely aware that he was completely rain-soaked.

She seemed shocked by the news of Brent's death, though not exactly saddened. That pioneer spirit that had been missing since the death of her husband was suddenly back. She was circling the proverbial wagons.

"Are you sure he's dead?"

"I haven't seen the body, if that's what you mean."

"Then how do you know that man wasn't bluffing?"

"He wouldn't break into the house and steal Dad's gun just to bluff. I can drive down Two-eighty-seven and take a look for myself, if that's what you want."

"No, don't do that."

Her tone alarmed him. "Why not?"

"Because the police could be there already. I don't think you should talk to them."

"Why not?"

"Because you have to think this through first. What are you going to tell them?"

"I was going to tell them I think I'm being framed for a murder I didn't commit. That way, I'll just beat Kozelka's thug to the punch."

"Please, don't do that."

"Why not, Mom?"

"Because if you tell the police you're being framed, you'll have to tell them *why* you're being framed."

"I think it's about time we just came clean on this."

"No."

Ryan cringed. "What do you mean, no?"

"It's not totally your call anymore, Ryan. I have a say in this."

"What are we arguing about, Mom? I'm being framed for *murder*."

"Not yet. They've only threatened to frame you. The only way you will be framed is if you tell the FBI what your father did. If you keep your mouth shut, Brent's just another unsolved murder."

His mouth opened, but words didn't come. He couldn't believe what his own mother was saying. "Mom, somebody was murdered here."

"Not *somebody*. Brent. I'm sorry, but I'm not shedding any tears over a human slug who took a fist to my own daughter. Brent's dead. You can't change that by telling the police you're being framed. And you can't tell the police you're being framed without ruining your father's good name and reputation. None of that can bring Brent back, even if we wanted him back."

"Mom, I've already done more than I should to keep this blackmail a secret."

"Damn it. It's not the blackmail I'm worried about. It's the *rape*. I can't have everyone in Prowers County thinking I was married forty-six years to a rapist!"

Ryan froze. "I thought you didn't know about the rape. You told me you didn't know what was in that safe deposit box in Panama. You said you didn't *want* to know."

Her voice was shaking, but she was no longer shouting. "Of course I knew."

"Why did you lie to me before I went down to Panama?"

"I'm sorry."

"Why didn't you tell me what you knew?"

"Ryan, please."

"*No*," he said sharply. "You knew. Why didn't you *tell* me?"

"I was afraid," she said softly.

"Afraid of what?"

"Afraid that you would never understand how I could forgive him. Please, Ryan. Let's not do it this way. Your sister's husband has just been murdered. She shouldn't hear about it through the Piedmont Springs grapevine. I need to go to her. Let me be the one to tell her."

"Don't try to hide behind Sarah."

"I'm not hiding. Not anymore. Meet me at her house. Then Sarah, you, and I will discuss this. Like a family."

"Or what's left of it."

"Please, son. See me on this."

A bitterness swelled from deep within—but he swallowed it. "All right, Mom. I'll see you there."

341

50

Ryan took the long way home, down the lonely gravel side roads he'd discovered years ago as a boy on a bicycle. It wasn't a shortcut by any means. It was a detour that would keep him from coming upon the scene of the crime on Highway 287. He assumed the police would already be there. After the promise to his mother, he didn't want to be tempted to stop and say something he might regret.

He drove faster than he should have, kicking up loose gravel that pelted the floorboards. Scattered potholes made the largely one-lane road even more treacherous. A few bumps were so big they brought his chin to his chest. It was a jarring ride at such high speed, almost like off-road. A sane driver would have slowed down. But not Ryan, not tonight. The bumps, the jolts, the disoriented sensation—it was a perfect complement to the jumbled thoughts in his present state of mind.

In all the confusion, the thought of Brent lying dead on the highway was foremost in his mind. He was no fan of his brother-in-law, especially after his testimony this morning. Still, the very thought of money in the attic leading to murder in the family was unsettling. He wondered what Liz would think. He could only imagine what her lawyer might make of it. Even without the gun and the audiotape Kozelka might use to frame him, Jackson was bound to point the finger at Ryan. Who else had such obvious motive?

Perhaps he even deserved some blame. Fact was, Brent was dead because Ryan had threatened Kozelka. That made him feel guilty in a way, mostly because of all the times in years past he had wished Brent were gone. Now he was.

The long dirt road fed into the highway near an old barn and wind-ravaged silo. Ryan steered onto the pavement without slowing down, reaching Sarah's house in record time. The truck skidded to a stop in the driveway, and Ryan jumped out. The porch light was on, brightening the rain-slicked path to the front door. He didn't bother to knock. The door was unlocked.

"Mom?" he said as he entered the living room.

"In here." The reply had come from the kitchen.

Ryan hurried inside. His mother was seated at the kitchen table. Sarah was a lump in the chair right beside her, leaning on her like a grieving widow. Ryan saw sadness in his sister's eyes. Slowly, it turned to rage.

"Oh, Ryan," she said with contempt. "How *could* you?"

"How could I what?"

"I'm giving birth next month. How could you do this to my husband?"

"I didn't do anything to Brent." He looked at his mother, pleading. "Mom, tell her."

"I did," said his mother.

Sarah scoffed. "Framed? Right. I don't

believe it for one second. Brent told me everything before he went to court this morning. He was afraid you might retaliate. But neither one of us ever imagined *this*."

"Look, I don't know what Brent told you, but—"

"He told me that you called him from Panama and asked him to beat up Liz's lawyer. He wouldn't do it, so you hired some thug."

"He said the same thing in court. It's a lie."

"Did you hire the same guy to kill my husband, Ryan? Or did you do this job yourself?"

"Sarah, I had nothing to do with Brent's murder."

"It all goes back to that night Brent asked you for some money at Mom's house. You went berserk and started burning it. You almost killed him then. Mom says you even had Dad's gun that night. You tried to hide it when she walked in, but she saw it. You were gunning for Brent!"

"I didn't kill Brent, so just shut the hell up!"

Sarah leaned into her mother, crying. Jeanette pulled her daughter close to console her, then looked at Ryan. "We all need to just calm down before we say things we don't mean. Let's get a good night's sleep and talk about this in the morning."

"No!" shouted Ryan. "You told me on the phone we would discuss this as a family. Well, the family's all here. Don't avoid this, Mom. We have to talk—*tonight*."

"Now isn't the time."

Ryan nearly exploded, but a knock on the front door checked his anger. The three of them glanced at one another, as if to ask who it might be.

"Are you expecting someone?" asked Ryan.

Both women shook their heads.

"Answer it, Ryan. Your sister is in no condition."

He sighed with exasperation, his feet pounding the floor as he left the kitchen. He yanked hard on the door, harder than necessary. It startled their visitor.

"Hello, Ryan," the man said timidly.

It was Josh Colburn, the old lawyer who had prepared his father's will. Ryan hadn't seen him since the funeral. He was wearing a bright yellow bowling shirt that bore the logo of the local hardware store. "Mr. Colburn," he said with surprise. "What are you doing here?"

"I was over at the bowling alley. Word is out about Brent. Poor fellow. I drove by your mother's house first, but there was nobody there. So I came here as quickly as I could."

"That's very nice of you," he said, bewildered. "But what's the hurry?"

"Well, I needed to talk to you. I'm having a little trouble interpreting your father's instructions."

"My father? What are you talking about?"

He leaned forward and whispered, as if sharing a matter of national security. "I have the envelope."

"Mr. Colburn, I have no idea what you're talking about."

"The *envelope*. Frank told me to send it straight to the *Denver Post* if anyone in the Duffy family was ever harmed."

A chill went down Ryan's spine. It was just like Norm had said. In any viable extortion scheme there had to be a safety valve—an unidentified third person who would automatically disclose the secret in the event the blackmailer or his family were ever killed. It was a way to ensure payment and prevent retaliation.

"Did you send it to the *Post* yet?" asked Ryan.

"No. You see, that's where I'm confused. I know how your father felt about Brent. He hated him more than you did. To be honest with you, I'm not sure if Brent is considered part of the Duffy family."

"Where's the envelope now?"

"Back in my law office. I keep it locked in the safe. Frank told me never to carry it on my person."

Ryan stepped outside, put a friendly arm around the old man's shoulder, and started down the porch. "Let's you and I talk about that," said Ryan. "On the way to your office."

The telephone rang after midnight. Amy was stretched across the couch in the living room, watching an old Audrey Hepburn flick. She snatched the cordless receiver from the cocktail table before the piercing ring could wake Taylor or her grandmother.

"Hello."

"Amy, this is Ryan Duffy."

She nearly jackknifed on the couch, spilling her steamy bag of microwave popcorn. "How did you get my number?"

"I found an old letter written by a woman named Debby Parkens."

She rose, stunned. "That's my mother."

"I figured. It was postmarked in Boulder. I dialed directory assistance on a hunch. There's only one Amy Parkens."

She suddenly regretted ever having told him her real first name. "What do you want?"

"I had to call you. Amy, my father didn't rape your mother."

"I know he didn't. He raped—" She stopped herself. She didn't want to drag Marilyn's name into this. "Just stop harassing me. Don't ever call me again."

"No, wait. I know why my father sent you the money."

She fought the urge to hang up. That was one question she definitely wanted answered. "Why?"

"If I tell you on the phone, you'll think I'm making this up. Meet with me, please."

"I'm not getting anywhere near you. Just tell me now."

"Amy, you have to see the letter. I don't want to share it with you or anyone else until I'm sure it's genuine. You're the only one who can verify it. Bring something that will help you identify your mother's handwriting. But please meet with me. As soon as possible."

She paused to think. He now knew where she lived. If she refused to meet him, he'd probably show up at her front door, which would give her one more thing to explain to the FBI. "All right. Come to Boulder. But we can't meet at my apartment."

"Unfortunately, Boulder won't work. I can't leave Piedmont Springs right now. I have some serious family issues I have to deal with."

"What kind of joke is this?"

"I just can't go anywhere right now. There's been a...another death in the family."

"I'm sorry. But do you really expect me to come all the way down to Piedmont Springs again?"

"Only if you want to find out why your mother would write to my father just two weeks before she died."

Chills ran down her spine. That was all she needed to hear. "I'll be there in the morning," she said, then hung up the phone.

51

A firm knock on the door landed just after dawn. Sarah lay on her side in the fetal position, trying to relieve the stabbing back pain that came with her pregnancy. Her bleary eyes focused on the orange liquid crystals on the alarm clock beside her bed. 6:22 A.M. She rolled out of bed, slipped on her robe, and started downstairs.

The night had taken its toll. She had slept little, wept often. The tears were not those typical of grief. They were laden with self-pity and apprehension about her future. She thought about the long term, but it was the short term that created the most anxiety. Her mother had run interference for her last night, telling the police that Sarah was an emotional wreck and couldn't talk to them. Very soon, however, she would have to talk to the homicide detectives. They'd surely ask her if she was aware of any reason why someone might want to kill her husband. One question had kept her awake most of the night: What would she tell them about her father's money?

The knocking continued.

"Coming," she said, shuffling to the front door. She instantly regretted having said a word. It took away the option to peek out the window, see who it was, and pretend not to be home. She pulled back the curtain for a discreet peek anyway.

The man standing on the porch was facing the driveway, his back to the house. His profile was unfamiliar to her. He seemed handsome and was dressed casually but smartly. The wristwatch looked to be the expensive kind. Inasmuch as she didn't feel ready to talk to police, she was certain that no one at the sheriff's department could afford a Rolex. She unlocked the deadbolt and opened the door.

"Mrs. Langford," he said in a soft, sympathetic tone. "I'm Phil Jackson."

She knew the name but was unsure of her feelings. "You're Liz's lawyer."

"That's right. I'm very sorry about your husband. I know this is a very difficult time for you, but it's very important that we talk."

"What about?"

"May I come in, please?"

"No."

He took a half-step back. "Mrs. Langford, I can understand how you might have some unresolved feelings about me. But the sooner you recognize I'm on your side, the sooner we can get to the bottom of what happened to Brent."

"I know what happened to Brent. He got himself in the middle of something he should never have gotten involved in. And he got himself killed."

"But he did it for you. And your baby."

"I doubt that."

"It's true. After Brent testified in court yesterday morning, he and I had a nice talk. One of the last things he said to me was that he knew he hadn't been a very good husband to you over the years. He always thought you deserved better."

Her eyes clouded with emotion. She was suddenly less defensive. "He really said that?"

"Yes, he most certainly did. He knew he hadn't provided for you. He regretted that, terribly. His testimony in court yesterday was his way of making it up to you."

"It sounded to me like he was just trying to hurt Ryan."

"No. The goal wasn't to hurt Ryan. The goal was to protect *you*."

"I don't understand."

"Let me be up front with you. I know all about

the three million dollars in the Banco del Istmo in Panama City. A law enforcement source verified that for me. Brent knew about it, too, obviously. His biggest fear was that Ryan—Mr. Goody Two-shoes—was going to screw things up and lose the money for the whole family."

"That's always been my fear, too."

"It's a reasonable fear. Your needs are different than your brother's. He's a doctor who can make a ton of money on his own, if he so chooses. But just like you, Liz needs and deserves the money. So when Brent came forward to help Liz, he was really looking out for you. By the same token, whatever I do for Liz also helps you."

Her eyes narrowed. "What can *you* do for me?"

"I can help you make sure that Brent didn't die in vain."

"What does that mean?"

"That means I intend to honor the agreement Brent and I reached. So long as his widow will help me reach the same objectives."

"I need specifics."

"Very simple," said Jackson. "There's three million dollars in the bank. According to Brent, you and Ryan were going to divide it fifty-fifty. Liz was supposed to get nothing."

Sarah blinked. The way he said it made it sound like they really were cheating Liz.

Jackson continued, "So here's the deal. You keep your share of the inheritance. And as an added incentive to make sure Liz gets her fair share, you get twenty percent of whatever you help Liz take from Ryan."

"Mr. Jackson, this is my brother we're talking about."

He stepped closer, pointing out the purple bruises beneath his facial makeup. "Your brother hired someone to beat the crap out of me. And he may have gotten your husband killed."

"We can't be sure of that."

"We don't have to be sure. I'm not trying to put him in jail, and I'm not asking you to go that far, either. All we have to do is make the judge in the divorce case think Ryan could possibly have been connected to either act of violence. If the judge so much as *suspects* that's true, we all come out winners."

"I don't know," she said, wincing.

"Okay," said Jackson. "You get *thirty* percent of whatever Liz takes from Ryan. After my fee is paid, of course."

Sarah felt a rush of adrenaline. After years of abuse from Brent, the very act of negotiating gave her a sense of efficacy she'd never felt before. The best part was, Jackson still didn't even seem to know about the other two million in the attic. Brent must not have told him.

"Tell you what," she said coyly. "I will definitely think about it." She stepped back and started to close the door.

Jackson stopped her. "When can I expect to hear from you?"

"When I'm good and ready," she replied, then swung the door shut.

A deputy from the Prowers County Sheriff's Department was at the Duffy homestead well before breakfast. On Norm's advice—insistence, really—Ryan had called to report the break-in. The deputy was a high school classmate of Ryan's, dressed in the familiar light green summer uniform with short sleeves. Ryan spoke to him alone, keeping his mother out of it as the two men walked around back to the kitchen door. The broken glass pane had the markings of typical Prowers County criminal mischief, according to the deputy. Juvenile crimes consumed three-quarters of his time.

Ryan offered no opinions as to the age of the perpetrator. The trick was simply to report the break-in without digressing into the murder, the money, or the blackmail.

"Was anything taken from the house?" asked the deputy.

"I don't know for sure," said Ryan. It was the truth. He had yet to check his father's dresser drawer to confirm that the gun had actually been taken.

"When did you first notice the broken glass?"

"This morning." Again, the truth. It had been after midnight by the time he had gone to Josh Colburn's office, phoned Amy, and returned home to inspect the window.

The report was finished in just a few minutes. Out of sympathy for the family tragedy—meaning Brent—the deputy didn't detain Ryan any longer than necessary. Ryan thanked him and watched him pull out of the driveway, shielding his eyes as the squad car disappeared into the low morning sun.

Ryan climbed the front stairs, stopping on the porch. Out of the corner of his eye, he caught sight of an approaching car up the road. A truck, actually. It was coming quickly, splashing through muddy puddles of last night's rain. A hundred yards away he could see the driver. It was Amy.

She really came.

He jogged to the end of the driveway to head her off. Having yet to tell his mother anything about Amy, he didn't want a scene. The truck stopped at the mailbox. Amy rolled down the window. Her expression was guarded, neither friendly nor hostile. Her eyes seemed puffy from the all-night drive.

"Thanks for coming," said Ryan.

"Please, don't thank me. Do you have the letter?"

"I locked it in the wall safe over at my clinic. Like I said on the phone, I didn't want to show it to anyone until you confirmed it was genuine. I haven't even told my mother about it."

She pushed the clutch, ready to go. "Let's head into town, then."

"You can ride with me, if you want."

"I'll follow you."

He sensed more than a little distrust in her voice. "Okay. Follow me."

52

They had never found a suicide note. That had been Amy's first thought when Ryan had mentioned a letter from her mother. The absence of a note had been one of the precious things she had clung to all these years. It was the cornerstone of her denial that her mother had killed herself. It was what had spurred her to drive down from Boulder all night. As she took the letter from Ryan, it was the cause of the butterflies that stirred in her stomach.

Amy handled it carefully, delicately, as if the parchment were as priceless and fragile as the original Magna Carta. She unfolded it and laid it on the desktop before her. The process felt ceremonial, a sacred connection to her mother's past. She checked the date. Ryan had been truthful. It was just two weeks before she had died.

Amy read in silence, the eyes leading her down an uncharted path. She struggled to keep her composure. She knew Ryan was studying her from the other side of his desk, though her eyes never met his, never left the pale green stationery that bore her mother's initials.

She glanced up only once, as if suddenly aware of how stifling it was in the back office of Ryan's clinic. The air conditioner hadn't been run in days. The lone window was blocked by a set of floor-to-ceiling shelves jammed with patient files. The faux wood paneling was the cheap kind typically found in basements. Directly over Amy's head was a long, bent-arm lamp that belonged over a physician's examining table, not a desk. It threw more heat than light.

It was the emotional heat, however, that was starting to consume her, rising with each sentence, heightened by each word. Halfway through the letter, tiny beads of perspiration gathered above her lip, making her mouth dry and salty. She read to herself, allowing her mind to put the words to the tune of her mother's voice. She tried to envision her mother actually saying such things aloud. It was a frustrating exercise. The imagined voice kept changing. Amy reached back in time for the soothing voice she remembered as a very small child, but the anxious tone of her mother's last days was a constant interruption. It was like listening to a radio with a faulty antenna. At times, the interference was so great she couldn't even remember what her mother had truly sounded like, happy or sad. Her confusion turned the narrator into someone altogether different. She could hear Marilyn, Gram, and even herself. The distractions made her angry. It was misdirected anger, an unfocused rage she had harbored her entire life—the anger of an eight-year-old robbed of her mother.

Her hands were shaking as she neared the bottom of the page. She finally had reached a silent rhythm, reading in her mother's voice, loud and strong. It was strange, but she finished with one overwhelming impression.

"This can't be true."

Ryan looked at her quizzically. "You mean everything in the letter is false? Or do you mean your mother didn't write it?"

"Both."

Ryan disagreed. But he tried not to sound disagreeable. "Let's focus on the authenticity first. Did you bring something with your mother's handwriting that we can compare to this letter, like we agreed?"

"Yes. But I don't need to make any comparisons to tell you this letter is bogus."

"That's your opinion. I'd like to see for myself."

"What are you, a handwriting expert?"

"No. But if you're so sure it's a phony, then what's the downside to letting me lay the two side by side and compare?"

Amy clutched her purse. She didn't feel threatened, but his tone had definitely challenged her. "All right."

She unzipped her purse and removed an envelope. "This is a letter my mother wrote me when I was seven years old, at camp. As you'll see, the handwriting is totally different."

He took the letter a little too eagerly, embarrassed by the grab. He opened it and laid it beside the other letter, the one to his father. He didn't really focus on what the letter to Amy said. Instead, he was checking the loops in the penmanship, noting the way she dotted the letter "i" or crossed the letter "t." He compared individual letters, groups of letters, words, and groups of words. He did all the things Norm had told him a handwriting expert would do. Finally, he looked up.

"I'm no expert, but I would say that these two letters were written by the same person."

"It's not even close."

Ryan backed away in his chair. Her tone was getting hostile. "Look," he said, trying to appeal to reason. "The penmanship in this letter to my father is a little shaky, I'll grant you that. But they look very similar."

"You think it's similar because you *want* it to be similar."

"I'd like to copy this and have an expert tell us one way or the other."

"No."

"Why not?"

"Because I've worked at a law firm long enough to know that people hire experts who will tell them what they want to hear."

"I'm just after the truth here."

"You're out to clear your father's name."

"What's wrong with that?"

"What's *wrong* with that?" she said, raising her voice. "Marilyn Gaslow was my mother's best friend. Your father raped her. And now, forty-six years later, you expect me to believe that Marilyn made it all up?"

"It's right there in the letter. According to your mother, my father was convicted of a rape he never committed."

"That's why I say the letter's a fraud. Why would my mother write a letter like that?"

"Because it's the truth, that's why."

"It's not the truth. If it were, your father would have told the whole world he had been falsely accused. Any normal human being would do everything possible to clear his name."

"There was no need to clear his name. He was convicted as a juvenile and the record was sealed."

She smiled sardonically. "How convenient. Marilyn works hard all her life, never so much as a hint of scandal in her life. But the very week of her presidential appointment, out pops a letter saying that she falsely accused a man of raping her."

"I can't account for the timing."

"Well, I can. It's a lie. It's designed to hurt Marilyn. And it's at the expense of my mother."

"If it's a lie, then why did my father send you two hundred thousand dollars?"

"What does that have to do with this?"

"I believe my father sent you that money out of gratitude to your mother. She was Marilyn's best friend. Marilyn confided in her and told her the rape never happened. Your mother did the right thing and wrote a letter to my dad, telling him just that. It finally gave my father the corroboration he needed to prove himself innocent."

"I don't believe that."

"Do you have a better explanation as to why my father would send you that kind of money right before he died?"

Amy glared, but she had no response.

Ryan said, "I didn't think you did."

Her voice shook with anger. "All right. I'll play along with your little fantasy for a minute or two. Let's say my mother wrote that letter. Let's say Marilyn Gaslow falsely accused your father. Where in the hell did your father get the two hundred thousand dollars that he sent to me?"

"That's a fair question," he said softly. "And I'll answer it on one condition. I want to make a copy of that letter you brought, so I can have an expert compare the two."

"What if I say no?"

"Then I guess you'll never know where the money came from."

Amy paused. The letter she had brought contained nothing embarrassing or too personal. There was no guarantee Ryan would tell her the truth, but there was one way to make sure she was getting *something* out of the deal. "I'll swap you. You can copy the handwriting sample I brought. If I can copy the letter to your father."

"Deal." He rose from behind the desk, leading Amy to the copy machine in the next room. He reached for Amy's letter, but she pulled away.

"Yours first."

Ryan didn't argue. He made a quick copy and handed it to Amy. She shoved the duplicate in her purse.

"Now yours," he said.

She handed it over. Ryan shot the copy, then reached for the duplicate feeding out of the other end. Amy stopped him.

"Not so fast. This isn't a one-for-one trade. Where did the money come from?"

His throat tightened. It had been hard enough to tell Norm, his friend and lawyer. Amy was altogether different. Maybe it all went back to the spark he'd felt the first time they'd met, but for whatever reason, what she thought of him *mattered*. "I don't know for sure."

"Where do you *think* it came from?"

"I think...my father used your mother's letter to get the money."

"Used it? What do you mean?"

He removed the copy from the tray. "I'm talking about extortion. That's where the two hundred thousand dollars came from. And lots more."

"He extorted Marilyn?"

"Not Marilyn. A very wealthy businessman named Joseph Kozelka."

Amy stepped back, suddenly eager to leave. "This is getting way too crazy."

"Just listen to me, please. I know it sounds horrible to say my dad was a blackmailer. But put yourself in his shoes. I think the only reason he became a blackmailer is because he was falsely convicted of rape."

"Your father was a blackmailer *and* a rapist."

"That's not possible. The only way this makes sense is if he *didn't* commit the rape."

"You wish."

"It's mere logic. Ever since I learned about the rape conviction, I've asked myself: How does a man rape a woman and then turn into a blackmailer? Could the rapist extort the victim? No way. Unless the rape never happened—and the alleged rapist could prove the victim had made it all up. Your mother's letter proves exactly that."

"The only thing this whole visit proves is

that I should have listened to Marilyn Gaslow. You Duffys are despicable people, and I need to stay as far away from you as possible." She grabbed the photocopy from his hand. "And I'm not going to let you use this to prove your phony point."

"Amy, wait!" He ran after her as she hurried toward the door, grabbing at the letter in her hand and ripping it in half. She screamed and swung at him. He stopped in his tracks. She looked him straight in the eye, her fist clenching pepper spray for self-defense.

Each watched the other, waiting for the next move. Neither one flinched. For an instant, they seemed taken with the irony. It was their parents, after all, who had predestined their meeting, watching from another world as the children moved from subtle flirtation at the Green Parrot to outright confrontation in Ryan's office.

Amy said, "Stay away from me. I don't want your money. And I don't need your lies." She turned and quickly let herself out.

He felt the urge to follow but didn't. He'd taken his best shot. He should have known there would be no persuading her. At least he had a handwriting sample—half of Debby Parkens's letter to her daughter. It was surely enough to allow one of Norm's experts to verify she'd also written the letter to his father.

He laid his torn copy on the table and flattened the creases so that it would run through the fax machine. He scribbled a short message on a cover sheet, punched Norm's number, and fed the documents into the slot.

Second thoughts gripped him as the machine slowly swallowed the letter. It wasn't as if the handwriting analysis would be dispositive. Experts could only render opinions. Neither experts nor Amy could confirm for a *fact* that Frank Duffy had been falsely accused of rape. Only one person alive could do that. Her name was Marilyn Gaslow. The next chairwoman of the Board of Governors of the Federal Reserve.

The fax machine beeped, signaling the transmission was completed. Ryan stared at the documents, chilled by his own sudden resolve.

He picked up the phone and dialed once again.

53

Ryan stopped for breakfast on the way home. After the blow-up with Amy, he wasn't ready to deal with his mother. He pulled into C.J.'s Diner, a converted gas station that had become a popular spot for the most unhealthy Sunday breakfast around. The buttermilk biscuits alone were enough to make anyone forget there was more grease in this establishment now than when they were doing lube jobs. As usual, the line for a table stretched out the front door. Ryan was about to check on availability at the counter when his pager went off. He checked the number. It was Norm.

Ryan had to think for a second to remember where on the learning curve he had left his lawyer. Apart from this morning's fax, they had talked by telephone last night, just after the discovery of the letter. That letter was the first time either of them had heard that the alleged rape victim was Marilyn Gaslow. Like the rest of the country, they had heard her name on television in connection with her recent appointment. Their interest, however, lay in a part of her life that wasn't in the news. At least not yet.

Ryan went to a pay phone outside the restaurant and eagerly dialed the number.

"Did you get my fax this morning?" asked Ryan.

"Yeah. I'll give some thought to a hand-writing expert. But that's not why I'm calling."

"You find something on Gaslow already?"

"Plenty. First, the small stuff. Marilyn Gaslow is exactly your dad's same age, lived near Boulder when he did. She went to Fairmont High School, which was the other one in the area. It's still conceivable they would have known each other, or at least met."

"Which means she also could have known Kozelka."

"That's an understatement. Here's the biggie: They were married."

"What?"

"Joseph Kozelka is Marilyn Gaslow's ex-husband."

"How long were they married?"

"Long time. Tied the knot just two years out

of high school. Lasted twenty-two years. Been divorced almost twenty."

Ryan nearly burst through the phone. "This is it!"

"This is what?"

"The connection I've been waiting for. Marilyn Gaslow accuses my dad of rape. She marries a rich guy. Turns out the accusations are false. He has to pay. It means my dad is innocent!" He could have hugged his friend. "He's *innocent*."

Norm was silent. Ryan asked, "What's wrong?"

"I just think the celebration is premature."

"Norm, don't deprive me of this."

"Do you want my honest opinion or don't you?"

"Yes. But all along, you've never wanted to even entertain the possibility that my dad was innocent."

"That's not true."

"It *is* true. What are you—jealous that maybe now I'll keep the money?"

"Ryan, I'm your friend."

"Some friend. You of all people should know that innocent people do get convicted."

"Not very often."

"It's possible."

"In some cases, yes."

"What the hell do you have against my father?"

"For God's sake, Ryan! If your old man was innocent, don't you think he would have looked you straight in the eye and told you?"

Norm's voice slashed with a cutting edge, as if he were grabbing his friend and shaking him by the lapels. It was a heated moment that left them both cold.

"I'm sorry, Ryan."

The phone was shaking in his hand. "No, you're right. We need to think this through. There must be something we're overlooking."

"Well, we need to think fast. Agent Forsyth called me at home this morning. Now more than ever, the FBI wants our meeting to go forward tomorrow."

"Let's put that off. Just tell them I need a few days to bury my brother-in-law."

"Any more stalling and Forsyth implied the U.S. attorney would initiate a forfeiture proceeding against the Panamanian account. That's an added three-million-dollar headache we don't need right now."

"Who do they think I am, Al Capone?"

"No. But they don't see you as the typical grieving family member, either. The FBI doesn't normally get involved in murder cases. But when a witness is murdered and an attorney is beat up in a pattern of criminal activity that may include extortion and money laundering, that can add up to a federal racketeering charge."

"Wait a minute. You mean they've already linked me to Brent's murder?"

"You're probably the number one suspect, Ryan. And that's just based on what happened in court yesterday. They don't even have the gun yet."

"Great. Kozelka is going to *give* them the damn gun if we go forward with tomorrow's meeting with the FBI."

"Kind of a catch-twenty-two, I know. But there's one sure way to beat it."

"What?"

"Just tell the FBI you're being framed."

"I can't. It's like my mom said. If I tell them I'm being framed, I have to tell them *why* I'm being framed—which means telling them all about the rape and the extortion. And you know what, Norm? You may have your doubts about my father, and those doubts may be reasonable. But if that letter from Debby Parkens is true and my dad didn't commit the rape, then he *did* deserve the money. That money was his justice. Turning it over to the FBI and telling them it's extortion isn't just stupid. It's a betrayal."

"I can see how you feel that way. But there comes a point where it may be too late to claim you were framed."

"I haven't even been formally accused yet, Norm."

"True. But as more time passes, the tighter Kozelka can weave his net."

"Why the hell is he going to all the trouble of framing me, anyway? If he wanted to keep me from talking to the FBI, why not just kill me outright?"

"My guess is that the trip you made to K&G Enterprises saved your life. It would have been very incriminating if you were to turn up dead right after paying Kozelka a personal visit."

"That makes sense, I guess."

They paused to collect their thoughts. Finally, Norm asked, "What are you thinking?"

"I was thinking about timing. You said Joe Kozelka and Marilyn Gaslow were divorced twenty years ago. Was it before or after Amy's mother wrote this letter to my father?"

"After. The divorce was final within a year, actually."

"So they were still married when Kozelka started making the first few extortion payments to my father."

"That's right."

Ryan asked, "Why would he keep paying after they were divorced?"

"Probably for the same reason he's so determined to keep you from talking to the FBI."

"But speaking from personal experience, if someone were blackmailing Liz, I'm not sure I'd feel obligated to keep paying after our marriage was over. What kind of thing could he have going on with his ex-wife?"

"Something's screwy there."

"You're telling me." Ryan thought for a moment. "Push our meeting with the FBI to the end of the day, at least. I need some extra time."

"Oh, shit. Last time I heard you talk like this you nearly landed in a Panamanian prison."

"Don't worry. This time I'll wear my running shoes. Talk to you later." He hung up the phone and hurried to his truck.

54

Sunday was a workday for the presidential appointee. Marilyn Gaslow had just a few days to prepare for her Senate confirmation hearings, and she was wasting not a minute.

Her advisors were working with her at her home in Denver. Some were her friends, some were paid consultants. Today, they would engage in role-playing. Five partners from her law firm pretended to be the Senate Judiciary Committee, firing questions. One of them even showed up with a hangover to lend an added element of authenticity. Marilyn would answer as if it were the real thing. No one was to pull any punches. They assured her that this mock exercise would be much tougher than the real thing.

Marilyn prayed they were right.

To say that head of the Federal Reserve had been a lifelong dream wouldn't be entirely correct. Marilyn was too much of a realist to dream for things that didn't seem attainable. True, she had been one of the President's earliest supporters in Colorado. Her law firm had raised millions for his two campaigns. It didn't take a cerebral hernia to figure out that someone at Bailey, Gaslow & Heinz was due a political plum of an appointment. The buzz at the law firm was something along the lines of an assistant cabinet position or perhaps an appointment to the federal appeals court in Denver. But not the Board of Governors of the Federal Reserve—

and certainly not the chair. Some of her colleagues had kidded her, saying she must have had influential friends she wasn't telling them about. Marilyn took it as good-natured ribbing. She simply smiled and said nothing.

"I need a break," said Marilyn. By 9:00 A.M., they had already been role-playing for ninety minutes. Marilyn's head was beginning to hurt.

"You okay?" asked her consultant. Felicia Hernandez was one of the paid assistants, a young and wiry go-getter who survived on caffeine. Marilyn thought of her as a cheerleader with a Ph.D. in psychology.

"Yeah," she said, massaging her temples. "I think I'd just like to get some aspirin."

"All right. Everybody take five."

The group disbursed, most of them heading toward the coffee and bagels. Marilyn headed down the hall toward her bedroom, alone. She was prone to headaches, though not usually this bad. The excitement over the presidential appointment and the apprehension over the approval process was a deadly combination. Although she had passed Senate confirmation once before, years ago, when she was approved for her position on the Commodities Futures Trading Commission, she knew that wasn't dispositive. Professor Bork had been approved as a federal appeals judge before Reagan had appointed him to the Supreme Court. That didn't keep his enemies from running down to Blockbuster Video to see what movies he'd been renting—anything to dig up dirt and keep him from getting the higher appointment. And they succeeded.

Marilyn went straight to the medicine cabinet and swallowed two Tylenol. As she screwed the cap back on, a noise startled her. From the bathroom off the master, she could hear the fax machine in the bedroom. Curious, she cut across the room. Sure enough, two pages were resting in the receiving bin. They were still warm to the touch.

She checked the first page. It confused her at first. Every other word was blacked out, so that it made no sense to anyone—except to someone who had seen the original. A closer look took her throbbing headache to yet another level. She could see it was a letter addressed to Frank Duffy. And she recognized the signature of her old friend Debby Parkens.

Amy's mother.

She quickly turned to the second page. The message was brief: "Meet me at Cheesman Dam. Monday. Two A.M. Alone."

Her consultant appeared in the doorway. "Marilyn?" she said in her perky cheerleader voice. "You coming? Lots of work to do."

She folded the letter and quickly tucked it in her pocket. "Yes," she said nervously. "Lots of work."

A trail of dust followed Ryan up the driveway. The morning sun had already baked the back roads, leaving no sign of last night's rain. As he stepped down from his truck, he heard the screen door slap shut. He looked toward the house. His mother was standing on the front porch.

"You ready to talk?" she asked as she lowered herself into the chair.

He climbed the stairs, saying nothing, the answer being obvious. Ryan still wasn't convinced that last night's timely arrival of Josh Colburn was coincidental. Nor was he convinced that Sarah's tears were genuine. It all had the makings of a big diversion his mother had created to preempt the family meeting she had promised. Ryan had the unsettling feeling that for whatever reason his mother might never tell him the whole story. Perhaps it was just easier for her, emotionally, to tell him a little at a time. At this point, he'd take whatever he could get.

He leaned against the railing, his back to the yard. "An interesting night," he said. "Mr. Colburn took me by surprise."

"Me too."

"Why do I doubt that?"

"You shouldn't," she said.

"Are you telling me you knew nothing about the letter in Mr. Colburn's safe?"

"Ryan, I swear on your father's soul I know nothing about anything that was part of the blackmail."

"But you knew about the rape."

"Yes.

"Why didn't you tell me about it?"

"Because I believed it never happened."

He made a face, confused. "Why did you believe that?"

"Because that's what your father told me."

"And you just accepted it?"

"It took time. A long time."

"You must have had a reason. Did Dad show you something, say something?"

"Nothing. I didn't want a fancy explanation in some signed and sealed affidavit. Too much time had passed to dig it all up again. I believed him for one reason only, Ryan. Because I *wanted* to believe."

Ryan looked at her skeptically. "Mom," he said in a voice that shook. "I've never said this before, but I have to say it: I don't believe you."

"What don't you believe?"

"I don't believe you just took it on faith that the rape never happened. Dad was *convicted.* You don't just take a convicted man's word for it that the crime never happened."

"You do if that man is your husband, the father of your children."

"No." He started to pace, trying to contain his anger. "You saw the letter, didn't you?"

"I never saw anything, Ryan."

"That's why you believed Dad. You saw the letter from Debby Parkens."

"I told you, no."

"You're the reason he got the letter, aren't you?"

"What?"

"Dad told you it never happened, and you didn't believe him. So he had to go out and get the letter from Marilyn Gaslow's best friend saying she made it all up."

"I never saw the letter."

"But you *knew* about it."

She paused. "Your father told me he had proof it never happened. He said he was going to use it to get even with the bastard who had framed him. I never saw the proof he had. Just, all of a sudden, money started pouring in. Millions of dollars. That was enough for me to believe him."

"Why didn't you just look at the letter?"

"Because I believed him without seeing it."

"You *refused* to look at it, didn't you. You felt guilty for not believing *him*."

"Ryan, you're getting this all backwards."

"I don't think so."

"Ryan, did it ever occur to you that I didn't want to see the proof because I believed him just fine without it? That maybe my greatest fear was that seeing the so-called proof would just raise more questions in my mind?"

Ryan searched her eyes. Her agony seemed genuine. He wanted to console her, but he was suddenly thinking back to a pointed question Norm had raised: If his father was innocent, wouldn't *he* have told Ryan? The answer might have been right before him all along, deep in his mother's eyes. Maybe Dad couldn't face the pain of yet another loved one who *said* "I believe you" but in the heart harbored doubts.

Then another possibility chilled him.

He got down on a knee and took her hand. "Mom, I'm going to ask you something very important. I want a completely honest answer. Do you think it's possible that Dad made up the proof? Would he go so far as to forge a document to prove he was innocent?"

Her reply was soft, shaky. "I don't know,

Ryan. But this is the way I've always looked at it: Would a phony document make somebody pay five million dollars?"

It was the kind of question that needed no answer. Until he thought about it. "Depends on how good the fake is." He rose and retreated into the house, letting the screen door slap shut behind him.

55

Liz slept late on Sunday. She'd had trouble falling asleep. Yesterday's court appearance had given her the jitters. They'd lasted all day, keeping her up most of the night. Not even a bottle of Merlot had calmed her nerves. She'd never testified in court before. Jackson had told her she was terrific, but she didn't have the stomach for it. Thankfully, Ryan's lawyer hadn't come after her. She knew that wouldn't be the case, however, if the legal battle continued. Yesterday had been a victory for sure. But it had taught her something. She was far less interested in courtroom warfare than her lawyer was.

Still, she wasn't about to back down. Last night, drifting in and out of near-sleep, her mind had wandered to places she hadn't visited for some time—scenes from her childhood. She was at the Prowers County Fair, and she was nine years old. It was funny how so many of the games at the fair revolved around money, at least the way Liz remembered it. There used to be a flagpole smeared with grease, with a twenty-dollar bill taped on the top. Kids would line up all day to take a shot at climbing up for the prize. Liz was the one who got it. Instead of wearing old shorts like most of the kids, she'd worn a skirt with her bathing suit underneath, using it like a rag to wipe off the axle grease as she climbed so she wouldn't slide down. Her mother had slapped her face afterward. "What kind of stupid fool are you, Elizabeth? You don't ruin a twenty-dollar skirt to get a twenty-dollar prize." Liz understood the logic, but it seemed beside the point. *Nothing* could dim the feeling of winning that twenty bucks.

The phone rang on the nightstand. Liz rolled across the bed and answered. It was Sarah.

She sat up quickly, wiping the sleep from her eyes. She listened in shock as Sarah told her about Brent.

"Sarah, I had no idea."

"Then why was your lawyer down here this morning?"

"Phil was in Piedmont Springs?"

"Came right to my house to offer me a deal. He wants me to help you squeeze more money out of my brother. Says you'll give me a cut of whatever I can get you."

Her mouth fell open. "Sarah, I swear to you, I never even talked to my lawyer about this. I wouldn't. I would never try to turn you against Ryan. All I'm looking to get is my fair share. I'm not looking to destroy you guys."

"I'd like to believe you."

"You have to believe me. Please. Let's work this out."

Sarah fell silent for a moment. Finally, she said, "I'll make you a deal."

"What?"

"The way I see it, that snake you hired is going to cost us all a fortune. You're going to spend a lot of money trying to get your share, Ryan is going to spend a fortune trying to protect the estate."

Liz nodded to herself, seeing the logic. "Okay. I'm listening."

"I think Jackson uses people. He used Brent. He'll use you. And he won't stop until every dime my father stashed away is lining the pockets of his three-piece suit."

"He is aggressive."

"He's a shark, Liz. And he's circling all of us."

"What are you proposing?"

"From what I've been able to tell, it seems Dad wanted you to share in the family fortune. I'm willing to honor those wishes. On one condition. Fire Phil Jackson."

"You want me to fire my lawyer?"

"Immediately. Jackson is going to screw everything up for everybody. And in the end, the only winners will be the lawyers."

Liz said nothing, but she couldn't disagree. For a split second she was nine years old again, thinking of that twenty-dollar skirt she'd ruined to get the twenty-dollar prize. One Pyrrhic victory was enough for anyone's lifetime.

"Let me think about it," said Liz. "This might just work."

Amy drove nonstop back to Boulder, returning just after noon. Taylor was having a tea party in her room with Barbie. Amy was just in time to join them, but she was able to convince Taylor that the affair was much too formal for someone who had traveled clear across the state without showering. Taylor pinched her nose, hugged her as if she were covered with garlic, and sent her mommy marching off to the bathroom.

Amy had just about made a clean getaway when she heard Gram's voice.

"Not so fast, young lady."

Gram was leaning against the headboard, reading in bed. Amy was almost too tired to talk, but that was irrelevant to her grandmother. She wasn't about to settle for the *Reader's Digest* version, let alone a simple "Tell you later." It took thirty minutes, but Amy sat obediently at the foot of the bed and recounted every detail. She even let Gram read the letter. At first it was difficult, but telling the story seemed to energize her. By the time she'd finished, her second (or perhaps third) wind had kicked in and she was ready to brainstorm.

"Why would Marilyn make the whole thing up?" asked Amy.

"Why does any woman make a false accusation of rape? Maybe they had sex and he dumped her. Maybe she got pregnant and couldn't tell her parents she'd engaged in consensual sex. This was the 1950s, after all. Marilyn did come from a very proper family. Her grandfather founded the biggest law firm in Colorado."

"But the letter doesn't explain any of that."

"Probably because Frank Duffy *knew* why she had lied. He just never was able to prove it."

"What does this prove, though? It's just a letter from my mother saying that Marilyn was never actually raped by Frank Duffy."

Gram took another look at the letter. "It's more than that. It says Marilyn and your mother attended their twenty-fifth high school reunion together. They had a few drinks, got to talking about old boyfriends. And then Marilyn admitted to your mother that Frank Duffy didn't rape her."

"What's the difference?"

"To me, it makes the letter more believable. It's not a secret your mother kept bottled up for twenty-five years and then, for no apparent reason, she decided to write a letter to Frank Duffy. She apparently wrote this letter not too long after Marilyn told her the truth."

"Do you believe she wrote the letter?"

"What reason would I have to doubt that?"

Amy took the letter back. "I don't think the handwriting looks all that much like Mom's. Look at it. It's shaky."

Gram took another look. "There could be any number of reasons for that. Maybe she wrote it the night she came back from the reunion, when it was fresh in her mind. She could have been dead tired or even drunk."

"Or scared," said Amy.

"Scared of what?"

"This was a very courageous thing to do. Marilyn Gaslow was married to Joe Kozelka at the time. That's a pretty intimidating duo. Not everyone would do the right thing under those circumstances."

"Meaning what, Amy?"

"Meaning that she might have feared some retaliation. She could have been afraid...afraid for her life."

Gram groaned. "Now you're going off the deep end again."

Amy was even more serious. "I don't think so. Look at the evidence. I never believed Mom really killed herself. Not the way she talked to me that night, the way the door was tied shut even though she knew I could crawl out through the attic. I never knew why anyone would want to kill her. But this letter—that's a reason, isn't it?"

"Nobody killed your mother, Amy. Your mother killed herself."

"I don't believe it. She wasn't the type to just check out on an eight-year-old daughter."

"Amy, we've been over this so many times. Your mother was terminally ill with a very aggressive cancer. By the time she took her life, she had only weeks to live."

"According to one doctor. Another gave her as long as three months."

"Who told you that?"

"Marilyn. Years ago."

"That's not *her* place," snapped Gram.

"Wrong. It's not *your* place to keep things

like that from me. The longer Mom had to live, the less likely it was she killed herself."

"You're grasping at straws."

Her eyes blazed with anger. "Just because you're convinced it was suicide doesn't give you the right to hide the true facts from me."

"I just didn't want you to see your mother as a coward who left her little girl sooner than she had to. How can you fault me for that?"

"Because she's my *mother,* that's why. I have a right to know what happened."

"And I had a responsibility. I didn't want you to end up in counseling all your life. I was just looking out for you."

"Well, damn it, just *stop* already. I'm twenty-eight years old. Stop treating me as if I were Taylor's age!"

Tears welled in Gram's eyes. "I'm sorry. It was a decision I made for your own good."

"Let *me* make those decisions," she shouted, rising from the bed.

"At least let me explain."

Amy felt the urge to bolt, but the weary look in Gram's eyes wouldn't allow it. She sat back down on the edge of the bed.

"When your father was killed in Vietnam…" Her grandmother paused, struggling. "I had to know what happened to my son."

Her voice was cracking. Amy touched her hand to console. Gram continued. "It wasn't enough just to hear he'd been killed in action. I needed specifics. I asked everyone who knew him, other boys in his platoon. Most of them gave me vague answers. I wouldn't stop until I found someone who would be completely honest with me. Finally, I found someone. To this day, I wish I never had. I thought it would give me closure to know exactly how it had happened." She dabbed a tear, then looked her granddaughter in the eye. "There's no closure in the details of violent death, Amy. Only nightmares."

Amy leaned forward and embraced her. Gram squeezed back with all her strength, whispering in Amy's ear, "You're the child I lost, darling. I love you like my own."

Amy shivered. It had surely come from the heart, but perhaps it was one of those self-evident sentiments that was awkward to articulate and best left unsaid. They hugged a little tighter, then Amy tried to pull away. But she couldn't move.

Gram would not let go.

"Mommy?"

Amy broke away at the sound of Taylor's voice. She was standing in the doorway, wearing Gram's big pink apron. "What, sweetheart?"

"Are you coming to my tea party now?"

She smiled. "Mommy still has to shower."

Gram grabbed her by the dangling apron strings. "Come here, Taylor. Let me tie your apron before you trip and hurt yourself."

It was too big to tie in the back, the way it was supposed to tie. She wrapped it around Taylor's waist and tied it in the front. Taylor watched carefully, still at the age where something as simple as tying a knot was utterly intriguing.

"You tie funny," said Taylor.

Amy said, "That's because Gram is right-handed. You're left-handed, like me. And like my mommy was." She stopped for a second, as if struck by lightning.

Gram watched with concern. "Taylor, go check on Barbie. I'll be there in a second."

"Okay," she said as she hurried from the room.

Gram asked, "Amy, what's going on in that head of yours?"

"The knot."

"What knot?"

"I was just thinking about the rope that was tied to my bedroom door—that kept me in the room the night Mom died. The theory is that Mom tied me in my room so I wouldn't find the body after she killed herself."

"Right."

"If she tied the knot, then it would have been tied the way a left-handed person tied it."

"Nobody ever said it wasn't."

"But did anyone ever say it *was*?"

Gram just sat there, silent.

"I didn't think so." Amy looked off to the middle distance, deep in thought. Finally, she glanced back at her grandmother. "I have to go back there."

"Back where?"

"Our old house."

"That's crazy. You don't even know who lives there now."

"I have to try. Don't you see? I'm not saying I'm going to go back and remember which way a little knot was tied. But this just drives home the point that I'm missing the details. If I could just remember more about that night, maybe that would resolve the questions I have. Going back there is the only way I can think of to jar my memory."

"Amy, accept what I'm telling you. Your mother made a quick escape from a long and painful illness."

"Lots of people get cancer and don't kill themselves."

"That may be. But doesn't what I just told about your father mean anything?"

"Yes," she said sincerely. "It means we're all different. Some of us are better off not knowing. Some of us would rather die than carry on without knowing. You've known me all my life. Deep in your heart, which kind of person do you really think I am?"

Gram showed no encouragement, but the fight had drained from her eyes. "All right. But I'm going with you."

56

Marilyn lacked focus. That was the consensus opinion of her prep session experts. They offered numerous explanations for her subpar performance. She was too serious. She was too flip. She was overprepared. She was under-prepared. All of them were off the mark.

Way off the mark.

It was only midafternoon, and already

Marilyn had been at it for a full eight hours. A fresh group of interrogators had replaced the morning team at lunchtime. The procedure had remained the same, however, and it was getting tedious. Each member of the mock Senate Judiciary Committee would ask a question. Marilyn would answer. The experts would critique. It was enough to fry a woman with a clear head. It was unbearable for someone as preoccupied as Marilyn.

"Let's take a break," said Marilyn.

"Second," shouted one of the mock committee members. The chairman banged his coffee cup like a gavel, and the others eagerly shifted out of role. Some stood up and stretched, while the others drifted toward the leftover sandwiches and chocolate chip cookies at the lunch buffet table. Marilyn headed in the other direction.

"You're doing great, Marilyn," said her consultant.

Marilyn forced a smile. She knew she was lying. "Thanks. If you don't mind, I think I'm going to lie down for about a half hour. Clear my head."

"Excellent idea. We won't go much longer today. I promise."

"Good," she said, then headed back to her bedroom.

The walk down the hall was her first real opportunity to think. The effect was immediate. Her headache was back before she even reached the bedroom door.

She stepped inside the master and closed the door. This time she locked it.

The bedroom was her sacred sanctuary, a place for retreat. More than any other place, it reflected her own tastes and preferences. Here, she didn't need the power look of her corner office. She didn't even feel the decorating constraints that governed the rest of the house, where furniture was arranged to accommodate party flow and rugs were selected on the basis of whether they were resistant to red wine and shrimp sauce. This was her space, and hers alone. There had been men, of course, some of whom she wished she had never invited. But that was the point. Pleasant or not, they had been *invited*. This morning's fax was altogether different. In this room, nothing could have been more intrusive.

She opened the top drawer of the nightstand and removed the fax. The choice of venue was interesting. Cheesman Dam. It wasn't the makeout spot Cherry Creek Dam was for Denver teenagers in the fifties, but it was one of the more remote spots to watch the proverbial submarine races. Marilyn hadn't been there in over forty-five years, since she was fifteen. Her one and only visit. She and her boyfriend, Joe Kozelka, on a double date with Joe's friend Frank and some ditz named Linda. The four of them had taken a day trip down to Pikes Peak in Frank's car, as Joe didn't have a license yet. Two other couples followed in another car. On the way back to Boulder, they stopped at Cheesman Dam, sharing a bottle of hundred-proof Southern Comfort as the sun set. They ended up staying longer than they'd planned. Longer than they should have.

The headache was getting worse. Her temples were throbbing, and a blinding light pierced her eye. It felt like a migraine. She tried to focus on the pillow across the room, but it only made her dizzy. Her mind swirled with memories. She shook her head, trying not to go there, but it was too late. The woozy feeling, the blurred vision—it was much the way she'd felt more than four decades ago on that warm summer night in the back seat of Frank Duffy's Buick…

"I'm *drunk!*" Marilyn snorted as she laughed, smiling widely.

"I'm *glad*," said Joe. He took a swig straight from the bottle of Southern Comfort, then moved closer.

Marilyn scooted forward. The view through the windshield brought a gleam to her eyes. Cheesman was an old stone masonry dam that rose more than two hundred and twenty feet above the streambed below. Tonight, the moon hung low over the gaping canyon. Bright stars blanketed the sky. They glistened off the placid waters of the reservoir behind the dam. With all she'd had to drink, it was hard to tell where the stars ended and their reflection began. "So pretty," she said. "Let's go for a walk."

"That's a great idea," said Joe. "Frank, why don't you and Linda go first."

Frank was resting comfortably behind the wheel, his girlfriend's head on his shoulder. "I don't want to go for—"

Joe thumped him on the back of the head, knocking sense into him. Frank looked back

387

and glared, then smiled thinly. "You know," said Frank, "I could use some air. Let's go, Linda."

The door opened. Frank and his date slid out. The door slammed shut. Marilyn and Joe were alone in the backseat.

"Let's go, too," said Marilyn.

He took her arm and stopped her. "Have some more to drink."

"I don't want any more."

"Just have some."

"It's making me kind of sick."

"That's because you're mixing in too much Seven-Up. You have to drink some straight whiskey. If you don't get the right balance, you get sick. Come on. Drink up."

"I don't think I can drink it straight."

"Don't think about it. Just chug it." He handed her the bottle. She hesitated. He tipped the neck toward her, helping it along. "Go on. Trust me, Marilyn. Just trust me."

She brought the bottle to her lips. Her head went back. The whiskey touched her lips. It burned her throat. She wanted to stop, but Joe held her head back and kept the bottle in place. She swallowed once, twice. She was losing count. The burning stopped, but the whiskey kept flowing. She was feeling dizzy, then totally numb. She pushed the bottle away. She blinked to focus, but Joe was a blur. He was smiling and moving closer. Her mouth moved, but she couldn't even form a sentence in her head, let alone with her lips. Her body tingled, then she lost all sensation as her head rolled back and the lights went out...

Marilyn opened her eyes. She was lying on the bed. The headache had lessened somewhat. Slowly, she sat up and glanced across the room. She could see again. Her gaze landed upon the fax machine across the room. The receiving bin was empty, which came as a relief. No more threats.

It *was* a threat, she'd decided. On the heels of her appointment, there was no other way to interpret it. The timing could not be coincidence. The header on the fax said it was from the 719 area code, which included Piedmont Springs. At the lunch break she'd confirmed it was from a drugstore in Prowers County, one of those places that will let anyone send a fax for a couple of bucks. She figured it had to be from *someone* in the Duffy family, which could not be good. True, the message was vague. It didn't say, "Do this, or else." But it didn't have to be explicit to be threatening. And she knew what she was supposed to do if ever she felt threatened.

She drew a deep breath, then picked up the phone and dialed Joe Kozelka.

57

Sheila was beginning to worry. Rusch wasn't happy with her work. One little mistake—a stupid cocktail glass left behind in a Panamanian hotel. It was such a tenuous link to Kozelka anyway. Even if the FBI got a match on her fingerprints, they would still have to make her buckle under pressure and finger Kozelka. She was no snitch, but her roots as a hooker must have made Rusch nervous. Clearly he was assuming she would deal with the FBI the way she used to deal with him.

Everything was negotiable.

Her survival instincts were kicking in. When Rusch had said they would "reevaluate," she knew what that meant. If the frame-up didn't keep Ryan Duffy from taking that glassful of fingerprints to the FBI, Sheila was dead. One way or another, Rusch would make sure she was never subjected to FBI interrogation.

Sheila herself had been reevaluating things all afternoon, ever since she and Rusch had stopped to rest in a cheap roadside hotel. It was time to get out of Dodge. But not without a piece of the action.

Late Sunday afternoon, she picked up the phone in her hotel room and dialed Ryan Duffy. She tried his clinic, but no one answered. She tried his mother's house and hit pay dirt.

"Remember this voice?" She used the same seductive voice she'd used in Panama.

Ryan felt a chill. He was alone in his mother's kitchen, standing by the counter. "Where have you been?"

"Closer than you think. I've got something for you."

"What?"

"Your father's gun."

His pulse quickened. "I want it."

"How bad? Or should I say, how much?"

"Are you saying it's for sale?"

"That's a keen grasp of the obvious you've got there, Doc."

"How much?"

"A bargain. According to my sources, you've got another two million dollars cash somewhere. Just a hundred grand is all I want."

"How do I know you really have it?"

"Because I took it."

"From Kozelka's thug? Right. The guy's a Goliath."

Sheila glanced over her shoulder. Rusch lay naked on the bed behind her, flat on his back. He was still erect—a bigger stud unconscious than he was wide awake.

"He's not so tough," she said with a smirk.

Ryan's interest piqued. He sensed a crack in the alliance. But he also feared a trap.

Sheila said, "What's it gonna be, Doc? You want the gun or don't you?"

"Of course I want it."

"Then you gotta pay."

He froze, undecided. Then an idea struck. This was a chance to pull it all together—to put Marilyn Gaslow and Kozelka's goons at the same place at the same time. It would be telling indeed to see how they treated one another. "All right," said Ryan. "Meet me at Cheesman Dam. Two A.M."

"See you then," she said, then hung up the phone.

Yeah, thought Ryan. *See* us *then*.

The phone rang in Marilyn Gaslow's bedroom. She hadn't moved from the edge of her bed since dialing Joe Kozelka's pager. She checked the caller identification box on her nightstand. It was him.

"Joe, thanks for calling back."

"What's going on?"

"Trouble." She told him about the faxed invitation to Cheesman Dam.

He was silent, the way he usually was whenever he got angry. Hundreds of times during their marriage, Marilyn had watched him internalize his rage. Joe was a pressure cooker that totally blew about every ten years. The first time, she'd forgiven him. The second time she'd decided not to wait for a third. She was afraid she wouldn't live through the third.

"Who sent it?"

"It came from the seven-one-nine area code. I assume it's from the Duffys."

"Probably. But Amy Parkens was down that way this morning, too."

"How do you know?"

"We know. Rusch put a tracking device on her truck."

"Amy wouldn't send a fax like this."

"No, but she and Duffy could be cooking something up."

"Let me call Amy."

"No," he said sternly. "Just let me handle it."

"What are you going to do?"

"Leave your Mercedes in the driveway with the keys in the glove box. I'll arrange for someone to pick it up this evening and drive it to the dam."

Marilyn blinked nervously. "And then what?"

"Whoever sent this has to be taught a lesson. I had a deal with the old man. Frank got five million dollars. His family was never supposed to see the letter. He obviously broke his end of the deal. Now the family has to deal with the consequences."

"Please don't get carried away here."

"Don't tell me what to do," he said, his voice tightening. "I've paid a lot of money to call the shots, Marilyn. Five million to Duffy. Millions more in campaign contributions to get you in line for some useful presidential appointment. It took a long time for the right opportunity to come along. To be honest, the Board of Governors was even beyond my expectations. But now that it's for the taking, we are not going to be denied your one and only shot at the chair."

"You mean *your* shot," she said bitterly.

"I will never influence a decision of yours, Marilyn. I just want to know what your decisions are. Before anyone else does."

Her stomach wrenched. A man as wealthy as Kozelka could make billions of dollars knowing that the Fed was going to raise interest rates a day before the public announcement. "Do you have to rub it in my face? I'm well aware that you're the one who stands to gain."

"And if you resist me, you're the one who stands to lose. That's the real beauty of it, Marilyn."

She said nothing, knowing it was true.

"I'm counting on you," he said. "Study hard for your confirmation hearing. And leave the rest to me."

The dial tone hummed in her ear. Marilyn felt numb as she hung up the phone. She was poised to assume one of the world's most powerful positions, yet she was a puppet. Worst of all, a puppet under the control of her ex-husband. In hindsight, she would never have paid the extortion. Once she did, however, there was no going back. She knew of no public official who could survive a teenage rape scandal that involved the payment of hush money.

Back then, saving her career had seemed like the only thing to do. Right now, however, it wasn't her career she was worried about. It terrified her to think that Amy might show up with Ryan Duffy at Cheesman Dam. Had she known Amy had been in Piedmont Springs this morning, she would never have called Joe. As it turned out, she might well have signed Amy's death warrant. *That* was something she could never live with.

She reached for the phone, then put it down. There was too much to tell, too much to explain. She grabbed her purse and started for the door.

It was time she and Amy had a very frank talk.

58

It was Amy's first trip down Holling Street since the night her mother died. For over twenty years she had avoided the old house, the street, and pretty much the entire neighborhood. She recognized the contradiction—a *scientist* who refused to look at the data. As much as she wanted the truth, her intellectual curiosity had always yielded to emotion whenever she came too close to her past. The house had become like the Ring Nebula, the dying star she had captured on that tragic night in her telescope. She just couldn't look at it again.

Until tonight.

Amy parked at the curb, beneath a streetlight. The two-story frame house sat in relative darkness on the other side of the street. Just one light was on. It came from the dining room, or at least what used to be the dining room. As her eyes adjusted to the moonlight, she noted all the things that had changed. The tiny Douglas fir she and her mother had planted in the front yard was now over twenty feet tall. The front porch where they used to swing had been enclosed in makeshift fashion. The clapboard siding needed a fresh coat of paint, and the lawn needed mowing. Cracks in the sidewalk seemed more plentiful. Amy remembered how she used to skip over them as a child, determined not to break her mother's back.

"You sure you want to do this?" Gram asked from behind.

Amy nodded. She started up the sidewalk, ignoring the cracks, letting her feet fall where they may.

As she climbed the front steps, the night could no longer hide the telltale signs of aging and neglect. Several broken windows had been boarded rather than replaced. The front door bore the scars of a previous break-in, or perhaps just a tenant who had forgotten his key. The porch railings had nearly been consumed by rust. The basement window was framed with water damage. Amy had expected some disrepair. Her mother's violent death had stigmatized the property. Gram had tried to sell it after the funeral, but no one wanted to live there. An investor finally picked it up for less than the remaining mortgage. For the past twenty years, it had been rented to college students for less than half the going rate for a three-bedroom house. The owner was apparently content to let it deteriorate to the point where it could be razed and replaced by ghost-free new construction.

Amy knocked firmly. Gram touched her hand as they waited. Finally, the chain rattled on the door, and it opened. A young man wearing blue jeans and a white UC Boulder T-shirt stood in the open doorway. Something that resembled a mustache covered his upper lip. He was like a big kid who had grown a little facial hair to make him look like college material.

"You're the lady who called?" he said.

"Yes." Amy had called in advance to explain who she was. The students who lived there had no qualms with her visit. They actually thought it was pretty cool. "This is my grandmother," said Amy.

"Cool. I'm Evan. Come on in."

Amy stepped inside. Gram followed. Amy stood in the foyer, nearly breathless. It looked almost as bad as Amy's apartment after the break-in. The fireplace had been boarded up to keep out the weather or worse. In traffic areas, the vintage seventies shag carpet had worn through to the floorboards. Wires dangled from the ceiling where there used to be a chandelier. A collage of posters covered the cracked and dirty walls. A mattress lay on the dining room floor.

"You sleep in the dining room?" she asked.

"No, there's three of us. We made that into Ben's room. Jake gets the back bedroom downstairs. I get the small bedroom upstairs."

"Who gets the master?"

He made a face. "Nobody. No offense, but nobody even goes in there."

"None taken," she said, seeming to understand. "Is there anybody upstairs now?"

"No. My roomies are out sucking down margaritas at Muldoon's."

"You mind if I have a look around?"

"That's what you came for, isn't it? Be my guest."

"Thanks."

Gram asked, "You want me to come with you?"

397

"Oh, by the way," said Evan. "Don't mind the pet tarantula at the top of the stairs. He looks mean, but he's okay with strangers. Well, most strangers."

"On second thought," said Gram, "I'll wait here."

Amy said, "I think it's best I do this alone anyway."

Gram gave her a hug. Amy turned and started up the stairs.

She climbed slowly, deliberately. With each step, she felt a rush of adrenaline. Her pulse quickened. Her hands began to tingle. The feelings were coming back to her. She remembered having lived there. Flying down the stairs on Christmas mornings. Racing up the stairs to her room each day after school. She stopped on the landing at the top of the stairway. Down the hall to her right was her old room. To the left was her mother's. She tried to pinpoint her memory and focus on that night. Her mind wouldn't take her there. Too much distraction. A strange mountain bike in the hallway. The pet tarantula in the tank. The lights had to go. There had been no lights on that night.

She flipped the switch. The present disappeared. She stood alone in darkness.

Fear filled her heart. Not the fear of tarantulas or other things that were there. She was feeling the fear of an eight-year-old girl. She stood frozen in the darkness, waiting for it to subside. It wouldn't. As her eyes adjusted, the fear only grew. She could see all the way down the hall, through the darkness, right up to the door that led to her mother's room. The fear was much worse than it had been twenty years ago. This time she knew what lay on the other side.

Her foot slid forward and she took the first step.

She felt the carpet between her toes, even though she wore shoes. She was eight again and barefoot, creeping down the hall toward her mother's room. Her knees felt scratched from the crawl through the attic—the escape from her room. Another step forward and she could hear the oscillating fan. The door was now open. She saw the clump of blankets atop the bed. Finally, she saw the hand again, hanging limply off the mattress. Words stuck in her throat, but her mind heard them anyway. *Mom?*

A chill went down her spine as she was sucked from the room. She was spiraling down the hall, screaming helplessly, caught in some kind of cosmic explosion that lifted her from the hallway, the house, the planet.

Dust and debris clouded her vision as she raced though the night at such incredible speed that the stars converged into an endless beam of light that seemed to bend with her movement and wrap around her fears. It wrapped tighter and tighter, until the fear subsided and she could make herself think. Thinking slowed the pace. Thinking dimmed the intensity. She was no longer going anywhere. She was back on the planet, a distant and dispassionate observer, a scientist logging what she'd seen on that horrible night.

The Ring Nebula. M 57. The fifty-seventh object in Charles Messier's eighteenth-century catalog of fuzzy objects in the sky.

"Amy?"

She turned. Gram was right behind her on the steps. She had never left the landing.

"You okay?" asked Gram.

Amy's hands were shaking. She was sweating beneath her jacket. She wanted to lie and say yes, but she was too overwhelmed.

Gram asked, "Are you going to go in?"

Amy looked at her grandmother, her eyes filled with emotion. "I already did. Come on," she said, taking Gram by the arm. "Let's go home."

59

Trumpets blared. Violins wept. Joe Kozelka was seated in a leather wing chair, allowing a glass of Chivas Regal to help him through Beethoven's Ninth Symphony.

Music helped him sort out his thoughts. Whenever life seemed without order, he would put it to music. The Ninth Symphony was his favorite, particularly the fourth movement. Experts thought it contained some of the master's ugliest music. Kozelka had only the highest admiration for a man who could successfully incorporate his most controversial moments into his greatest overall achievement.

The music was suddenly soft. His thoughts turned toward Marilyn. In the nearly fifty years they'd known each other, they'd shared many memories. Strangely, the most memorable night for him was one of which Marilyn had no memory. It was the night Frank Duffy had driven them to Cheesman Dam. The night they'd all gotten drunk and parked on the canyon ridge.

His eyes drifted toward a Russian cut-crystal vase on the mantel. It sparkled beneath the track lighting, like the blanket of stars reflecting off the Cheesman reservoir. He sipped his Chivas, but it suddenly tasted like Southern Comfort. He remembered everything about that night, every little detail. He could smell the sweet bourbon, feel the warmth of his own erratic breath. He could see Marilyn passed out in the backseat of Frank's car, watch himself get out and walk up the path toward his unsuspecting friend...

"Frank, hey," said Joe.

Frank Duffy and his girlfriend were sitting on a fallen log, facing the moonlit canyon beyond the ridge. Joe was out of breath as he caught up with them.

Frank rose. "What's wrong?"

"It's Marilyn. She passed out. And—"

"And what?"

Joe made a face. "She tossed her cookies all over your backseat."

"Aww, man."

"Hey, it's not her fault. She never drank before."

"How bad is it?"

"Pretty bad. Look for yourself."

The boys ran toward the car. Linda followed behind. Frank opened the car door and immediately recoiled. The pungent odor was unmistakable. "Oh, gawd!"

Joe looked inside. Marilyn was lying on her back across the seat. A pool of vomit lay on the floor behind the driver's seat. "At least she didn't get any on her."

"What about my car?" said Frank. "I'll never get that smell out."

Linda stuck her head in, sniffed, and stepped back. "Yuck. You're on your own, Frankie boy. I'm not riding all the way back to Boulder in that. I'll catch a ride with the others."

"Linda, come on."

"No way. I'm squeezing in the other car." She hurried away before Frank could stop her.

Joe had an impish expression. "I think I'm going to ride back with the others, too."

"No way! She's your girlfriend."

"Frank, I'm feeling kind of sick myself. If I ride back with you and that smell, I'm going to lose it, too. You want double the mess in your car? Just take her home for me, will you, please?"

"I can't believe you're bailing on me like this."

"Come on, man. I can't let Marilyn's parents see me like this. They're good friends with my old man. They'll kill me."

"What about me?"

"The worst that will happen is that her parents won't let her double-date with Frank

Duffy anymore. That's no big deal. You're not the one who wants to marry her."

Frank's eyes widened. "You're in love with this girl?"

"Please. Just take her home. If her dad knows I got her drunk, I—I don't know what I'll do if he won't let me see her anymore."

Frank groaned, then said, "All right. What am I supposed to tell her parents?"

"I don't know. Tell them she got food poisoning. Just don't mention my name. Promise?"

"Yeah, I guess so." Frank dug for his car keys and opened the door. "But you owe me, Joe. Big time."

Joe slapped him on the back, nearly shoving him into the driver's seat. "Yeah, buddy. You have no idea."

...The phone rang, drawing Kozelka from his memories. Beethoven's symphony was in its fourth movement. The tumultuous Horror Fanfare had just begun when he hit the mute button and grabbed the phone.

"Yeah," he said.

"It's me," said Nathan Rusch.

"Where the hell have you been? I've beeped you a dozen times."

"I've been...indisposed."

"What is that supposed to mean?"

Rusch shook his head. Ex-prostitutes were like walking pharmacies. The effects of whatever Sheila had slipped him had not yet passed completely. "Long story."

"I need you back in Denver tonight. Duffy contacted Marilyn directly. He expects her to show up at the Cheesman Dam at two A.M."

"Why there?"

"Never mind, Rusch. Just get over here. I need you at the dam."

"You don't suspect an FBI setup?"

"No. It's a clear case of like father, like son. The boy wants more money. He isn't going to bring in the FBI to bear witness to his extortion. Besides, we have him boxed in so long as we have his father's gun."

Rusch rubbed his throbbing head. "One thing I should tell you. The gun is gone."

"Gone?" he said incredulously.

"The girl stole it, I think. She's gone and the gun is gone."

"Damn it, Rusch. The frame-up was our way of making sure that Duffy doesn't talk to the FBI."

"I realize that, sir."

Kozelka guzzled the rest of his scotch. In a rare surge of rage, he squeezed the crystal so tightly it nearly crushed in his bare hand. "That leaves us one option. Scorched earth. Take out the targets who are pushing the hardest."

"Meaning?"

"The lawyer and the ex-wife have to go. Preferably in one hit. Tonight."

"Easy enough. I'm thinking maybe an urgent package marked personal and confidential, addressed to Liz Duffy but delivered to Jackson's house. The lawyer shouldn't open it without his client's permission. Decent chance they'll open it together. I guarantee, it'll be the last thing that twosome ever does."

"Good." He tucked the phone under his chin

and refilled his scotch. "Get it done before you meet Duffy at the dam. I want this to look like the boy went berserk. Killed his brother-in-law, his ex-wife, her lawyer."

"And then?"

"Then he drove to the dam where his father raped a woman and blew his brains out."

Rusch smirked. "My specialty."

"Just don't screw it up. I have *everything* riding on this." The words lingered for a moment, then he hung up the phone.

60

Ryan reached Denver long after dark. He'd been thinking about the meeting on the long drive up and was starting to feel vulnerable. He stopped at Norm's house in Cherry Creek before heading out to the dam.

"What now?" asked Norm. He was standing at the back door, dressed in a T-shirt and shorts. He was wearing his eyeglasses, having removed the contact lenses for bed.

"I need a favor," said Ryan. "Can I come in?"

He stepped aside. "Just be quiet about it. Kids are asleep."

"It's just me, not the prize patrol." Ryan went to the kitchen, opened the refrigerator, and borrowed a Pepsi. Norm sat at the table.

Ryan sipped his soda. "I have a meeting tonight."

"Who with?"

"Marilyn Gaslow."

"You just have to ask her about that letter, don't you." Norm was practically groaning.

"Of course."

"Isn't it enough for you to have it in writing?"

Ryan came to the table. "The letter is no good until someone confirms it's true. I want to hear it straight from her that my father never raped her."

"Why wouldn't it be true?"

Ryan sat across from the friend, his expression solemn. "Have you ever stopped to think what stake Amy Parkens's mother might have had in this?"

"How do you mean?"

"I'm talking about motive. Why would she write that letter to my father?"

"Because Marilyn wouldn't do it. And it was the right thing to do."

"That's one explanation. Another is that she and my dad were in this thing together."

"What are you talking about?"

"Maybe that two hundred thousand dollars my father sent Amy Parkens wasn't just an unsolicited expression of gratitude for the way Debby Parkens stepped up to the plate and did the right thing. It could have been part of their deal. My dad and Amy's mother, co-conspirators."

"You're saying Debby Parkens betrayed her best friend Marilyn Gaslow?"

"For money."

Norm shook his head. "That would be like me selling you out."

"Or like Judas, who took his money and then hung himself from a tree. Betrayal always has consequences. Did you ever think maybe that's why Amy's mother killed herself?"

"Or why somebody killed her."

Ryan paused, then said, "Somebody like Marilyn."

They looked cautiously at one another, each waiting for the other to say they were talking crazy. Neither said a word.

"What's your plan?" asked Norm.

Ryan smiled with his eyes. "I knew you'd see it my way. I told her to meet me at Cheesman Dam. I figured if I was going to get an honest answer—or at least an honest reaction—from her, it made sense to get her back on the spot where the rape either happened or didn't happen."

"And if she says what you want her to say...then what?"

"I want my father's name cleared forever. I want Marilyn's voice on tape. I need to be wired."

"You can record it, but I want you to understand that it's not something you could ever use in court against her. The only way to do this legally would be to work with law enforcement."

"I'm not looking for something I can use in a courtroom. This is for me and my family. I want my mother to hear it."

"So do I," said Norm. "Let me call my investigator. He'll fit you up, no problem." He rose and stepped toward the telephone on the kitchen counter.

"I want a bulletproof vest, too. Just in case. And I need to borrow your gun."

Norm held the phone, poised to dial. "Marilyn Gaslow is not going to shoot you."

"No. But I've invited someone else to the meeting besides Marilyn. Someone a little less predictable. Someone who says she can return my father's gun to me."

Norm hung up the phone and returned to the table. "Let's talk about this."

"Yeah," said Ryan, "let's talk."

61

They returned to the Clover Leaf Apartments after ten o'clock. Gram went inside to turn down Taylor's bed while Amy went up to Mrs. Bentley's to pick her up. Rather than take her impressionable daughter to the old house, Amy had left her with their usual sitter.

Amy knocked once. The door opened. Mrs. Bentley was standing in the doorway. Marilyn Gaslow was standing right behind her, flashing a look that bordered on terror.

"Marilyn?" she said. "What are you doing here?"

"I stopped by your apartment, but no one was there. Your neighbor said to check with Mrs. Bentley."

"Is Taylor okay?"

Mrs. Bentley answered. "She's fine. Asleep since nine o'clock."

Marilyn said, "I have to talk to you. In private."

Amy was confused but curious. She got Mrs. Bentley to watch Taylor for a while longer, then stepped into the hall with Marilyn.

"What's this all about?"

Marilyn glanced over her shoulder, almost paranoid. "Can we talk someplace private?"

"My apartment's right upstairs."

"I mean totally private. Not even your grandmother."

The tone worried Amy. She led Marilyn down the hall to the laundry room, dug her key from her purse, and opened the door. "Nobody comes in here after ten o'clock. It closes then."

She pushed the metal door open and stepped inside. Marilyn followed. A bare fluorescent light made the tiny room too bright. The walls were yellow-painted cinder block, no windows. Six white washing machines lined one side. Stacked dryers lined another. A few mateless socks lay scattered on the linoleum floor. Amy closed the door and locked it. An empty chair waited by the soda machine, but neither one took it. They went to the folding table in the center of the room and stood at opposite ends, facing each other.

"Okay," said Amy. "Now tell me. What's going on?"

Marilyn struggled for words, struggled to look at Amy. "I haven't been honest with you."

"No kidding."

"I wish there was some unselfish explanation for my dishonesty. I'd like to be able to tell you it was for your own good."

"Please. I've heard that one enough for one lifetime."

Marilyn nodded, knowing the old story. "That always sounds so hollow, doesn't it? Rarely is it ever for the benefit of anyone but the person who is being dishonest. But I was able to fool myself for years. I told myself it was for your own safety that I didn't tell you the truth. Only tonight did I admit to myself that all the deception was for my benefit—for the good of my career. It took something pretty drastic to get me to realize that."

"What?"

"I realized that unless you know the truth, you are going to get yourself killed." She looked away, then back. "Just like your mother."

Amy went cold. "My mother was murdered, wasn't she."

"I don't know."

"Stop lying! Ryan Duffy showed me Mom's letter. I know the rape never happened."

"That's not what it says. It says Frank Duffy didn't rape me."

Her voice lowered, but the tone was just as bitter. "What's the difference?"

"I *was* raped."

A tense silence fell between them. "By who?"

She paused, then said, "Joe."

"You *married* the man who raped you?"

"I didn't know it was him. I thought it was Frank."

"That's ridiculous."

"Listen to me, please. It's not as ridiculous as it sounds." She quickly recounted the drive to Cheesman Dam forty-six years ago, the drinking that led to her passing out. "The next thing I knew, I was in the police station. My parents were there. A counselor was there. I had been raped. Joe denied ever laying a hand me. He made a real scene of it, accusing Frank of raping me when he drove me home. He even punched Frank in the face."

"And they believed Joe?"

"Frank ran with the rough crowd in high school. Never did anything major, but enough to make the police think he was capable of rape. Joe was the perfect kid from the perfect family."

"Couldn't they do a blood test from the semen?"

"They were both O-positive. Something like forty percent of the population is O-positive. And of course this was decades before they started doing DNA testing."

"So Frank got charged."

"And convicted."

"How did you find out the truth? What *is* the truth?"

"The truth is, Joe raped me after I passed out. Before any of us ever left Cheesman Dam. Before I got sick."

Amy stepped away from the table, taking it all in. "When did you find all this out?"

"Joe finally told me. Years after we were married."

411

"He just confessed?"

"No. Joe is one of those even-tempered gentlemen who blow a gasket every now and then. He could get pretty rough, especially if he drank. One time I actually had to hit him to keep him off me. He came back and said something like, 'I'll rape you again, bitch.' It was the *again* that hung him. I forced it out of him."

"What did you do?"

"I wanted to tell Frank Duffy how sorry I was. But if I ever told anyone, Joe swore he'd say our sex was consensual and that it was *my* idea to put the blame on Frank Duffy, just to save my reputation."

"But...you told my mother."

"Yes. I had to."

"I don't understand."

Marilyn tried to step closer, but Amy kept her distance. Marilyn said, "It was the same night your mother told me she had cancer. She was worried about you. She asked me to be your guardian."

Amy was confused, anguished. "What did you say?"

"I was torn. I wanted to. I would have done anything for Debby and you."

"But you didn't say yes."

"I couldn't give her an unconditional yes. I thought this thing with Frank Duffy was a potential noose around my neck. The absolute worst thing for you would be to lose your mother to cancer and then lose your guardian because she was embroiled in a rape scandal. I wanted Debby to know everything that

412

could possibly impact on my perceived fitness to be your guardian. So I told her I had decided to divorce Joe. And I told her why."

"You told her Frank Duffy didn't rape you. You told her it was Joe."

"That's right."

"And then she wrote to Frank Duffy and told him exactly what you said. Why?"

"I don't know why. Maybe she thought Frank might need the letter to clear his name someday. Whatever she was thinking, I've always felt somewhat betrayed by that."

The rage returned. "And that's when Frank Duffy started to blackmail you and Joe."

"Yes."

"And then my mother was shot."

"After. Yes."

"Oh, my God. It's like Ryan Duffy said. You and Joe are in this together. You killed my mother for telling his father the truth."

"No, I didn't."

"That's why Joe paid all that extortion. You weren't just hiding the rape. It was the murder. You killed my mother for writing that letter to Frank Duffy. And then you paid Frank Duffy to hide the letter and keep your motive a secret."

"Amy, I didn't kill her."

"Then Joe did."

Marilyn was silent.

Amy came around the table, ready to strike her. "Joe killed her, didn't he?"

Marilyn stepped back, on the verge of tears. "I don't know. I swear to God, I don't know."

"You *know*, Marilyn. In your heart, you know."

She covered her face, her hands shaking. "Don't you think it's been hell for me? Yes, in my heart I've suspected."

"Then why didn't you do something? Just go to the police."

"I couldn't. Not after Joe started paying the blackmail. The way he set it up, the whole scheme looked like it was designed to protect my reputation, my career. The police would have thought I was behind the murder. Not Joe."

"Why shouldn't I think the same thing?"

"Because now Joe's motive is finally apparent. It was a long-term investment for him. The blackmail, the murder. He controls me. And if I get this appointment to the Board of Governors, he'll control the Federal Reserve."

"You let him control you."

"I made a bad decision, and it snowballed. But I would never have done anything to hurt your mother. Or you. I'm a victim here, too. How do you think it feels after forty-six years? To be deceived into marrying the man who raped me. And to be manipulated by him still, twenty years after the divorce."

Marilyn wiped away a tear. Amy felt every right to be angry, but she felt sorry for her, too.

"All I want," she said, seething, "is to find the man who killed my mother. And make him pay."

"I can understand that. But if you're looking for an actual trigger man, it wouldn't have been Joe. Not personally, I mean."

"Who was it?"

"Probably a man named Rusch. He's been with Joe for years. He does the kind of work Joe never talked about, not even when we were married."

"How do I meet this Mr. Rusch?"

"Trust me. You never want to meet him."

She stepped closer, right in Marilyn's face. "Take me to him."

"Amy, the reason I came here is to make sure you *don't* meet him."

"Excuse me?"

"Somebody faxed your mother's letter to me this morning and said to meet them at Cheesman Dam tonight. I called Joe and told him about it. He's sending Rusch in my place, in my Mercedes. It's a trap."

"A trap for who?"

"For whoever faxed the letter to me. I was afraid it might have been you."

"I didn't fax you anything."

"Then it had to be Ryan Duffy." Marilyn stiffened, concerned. She dug her phone from her purse. "Somebody has to warn him."

Amy stopped her from dialing. "Let it go."

"But Rusch will be waiting for him in my car."

Amy's eyes narrowed, as if revenge were in sight. "And *I'll* be waiting for Rusch."

"He's a professional. He'll kill you like a fly."

"Not if you're with me, he won't."

Marilyn hesitated. She should have been afraid, but for over forty years she'd let fear control her. "All right. But we can't just walk into this without any backup. It'll cost me, but let me do that much."

Amy thought for a second, then nodded. "That makes sense."

"Of course it does," she said with a thin smile. "What's a guardian for, anyway?"

"Let's take a ride. Maybe we'll both find out."

62

The wrought-iron gate at the end of Marilyn's driveway was closed, but the old stone wall was easily scaled. Rusch cleared the cherry hedge on the inside and cut across the lawn, his black coveralls making him virtually invisible in the night. The silver 800 series Mercedes was unlocked, parked beneath the portico. He opened the door, dropped his black leather bag on the passenger side, and checked the glove box. As promised, the car key was inside, along with the electronic transmitter for the iron gate. Rusch fired up the engine, opened the gate, and backed out of the driveway.

He dialed Kozelka on the car phone as he pulled away. "Got the car. I'm on my way to the dam."

"Did Marilyn see you?"

"I don't think she's home. I peeked in the garage. Her Volvo was gone."

"Probably didn't want to be anywhere near her house when you came by. Just as well. Did you take care of the ex-wife and her lawyer yet?"

"Everything's in place. Package was delivered to Jackson's house around ten. That should take care of itself."

"Make sure of it. That goes double at the dam. Duffy's a smart guy."

"That's why I'd still rather take him out someplace else. Pop him by surprise."

"Can't do it. It's the same reason we had to frame him rather than kill him before. You never know when the FBI might be watching him."

"Like tonight."

"Not tonight," said Kozelka. "This is a business transaction for Duffy. He won't show up unless he's sure the FBI isn't following him."

"So this is our one and only clean shot at him."

"That's why I'm using my best man, Rusch. Do it right. And once it's done, don't call me for a month."

"Is this a paid vacation?" he asked as the car stopped at a traffic light.

"Anywhere you want."

"It's a toss-up. Fiji or Piedmont Springs," he said dryly, then hung up the phone.

Marilyn's Volvo took her and Amy back to Denver in well under an hour. Marilyn had phoned ahead before she and Amy left Boulder, so Jeb Stockton was expecting them. Jeb didn't ask for details on the phone, and Marilyn didn't offer. All she had to say was that she needed his help and was calling in the personal favors. Jeb agreed to meet them tonight at his downtown office.

Jeb headed the Denver office of a statewide private investigation firm, which sounded more impressive than it was. It was actually just a two-man operation, both retired ex-cops who would take a case anywhere in Colorado, so long as they could bring their fishing poles along. In that sense, it was "statewide." Jeb's law enforcement career had spanned nearly four decades, culminating with a twelve-year stint as Denver County sheriff. His election was due in no small part to the money Marilyn had raised for his campaigns. She considered him a friend, though she had politely stemmed his efforts to take it further than that. Jeb was handsome enough, but not her type. He had the rugged look of the Old West, with wind-burned skin and smoky gray hair. He rarely went anywhere without his cowboy boots and ten-gallon hat, even before his retirement. He wasn't the slickest ex-cop around, but slickness was no asset in places as far off the beaten track as Cheesman Dam. Outside the city lights, there was no one more dependable than Jeb. Most important, he could be trusted.

Marilyn followed the exit ramp off the expressway and steered into downtown Denver. It was after midnight, so the traffic lights had changed over to a string of blinking amber dots. Stores and offices on either side of the street were secured for the night, some with roll-up metal gates that resembled garage doors. A group of homeless people were haggling with a police officer on the corner. The Volvo cruised through one quiet intersection after another, passing only a handful of cars along the way.

Amy checked the street signs, then glanced back at Marilyn. "So, your friend Jeb will take us up to the dam, I presume?"

"Right. We'll use his van as a staging area. Park it somewhere out of sight. I'll be wired, so the two of you can hang back and listen from inside the van while I talk to Rusch."

Amy looked confused. "What do you mean, hang back? I'm talking to Rusch."

As the car slowly turned the corner, Marilyn caught Amy's eye. "Don't argue with me."

"There's no argument. This is something I have to do."

"Amy, this is a risk a young mother shouldn't be taking. It isn't necessary. It isn't even logical. Rusch won't tell you anything. He won't tell *me* anything if you're standing at my side. The only chance of getting him to say anything about your mother's death is if I go alone."

Amy wanted to argue, but she sensed Marilyn was right. "This wasn't the way I envisioned it."

"If you think about how this is likely to unfold, it's our only alternative."

"How do you see it?"

"It basically boils down to one likely scenario. When I talked to Joe this afternoon, he told me to leave the keys in my Mercedes, so I presume Rusch is going to use the car somehow. My guess is he'll park it out in the open for Duffy to see. Duffy will walk right up to the car, thinking it's me inside. When he does, Rusch will either shoot him on the spot or put him in the trunk and then shoot him somewhere else. I think it's fair to say that there are only two people on the planet who can walk up to that car and live to tell about it. Joe Kozelka is one of them. The other one is *not* you."

"How can you be sure Rusch won't shoot you?"

"First of all, he has no reason to think I'm not on his side. Not yet, anyway. Secondly, I'm too important to Joe. My appointment is too important."

"What if something goes wrong? What if Rusch somehow discovers you're wearing a wire."

"Then we kick into plan B."

"What's plan B?"

She pulled into a parking space and killed the engine. "I was kind of hoping Jeb might help us figure that out."

Amy tried not to look worried as they stepped down together and started toward Jeb Stockton's office.

Phil Jackson was still mad. Liz had phoned him at dinnertime, said she was thinking about finding a new lawyer. The ingrate. Without him, she would have gotten nothing.

Now she was at the doorstep of the mother lode. Of course, she couldn't completely stiff him. The judge would order her to pay him the fair value of his services so far. That wouldn't come close to the fees he would have racked up had he seen this battle through to the final chapter. Assuming he could get to the Duffys' Panamanian accounts, the contingency fee he and Liz had discussed would have earned him over nine thousand dollars an hour. And he was worth it.

Liz hadn't found the courage to utter the words, but he figured it was only a matter of days before she officially fired him. She'd probably do it by letter. *Backstabbing bitch.*

He'd been stiffed by clients before, but this one was especially hard to swallow. He'd worked hard on the case, but he always worked hard. He didn't mind the sweat. This case, however, had taken his blood. Almost a half-pint of it, spilled on the garage floor in the predawn beating.

The anger, the resentment, were not subsiding. If anything, he'd worked himself more into a dither as the evening passed. It was hard to concentrate, difficult to make decisions. One thing, in particular, had become a vexing quandary. The briefcase.

It had been delivered by courier to his doorstep around ten o'clock, marked "PERSONAL AND CONFIDENTIAL." It was addressed to his client. The return address indicated it was from Ryan Duffy.

He was naturally suspicious. After Brent's murder, he was at first afraid to touch it, fearing a booby trap. But the more he thought about it, the less likely that seemed. As much as he'd tried to make Ryan look like a gangster in the courtroom, he didn't seem the type to send his wife a letter bomb. He seemed more likely to send a peace offering—a settlement.

Jackson settled into the plush sofa in his family room, staring at the briefcase on the coffee table before him. He noticed the tumblers near the latch. There were three altogether. A lock with a three-number combination. Just like the combination Liz had testified to in court. Three numbers: 36-18-11.

The realization hit like lightning. That was exactly what this was—Liz's share of the money. Ryan had very cleverly put together a settlement offer his greedy wife couldn't refuse: a briefcase full of cash. His instincts took over. This was his chance. Liz was trying to screw him, but he could beat her to the punch. He'd bet his life there was money inside. And he knew the combination.

He jumped forward and laid the briefcase flat. Eagerly he turned the tumblers into place, left to right. The first one, thirty-six. The next, eighteen. Finally, eleven. He flipped the latches, left and right. They popped up. His body tingled with a surge of excitement. This was *it*. He opened the briefcase. It opened just an inch, then seemed to catch on something, moving no farther. He heard a click. An ominous click. In a flash, he knew it wasn't a cash settlement offer and that it wasn't from Ryan Duffy.

Oh, shit!

A fiery orange explosion decimated the entire west wing of the Jackson estate. The impact rattled windows around the neighborhood, as a shower of glowing embers rained down on the brand-new windshield of his just-repaired Mercedes.

63

Two minutes after they met, Ryan already had a name for him: the gadget man.

Bruce Dembroski was a friend of Norm's, a former CIA agent whose specialty had been sniping. Though life after the agency didn't present many opportunities to use his laser range finder, suppressed weapons, or ultra-long-range .50-caliber sniper rifle, he had found a profitable niche in offering high-tech, high-quality private investigative services to an elite clientele, mostly security-conscious corporations. His bread and butter was in the latest surveillance and countersurveillance equipment, from simple cordless phone monitors to fax machine intruders. He had all the toys and wasn't afraid to use them. That bravado had occasionally taken him beyond the accepted limits of corporate espionage. It was Norm who routinely got him out of legal trouble. They had an old-fashioned barter arrangement. Norm got the services of an investigator he couldn't otherwise afford, and Dembroski got a top-notch lawyer free of charge.

Norm's garage was their meeting place. Both cars had been backed out to give them room. Norm was a bit of gadget man himself. A long wooden workbench stretched across the back. A wide array of tools was neatly arranged on the tool board, though most of them looked like Father's Day gifts that had never been used. The bare cement floor and white fluorescent light made the garage look cooler than it was. Maybe it was nerves, maybe it was just one of those sticky summer nights. Ryan, however, was sweating heavily beneath his Kevlar jacket.

"I'm roasting." Ryan was dressed in long pants and a full-length ballistic jacket. It looked like something he'd wear on an autumn hike in the mountains.

Dembroski zipped him up, checking the fit around the torso. "You want safety, or you want a fashion statement?"

"If I get any hotter, the choices will be white meat or dark. Will this really do any good?"

"Heck, yeah," said Dembroski. "You have a Kevlar lining in here that protects the full upper torso. It's less conspicuous than a vest, and it's better protection. Most vests don't protect against side entry. The jacket does."

"Let's just hope no one shows up with a bazooka."

"Actually," said Dembroski, "I could probably arrange for that."

"Stop," said Norm. "This is crazy enough as it is."

"I was only kidding." He reached in his duffel bag and removed a pistol and ammunition clip. "This is another advantage of the jacket. You can easily conceal a firearm. This is a Smith and Wesson nine-millimeter parabellum pistol. Four-inch barrel. Slide mounting decocking lever. I brought one with tritium night sights, which may come in handy in the dark. Fifteen-round magazine. We're talking serious firepower."

"I know how to use a gun. My dad was quite the hunter."

"Well, you can hunt elephants with this baby." He slammed the clip into the stock and checked the safety. "Keep it in the breast pocket. Don't take it out unless you intend to use it."

Norm said, "I'd rather you leave it here."

Ryan ignored him. He took the gun and placed it in the pocket.

Dembroski stepped back and checked out the ensemble. "Looks good, my man."

"I feel like a bulletproof flasher." He wiped the sweat from his brow. "Can I take this off now that we know it fits?"

"I'll do it," said Dembroski. "You have to be very careful not to disconnect your microphone."

Ryan slipped off one sleeve at a time. A small tape recorder was strapped to his chest. The microphone was clipped inside his shirt collar.

"Remember," said Dembroski. "The microphone is voice-activated, so you won't be recording a bunch of dead time. Just speak in a normal tone of voice and it will pick it up."

"It's not my voice I'm worried about."

"It should pick up anyone within a good fifteen feet of you."

"So I have to get reasonably close."

"You don't have to stick your tongue down anybody's throat. But yeah, reasonably close."

Norm began to pace, obviously concerned. "Ryan, I really wish you'd let Bruce come with us. Fifteen feet is getting too damn close to someone who may be armed and dangerous."

"I'm more than happy to go," said Dembroski.

Ryan shook his head. "There's a public figure involved. If you come with us, you're likely to recognize her. Nothing personal against you, Bruce, but I don't want you to know who she is."

"Why not?"

"Because I don't know you. And I don't know what you might do with that information."

"What?" he said, half smiling. "Do I look like a blackmailer or something?"

"In my experience, they can look like just about anybody."

Dembroski glanced at Norm, then back at Ryan. "You know, I do most of my jobs on a no-questions-asked basis. But you guys have me totally intrigued. Who is it?"

"Sorry. If all goes well tonight, you'll never hear another thing about this. That's my goal, to put this behind me forever."

"And if the shit hits the fan?"

"Then you'll probably read about it in the newspapers."

"Let's hope it's not the obituaries," said Norm, grumbling.

"Let's hope," said Ryan. "You ready, Norm?"

Norm nodded reluctantly.

Ryan grabbed his ballistic jacket and started toward the door. "Let's do it."

64

They rode with the headlights off, invisible in the night, shrouded in a virtual tunnel of Douglas firs that lined the steep and narrow road to Cheesman Dam. Jeb's van climbed slowly toward the summit, zigzagging up the switchbacks in the road. Scattered clouds dimmed the light from the waxing crescent moon. Clusters of bright stars filled the pockets of night sky that weren't hidden by the clouds.

Cheesman was the oldest reservoir of Denver's water system, some sixty miles south-southwest of the city. Built at the turn of the century, it was for many years virtually inaccessible to the public, situated in a scarcely populated government forest reserve and surrounded by mountains that soared from 9,000 to 13,000 feet. The arch-masonry dam was the first of its type in the country, faced with squared granite blocks that were quarried upstream by Italian stonemasons, floated to the site on platforms, and hoisted into place with a gas-powered pulley. It linked the steep canyon walls in dramatic fashion, like a huge V-shaped fan, barely twenty-five feet across at the narrow base and nearly thirty times wider at the crest. Rising 221 feet from the streambed below, it had been the world's highest dam at the time of construction. It was no longer the highest but was still the tightest in the entire water system.

Amy's ears popped as the van climbed to an elevation of over 6,800 feet, the high-water mark for the reservoir. She sat quietly in the backseat with the surveillance equipment. Marilyn rode in the captain's chair on the passenger side.

"When the moon is right," said Jeb, "this is the most beautiful canyon you'll ever see at night."

Amy glanced out the window. Beyond the guardrail was a sheer granite drop. Up ahead, beyond the dam, the gentle light of the moon reflected on the dark reservoir surface, flickering like quiet glowing embers on the plain. No argument from her.

Jeb said, "Back in the old days, guys used to come here with their sweeties to watch the submarine races. If you know what I mean," he added with a wink.

Marilyn glanced at Amy, then said, "Yeah, I know all too well what you mean."

Jeb steered into a turnout along the side of the road. The van came to rest at about a twenty-degree angle, slightly steeper than the road grade. Jeb applied the parking brake, then turned to talk business.

"The dam is less than a five-minute walk from here, straight up the road. If we get any closer, the engine noise will surely give us away."

"This is close enough," said Marilyn. "I definitely don't want them to know I came here with anyone. Especially you."

Jeb climbed out of the seat and maneuvered to the back of the van. A radio control panel with a recorder was mounted into the wall. On the seat beside Amy rested a medium-sized trunk. Jeb opened it and removed a tangle of wires and microphones. He spoke as he sorted the equipment. "We'll be as good as with you the whole time you're up there, Marilyn. Your radio has two-way communication. Amy and I will be able to hear everything back here at the van as it feeds into the recorder."

"How will you talk to me?"

"Earpiece. We'll have to work the wire into your hair to hide it. Should work fine."

"All right," said Marilyn. "How about a panic button or something like that?"

"Just scream. I'll keep the motor running. We can be there in thirty seconds."

Marilyn checked her watch. 1:30 A.M. Thirty minutes before the designated meeting time. "Let's get me wired," she said. "I need to get going if I'm going to get to Rusch before Duffy does."

Amy looked at her with concern. She had definitely noticed the look on Marilyn's face when Jeb had made the innocent comment about the submarine races. "Are you sure you're okay with this?" asked Amy.

"Sure. This will be just fine."

Amy squeezed her hand. She squeezed back, but it unsettled Amy. The touch was very unlike Marilyn. It was remarkably weak.

"I hope so," said Amy, her eyes clouded with concern.

Across the dam, on the opposite side of the canyon, Ryan and Norm waited in the Range Rover. The phone rang. Norm answered it on the speaker.

Dembroski's voice boomed inside the truck. "Hey, it's Bruce. I finished that handwriting analysis you asked for."

Norm snatched up the phone, taking him off speaker. Ryan grabbed the phone back and cupped his hand over the mouthpiece so Dembroski couldn't hear. "Norm," he said in an accusatory tone, "what's he talking about?"

"Bruce was trained in handwriting analysis when he was with the CIA. I asked him to compare the handwriting samples we have for Debby Parkens. The letter she wrote to your father. And the letter she wrote to her daughter—the one Amy gave you."

"Great. So now he knows Marilyn Gaslow is involved."

"No. I blocked out her name in the letter."

"What the hell did you do this for, Norm?"

"Because I don't want to see you get killed out here tonight, all right? I was hoping that

430

if Bruce could tell you the letter was fake or genuine, maybe that would be enough for you."

"I didn't come all this way to turn around and go home."

"Humor me. Let's just listen to what he has to say."

Ryan calmed his anger, then nodded once. He placed the phone back in the holder. Norm put the call back on speaker. "You still there, Bruce?"

"Yeah."

"What do you think?"

"Well, this was pretty quick. I'd like to study them some more."

"Yeah, yeah. What's your gut reaction?"

"My gut says the letter is genuine. Meaning that whoever wrote this letter to Amy Parkens also wrote the letter to Frank Duffy."

Ryan and Norm looked at one another.

"But," said Dembroski, "I'm somewhat troubled by a couple things in the second letter—the letter to Frank Duffy."

"What?" asked Ryan.

"The wording is a little off, for one thing. People tend to have a way of expressing themselves in letters. I see different word choices, different turns of the phrase in these two letters."

"That's probably because the one letter is written to my father and the other one is written to her seven-year-old daughter."

"That's a good point," said Dembroski. "But then there's the matter of the shaky penmanship. The handwriting in the letter to your father is a little unsteady."

Norm asked, "What do you make of that?"

"Could be a lot of things. She could have been drunk. Could have been tired. Or—it could be something else."

"Like what?" asked Ryan.

"This is a wild guess. But you take the shaky handwriting and combine it with the awkward phraseology, and I can offer one theory. She wrote the letter to your father, all right. But not of her own free will."

"What are you saying?"

"I'm saying somebody could have told her what to write. Forced her to write it."

"You mean someone had a gun to her head?"

"Yes," he said. "Quite literally."

There was silence in the truck. Ryan glanced at Norm, saying nothing. Norm picked up the phone. "Thanks, Bruce. If you can, stay by the phone tonight, just in case."

He hung up, then looked at Ryan. "That sure opens some new possibilities."

"Not really. It's a wild theory, if you ask me. And even if she was forced to write it, that doesn't mean it's false. Seems to me I'm in the same place I've always been. The letter isn't dispositive. Only Marilyn Gaslow can tell me if my father raped her."

"I'm thinking beyond rape."

"Huh?"

"Take a worst-case scenario. Let's say Debby Parkens was forced to write a letter saying Frank Duffy was innocent. Say the letter was false, which means your father really was a rapist. Say her death wasn't a suicide, meaning that somebody conveniently got rid of her. There's only one person who had motive to make her write that letter. And in my book, that leaves one prime murder suspect."

Ryan stared blankly, stunned at the thought of his father as a murderer.

Norm asked, "You sure you want to go down this road tonight?"

"Now more than ever." He opened the door and stepped down from the truck.

Norm stopped him. "Take this," he said, offering his cell phone. "You get into trouble up there, you call."

Ryan gave a mock salute, then started toward the dam.

65

Nathan Rusch was lying in wait. A cluster of gray boulders offered protection and concealment. A black Nomex body suit made him part of the night. Perched on a rock formation that overlooked the dam, he had a clear view of the entire area. He could see the parking lot and both entrances from the north and south ends of the dam. With a crest length of 670 feet—1,100 including the spillway—the dam connected the steep canyon walls that had been separated by thousands of years of erosion. Behind it was the Cheesman reservoir, a man-made vessel for over 70,000 acre-feet of rain and melted mountain snow. The glowing moon glistened on the mirrorlike surface. Rusch was close enough to hear the water flowing into the South Platte River hundreds of feet below. No water ran through the dam. Foresighted engineers had instead tunneled through the natural canyon walls adjacent to the dam to preserve the structural integrity of their man-made wonder. The highest opening was more than 150 feet above the stream. With the valve open, water shot from a hole in the granite wall like water from a hydrant, cascading down into the river. From above, it was a peaceful background noise, like a running stream in the forest.

His weapon was fully assembled. The rifle was the sleek AR-7, lightweight and accurate. It wasn't cut for a night scope, but with a little ingenuity the ridge on top easily accepted one. The thirty-shot clip was filled with hollow-point ammunition. The silencer was his own creation, made from a ten-inch section of an automobile brake line, common PVC tubing, fiberglass resin and a few other materials that could be purchased at any hardware store. It was cheap and disposable, two priorities in a profession where ballistic markings made it advisable to use your equipment only once and then grind it into dust.

He checked his watch. Phase one of his plan should already have unfolded. Considering the short notice, the exploding briefcase had been a stroke of genius. Setting the lock to the same combination Liz had testified to in court was an especially convincing touch. His only regret was that he couldn't be the fly on the wall when Liz and her greedy lawyer popped it open and blew themselves to bits.

Now, phase two was only minutes away.

He raised his infrared binoculars and canvassed the parking lot. Only one car in sight. Marilyn's Mercedes. He estimated it was forty yards away, exactly where he had parked it, well within range with his three-to-six-powered scope. He lowered the infrared binoculars and looked through the scope, running the plan through his mind. He found success more achievable if he imagined it first. This close to a kill, however, he more than imagined it. He relished it.

In his mind's eye, he could see it unfold. The target approaching the car, taking the bait. The crosshairs in the night scope converging behind his ear. One squeeze of the trigger. The head snapping back. The knees buckling. The lifeless body falling to the ground.

Rusch would approach and finish the job with a double-barreled, twelve-gauge shotgun. The boss wanted it to look like a suicide—Duffy blows up his wife and her lawyer, then blows his brains out. The barrel would go into the mouth, and a simple squeeze of the trigger would unleash enough buckshot to make it impossible for any medical examiner to determine that a sniper's bullet was the actual cause of death. The Mercedes would be his getaway car. He'd try to position Duffy at the perfect angle, so the blood, shattered skull, and flying bits of brain didn't splatter on

435

the paint job. But neatness wasn't essential. He would have to dump the car at a chop shop anyway.

Especially with what was already inside.

He saw someone coming up the road, heading toward the Mercedes. The fantasy was over. Back to reality. He got in position and braced his rifle for the kill. He peered through the scope. Locked in the crosshairs, the target crossed the parking lot. Sixty yards away, now fifty. His finger caressed the trigger. Forty yards and closing. He could fire any-time. He had a clear head shot. Then he froze. He lowered the rifle in confusion and grabbed the binoculars. His instincts were right. The scope hadn't lied.

It wasn't Ryan Duffy.

Marilyn approached the Mercedes cautiously, one step at a time. Loose gravel crunched beneath her feet. Water running beneath the dam was like static in the background. Or maybe that was static from the radio. She was so nervous that it was hard to tell if her earpiece was even working.

"Jeb, you there?" She spoke like a ventril-oquist, trying not to move her lips.

The reply buzzed her ear. "Stay calm, Mar-ilyn."

"I'm almost at the car."

"Then stop talking. If he thinks you're wired...well, that won't be good."

She swallowed hard. Jeb was a master of understatement.

She stopped a few yards from the driver's door. Dark-tinted windows made it impossible to see inside. She checked around the car for footprints in the gravel. She noticed none. That meant one of two things. Either someone had meticulously swept them away. Or he was in there, waiting. She waited, too. She glanced toward the reservoir, beyond the outer ridge of the dam. The trees had grown, but the slope of the land and rock formations brought back memories. At first it was a trickle. Then the emotional dam burst.

The Mercedes was parked in the very same spot—exactly where the rape had taken place, more than forty-five years ago.

It suddenly didn't seem that long ago. Her hands began to shake. She drew a deep breath to calm her nerves. She knew the car couldn't have been positioned there to taunt *her*. Rusch had had no way to know Marilyn was coming. It was there to fool Duffy, to give him all the more reason to think Marilyn was inside. That, however, was little consolation. Whether she'd been targeted or not, the past was staring her in the face. Though she had few memories of that night, returning to this place had torn open the wounds. She had been raped. It had started that night, and it had lasted forty-five years. He had physically assaulted her. Made her accuse the wrong man. Deceived her into marrying him. Kept her under his control to this very day.

And if her suspicions were correct, he might have killed her best friend.

The wave of fear turned to anger. She had

a wild thought—but one she had to act upon. She had an overwhelming instinct that it wasn't Rusch inside the car. It was Joe Kozelka.

On impulse, she charged toward the car and tried the door. It was locked. She dug her keys from her coat pocket. She still had the remote. With a push of the button, the lock disengaged. She pulled open the door.

The front seat was empty. The rear made her gasp.

A young woman lay across the seat. Lifeless. Her hand draped limply onto the floor. A trail of blood ran from a bullet hole in the left temple, having spilled onto the carpet.

Marilyn tried to scream but was mute, paralyzed with fear. Images flashed through her head. She saw herself as a teenager passed out in the back of Frank Duffy's Buick. She saw Amy's mother on her deathbed with a bullet in her head. She took a step back. Her voice was suddenly back.

Her scream pierced the night as she ran toward the dam.

The scream rattled the van, sending the decibel meters on the tape recorder well into the red zone. Jeb Stockton called frantically on the radio, but he got no response. "Damn it, Marilyn, where the hell are you?"

"Don't lose her!" said Amy.

"It's pure static."

"Rusch must have her. He must have ripped off her headset."

"Don't panic on me. She could have just run into a low tree branch or something that knocked off the headset."

"Keep listening," said Amy as she leaped into the driver's seat. The motor was already running.

"Can you drive this?" asked Jeb.

She slammed it into gear. Tires spun and gravel flew as the van shot from the turnout. It leaned left, then right, squealing around corners at three times the speed limit, barely gripping the road.

"Guess so," he said, holding on for dear life.

She skidded through the last turn, which was sharper than expected. Amy momentarily lost control. The headlights seemed to point in every direction, then finally locked onto the Mercedes straight ahead. A man was running away from the car. Amy steered the van around the back of the Mercedes and slammed on the brakes. The van fishtailed, nearly knocking the man to his feet.

Jeb jumped out, gun drawn. "Freeze! Hands over your head!"

The man raised his hands. Amy hit the emergency blinkers for better light. In the intermittent blasts of orange light, she could see it was Ryan Duffy.

"What did you do to Marilyn!" she shouted.

Ryan kept one eye on the gun, the other on Amy. "I never saw Marilyn. I just heard a scream and ran over here. The body was already in the car when I got here."

"Body?" Amy's voice was filled with panic.

She hurried toward the Mercedes.

"Don't look," said Ryan.

It was too late. The sight of the body sent Amy back on her heels. "Who is that?"

"It's a woman I met in Panama. She was supposed to meet me here tonight. Apparently somebody got to her before I did."

Jeb moved toward the Mercedes, took a quick look for himself. "You're lying. You killed that woman." He took aim at Ryan's forehead, cocking the hammer on his revolver.

Ryan swallowed hard. "What the hell are you doing, old man?"

"Pat him down, Amy. Check for a gun."

Ryan said, "It's inside my jacket. Check it, please. You can tell it hasn't been fired. I didn't shoot this woman."

Amy cautiously stepped forward, unzipped the jacket, and pulled out the pistol.

"Bring it here," said Jeb.

She handed it to him. His gun aimed at Ryan, he sniffed the barrel for fresh powder and checked the ammunition clip. It was still full. "He may be telling the truth."

A scream echoed from somewhere near the dam. All three of them froze, trying to pinpoint the exact location. It had been deafening and shrill—the kind of scream Amy had heard in her nightmares about the night she'd found her mother.

Another scream followed, even louder than the last. It seemed to have come from beyond the hill, along the hiking path that led to the dam.

"It's Marilyn!" Amy grabbed Ryan's gun

from Jeb, then turned and ran toward the opening in a stretch of woods at the edge of the parking lot.

"Amy, wait!"

Ryan watched as she faded into darkness, then looked desperately at Jeb. "If one of us doesn't go after her, she's going to end up like that woman in the car."

Stockton tightened his aim. "Just stay right there!"

Ryan thought fast. Even in the heavy ballistic jacket, he could probably outrun the old man. On impulse, he turned and ran in Amy's footsteps.

"Stop!"

Ryan only ran faster, never looking back.

66

Nathan Rusch was angry, not about to be outrun by a woman ten years his senior. He had come down from his hiding spot in a matter of seconds, chasing down the wooded path that led to the dam. Her sixty-yard lead had closed to less than twenty. He'd tried to make verbal contact, but his shouts on the dead run had only made her scream.

His lungs were beginning to burn. The hills and thin mountain air were taking its toll. He wondered if the drug Sheila had given him back at the hotel this morning wasn't still affecting him, making him fatigue faster.

Lucky for him she'd lacked the nerve to kill. Unfortunate for her he didn't have the same qualms.

He stopped at a fork in the footpath, unsure of which way to go. A canopy of trees completely blocked out the moonlight. He'd lost sight of Marilyn. He listened for footsteps cutting across the woods. All was silent, save for the water flowing beneath the damn.

"Freeze!" The voice had come from behind—an older man's voice.

Startled, Rusch wheeled quickly. Jeb Stockton was standing behind a rock, his gun aimed at Rusch. "Put the gun down," said Jeb, "hands over your head."

Slowly, Rusch obeyed. The gun dropped. His hands went behind his head. Jeb was obviously having a hard time seeing in the darkness, particularly with Rusch's black clothing. He stepped out from behind the rock and took five steps forward. He closed to within ten yards. "Lay on the ground, face down. Nice and slow."

Rusch lowered himself to one knee, his eye on Jeb's chest. In one blinding motion his hand snapped forward from behind his head, releasing a titanium throwing knife from the sheath on his wrist. The sleek blade whirled through the air and struck the target, parting Jeb's ribs. He groaned as the wound dropped him to his knees. He fired two erratic shots, then fell to the ground.

Rusch grabbed his gun and came to him quickly, checking the pulse. It was weak. He gave a moment's thought to finishing him with a bullet, but it wasn't necessary. He'd let the old man suffer. He yanked the knife from his ribs, cleaned it on Jeb's shirt, and tucked it back into his wrist sheath.

"Don't feel bad, old man," he whispered smugly. "No one ever looks for the knife when they think they're in a gunfight."

Stockton's left arm jerked forward. A loud crack erupted as he fired off a round from a small palm-sized revolver. Rusch was hit square in the chest and fell over in a heap.

Stockton collapsed, exhausted. "Don't feel bad, jackass. Nobody ever looks for the second gun, either."

The gunshots echoed like thunder in the canyon, drawing Amy and Ryan to the fork in the footpath. Amy arrived first, barreling down the hill. Ryan was close behind. Breathless and scared, she stopped at the first sight of the body on the ground. The boots she recognized as Jeb's. In the darkness, she hadn't noticed the man in the black body suit, but finally she did. He was completely still. She felt a wave of relief till she noticed the blood at Jeb's side. She ran to him and knelt close.

His eyes were glazed. He was barely conscious. Blood had soaked his shirt, covering his chest. He coughed, trying to speak. "Bastard, got me with a knife."

"Who is it?"

"Damned if I know."

Amy quickly went to the body, checked a pulse. Nothing. "He's dead." She pulled the hood off his head. The face was unfamiliar, but she knew it had to be Rusch. She came back to Jeb's side.

"Did you see Marilyn?"

He shook his head.

"Which way did he come from?"

"The dam."

Amy started at the pounding footsteps behind her. She rose and aimed her gun. Ryan stopped short and backed away.

"Easy," he said. "I'm on your side. I think."

Amy jerked her gun, directing him toward Jeb. "Other guy's dead. He stabbed my friend here. You're a doctor. Help him."

Ryan went to his side and checked the wound. It was a clean hole from an incredibly sharp knife. Air and foamy blood appeared around the edges with each expiration. "Thankfully it missed the heart. But definite signs of pneumothorax."

"Numo-what?"

"A sucking chest wound. I think the knife punctured a lung. This man needs a chest tube. We have to get him to the ER."

"I can't just leave Marilyn. What if this dead guy has a partner out there somewhere? She's wearing a wire. They'll kill her if they find it on her."

"Who is *they*?"

"The people who would have killed you if Marilyn hadn't intervened. They may have killed my mother."

For Ryan, it was a relief to hear that someone other than his father might have killed Debby Parkens. Jeb groaned. Ryan dug Norm's cell phone from his coat pocket. "I'll call Medevac. Somebody has to wait here with him."

"You're the doctor," she said. "I'll find Marilyn."

Jeb raised his arm, as if he wanted to say something. Amy leaned close but couldn't hear.

"What's he saying?" asked Ryan.

"I don't know. He's delirious."

"I can't leave him. He'll go into shock. But don't you go charging off by yourself. This is too dangerous."

"Sorry," said Amy. "You're the one with the Hippocratic oath."

Before he could speak, Amy darted down the path in the direction of the last scream. Low-hanging branches slapped her in the darkness. She was running on pure adrenaline, rounded a sharp turn, then stopped short. She had reached a clearing. The dam was straight ahead. A moonlit view of the canyon stretched beyond. The powerful sounds of rushing water rose from the depths. She took a step forward and nearly lost her footing. The gentle slope of the trail was at an end. It was a steep drop to the dam and observation deck, accessible only by a walkway of makeshift steps cut into the mountainside.

"That's far enough." It was a booming voice from the side.

Amy froze. Joe Kozelka stepped out from behind the rocks. He had sent Rusch to do the job, but this assignment was far too important to rely totally on a subordinate. He *had* to follow, arriving quietly by boat off big

Lake Cheesman, which stretched for miles behind the dam.

His gun pressed against the base of Marilyn's skull. He was standing right behind her, using her body as a human shield. Amy turned her gun toward him, but Marilyn was in the way.

"Drop the gun," he said.

Her arms stretched out before her. The gun felt heavy in her hands. But she didn't move.

"I said, *drop* it."

Amy squeezed her gun.

"Don't listen to him," said Marilyn.

"Shut up!" He wrenched her arm behind her back.

Marilyn cringed. "Don't give up your gun, Amy. He'll kill you."

"Lose it," said Kozelka. "Or I shoot her right now."

Amy couldn't move. She tried to take aim, but her hands were unsteady. She knew how to use a gun, but only because her mother's death had made her afraid of them. She had always tried to learn about the things that frightened her. This shot, however, was beyond her capabilities.

Marilyn squirmed. "He's bluffing, Amy. He can't shoot me. I'm too important to him."

"Drop it!" Kozelka was seething, nearly screaming. "I swear I'll pop her right here. Right in front of you. You want to see another woman with a bullet in her head, kid?"

The words were like explosives—not just

for Amy, but for Marilyn, too. On impulse, she fell back against him with all her force, knocking them both off the ledge. Together, they tumbled backward, head over heels, rolling out of control toward the observation platform.

Amy charged down the steps after them, but they were rolling too fast down the steep embankment, gaining momentum. They slammed against the rail at the edge of the platform, Kozelka taking the major blow. The wooden beams split on impact. Splintered chunks of wood fell two hundred feet down into the canyon, into the churning river water far below. Marilyn grabbed a railing to stop her fall. Kozelka grabbed the other, but his weight was too great. The bolts ripped from the footing. His body sailed over the edge, but he caught the bottom of the platform in a desperate lunge. He barely had a grip. His hand was slipping. He struggled to pull himself up, but couldn't. He looked down. The fall was straight down. He could barely see bottom.

Amy ran to the platform and grabbed Marilyn. "Are you okay?"

She dabbed some blood from her nose. "Yeah. I think so."

Amy peered over the edge and looked down at Kozelka. He was flailing at the end of the broken railing, like a hooked fish, trying to pull himself up. From this height, the fall alone would be deadly. Just below them, in a magnificent display of overkill, tons of running water shot from the open outlet tunnel that cut through the canyon wall.

447

Amy handed Marilyn her gun. "Keep an aim on him. If he tries anything funny, you know what to do."

Marilyn took aim. "What are you doing?"

Amy braced herself against the railing and leaned over the edge. She extended her hand toward him, but not all the way. It was just out of his reach.

Marilyn's voice shook. "Amy, get away. He'll kill you."

She ignored her. "You're going to die, mister. Unless you tell me the truth."

He groped desperately for her hand, but he couldn't make contact. He was out of breath, barely able to speak. "What. Truth?"

"Tell me, you bastard. Did you kill my mother?"

"No."

"You ordered her killed, didn't you!"

"No. I had nothing to do with it."

"You're lying! Don't play this game. Tell the truth and I'll help you."

"I *am* telling the truth. I didn't kill your old lady. I didn't have her killed. That's the truth!"

Amy nearly burst with anger. She wanted the confession, but she couldn't just let him fall. Mercifully, reluctantly, she lowered her hand.

Kozelka was suddenly rigid. His eyes were two narrow slits. "Don't look now, kid. But Marilyn Gaslow is about to shoot you in the back."

Amy gasped and turned quickly. Kozelka freed one hand and grabbed a fallen branch from the cliffside the size of a baseball bat. He was about to crack Amy's skull, as if betting that his beleaguered ex-wife wouldn't pull the trigger. She did. Twice. The booming gunshots ripped through the canyon.

His head snapped back in a violent explosion. Amy's heart was in her throat as she watched him fall away, a long and graceful descent into the gaping canyon, the blood trailing from his massive head wound like a fatal red jet stream. She looked away before his body splattered on the rocks in the stream below. Shaking with emotion, Amy slid back onto the platform. Marilyn scooted toward her, dropped the gun, and pulled her close.

They held each other in silence, overcome with shock and horror. Marilyn stroked her head. "It's okay. That bastard has had it coming since I was fifteen years old."

Amy's voice quivered. "He said he had nothing to do with my mom's death."

"I heard."

"It had to be him. How could it not be?"

"Just because he denied it doesn't mean he's innocent."

"I was looking him right in the eye, Marilyn. He was barely hanging on, scared for his life. So scared, he was believable. I don't think he killed Mom."

Their embrace tightened. Amy was looking past Marilyn, peering over her shoulder into the night sky. The clouds had cleared. Stars were everywhere, exactly the way they'd looked the night her mother died. The patterns began to swirl against the blackness, then finally came into focus. Amy felt a chill, struck by the sudden realization.

Marilyn said, "I don't know what to think."

"I don't either," she said quietly. "Except the unthinkable."

67

Amy left before the police arrived. With Marilyn's permission, she drove Jeb's van back to Boulder. Ryan and Marilyn had plenty to explain on their own, which would probably take all night. She, too, would have to give a full statement. That was fine with her. Before talking to the police, however, she had to do one more thing.

She had to unravel her latest suspicions.

It was after 4:00 A.M. when she arrived back at the apartment. It was dark inside, save for the night light in the hall. She peeked in on Taylor. She was asleep on her stomach in one of those lumpy positions that only a four-year-old could find comfortable, scrunched up like a turtle. She stroked her head lightly and kissed her on the cheek. Taylor didn't stir. Amy turned toward the door, then started. Gram was standing in the doorway. It was an eerie feeling, one that angered her inside. She rarely shared a tender moment with Taylor when she didn't feel Gram was somehow watching. She used to think it was out of concern. She was beginning to think otherwise.

Amy stepped into the hall and closed the door behind her.

"I heard you come in," said Gram. She was dressed in her nightgown and slippers, a silk cap protecting her hair.

"Did you wait up for me?"

"Of course. I was worried about you, darling."

Amy walked down the hall toward the kitchen. Gram followed and took a seat at the table. "What happened tonight?"

Amy opened the refrigerator and poured herself some orange juice. She leaned against the counter, leaving Gram alone at the table. "I found out who didn't kill Mom."

Gram looked confused. "What?"

"But I think I know who did."

"Who?"

She sipped her orange juice. "You don't want to tell me?"

"What are you talking about, Amy?"

Her tone sharpened. "Remember how I told you that I couldn't remember much about the night Mom died? Every time I got to a certain point, those numbers would pop into my head."

"Yes."

"I told you it was M 57. I always thought that was a form of psychological self-preservation. Whenever I got too close to my most painful memories, my adult brain would kick in and short-circuit everything, cluttering my mind with the astronomical designation for the star I was looking at the night Mom died."

"That would be logical."

"Except that I lied to you last night. I did see numbers when I went back to the house. But this time it wasn't M 57. It wasn't an astronomical designation at all."

"What was it?"

She stared at Gram, almost looking through her. "I saw numbers and letters. I'm not really sure which ones. The important thing I remember is that they were from a license tag."

Gram folded her hands nervously. "I don't understand."

"I didn't, either, until tonight, when it came back to me. When I looked through my telescope as a little girl, I didn't always look up into the sky. Sometimes I'd watch people in their yards. Sometimes I'd watch cars on the road. That night, I remember watching a car come toward the house before I went to bed. I remember it was a Ford Galaxie, black vinyl roof. I remember focusing on it, because it was your car."

Gram was ashen, more frail than Amy had ever seen her. "You must be confused."

"No. I had just blocked it out, suppressed it all these years. But since I went back to the house, the memory has become more clear. The funny thing is, I still don't remember you coming by the house that night. You were right in the neighborhood, but you didn't stop by the house."

"I stopped by after you went to bed."

Amy's glare tightened. "Yes. That's what I thought. I saw your car almost an hour before

I went to bed. But you came by after I went to sleep."

"Well, I—I don't know about the timing."

"I remember now," said Amy. "I remember thinking, Where's Gram? Where did she go? I was expecting you to come by any minute, but you never came."

"I don't really remember."

"I think you do. You were outside waiting for me to go asleep."

"That's silly. Why would I do that?"

"Because you came by the house to see Mom. And you didn't want me or anyone else to know you had been there that night."

Gram looked away, flustered. "I don't know what you're driving at," she said harshly. "But I don't deserve this."

"You killed her, didn't you?"

"No!" she said, indignant. "She killed herself, like the police said. That's why she tied the rope around your bedroom door, so you wouldn't find the body."

"*You* tied the rope, Gram. The police were right in one respect. The person who took Mom's life loved me so much she didn't want me to find the body. The cops thought it was Mom. Problem is, Mom knew I could climb out of my room through the attic. But you didn't."

"Amy, I didn't kill your mother."

She stepped closer, eyes narrowing. "It's like you said. When Dad was killed in Vietnam— your only child—I was the replacement."

"I was practically raising you anyway, even before your mother got sick. She was always so busy with one thing or another. I always loved you as my own."

"But that's not the guardianship Mom envisioned. Marilyn told me. It must have shocked you when she asked Marilyn to look after me, instead of you."

Gram shook with anger. "Marilyn Gaslow had no right to you."

"It was what Mom wanted."

"It was the *wrong* choice. I knew it. Your mother knew it. Even *she* was having reservations. She told me how Marilyn was afraid to take you because of the skeleton in her closet—the rape that didn't happen."

"You knew Frank Duffy was innocent?"

"Your mother told me exactly what Marilyn had told her. She was brutally honest," she said with a false chuckle. "I guess she wanted me to understand the risk she was taking by giving you to Marilyn. Maybe she even wanted my blessing. She wanted me to be ready to step in if the Frank Duffy thing ever exploded and the court found Marilyn unfit to be your guardian. Like I was second string or something."

Amy came to the table, glaring at Gram. "You sent the letter to Frank Duffy. That's why the penmanship was shaky in places."

"All I wanted was to expose Marilyn for what she was. An unfit guardian. I didn't expect him to blackmail her."

"You more than expected it. I think the two of you planned it. That's why he sent me two hundred thousand dollars when he died. Was that your cut, Gram? Is that why you

454

wouldn't let me call the police when the money arrived?"

Her mouth quivered. "This wasn't about money. I never asked for a cent."

"But he gave it to you anyway. Or maybe you wouldn't take it, so he made an anonymous gift to your granddaughter."

"I don't know what he was thinking. I don't *care* what he was thinking."

"So long as the letter kept Marilyn from becoming my guardian."

"Not the letter," said Gram. "The truth. *I* told the truth. It was better that way."

"Better for you."

"And for you."

Amy shook with disbelief. "Is that how your mind works? Just rationalize everything?"

"I'm not rationalizing anything."

"Then how do you live with yourself?"

Her eyes filled with tears. "I raised you the best I could. That's how."

"After you killed my mother."

"I didn't kill her."

"You killed her before she could meet with her lawyer and change her will to name Marilyn guardian."

"No."

"You came by the house and shot her with her own gun."

"That's not true."

"Admit it. You killed her!"

"For God's sake, she was already dying!"

They looked at each other, stunned, as if neither could fathom the words she'd just

455

uttered. Gram broke down, sobbing. "I'd already lost one child, Amy. I couldn't lose you, too. When your mother said she was giving you to Marilyn, something snapped inside me. It was like losing your father all over again. Only this time, I could stop it from happening. This was the only way to stop it."

Amy stared, incredulous. The rationale of a murderer. It was as good as a confession, but she felt no fulfillment. Only sadness—then anger.

"She deserved it, didn't she, Gram?"

"What?"

"In your eyes. Mom deserved to die a death as violent as Dad's."

"That's a terrible thing to say."

"Mom never grieved enough for your son, did she? I saw it in your eyes whenever she went on a date, the nights you babysat me. I saw it every time she brought another man through our front door. Your looks of contempt. You could have pulled the trigger right then and there."

"Amy, I did this for you."

Amy hurried from the kitchen and walked briskly down the hall. Gram followed.

"Amy, wait!"

She ignored the call and entered Taylor's room. Her daughter was still sound asleep. Amy snatched the tote bag from the closet and packed some clothes for Taylor.

"What are you doing?" She was shaking, desperate.

Amy strung the bag over her shoulder and lifted Taylor from the bed. Taylor's arms wrapped around her neck, but she kept right on sleeping. Amy held her tight as she blew right past Gram, crossed the living room, and threw open the front door.

"Please," said Gram, her voice cracking. "I swear, I did it for you."

Amy stopped in the doorway, looked Gram in the eye. "You did it for yourself. *Everything* you do, you do for yourself."

Amy slammed the door behind her. With Taylor in her arms, she headed for her truck—her mother's old truck.

Epilogue

"Robert Oppenheimer," the voice boomed over the loudspeaker. A beaming young man wearing a flowing black gown hurried toward the dais. It wasn't the usual rowdy crowd that filled Folsom Stadium on fall football Saturdays, but even in the silence of a sunny spring morning the excitement was palpable as each member of the class of 2000 had a personal moment of glory. For the big May class, no place but the stadium could accommodate the University of Colorado's combined ceremonies for all degrees, bachelors through doctorate. The doctoral candidates went first. Amy would be the fifth person across the stage. Right after Oppenheimer.

She felt goose bumps. Her friend and faculty advisor, Maria Perez, squeezed her hand as they climbed the steps to the left of the stage. The dean of the department of astrophysical and planetary sciences stood center stage, waiting. The field level was packed with students in full graduation regalia.

"Amy Parkens."

She stepped forward, smiling widely.

"Way to go, Mommy!"

Taylor was on her feet, standing on her

seat cushion in the tiered seating section. Maria's husband was seated right beside her, trying to get her down, but she was too proud to be controlled.

Amy gave a wink from afar, then shook hands with the dean, who presented her diploma. The traditional doctoral hood went over her shoulders. The tassel flipped as she crossed to the other side. She'd made it. She and Taylor, alone, had made it. Though not without a few bumps in the road.

Amy had told no one about her grandmother. She'd decided she never would. Her mother's death would forever be a suicide. Officially. Amy's silence was as much about mercy as it was about moving on with her own life. A sensational trial with Amy as witness against her own grandmother was no way to find closure. It seemed like punishment enough for Gram to know that Amy had uncovered the truth.

Over the following ten months, Amy had built a new life. Leaving the law firm had been easy. Forgiving Marilyn Gaslow had not been so easy. A brave night at Cheesman Dam couldn't overcome twenty years of deceit. After Marilyn had withdrawn her name from consideration for the Federal Reserve appointment, the two of them had simply seemed to pull away from each other.

The hardest part had been trying to explain to Taylor why they couldn't live with Gram anymore. The return to astronomy had helped the transition. She and Taylor had moved closer to the Meyer-Womble Observatory on Mt. Evans, where Amy could complete her doctoral research. Gram stayed behind in Boulder. They hadn't spoken since that night last summer, though her grandmother did write once. The letter was returned unopened. In her own controlling way, she undoubtedly hoped Amy would move back to Boulder after graduation. Amy wouldn't. Not ever. At least not as long as Gram was alive.

After the ceremony, the graduates gathered outside the stadium with their families. Amy filed out with Maria and waited for Taylor and Maria's husband. All around her, loving couples were locked in hugs and congratulatory kisses. Amy tried to hide the funny look on her face, but her tell-all expressions were not to be contained. Maria gave her an awkward hug that, in this setting, seemed a bit like a consolation prize.

Taylor came running through the crowd, brightening Amy's face. "Can I wear your funny hat, Mommy?"

"You betcha," she said as she lifted her from the sidewalk. She put her down and pulled the cap over her eyes. Just then, someone caught her eye through the crowd. He was standing near the stadium exit. Amy's smile faded. It was Ryan Duffy.

"It's too big!" shouted Taylor.

Amy was still looking at Ryan. He took a tentative step forward, then stopped.

"Maria, could you watch Taylor for a second?"

"Sure." She knelt on one knee and adjusted Taylor's mortarboard.

Amy weaved her way through the noisy crowd. Ryan slowly came forward, as if to meet her halfway. They had parted on decent terms last summer. The fact that Ryan's father was no rapist had taken away the bitterness. Amy had thought about him from time to time over the past eleven months, during many a lonely night at the observatory on Mt. Evans. Neither one had called the other, however. Circumstances had pushed them so far apart, only a lunatic would have picked up the phone. Or so she had thought.

Amy stopped right before him. "What brings you here?"

He gave a half-smile. "I felt like we had some unfinished business."

"Really?"

He rocked on his heels, as if he had something to say and wasn't quite sure how to say it. "It's been a strange year for me."

"Me too."

"Not all bad. I'm a new uncle. My sister Sarah had a little girl. Fortunately she doesn't seem to be taking after her mother or her father. That's a good thing."

"Congratulations."

"Yeah. It's nice."

"Somehow, I get the feeling you didn't come all this way just to tell me that."

"You're right." He looked away, then back, as if words were difficult. "I've been meaning to talk to you. I was just waiting for the divorce to finally come through before I did."

"Why?"

"Just wanted to see how everything shook

462

out with the money. Now that all the legal stuff is over, my share has finally been decided."

"Oh," she said, disappointed. "Still talking about the money."

"I never felt entitled to any of it, honestly. I've always thought that if there was an innocent victim, it was you." He pulled a paper sack from his pocket and offered it to her. "I want you to have it."

She backed away, surprised. "I can't take your money."

"It's not much. Like I said, the government took a big cut. The FBI, the IRS. Do you have any idea what the penalties are for taxes that should have been paid over twenty years ago? Turns out my dad had quite a few other debts, too. Off-track gambling was apparently quite a weakness for him. Me, my sister, and my ex-wife split what was left three ways. Out of the original five million, I'm left with exactly six hundred and forty-two bucks."

Amy almost giggled, then brought a hand to her mouth in embarrassment. " I'm sorry. I don't know why I think that's so funny."

"Because you can finally look back and laugh at all this. I was hoping that would be the case."

Their eyes met and held. It could have been an awkward moment, but it wasn't. Finally, Amy said, "So, you're really divorced now?"

"Yeah, thank God. Looking back on it, it's amazing we lasted as long as we did. Not sure what we had in common. Guess it's like they say, opposites attract."

"Only if you're a magnet."

"Yeah." He chuckled.

"Of course, if you want a more instructive scientific analogy, the true opposites in our universe are called matter and anti-matter. Whenever they come into contact, they shoot off deadly gamma rays, and instantly annihilate each other."

"Now you're showing off, Dr. Parkens."

"I guess I am." She glanced over her shoulder toward Taylor. She was doing the five-year-old version of tapping her foot, waiting. "I should get back to my daughter."

"Sorry. Didn't mean to hold you up."

"Not at all." She clutched the paper bag, then looked at Ryan with soulful eyes. "This was...a nice gesture. But please, keep your money. I don't think I'm any more entitled to it than you are."

"Just take it. After going back to school, you can use it, I'm sure."

"Believe me, I'd still need the life expectancy of a redwood to pay off those debts."

Gently, she pushed it back toward him, touching his hand lightly. "Thanks for coming all the way up here. And you take care of yourself." She turned away slowly.

"Hey."

She glanced back one last time.

Ryan shrugged, as if he didn't know what to say. "Good luck to you, Amy."

She smiled sadly, feeling chills as she walked away. She was too confused to say whether she was glad he had come. But it didn't warm her heart to pull herself away.

"Can I put on your robe, too?" Taylor was tugging on her sleeve.

"After we take some pictures."

"Okay!" said Taylor, almost squealing.

Amy took her daughter's hand and started toward the lawn. She didn't want to be obvious, but as they passed the last stadium exit she checked to see if Ryan was still around. She glanced left, then right. He was gone.

"Mommy, why don't you look happy-faced like everybody else?"

"I'm very happy, sweetheart. Let's take pictures."

They flowed with the crowd toward a picturesque spot with the mountains in the background. On a bench near the stadium, she noticed the paper sack just sitting there. It was definitely Ryan's, but she didn't dare touch it. She turned and, through the crowd, saw the back of his head. He was walking the other way. She hurried to catch up, pulling Taylor by the hand. "Ryan!" she called. "Dr. Duffy!"

He stopped and turned.

Amy said, "I think you forgot something, didn't you?" With her eyes, she pointed back to the paper bag resting on the bench. But Ryan's eyes remained fixed on her.

"Actually, I did forget something. I forgot to remind you. We never did get that second cup of coffee at the Green Parrot."

Her mouth opened, but there was a few seconds' delay. "That's, uh, true."

"You think maybe we could fix that?"

She smiled with her eyes, recalling their meeting and how she had wanted to say yes when he'd asked if he might see her again. Instead, she had said something coy like *You never know*. This time she wanted to do better. "I'd like that," she said. "I'd like that a lot. In fact, I know a place not too far from here."

"I can follow."

"Okay," she said happily.

"Lead on."

They started down the sidewalk together, Ryan on the left, Amy and her daughter on the right. They had to retrace their steps past the bench where Ryan had left the money. The paper sack, however, was already gone. Two young graduates were engaged in heated conversation. The short guy was holding the bag. The other was trying to take it from him.

"We have to turn it in," said the taller one. "It doesn't belong to us."

"It's cash," snapped the other. "Found money. Finders keepers."

Their voices rose as the argument intensified. People were starting to gather round them and gawk, as if anticipating a fistfight.

Amy and Ryan exchanged knowing glances as they passed the commotion, but neither said a word. She struggled not to burst out laughing. He grinned and shook his head.

Their smiles only widened as they kept right on walking.